A Labyrinth of Scions and Sorcery

A Labyrinth of Scions and Sorcery

CURTIS CRADDOCK

TOR

A TOM DOHERTY ASSOCIATES BOOK • NEW YORK

A LABYRINTH OF SCIONS AND SORCERY

Copyright © 2019 by Curtis Craddock

A Tor Book
Published by Tom Doherty Associates
175 Fifth Avenue
New York, NY 10010

www.tor-forge.com

Tor® is a registered trademark of Macmillan Publishing Group, LLC.

The Library of Congress Cataloging-in-Publication Data is available upon request.

ISBN 978-0-7653-8962-6 (hardcover)
ISBN 978-0-7653-8964-0 (ebook)

Our books may be purchased in bulk for promotional, educational, or business use. Please contact your local bookseller or the Macmillan Corporate and Premium Sales Department at 1-800-221-7945, extension 5442, or by email at MacmillanSpecialMarkets@macmillan.com.

First Edition: January 2019

Printed in the United States of America

0 9 8 7 6 5 4 3 2 1

To Donna Hume.
For making my world a better, saner, and sillier place.

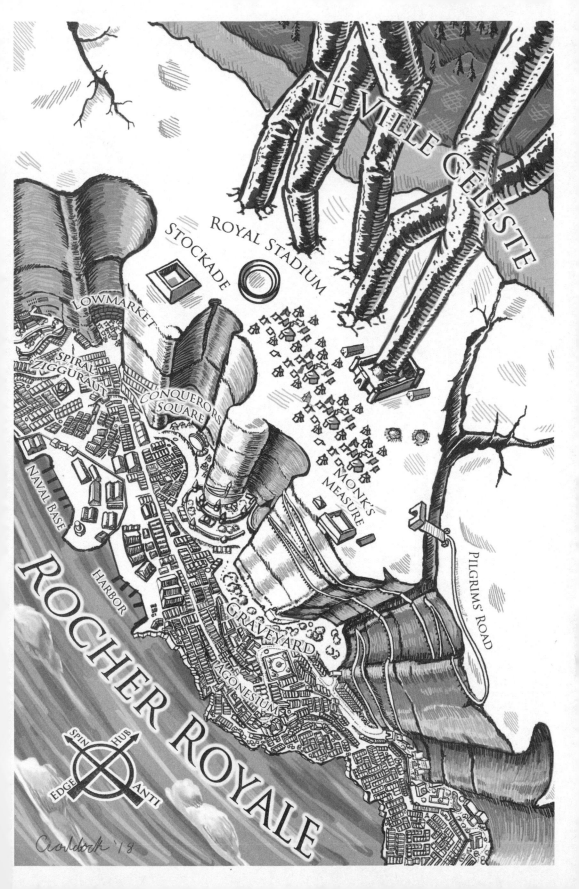

LE VILLE CÉLESTE

ROYAL STADIUM

STOCKADE

LOWMARKET

SPIRAL
ZIGGURAUT

CONQUERORS
SQUARE

NAVAL BASE

MONK'S
MEASURE

PILGRIMS' ROAD

HARBOR

GRAVEYARD

AGONESIUM

ROCHER ROYALE

SPIN HUB

EDGE ANTI

Craddock '18

Acknowledgments

Innumerable thanks go to Susan Smith, Carol Berg, Brian Tobias, Courtney Schafer, and Saytchyn-Maddux Creech, without whose good and abundant advice this book would not have become half of what it is. Special thanks to my editor, Diana Pho, for taking me on and for all her invaluable work and insight. Thanks to Caitlin Blasdell for her skillful work and dedication.

A Labyrinth of Scions and Sorcery

CHAPTER

One

Jean-Claude rubbed two copper pennies between his fingers. He was in the market for information, the collection of such being the greater part of his job. Unfortunately the particular salesman with whom he was faced, a nervous tic of a man named Pacy, was a bit of a junk merchant, selling rusty, secondhand rumors often cobbled together out of entirely different stories and missing critical pieces.

"What scandal are you talking about?" Jean-Claude asked, having been pursuing this topic for some time.

Pacy crouched at the mouth of his alley, looking around with the furtive air of a mouse who expected to be eaten by a cat at any moment. It would have to be a lower-class cat, probably a one-eyed stray with a yowl that could strip paint.

"If I knew that, I'd be selling that," Pacy said peevishly. "All I know is that Mistwaithe talked about auctioning off a scandal to get even with des Zephyrs. Now where's my coin?"

Jean-Claude, King's Own Musketeer, had been guardian to Princess

Isabelle des Zephyrs since the day she was born. She was his daughter in all but blood and woe betide anyone who sought to harm her.

"Getting even for what?" Jean-Claude asked. Isabelle was Ambassadress to the Grand Peace. She'd spent the last year stitching together a treaty between l'Empire Céleste and the neighboring kingdom of Aragoth. This attempt to preemptively stop people from killing each other had naturally earned her many enemies amongst those who likened peace to weakness.

"How should I know?" Pacy stared at the coins in Jean-Claude's hand. He bounced up and down like a nervous squirrel, his fingers twitching. "He just said the comte and his children would regret double-crossing him."

"Le Comte des Zephyrs?" Jean-Claude asked, surprised. Isabelle's father was a vile, twisted villain, but he was also dying of the red consumption hundreds of kilometers away on a remote skyland. What in all the ten thosand Torments was a scandal of his doing here?

"Yes," Pacy whined. "C'mon. I've told you all I know."

Jean-Claude tossed him the coins, which he managed to drop. Pacy spent the next several seconds chasing the coins around on the cobbles and panting in panic as if they were running away on purpose. He then counted his haul, both of them, several times before slinking into the alley.

Jean-Claude couldn't care less about Isabelle's father—the sooner the man died, the better—but men seeking revenge frequently targeted the families of the ones they hated. Lord Brandon Mistwaithe, Goldentongue sorcerer and rumor monger of scurrilous reputation, must be dissuaded from taking any such action against Isabelle.

Jean-Claude therefore exerted himself to obtain an invitation to the auction. The event was to be held this hour at an inn called the Golden Swain.

Since showing up in a den of thieves and whisperers in uniform was likely to spoil the party, Jean-Claude had exchanged his blue-and-gold musketeer's tabard for merchant's garb: a floppy beret, a padded green doublet, and a pair of spectacles that he kept telling himself he didn't really need.

At the appointed hour, Jean-Claude mounted up and rode to the Lowmarket. The main portion of the city rested on a narrow shelf of land between the deep sky and an immense cliff called the Rivencrag, which rose two kilometers straight up from the coastal apron. He passed beneath a wide stone archway, one of the many that cut through the buttresses the great cliff thrust out onto the plain, and emerged into the market circle. Here was a gladiatorial arena where great battles of commerce were daily enacted. Hundreds of merchant stalls selling everything from flake-bread to glimmer oil to drag-onweed were staked out in mostly regular concentric rings around the open hub. More permanent structures were carved into the terraces that climbed the steep walls of the surrounding bowl.

The market was as packed as a pickle barrel. Pedestrians only made pro-gress by sliding and bumping, shuffling past each other like cards in the hand of a clumsy dealer. Merchants dickered with customers, whores flashed tempt-ing bits of skin, and troubadours strove to be heard over the din of a thou-sand voices. Beggars pleaded for alms and gangs of urchins worked the crowd looking for purses to cut. A crowd had gathered around the stone platform in the center of the square to watch a troupe of dwarf acrobats perform.

The Golden Swain was a large, open-fronted inn near the livery stable on the far side of the market. A hanging sign depicted a gallant youth dressed in yellow dancing with a young woman in a blue dress.

The back of Jean-Claude's mind kept busy trying to puzzle out just what scandal this Mistwaithe person might be trying to sell. Le Comte des Zephyrs had only left his skyland once in all the years Jean-Claude had known him, and that was to attend his wife's funeral here in Rocher Royale. Isabelle had no interest in scandalous behavior, unless one counted being a female math-ematician, a fact which she did not advertise. Perhaps Isabelle's brother, Guil-laume, had committed some faux pas, like opening his mouth in the presence of functional adults.

Jean-Claude's horse gingerly forded the human tumult toward the inn across the widest part of the square. Jean-Claude had chosen a long approach specifically to see if anyone took note of his arrival. It was always a good idea to know where the lookouts and toughs were perched.

Jean-Claude had just passed by the dwarf-occupied platform when a man in fine clothes burst from the Golden Swain's back room into the open com-mon area. His face was white and his mouth gaped in terror. A piercing in-human scream followed him out the door and cut the noise of the market to ribbons. Several patrons in the Swain's common room lurched to their feet, upsetting the trestle tables and knocking their compatriots to the floor.

From the open door lurched a horror. It had the shape of a man, if that man had been dipped head to heels in fresh-spilt blood. He was a Sangui-naire sorcerer in the midst of a horrible derangement of his powers. His whole body glistened crimson, and his scarlet shadow flailed about his feet like a maddened kraken. Carmine tendrils slithered across the floor, climbed the walls, and raced across the ceiling. One of them touched the fleeing man's shadow, and he toppled as if he'd tripped over a physical thing.

The bloodshadow pierced the man's ordinary umbra and spread through it like ink through water. The victim's spine twisted in spasms of agony. His body lost its crisp edges, slumped like a butter sculpture in the sun, and dissolved away until there was nothing left but a russet stain on the ground, a soul smudge that writhed of its own accord.

The screaming, sobbing Sanguinaire rampaged through the tavern, his bloodshadow consuming patrons on every side. His ululating wail shattered into forsaken sobs. It was the sound of a soul being shredded on the Breaker's wheel.

Panic swept through the square. Frightened souls near the Golden Swain turned and ran headlong into people farther out. The terror boiled up into a stampede. People thundered across the market. The unlucky fell and were trampled. The dwarf acrobats abandoned the stage and bolted for their wagon. Merchants ducked into their shops.

The human tide surged toward Jean-Claude. He raced after the dwarves toward their sturdily built, brightly painted carnival wagon. His mount plunged through the crowd as if through high water. A woman went down under his horse's hooves. The horse stumbled, righted itself, thrust forward. Jean-Claude dared not even look back.

He skidded into the lee of the wagon as the mob broke around it. Wave after wave of bodies bashed against the timbers. People screamed, but above all the noise rose the sobbing shrieking howl of the mad Sanguinaire.

In an instant of respite, Jean-Claude looked for a clear path to the monster. He was a King's Own Musketeer, versed in the means of disposing of sorcerers. He could not look himself in the mirror or Isabelle in the eye if he let this slaughter continue.

An alchemical lantern hung on the cart's lamp hook. Jean-Claude deftly lifted it and lit it with his sparker. A clear flame jumped up, giving off a blue-white light. He clapped the front pane shut, then wheeled his mount.

The Lowmarket was still emptying of people, but the greatest surge had passed him by, and many of those left behind were wounded stragglers. The Sanguinaire had cleared out the inn and stumbled into the open. His blood-shadow reached out long threads into the square, consuming the lame and unconscious.

Outside the square, alarm bells called the city watch to arms.

Jean-Claude drew his pistol. He had only one shot, and he'd need to be close. He kicked his horse to a gallop toward the Sanguinaire. There was no point in subtlety; the man seemed lost in his own agony, gyrating like a drunkard with his horrible shadow flailing all around.

Jean-Claude whirled the lantern on its short chain. There were only two absolute defenses against a bloodshadow. One was total darkness. Bloodshadows couldn't manifest without light.

He hurled the lamp. Tendrils of bloodshadow reached toward him. He tucked down and hung off the saddle, hiding his shadow in the horse's.

The lantern hit cobblestone. Glass shattered. Lumin vapor sprayed. The bloodshadow grabbed the horse's shadow. The poor beast squealed and pitched forward. Jean-Claude launched from the saddle. His shadow touched the bloodshadow and his body wasn't his own anymore. He could not feel his flesh at all. Terror swelled in his chest. He'd misjudged his timing—

There was a hissing *whump* and a white-hot flash as the hypervolatile lumin vapor ignited. An expanding ball of fire drove every shadow from the square.

The other way to fight a bloodshadow was with blinding light.

Sensation returned to Jean-Claude's body just as he crashed to the cobbles. He tucked hard and rolled across his shoulders, narrowly avoiding being crushed by what was left of his horse.

He heaved to his feet, spectacles askew. The Sanguinaire, covering his eyes, blundered toward Jean-Claude. Already, the bloodshadow re-formed.

Jean-Claude raised his pistol, aimed, squeezed the trigger.

Fire and smoke. The gun kicked. The Sanguinaire jerked. The bloodshadow twitched and then dissolved as whatever mad mental faculty had been driving it retreated, and the sorcerer's whole attention focused on the hole in his chest. He was a ragged man, skin and bones and tattered clothes and no shoes. He fell over backward. His bare toes were bloodied with missing toenails.

Jean-Claude took a step and nearly fell over again as his body reminded him that he'd just been shadowburned and thrown from a charging horse. Every muscle that wasn't bruised was strained, and he'd bashed his game leg. Nevertheless, he stumbled onward, pushing his glasses back into place and drawing his rapier to finish the job.

The sorcerer looked even worse close up. One of his eyes was white with blindness, as his flesh was pocked with running sores. His face was an effigy of poverty, thin and scabrous, with fewer teeth than gaps. There was nothing to him but papery skin and twisted bones. His forearms had been scarred by countless bleedings, and there was an open trepanning wound over his temple, his brain clearly visible within. Aside from the bullet hole in his chest, only the trepanning wound was fresh. He lay with his hands clasped over the wound in his chest. Blood bubbled between his fingers and his breathing gurgled like a downspout. Of his bloodshadow there was no sign. His shadow was the same thin gray as any other man's, and that didn't make any sense. From all Jean-Claude had ever learned or witnessed, it was not until a Sanguinaire's last breath had left his body that his shadow became normal.

"Who are you?" Jean-Claude asked, not expecting an answer.

The man's eye didn't focus, but his broken mouth spat out blood-flecked words. "Gloom rises, brother. Harvest king. Look at the cracks. Voices in the dark have feathers, tell the saints what to do. Their eyes see for harvest king. He wears their scars. Brother . . ." There was another spasm of coughing and then stillness.

The words meant nothing to Jean-Claude, and what of this rampage? The Sanguinaire had erupted from the Golden Swain where Lord Mistwaithe's auction was to have taken place. No one else had come out, so Jean-Claude would have to go in.

First, he turned his attention to the immediate, necessary, and grisly business of dispatching his wounded horse. The poor beast hadn't been absorbed by the bloodshadow, but it lay on its side, thrashing and kicking, eyes rolling and sightless. Humans could recover from brief exposure to a hunting bloodshadow, but beasts had to be put down.

Careful of the poor animal's thrashing, Jean-Claude stepped in and put his sword through its eye. It shuddered and went still.

After that, the square was eerily quiet and empty. Even the swarms of corpse flies that were usually the first to arrive on a battlefield were absent. Most of the dead left no corpses, only soul smudges. There were a few survivors, people who had been trampled or only lightly shadowburned. Jean-Claude knocked on doors and called people out to lend aid and comfort where possible. More than a few, still filled with fear, rebuked his command, but enough came that he reckoned no more would die for want of aid.

The first watchman to arrive was a grizzled sergeant with a boot-leather face, gray hair, and aggressive eyebrows. He quick-marched into the square, musket at the ready, with half a squad of younger watchmen trailing behind him. He took in the scene at a glance before his attention landed on Jean-Claude, standing in the center of it, giving orders.

"You there. What's your name?" the watchman called.

"I am Jean-Claude, King's Own Musketeer," Jean-Claude said. He opened his wattle pouch, which hung on a chain under his cravat, and pulled out his creased, stained letters of authority. He probably ought to get a new set while he was here in the capital, but these carried with them a patina of luck along with the stains of blood, oil, and beer.

The watchman took the papers and scanned them with the suspicious care of the barely literate. Finally he handed them back to Jean-Claude. "Near as I can reckon, those are real. So that being the case, may I ask what in all the foul-hearted, stink-headed names of Torment happened here, sir?"

Jean-Claude grinned, for he recognized a true sergeant's manner of chivvying his superiors. "First your name, sergeant."

"Sergeant Pierre, but just Sergeant if it's all the same to you."

"Fine by me, Sergeant. Do you know this man?" He gestured at the dead Sanguinaire.

Sergeant looked down at the corpse. "Blasted balls."

"That would be a 'Yes.' Who is he and how do you know him?"

Sergeant knelt down and shook his head. "His name's Orem. Everyone in a uniform's run into the spindle-legged, rot-mouthed, piss-drinking blighter at some point. Vagrant, beggar, heard voices in the ground, claimed the Gloom was calling him. Old folks thought he had a Torment in him, but the Temple said it's just a mind built on chalk. It cracks, it crumbles, it falls away. We used to run him out of town about once a week until they opened up Screaming Hall."

"Screaming Hall?"

Sergeant spat on the ground. "It's the Royal Agonesium for the Deranged, but everyone calls it Screaming Hall. Most folk here take care of their own, but the Agonesium takes in the really bad ones, the ones no one can handle. The lock-ups escape every now and then and we have to drag 'em back in."

"A few moments ago, he was rampaging through the market with the powers of a Sanguinaire, snuffing people like candles."

"You're daft. Orem's mad as a moon-dog, but common as sin, only more so."

Jean-Claude stared at Orem, willing the corpse to yield up information. Could something have happened in the Agonesium to cause him to manifest long-buried powers? Saintblooded children usually manifested their sacred gift about the time they turned eight. Occasionally one would bloom after puberty. Those were called the lateborn. An unhappy minority, the unhallowed, never manifested their powers at all. Jean-Claude had never heard of someone Orem's age discovering their gift. Isabelle hadn't discovered her sorcery until she was twenty-five, but her gift had been deliberately suppressed.

"Whatever he was during the rest of his life, he was a Sanguinaire at his death. His bloodshadow devoured at least a dozen people. Watch that you don't tread on the soul smudges."

Sergeant yelped and took several mincing steps to avoid treading on a smudge that oozed toward him, like the shadow of a fish under ice. Soul smudges yearned toward the shadows of the living, gathering around them like moths to a flame. As far as anyone could tell, their touch was harmless, weightless, but no one stayed long where the suffering things had been created. One could not bring justice to the dead, but there were dozens of victims here, men and women with families who deserved an accounting.

"Breaker-cursed, skin-shriveling . . ." Sergeant muttered. Jean-Claude had learned to swear proficiently, but clearly he had stumbled into the presence of a master.

Jean-Claude said, "Sergeant, do me a kindness, and put Orem on ice. I want to have a friend of mine examine the body later." Isabelle had the sharpest mind in the Risen Kingdoms; if anyone could extract a confession from a dead man it was she.

Sergeant frowned, but shrugged. "If it pleases le roi."

"Orem mentioned the Gloom and something called the harvest king."

Sergeant waved this away. "Means nothing. Orem never stopped muttering, even in his sleep. Thought the Torments under the street were out to get him, claimed the cobblestones moved around at night on hundreds of tiny legs, like beetles."

"No help there, then." Jean-Claude knelt and searched the wasted body for anything he might have been carrying to explain his presence and his sudden bout of sorcery. The manacle scars on wrists, ankles, and throat probably came from his stay at the Agonesium. But then how had he escaped, and how had he ended up with the Builder's gift? Jean-Claude must report this to Grand Leon, but he damned well better have an explanation to offer up along with the mystery.

"Where is Screaming Hall?" Jean-Claude asked.

"Over by the tombs off Dousing Street in Cliffside."

"So somehow Orem escaped from Screaming Hall, wandered all the way to the opposite end of the city unnoticed, and then broke out in bloodshadows. I am going to have to have a word with his keepers. In the meantime, if you'd like to make a little scrip on the side, I'll pay for good information on who saw what before this got started, who's missing and who isn't." Jean-Claude certainly wasn't going to have time to talk to everyone himself.

Sergeant's eyes narrowed. "And how do I know what you'll think is good information?"

"It'll be the kind that makes your arse pucker." Jean-Claude slapped a silver *denier* into his hand, probably as much money as he saw in a season. "Consider that a down payment. I'm staying at the Rowan House in the Rookery."

Sergeant made the coin disappear with the alacrity of a seasoned pickpocket. "I know the place."

"In that case, I'll leave you to sort this out," Jean-Claude said. He touched his fingers to his hat and limped into the Golden Swain. His leg throbbed and kept trying to seize up on him. In the open taproom, a whole shoal of soul smudges yearned toward him. His skin crawled. The next good day of bright sunshine should burn away the ones outside. The ones beneath the eaves would need a pyre built.

The doorway from which Orem had emerged led directly into a room set up with rows of benches as if for a lecture or Temple instruction. Most of the seating had been overturned. The floor was awash with soul smudges, though their squirming made them hard to count. The one wriggling across the table at the front might be Lord Mistwaithe, or it might not. Orem hadn't left any identifiable corpses behind.

What remained were two capes, a broken sword, a drinking horn, a pistol, a few coins, three hats, and a glass rod like the kind Isabelle used to stir alchemical compounds when metal or wood wouldn't do. They were all things that could have been easily dropped. The stink of gun smoke lingered, and there were splashes of blood on the walls and floor as if there'd been a fight. But who'd been fighting who? A Sanguinaire's bloodshadow left no wounds on its victims.

"Does that offer for information apply to anyone, or just greedy old guardsmen?" asked a voice from the doorway.

Jean-Claude turned and looked down at one of the dwarf acrobats, a man with a lopsided face, brown hair cut close, and a fool's motley in yellow and purple. Unfinished clay, as Jean-Claude's mother would have said. Jean-Claude pulled out his coin purse and flipped the dwarf half a copper penny. "That's for your name. And more to come if you know anything of what happened here."

The dwarf plucked the coin from the air with a stubby hand, then made it do acrobatic flips through his fingers before tucking it away. "Name's Sedgwick. You have a heavy purse."

"I work for le roi," Jean-Claude said. Not that his bribe money came from le roi. It was all corpse money, gleaned from dead men.

"I hear the royal coffers are bare," Sedgwick said. "And even Grand Leon can't thread silver out his arse."

"The penury of kings is still plenty for the common man. You could probably find enough coins twixt the floorboards of his gambling parlor to set yourself up as a baronet. Now do you want to earn some of that bounty or not?"

"Have it your way, squire," Sedgwick said. "Before that bloody ruckus broke out, I saw something nobody else did. I was up on the roof getting ready to slide down the wire into the square and make a big ol' entrance, when I saw two folks go in the back way."

He paused, expectantly.

Jean-Claude huffed, amused, and pulled out a *denier*. "For the whole story and no mucking about."

"Done."

Jean-Claude flipped him the coin.

Sedgwick said, "There was two of 'em, a man and a woman. Nothing special about him, but she was a sorcerer, one of the feathered ones. Fenice."

All the hairs on the back of Jean-Claude's neck stood up and he resisted the urge to look around. All sorcerers were dangerous, but few more so than the eternally reborn Fenice. Each one was strong as a dire-bear and tough enough to shrug off grapeshot. Add to that skills honed over several lifetimes and you had an absolute terror in battle. That could certainly explain the blood on the walls.

"Was the man who was with her a Sanguinaire?"

"No, he were covered up real good. Hood, cloak, and all, but you can't hide that red shadow."

"Did either one of them come out again?"

"I don't know. I had to take my run off the bloody roof, didn't I?"

Jean-Claude made another circuit of the room but saw no way to determine whether the Fenice sorceress had stayed and died, or escaped. There were several soul smudges near the back, as if they had been trying to escape. The thick door boards were cracked from heavy impact, the fists of a Fenice, perhaps? Jean-Claude put his shoulder to the door, but it was blocked from the outside.

Jean-Claude asked, "How long between the time you saw the Fenice go in and the massacre in the square?"

Sedgwick considered his answer carefully. "We were in the middle of an act. There was only the stacking stools routine in between 'em, so no more than five minutes."

"Did you hear a fight? A gunshot?" The gunsmoke smell was recent and the shot should have been audible for blocks around.

"Can't say that I did."

Jean-Claude exited the front door. Like most of the permanent structures here, the Golden Swain was built partially into the cliff face, but there was still a foreshortened alley between it and the neighboring building. Someone had wedged the alley door shut with a heavy wooden beam. He pictured a scene where someone had tossed in a mad Sanguinaire like a grenade and barred the door, knowing that no one in that room would escape. But who had been the target? Had it been Mistwaithe, the Fenice, or someone else? Had the grenadier been interested in silencing Mistwaithe, or obtaining his secrets? And what did this say about the significance of the des Zephyrs scandal?

Sedgwick leaned against the corner of the building, flipping the coin with his thumb and catching it again and again. "So what's all this to you, squire? King's Own Musketeer, I get that, but what does le roi care if some Sanguinaire goes poppers and melts a bunch of clayborn? It's not like the nobs don't feed on common folk all regular."

"Grand Leon strongly discourages his nobles from actually killing anyone when they feed their bloodshadows," Jean-Claude said. That prohibition had spawned a whole new industry of shadelings, shadow whores who got paid handsomely to have their shadows periodically grazed.

"If you say so," Sedgwick said.

Jean-Claude said, "Come, I need to run a quick experiment."

Sedgwick regarded him suspiciously. "What sort of experiment?"

"One that involves shouting at each other like an old married couple."

"I don't like you that well," Sedgwick said, but he followed Jean-Claude inside.

There had been a fight before Orem killed everyone in the room. Someone had discharged a pistol. There was blood on the walls. The scrum would have made noise—lots of noise—but no one in the common room outside had so much as stirred until the door had opened and all Torment broke loose.

"Wait here," Jean-Claude said, indicating a spot outside the backroom door, "and come in when I call."

"Do I have to balance a ball on my nose, too?"

"Only if it improves your hearing." Jean-Claude stepped inside and closed the door. The wall was made of cut stone, but the door was thin, ill-fitting wood that should not have contained the sound of a commotion.

"Sedgwick!" he bellowed. "Sedgwick, come in here!"

Nothing happened. Jean-Claude opened the door. Sedgwick folded his arms and stared up at Jean-Claude questioningly.

"I take it you didn't hear me," Jean-Claude said.

"You need to fart louder," Sedgwick said.

"Have you ever considered becoming a mime?" Jean-Claude replied.

Sedgwick snorted and made an obscene gesture. "So what was all that about?"

"My old mother, saints keep her, had a saying, 'Once is happenstance, twice coincidence, thrice shenanigans.'"

"Thrice what?"

"In this case, sorcerers," Jean-Claude said. "Three went in but how many went out?"

When a much younger and sprier Jean-Claude and his boyhood friends had talked about what type of sorcery they might like to have been born with, most patriotically argued on behalf of l'Empire's native Sanguinaire sorcery. A sizable minority had argued for the bestial shapeshifting abilities of the Seelenjäger, but Jean-Claude had always picked Goldentongue sorcery, the ability to craft illusions so convincing that they could even upend nature for a time. There was no end to the possibilities such powers represented to such a clever and daring mind as his younger self imagined he possessed. Later, at l'École Royale des Spécialistes, he had studied sorceries of all types and the few ways ordinary men might combat them. Goldentongue sorcery required the illusions be crafted into charms that were vulnerable to disruption by cold iron, arcanite, and water; and no Goldentongue could cast an illusion over himself.

The fact that sound could not escape this room suggested a charm of silence was in play. Jean-Claude searched carefully. The charm would be worked into something symbolic and probably something durable. Goldentongue glamours took a toll on whatever it was put into, so charms were typically stone, crystal, or metal.

Even knowing what he was looking for, it took Jean-Claude some time to find the charm. The room had been fitted with a hidden listening tube whereby the innkeep could spy on his guests, but Earl Mistwaithe had flipped the board on him. Into the tube had been stuffed a bat of wool wrapped around a silver bodkin. Such was the nature of a glamour that, as the tube was gagged, so was the rest of the room. No sound could get out at all. Jean-Claude extracted the charm from the tube's throat and repeated the shouting at the door experiment.

As he expected, the charm of silence had been broken, and Sedgwick heard him clearly. The fact that the charm had been working when Jean-Claude found it all meant Mistwaithe was still alive, for with the rare exception of true reliquaries and storied artifacts of renown, the effects of sorcery died along with the sorcerer who created them.

Orem and Mistwaithe had left this room alive. So what happened to the Fenice? Rarely did Jean-Claude wish for more corpses, but if these people were going to be dead anyway, the least they could do was leave identifying information.

He nodded to Sedgwick and said, "Thank you for your help. I'm always in the market for good information."

Sedgwick considered Jean-Claude. "You're an odd noggin, squire. No pushing, no threats, no short jokes. You're not daft but you pay more than the work's worth."

"Or it's worth more than you think."

"So who got killed that's so important?" Sedgwick gestured to encompass the whole scene.

"It's not the slaughter. It's what the slaughter is meant to cover up."

"Which is?"

"Shenanigans," Jean-Claude said, "whole fleets of them."

CHAPTER

Two

Crows' Feast Square, in the narrow canyons of the lower city, was little more than a junction wide enough to turn a donkey cart around in. Four-story tenements with overhanging eaves cast the place in a permanent twilight. Its only notable feature aside from its general awkwardness of shape was the gallows set up in its center.

Atop the gallows, standing on a small block of wood, with a noose around her neck was Hysia Dominguez, tried and convicted of murdering her employer, Ambassador Cubilla of Aragoth. Tears streamed down her face as the executioner approached her with a hood and a gag. Nobody liked a blubbering murderess. It took away from the solemnity of the occasion.

"Please, señor," she wailed. "Please, I beg you. I am innocent."

"Consul de la Vega! Wait!" Princess Isabelle des Zephyrs, Ambassadress of the Grand Peace, and cousin once removed to the emperor Grand Leon, pushed her way through the crowd toward the gallows. Her handmaid, Marie, followed close behind. Thank all the saints they'd arrived in time.

Consul de la Vega, Isabelle's counterpart in the Grand Peace negotiations, turned from the spectacle to meet Isabelle.

"Mademoiselle Ambassadress," he said. "I'm glad you could make it, though of course I am sorry about the circumstances."

Isabelle wanted to bend over with her one flesh-and-blood hand on her knee and just breathe for a minute or two, but neither time nor dignity would allow it. Instead, she squared her shoulders and said, "It is the circumstances about which I need to speak with you. You need to call off the execution."

De la Vega was a stocky man with graying temples and the silver eyes of an Aragothic Glasswalker. She'd always found him a reasonable interlocutor and a hard bargainer, and she was surprised when his face turned scarlet.

"That clayborn murdered my cousin."

Isabelle made a calming gesture with both her normal left hand and her spark-hand. Her right arm had been amputated at the shoulder, but in its place manifested a sorcerous limb, the blazon of her unique l'Étincelle sorcery. It was an arm-shaped volume filled with luminescent clouds in which pink and purple sparks like fireflies swarmed. Most people made signs against evil when they saw it and called her the Breaker's get.

"That's just the thing," Isabelle said. "Hysia Dominguez didn't murder anyone."

Consul de la Vega held up a scroll of thick paper, crushed and wrinkled in his vengeful hand. His face was purple as an overripe plum. "She confessed of her own free will." He was surrounded and supported by half a dozen Aragothic noblemen, Glasswalker sorcerers, and embassy guards. Isabelle had only Marie.

"Nevertheless, it is impossible," Isabelle insisted. "Your cousin was sitting in a chair. The bullet went in his mouth and came out the top of his head—"

"She confessed and she will pay for her crime!" de la Vega screamed, tears running down his cheeks.

A deeper shadow loomed as the Aragothic judge who'd witnessed the confession advanced as if to push Isabelle back, but Marie stepped swiftly in front of him, her maidenblade appearing in her hand. The tiny weapon seemed wholly inadequate against the man's superior bulk, but Marie had a talent for unnerving people.

Marie had spent a decade as a mindless bloodhollow slave. The ordeal had stripped her of color. Her flesh and hair were as white as bleached bone. Shadows did not stick to her so that in all but the most abject darkness she seemed to glow like the white moon Kore. Her face was as expressionless as a porcelain doll's, and few people could endure her stare.

The judge squeezed in close to de la Vega and said, "The facts of the matter are already settled. She has taken responsibility for the crime and will be punished accordingly."

"She was bullied into confessing," Isabelle said. "She knows she didn't do it."

The judge said, "In her confession she states jealousy as a motive. She was upset that Cubilla took another lover."

"And who put that idea in her head, pray tell?" Isabelle snapped. "It certainly didn't come from her lips. You wrote the whole script for her."

"Irrelevant," de la Vega said. "This is an Aragothic matter. She is an Aragothic subject who committed the murder of an Aragothic ambassador on Aragothic soil. She is bound by laws which you are bound to respect by the very treaty you signed this morning."

How long ago this morning seemed. Isabelle and de la Vega had been celebrating the successful completion of their negotiations on a treaty to guarantee peace between their kingdoms when tragedy struck. De la Vega's cousin had been murdered. Isabelle accompanied the consul to Cubilla's townhome, just in case the murder turned out to be political, and she had found herself caught up in an avalanche of miscarried justice. By the time she'd arrived, Hysia had been arrested for murder, and the judge had extracted a confession from her. He had witnesses saying her words were voluntary. The fig leaf of protocol thus satisfied, the Aragoths had dragged Hysia away to be hanged.

Isabelle, having no taste for blood or vengeance, had stayed behind and gone into the room where the ambassador had been killed. She saw there, painted in blood and bone, a picture utterly unlike the one the judge had framed. She'd been stunned, disbelieving her own senses. How could the judge have been so blind, so wrong? She'd intruded on the women preparing the body for cremation. They cursed her for her rudeness, but she'd found what she needed to convince herself of the truth. Then she and Marie had raced for Crows' Feast Square like falcons on the wing, only to encounter this impervious wall of bombast and denial.

Isabelle said, "Even in Aragoth, the law allows counsel for the accused. Who was there to speak for her?"

De la Vega said, "No one can force an advocate to speak for a criminal who they believe is guilty."

"I would speak for her," Isabelle said.

"You are not an Aragothic subject," de la Vega said. "Not yet."

The judge leaned forward as far as he could without earning a stab from Marie. "If you do not wish to imperil your betrothal, I suggest you withdraw. There are those on the small council who will be incensed if you hold Aragothic law in contempt, especially for the sake of a mere clayborn."

Isabelle's rage burned incandescent, and her spark-arm shed plumes of cold embers. All of her dearest friends were clayborn, and the saintborn treated them all with contempt. On top of that, the judge threatened her long-planned marriage to Príncipe Julio de Aragoth, el rei's brother.

Isabelle wanted to argue, to persuade them with facts and appeals to justice and mercy, but there was no reason sharp enough to breach the Aragoths' contempt, no words that would deflect their misplaced revenge. Isabelle might present the facts to Julio later and have de la Vega punished, but that would be far too late for Hysia.

"Marie," she snapped. "We're leaving."

Marie glanced up at her. She and Isabelle had learned hand speech from their deaf friend Gretl, and Isabelle signed, "Prepare for ambush."

Marie gave the barest nod. Isabelle pivoted from de la Vega, striding away in what she hoped was a convincing huff. Given that they were hoping she'd go away, the ring of guards let her storm through without impediment. When she reached the staircase up to the gallows, she made a sharp turn and took the steps two at a time.

"Stop her!" de la Vega shouted, and his guards rushed for the gallows' stair. The executioner in his gray hood, the broken gear symbol of the Breaker emblazoned on his ash-colored robes, rushed to kick the wobbly block from under Hysia's feet. Isabelle lunged for him, spark-arm extended.

Jean-Claude had occasionally regaled her with gruesome gallows tales, and so she'd heard that executioners wore chain shirts under their vestments to protect themselves from vengeful brothers, sons, and uncles.

Isabelle's hand passed through the executioner's robes and smacked hard chain-mail links. She took a grip and hauled back with all her might. In the months since her l'Étincelle sorcery had manifested, she'd worked hard to puzzle out what it could do. Being the first to possess this particular brand of sorcery since before the Annihilation of Rüul had left her with nothing but scraps of old legend to guide her study.

So far, she had just one trick. Her heart pounded as if it were about to burst, and needles of agony lanced through her mind, but her spark-arm flashed with inner streaks of pink lightning, and her fingers sank into the chain as if it was so much wet wicker. Her spark-arm wasn't a physical thing, as such. It didn't care about mass or momentum. The executioner jerked to a stop as if he'd hit a stone wall, and Isabelle's feet didn't even budge. She lifted the executioner as if he were a paper doll and flung him at the guards lumbering up the stairs. The lot of them went down like ninepins, rattling and crunching on the cobbles below.

Oh but it cost her. Isabelle fell to one knee, sucking wind as if she'd run for an hour with a bag over her head. Her vision constricted around the edges and her spark-arm dimmed. Worse, the impact jarred the gallows. Hysia lost her balance and slipped off the box. The strangling noose snapped taut about her neck. She squirmed and kicked though her feet were tied together. Marie darted in, seized Hysia by the waist, and lifted.

"Some help here," Marie said, her voice still ghostly.

Isabelle wobbled to her feet as if drunk in her fatigue and staggered to their aid. She pulled her maidenblade with her spark-hand, grabbed the rope with her left, and sliced through it with desperate strokes. Marie and Hysia tumbled to the platform, and Isabelle nearly fell atop them. Bootsteps thumped up behind her. De la Vega and the judge achieved the platform.

De la Vega brandished his rapier. "You dare interfere in Aragothic law! I will see you hanged for this."

Isabelle wheeled to face him. She wished the world would stop sloshing around. A manic grin strained at her cheeks. "To do that, you would have to be able to extradite me, and to do that you would have to ratify the Grand Peace."

The judge circled, his own blade drawn. "Foolish wench, you've achieved nothing here but shame and dishonor for your people. The murderess will still be hanged."

Isabelle pivoted so that neither man could get behind her. She'd lose if this came to blows.

Isabelle slowly drew herself up straight, and raised her voice so that the whole crowd could hear. "All my childhood I endured a man like you, a monster who killed to stroke his pride, a Torment who saw the clayborn as cattle. But I am not a child anymore. I am a woman grown, and never again will I stand by and let an innocent woman be murdered to soothe your wounded vanity!"

She took her gaze off the Aragoths long enough to sweep the crowd, enflamed in their passion and engaged in the drama. "Lest you forget, I am

Princess des Zephyrs of l'Empire Céleste, and I will not be cowed by a pair of Aragothic dogs! *Vive l'Empire!*"

"Vive l'Empire!" roared the crowd, shaking their fists and waving their truncheons in a great ecstatic cry. "Vive l'Empire!"

De la Vega and the judge grew pale as they took in the roiling ranks of clayborn commoners arrayed against them, and realized just how swiftly the wind had shifted against them. The terrible urge welled up in Isabelle's breast to whip the mob into a killing frenzy . . . but that would only lead to reprisal upon reprisal and the unraveling of all hope.

Marie cut Hysia's bonds and helped her to her feet. Hysia wheezed, still disoriented.

Isabelle took a deep breath just to keep from passing out. She gave de la Vega her coldest stare. "Shall we continue, or would you like to retreat in good order?"

De la Vega growled at her, but sheathed his sword. "You have not heard the last of this, Breaker's get."

Isabelle just smiled at his taunt. She'd been enduring that insult since before she could pronounce it. These days it merely reminded her of pain.

She extended her spark-hand, palm down. "Builder keep you safe from harm."

De la Vega spat on the vaporous apparition, then stalked away, his guardsmen making a tight cordon and wedging their way through the crowd. Isabelle watched them out of sight, then assisted Marie in lowering Hysia from the gallows platform. It was a long walk yet back to Isabelle's townhome.

—

"Marc, bring me a horse, I'm riding to le Ville Céleste," Isabelle said. Barely an hour had passed since she'd arrived at Rowan House, drained of all but a nervous energy that refused to be stilled. Hysia was sleeping, drugged out of her misery by a potion concocted by Isabelle's physician, Gretl. Isabelle had already sent dispatches to her diplomatic subordinates warning them of possible reprisals from the Aragoths, and now she must report her misadventure to Grand Leon.

"Make that two horses," Isabelle said. "One for me and one for Marie." She was going to need all the support she could get. Grand Leon would be furious with her. The only question was what form his wrath would take. The only guarantee was that it would be worse if she didn't deliver the news herself and of her own volition.

Marie stepped up beside her. "Three horses, Marc. One for Isabelle, one for DuPont, and one for you. I'm not going."

Marc looked to Isabelle for clarification of this contradiction.

Isabelle was stung by Marie's refusal. "I need you."

"You need guards in case de la Vega or one of his partisans decides they can't wait to plot a proper revenge," Marie insisted, her voice like a grave oracle. "You need me to go find Jean-Claude and let him know what happened."

"Ah, yes," Isabelle said. Marie was thinking more clearly than she just now. With her perfect memory, another legacy of her time as a bloodhollow, she could relate the day's events to Jean-Claude in exacting detail.

To Marc she said, "Do as she says."

"Yes, Mademoiselle des Zephyrs," Marc said, and took himself off. Marie departed on her quest.

Valérie, Isabelle's secretary, came in with her infant in one arm and Isabelle's winter riding coat in the other. "There's a storm coming," she said.

"Wouldn't want me to get sick on the way to my execution." Isabelle accepted the cloak, keenly aware that whatever punishment befell her would splatter onto her household. Her status was a resource upon which they all depended.

Valérie tsked dismissively. "I'll bet you haven't eaten today. You only ever get glum when you're starving."

"I am not glum," Isabelle protested. "Or starving." Isabelle's stomach rumbled, betraying her lie, but Valérie had already wheeled away, calling the kitchen to prepare riding meals.

Isabelle pulled on the cloak, and its weight settled on her like a warm hug. She paced the marble foyer, rehearsing explanations that might appease His Imperial Majesty. Grand Leon was not noted for his appreciation of failure or calamity, especially on the eve of his birthday celebration. He expected his subordinates to solve his problems, not bring him theirs.

A bell chimed from the library down the hall. A Glasswalker had arrived at the traveling mirror, but was this visitor friend or foe? No doubt de la Vega had taken the mirror path back to Aragoth to inveigh against her. If he'd been savvy about it and collected partisans on the way in, it would be rain-ing angry Glasswalkers in el rei's throne room by now. It was not out of the question that some zealous hothead might decide to take a stab at Isabelle, so to speak.

But would an assassin ring the bell?

"Gaston!" she called to the third of her six allotted men-at-arms. Tall and grim, he appeared with alacrity from the direction of the kitchen. "Someone calls at the mirror gate." She prayed it was not an enemy, but prayer had yet to prove the right tool for any job.

Gaston nodded and peeked inside.

Gaston said, "It's the príncipe."

"Tell him I'll meet him in the drawing room," Isabelle said, relieved and resigned at the same time. Julio loved Aragoth with the same self-immolating devotion as blessed martyrs loved the Savior. He certainly spoke of his homeland and toiled on its behalf with more passion than he ever did for her, but then it had been the focus of his life since he was a child, and he had known her but a year. Would he ever feel the same for her? There had been a brief spark between them after he'd helped her save Aragoth from civil war, but it had not kindled any of the fire that poets called love.

Isabelle didn't necessarily need fervor, though. It seemed antithetical to stability. As a woman of high status it had always been made plain to her that any marriage she might make would be a business arrangement, with duties and benefits for all sides strictly codified and enforceable.

Yet now she'd interfered with Aragothic sovereignty and come between Julio and his kingdom.

"Is it wise to let him in?" Gaston asked.

"Yes," Isabelle said. Julio was neither berserker nor assassin . . . especially not an assassin. She needed to give him her version of events and find out how the story was being told in Aragoth. She also needed to find out just who he would blame for the whole fiasco. Would he still agree to marry her?

Isabelle centered herself in the drawing room, faced the door, and pulled on a mantle of serenity.

A moment later, Gaston appeared at the door and said, "His Royal Highness Príncipe Julio de Aragoth."

Julio entered on cue. He was broad of shoulder, narrow of hip, chiseled of feature, overtopping even lanky Isabelle by a handspan. Yet this was not Julio's born body. His flesh and blood remained in faraway San Augustus, the

Aragothic capital. This was instead his espejismo, the manifestation of his Glasswalker sorcery. The real Julio was shorter than Isabelle, wiry of frame, but this paragon was how he saw himself, or what he expected of himself.

His silver eyes looked on Isabelle with concern. "Are you injured?"

The tone of the question relieved Isabelle's worst fears. He had not come here to condemn her. "I am uninjured," she said. Exhaustion and hunger did not count. "I am guessing you have heard about the debacle."

He snorted. "The news went off like a bomb in a magazine. The capital is in an uproar, but I wanted to hear your side of it."

Isabelle told him, starting with the gunshot and ending with her running de la Vega out of Crows' Feast Square. "What I don't understand is why he was so determined to hang Hysia. She's innocent."

Julio ran both his hands through his slicked-back hair, a gesture of frustration. "It's a matter we don't talk about. Aragoths, that is."

"What isn't?" Isabelle asked.

"Suicide," he said, as if even uttering the word hurt. "If what you say is true, de la Vega's cousin killed himself, and that is a terrible dishonor for his family."

Isabelle winced, for in Aragoth the word *family* claimed a territory stretching out to the hinterlands of seventh and eighths cousins.

Julio said, "It's a common belief that a man who kills himself has turned his back on the Builder, lost his place in Paradise Everlasting, and burned his soul to ash. Even the clayborn will get souls and be released from Torment when the Savior comes, but suicides will not, and so de la Vega and his whole family will live under a shadow in Paradise, with an unfillable absence in their sacred number." He quivered like one just cut down from the whipping post, as if even describing the taboo was painful.

Isabelle was disgusted. "So de la Vega and everyone else there was willing to kill an innocent woman just to save face. It doesn't even make sense theologically. Even if this belief is true, killing Hysia wouldn't restore the man's soul; the Builder knows how he died. How is that not a greater dishonor?"

Julio's hands clenched and relaxed. "Stop. Just stop. This isn't a puzzle logic can untangle. The important thing is my brother has backed the Grand Peace to the hilt, but it's not universally loved at home. While you have been stitching together the treaty here, there are factions in the Sacred Hundred who are trying to unravel it behind you. We've managed to hold them off, mostly by turning them against each other, but this . . . libel as they see it, will give them a cause around which to unite."

"This had nothing to do with the treaty," Isabelle protested. She'd ridden through every duchy, county, barony, and shire in two kingdoms. She'd negotiated, placated, and argued with everyone from grand ducs to hedge knights, to weave together a tapestry of law by which everyone would profit. It could not, must not come apart because of this.

"Except for the bit about you violating Aragothic sovereignty," Julio said. "It doesn't matter how wrong de la Vega was in his rush to condemn the woman; they will argue you had no right, no standing to interfere."

"Because I'm not yet an Aragothic subject," Isabelle said, and then asked one of the several questions screaming loudest in her mind. "Will there still be a yet?" She'd asked for a year of courtship, a year to find her footing in the wider world, and he'd granted it. True, his actual courtship had been desultory and pragmatic. They'd spend evenings discussing land acquisition, tax structures, and distribution of incomes, not exactly the stuff to inspire poets. Yet a pragmatic marriage was all she'd asked for and all she really wanted.

"Yes," he said. "The marriage is between you and me. I made you a promise, and I keep my word, no matter what."

Isabelle did not quite grimace. He always spoke of their betrothal in terms of keeping his word. There was nothing wrong with that, she supposed, but it made her feel like an item on an accounting table.

"And the treaty?" she asked.

Julio's hands flexed in agitation. "I'll return to Aragoth and start cutting a fire break. I'll tell my brother and anyone else who will listen that de la Vega misunderstood you. You meant to say Cubilla accidentally shot himself while cleaning his gun."

"Will the Sacred Hundred accept that?"

"Our allies will. Our enemies won't. De la Vega definitely won't."

"Why not? He's worked as hard on the Grand Peace as anyone. I can't believe he'd scuttle it all just because he didn't get to murder an innocent woman."

Julio winced. "You made a fool of him in public, stained his honor—"

Isabelle's anger rose. "He stained his own cursed honor."

Julio held up his hands defensively. "I agree with you. I'm just explaining how he will see it. He won't be reasoned with, but now that I have your side of the story, I can work to contain the damage. The sooner I get to it the better. In the meantime, please keep your head below the palisade."

"I have to report to Grand Leon," Isabelle said, "but after that, yes." Assuming there was an after.

Julio took her hand and squeezed it gently. His espejismo fingers were cool as glass. He opened his hand palm down. "May the Builder keep you safe from harm."

She completed the gesture palm up. "Until the Savior comes to take you home."

Isabelle saw him out the traveling mirror. He passed through its surface as if it were an open door, acknowledged her with his hand over his heart, and then stepped out of the frame. Isabelle covered the mirror with a decorative tapestry. If there was no light, there was no reflection, no room beyond the mirror, and no portal from this realm to the other through which an assassin might step. She closed and locked the iron gate that caged the mirror, just in case.

At last, with no more reasons to delay, she collected Marc and DuPont and set out for le Ville Céleste and whatever judgment Grand Leon would lay upon her.

CHAPTER

Three

Jean-Claude rescued his saddlebags and saddle from his dead horse and donned his musketeer tabard with the thundercrown emblazoned fore and aft. He generally eschewed the uniform as it tended to put people on their guard, but he was about to be calling on men in official positions, so it was good to have a sartorial trump card.

He commandeered a horse that had been left in the Lowmarket when its owner had either died or fled, then rode as fast as traffic would allow to Screaming Hall. Meanwhile, the sky closed in, stealing away any sense of the horizon, and it started to snow.

The Royal Agonesium for the Deranged was a square-fronted building carved into the cliff face. It had all the aesthetic appeal of an abscessed tooth. Its neighboring structures seemed to shrink away, as if it was contagious. There were no windows on the ground floor and all the openings higher up were narrow slits fitted with even narrower grills. Even the two statues standing out front, likenesses of Saint Isaac the Mad, looked like they were on punishment detail.

So how had Orem gotten out, why had he shown up at Mistwaithe's auction, and how had he acquired the powers of a Sanguinaire? Could he be a lateborn who had bloomed at precisely the wrong moment? It seemed unlikely.

Jean-Claude dismounted in the tiny foreyard and hitched the borrowed horse to the wrought-iron rail. The Agonesium's black-painted door was tall and narrow, like a gash in a skull. There was no doorman, so he let himself in. He traversed a claustrophobic entryway into what he took to be the main hall, a long, low room only patchily lit by three alchemical lanterns. Off to one side was a small shrine. There before a statue of Saint Isaac knelt several gaunt and shoeless men in robes so colorless they no longer even counted as gray. Vacant-eyed and muttering, any one of them could have been Orem. They were closely watched by a tall monk in mendicant's robes who droned on in Saintstongue, apparently trying to drill the ancient words in through the back of their heads. His black sash was marked with the sigil of Saint Isaac, a stylized screaming man with faces all over his body.

"Ho there," Jean-Claude called, his voice echoing in the gloom.

The chanting monk ignored him. Likely he imagined that his liturgy was more important than le roi's business.

"Who goes there?" Another monk appeared through a side door, his alchemical lantern giving a brief glimpse of a long dark hallway behind him. Short and stocky, he peered up at Jean-Claude with a squint that suggested a cave dweller confronted by the Solar.

"I am Jean-Claude, King's Own Musketeer, and who might you be?"

"Brother Houlen," he said. "How may I help you?"

"I need information about one of your former residents, a man named Orem."

"What is it you need to know, exactly?"

"I need to know the circumstances under which he departed," Jean-Claude said.

Houlen's brows beetled as if Jean-Claude had just asked him to solve one of Isabelle's equations. "You . . . why would you want to know that?"

"Because it's an important fact," Jean-Claude said. "I'm a collector of important facts, and a rather impatient collector at that."

"I'm afraid I don't know."

"Who does?" Jean-Claude asked.

"Prior Ingle," Houlen said. "But I'm afraid he's indisposed."

"Then I suggest you un-indispose him. I am on crown business." As a

King's Own Musketeer, he was the hard leading knuckle on le roi's right hand. No door could be barred to him, and there was no one he could not arrest, even the high and mighty, which was more or less how he'd got the post in the first place.

Brother Houlen made a strangled squeak, as a mouse might when cornered by a cat. "I'll see what I can do." He scurried off muttering, "Oh my. Oh my."

After giving the runner a five-second head start, Jean-Claude followed. In his experience, the word "indisposed" was synonymous with "up to no good." There were endless forms the no good could take—anything from embarrassing personal habits, to peculation large and small, to full-blown treason—but in all cases, Jean-Claude generally found it most advantageous to catch the up-to-no-gooder in the act. People were more scared of their own secrets coming to light than of anything he could invent.

Tailing the bright light in the gloomy building was easy. He followed bobbing shadows up three flights of stairs to a landing. It opened up on a cross hall that was as ostentatious as the rest of the building was austere. The floor was parquetry covered in thick rugs. The walls were wood-paneled with patterned wainscoting, and alchemical lamps in decorative sconces drove away all shadows. Across the hall stood a pair of ornately carved double doors.

Houlen hesitated outside the door, dancing from foot to foot as if he had to pee. Just as he raised his hand to knock, a low piteous wail came from the other side. A woman in pain. Houlen flinched, raised his face to the sky, closed his eyes, and mouthed silent words of prayer.

Anger rose hot in Jean-Claude's heart. He drew the bag of coins from around his throat, slipped into the hall, and coshed Houlen on the back of the head. Houlen dropped like a pudding.

The woman's whimpering came again, followed by gagging noises. Jean-Claude's blood simmered to a boil. He rolled Houlen over and snagged his keys from his belt. It was easy to see which one fit this ornate lock. Jean-Claude pushed it in, turned it hard, and yanked the doors open.

Bright light dazzled him. Many dozen alchemical lights filled the room with an eye-watering glare.

"Who are you?" snapped a deep, heavy voice from the unexpected light. "What are you doing here?"

Jean-Claude pulled his hat down to shade his eyes and saw the bottom half of a man wearing a blood-soaked butcher's apron over monastic robes. His feet were clad in heavy workman's boots.

"I am Jean-Claude, King's Own Musketeer, and I am here to see Prior Ingle on crown business." But where was the woman whose anguish he'd heard?

"I am Prior Ingle and this is my domain," said the voice.

Jean-Claude forced himself to look up, his eyes slowly adjusting to the burn. There was a girl strapped to a strange sort of table that held her propped up at an angle, her arms and legs akimbo. Her head extended off the table but was held firmly in place by a metal brace. Her mouth was stopped with a cruel gag, and a set of clawlike spreaders forced her eyelids back until her eyes were fully exposed in their sockets. Floods of tears, pink with blood, streamed down her cheeks. Even more grotesque, her scalp had been cut back to reveal the hemisphere of her skull, and a section of that had been cut away to reveal her brain.

"Breaker's Blood," Jean-Claude spat, his shock rotting quickly into revulsion. It was the exact same wound Orem bore.

"Glorious, isn't it. To think the body receives the Builder's word through this spongy filter." Ingle placed the extracted piece of skull on a nearby stand. He was bald-headed with a full beard, braided and pulled into a long fork. He wore brass-rimmed goggles with dark lenses. He prodded the woman's brain with a glass rod. A galvanic spark flashed. Her whole body gave a giant spasm that made every tendon stand out against her skin. Another ghastly scream found its way around the gag.

"Stop that!" Jean-Claude stepped in and swatted the rod from the man's hand.

Ingle lurched back. "Stand down! This woman is my patient. You have no right—"

"I am a King's Own Musketeer. I have whatever rights I need." He extracted his papers of authority and held them out like a talisman to ward off this Torment-fiend.

"Rubbish. Even a King's Own Musketeer needs more justification than mere whimsy."

"Do I not have justification?" Jean-Claude asked, glancing at the woman. She was breathing as hard as she could through the gag.

"Indeed you do not," Ingle said. "This is sensitive research."

"Cutting holes in people's heads is not research," Jean-Claude snarled.

"How else are you going to find out what goes on in there? Did you know each section of the brain regulates a different function of the body? I could not have discovered that without cutting open a few skulls." He gestured toward the far wall where stood shelf upon shelf of glass bottles, each one with a human brain inside.

While Jean-Claude gawped in horror, Ingle continued. "This unfortunate woman carries the Builder's gifts, but she is subject to visual and auditory hallucinations. I am vivisecting her visual and audible domains in an attempt to isolate the precise nodule wherein the defect is located. In order to do that, I must stimulate the brain to bring on a hallucinatory period. Otherwise it would be like trying to study rain during a drought."

He stooped to pick up his galvanic rod, and came up to find the barrel of Jean-Claude's pistol pointed squarely between his eyes.

"No," Jean-Claude growled. That could be Isabelle on that table. That could be her brilliant brain shriven of its armor.

Ingle backed up a step. "Are you mad? Put that thing away!"

"Put her back together," Jean-Claude said, backing Ingle up against the wall of brains.

"Impossible," Ingle said, standing on tiptoes trying to get away from the gaping mouth of the pistol's barrel. "The operation has already gone too far. If I don't finish it, she'll just linger a few days in agony before dying, and she won't even yield any information. And even if she doesn't die, she'll still be mad. Her life has no value, but her death will help me unlock the Builder's secrets. This is the kindest thing—"

Jean-Claude kicked him in the knee, driving him to the floor. He howled in pain.

"You misunderstand your position. This is not the point where you argue with me. This is the point where you put this woman back the way you found her."

"Your master will hear of this!" Ingle warned. "He'll have your head off."

Jean-Claude seized Ingle by his forked beard and yanked him to his feet. "You are damned right he'll hear about this, because I will report it, and if I were you I would be well out of the city by then. I wouldn't even take time to pack. If I were you, I would run and find a deep dark hole to hide in and then find a rock to pull in over my head. Grand Leon may be a sneaky, manipulative, ruthless bastard; he may toy with the wealthy, frustrate the powerful, and squeeze the capable for every advantage they can give him; but if there is one thing he despises, if there is one thing that will earn his instant and unyielding contempt, it is a cowardly cur who torments the helpless. Now get to work or we'll see how well your brain works with a three-finger hole through the middle of it."

Ingle clung to Jean-Claude's arm. "I've never put one back together."

Jean-Claude shoved Ingle toward his tray of implements. "Then now is your chance to learn a new skill. If she dies, you die." By all rights, Ingle should die anyway, for any of the hundred murders stacked on his shelves. More likely Grand Leon would find some more political use for the prior in his endless sparring with the Temple. Jean-Claude only prayed Ingle suffered for his sins.

Jean-Claude moved to the opposite side of the tilted table from Ingle. The poor woman's stretched-open eyes followed him. She seemed to be trying to weep and hold perfectly still at the same time. He was astounded she was still conscious, apparently aware.

Jean-Claude inspected the eye clamps, found the pin that held them in place, and ever so carefully disengaged them. The instant they could, her eyes snapped shut, displacing another flood of bloody tears from her contracting eye-wells.

"I'm going to get you out of here," he said in his most soothing voice. Even if his efforts came to nothing else, she would not die like this, not strapped to a table, alone and afraid.

Ingle's hands were shaking as he picked the discarded section of skull from the plate and gingerly replaced it. "This won't work, you know. It's pointless. The wound will fester—"

"And you will become food for worms."

Ingle took several deep breaths, trying to calm his nerves. "Very well. I need an extra hand here. Hold the skull in place while I stitch the scalp back on."

Jean-Claude regarded him suspiciously, but was forced to acknowledge the logistical problem he faced. He replaced his pistol in his belt sash and circled the table.

"Just hold it in place. Touch lightly."

"I should wash my hands," Jean-Claude said. Isabelle's physician, Gretl, who was the most talented surgeon he'd ever met, was a tightly packed powder keg on the subject of wound sanitation.

"What for?" Ingle said. "They're just going to get dirty again. Press here."

Jean-Claude stretched his fingers out to touch the bone. His stomach got queasy even before his fingers made contact. He'd seen all manner of blood and gore and splintered bone in his time. He could walk across a field of dead and dying men and blot out the tangible clouds of pain and despair that overhung such carnage, but this was different. He was but a bone's breadth from this living, alert woman's thoughts, her soul. Ingle had meant to dissect who she was, to cut away pieces of her memory, her dreams, her secrets. Jean-Claude could imagine no more intimate or terrible violence.

His fingertips contacted the bone. It was slightly slimy. He choked down his gorge.

Ingle said, "Now just hold still."

It was the sudden tightness in Ingle's voice that gave him away. Jean-Claude lunged sideways, leaving the bone behind. Ingle's scalpel sliced Jean-Claude's collar instead of his throat.

Jean-Claude's bad leg twisted and he sprawled on his back.

Ingle charged him, snarling in rage and fear. Jean-Claude grabbed his apron, tugged him off-balance, thrust a boot heel into his gut, and flipped him through the double doors. The move was supposed to end with Jean-Claude completing a backward somersault and rolling gracefully to his feet. Alas, grace and flexibility had left him years ago. He flopped onto his belly and scrambled to his feet in time to see Ingle bolting for the stairwell. Jean-Claude pulled his pistol, aimed, and squeezed the trigger.

The pistol barked, spat fire and smoke. Ingle howled, staggered through the doorway, and then screamed. Jean-Claude rushed forward and reached the landing in time to see Ingle caroming down the steep stairway in a series of fleshy thumps, his body an increasingly disorganized sack of limbs. He bounced off a support post and fell into the central well. What landed at the bottom resembled a splattered jelly-floater.

Jean-Claude limped back into the surgery, cursing under his breath. Damned idiot. He'd lost Ingle, and with him the best thread of hope this woman had, not to mention losing his best lead on Orem.

He approached the table. The woman's eyes were open. The whites were bloody but her irises were a pale shade of gray, her pupils pinpricks in the dazzling light. She watched him, but the gag in her mouth and the wrinkles caused by the relaxation of skin caused by her scalping made her expression impossible to read.

"My name is Jean-Claude," he said. "I'm going to help you. You're going to live."

Was it a sin to tell such a gross lie when he had no other comfort to give? How could anyone live with their scalp peeled and their skull pierced? He tore off his cravat and turned the damned frilly thing into a field-dressing, folding her scalp back into place and fastening it as snugly as he could.

"I'm going to take that gag out," he said, releasing her mouth.

She coughed, bringing up gobs of blood and slimy spit that he brushed away with his sleeve. He prayed she didn't choke to death. When at last the paroxysm had passed, she looked at him through blood-smeared eyes. "He tried to cut my head off," she rasped.

"Yes, but I'm going to have someone sew it back on again." There was only one person who would do for that: Gretl, who had learned medicine from an evil genius with the knowledge handed down from the saints themselves. "I'm going to have to summon help."

"Don't leave me!" she squealed.

"What's your name?" Jean-Claude asked.

"Niñon," she said. "Lady Niñon du Grace."

"Niñon," he said. "I must go, but I swear to you as a King's Own Musketeer I will return at once."

Only as Jean-Claude rushed out the door did he wonder why a lady of pedigree was locked up in this madhouse. Sometimes excess daughters of such houses were given up to nunneries, but never to any place like Screaming Hall. No noble family would want the taint of madness associated with their name.

Ingle had said she bore the Builder's gift of sorcery, but clearly she was no Sanguinaire. Was she blessed of some lost sorcery like Isabelle, or was she possessed of the blood of two sorceries, an abomination in the eyes of the Temple?

He reached the stairwell landing and looked down to see a gaggle of monks and a pair of city guardsmen milling around Ingle's body.

"You there!" Jean-Claude shouted. "Guardsman!"

Everyone looked up. A familiar pair of eyebrows bristled up at Jean-Claude.

"You again!" shouted Sergeant. "Ill-fated, misbegotten, spawn of spittle, how many bodies do you intend to roll through my streets today? You're worse than the Breaker-be-damned plague."

"One less if I can help it. In the name of le roi, send your swiftest runner to Rowan House. Fetch a woman named Gretl. Tell her Jean-Claude needs her. We have an open head wound that needs her utmost skill."

Sergeant gave him an incredulous look and pointed at Ingle. "No surgery is going to bring this one back, le roi's command or no."

"Not him. His victim. She's up here. Send the runner. Now!"

CHAPTER

Four

The Pilgrims' Road zigged and zagged like a demented squirrel up the sheer cliff of the Rivencrag. In some places the road cut into the stone or bored through it, but most of its length was an exposed wooden shelf road. Endless antlike streams of people trudged along, hauling supplies, bearing messages, and making pilgrimages both sacred and political.

Isabelle, Marc, and DuPont plodded along with the upward stream. If nothing else, the long slog provided a brilliant view of the deep sky. Swarms of skyships dipped and turned just off the coast, swooping in to load or unload, but a storm was brewing off the coast. By tomorrow morning, those ships that could not fit in the scant safety of Rocher Royale's tiny harbor would be forced to flee antiwise along the Craton Massif's rim to more sheltered ports.

Already the sky closed in, and a thin cold wind clawed at Isabelle's skin and made her eyes water. The first flakes of a new snow bounced off the sheer cliff wall and skirled around her horse's hooves.

Isabelle craned her neck to count how many more switchbacks there were to the top. It was hard to see much of anything from this angle, save the over-hanging branches of the imperial residence, le Ville Céleste.

Grand Leon's abode had not been built by human hands. It was a relic of the Primus Mundi and had survived the Breaking of the World. Five great crooked shafts of quondam metal erupted from the rock and kinked skyward. They stretched several more kilometers above the cliff tops, like the grasping fingers of a dead and buried god, forever clawing at the whistling wind. Their metal skin was dull gray in this light.

Once those structures had been a venerated shrine to the Builder main-tained by an order of Arcanist Monks, but when the Temple had refused to acknowledge Grand Leon as Defender of the Enlightened and rightful ruler of l'Empire, le roi had confiscated the shrine and the monastery and added it to his demesne, just to make a point.

He could very well make another point of ruining Isabelle. He had ele-vated her to this rarified position, Ambassadress to the Grand Peace, and he could destroy her with a word. All he had to do was withdraw his favor and she'd fall. Would Julio be able to catch her? Would he be allowed to?

And what would happen to Isabelle's household? Valérie was clayborn gen-try, but she had neither land nor stipend. Marie was dead to her family, and Gretl had been born a peasant. Jean-Claude would do all he could, she was sure, but he could not support so many people.

More than anything, Isabelle wished Jean-Claude were here. He knew Grand Leon's mind better than anyone. She kept hoping against all expec-tations that Marie had found him, and he would pop out of the crowd and greet her with one of his familiar alliterations. Alas, though the path was packed with pilgrims, porters, partygoers, and a plethora of other persons starting with "P," there was no sign of her musketeer.

By the time she crested the high plateau, the blizzard had made its en-trance, sweeping in like a white shroud to cover the festival grounds. Pavil-ions, platforms, and gonfalons faded into and out of view through curtains of snow. Menials hurried hither and yon with rolls of bunting, barrels of water, and Builder only knew what else in the service of last-minute preparations for the opening act of Grand Leon's birthday celebration tomorrow. Isabelle prayed he could summon grace enough to postpone the affair if the weather failed to abate. If he commanded it, people would stand for hours in the snow, cold, and wet, and many would die for his vanity.

Beyond the fairground loomed le Ville Céleste. The bent and twisted columns glowed faintly in the gathering dark like bolts of lightning frozen as they crashed from the heavens. Isabelle's party passed through the gates of the stone wall surrounding the nearest spire. The masonry would have been impressive anywhere else, but here it only served to emphasize the immensity of the quondam structures it encircled.

Hoardings, balconies, buttresses, and bridgeworks had been built up around the spire itself, wood and stone hugging the primeval metal like the last bark clinging to the smooth core of a dead tree. Isabelle dismounted, handed her reins to DuPont, and told her men to seek shelter.

She joined the line of people climbing the broad staircase toward the spire's nearest opening. Grand Leon and his court dwelt inside the ancient edifice, the royal halls, imperial courts, and extremely important antechambers built like an inside-out tree house within the mostly hollow trunk.

Isabelle's every step was heavy with dread and fatigue. She had done the right thing at Crows' Feast Square, or at least she'd done the best she could with no time to devise an elegant solution. Would Grand Leon see it that way? She'd stood up to le roi before on a matter of principle, but that time her determination had worked in favor with his political aims.

The entrance into the quondam spire was an asymmetrical pentagon tilted slightly to the right and short enough that Isabelle had to duck when walking through. The architect in charge of humanizing the entrance had outdone himself building a stone arch to frame the opening and hanging curtains to visually straighten the crooked edges, but there was ultimately no disguising the fact that humans had to adapt themselves to this ancient marvel, not the other way around.

Isabelle captured a page's attention. "I need to speak to the chamberlain."

An hour later, Isabelle was admitted into Grand Leon's presence. She climbed a spiral stair somewhere in the twisted innards of the spire. With a rattle of chains and a rumbling of tracked wheels, the ceiling above her head split and the sections parted.

Isabelle's nerves hummed like overstretched sheets in the wind as she climbed into the audience chamber. The exact size of the room was impossible to tell as its perimeter was lost in shadows. The floor was parquetry and the wooden pillars for the vaulted roof were graven with images of conquering armies, bountiful fields, and beautiful landscapes.

Harsh alchemical spotlights illuminated a glade in the center of this artificial forest, near the center of which stood a dais and a throne. Grand Leon, resplendent in cloth of gold and blue silk damask, nearly overflowed his audience throne. Thick ringlets of black hair, originally somebody else's, cascaded down his shoulders like ash from a volcano. His face was old and papery, with sagging eyelids and heavy jowls. His fingers were liver-spotted, with knuckles like the knots in mountain pines, but his legs, sheathed in close-fitting tights, retained a manly solidity. Most importantly, his blood-shadow pooled at his feet like an obedient hound, thicker and more liquid than any shadow had a right to be.

Isabelle nearly stumbled over her own misgivings, but she forced her stride to lengthen. She emerged into the circle of light and curtsied on her mark. "Monsieur."

"I had such high hopes for you," Grand Leon said, his tone as cold as the blizzard outside. He did not bid her to rise. "I gave you a measure of my power. I put you in charge of a great and necessary project. I defended you against those who said you were too young, too weak, too foolish, too female. Never in my wildest imaginations did I imagine that you would embarrass me so. In a single morning, you scandalized the Aragothic delegation, unilaterally voided a lawfully obtained confession, overturned a legal verdict, absconded with a condemned criminal, and wrongfully accused the murder victim of committing suicide. Is that broadly correct, or have I left anything out?"

Isabelle's heart quailed, but he'd tested her like this before, when he'd made her his ambassador. She held her ground. "The accused was innocent. The trial was a sham, its conclusion a farce, and Ambassador Cubilla did commit suicide whether Consul de la Vega wants to admit it or not. Facts are facts no matter who denies them."

"And the consequences? You have endangered the Grand Peace, and if the peace fails, the killing resumes, and l'Empire risks the death of a thousand skirmishes. Was it worth it? One clayborn life weighed against the countless lives the Grand Peace means to save?"

Isabelle clenched her teeth, for she knew where this line of argument must lead. Saving Hysia had been political folly, but she could not have left that poor woman to die.

"Worth it to whom?" Isabelle asked. "To Señora Dominguez it was, for she would otherwise be dead, murdered by her own countrymen. De la Vega broke his own laws in convicting her, and allowing her to die when I could have prevented it would have made me complicit."

"Execution is not murder, and Aragoth's laws and courts are not yours to judge," Grand Leon said. "Did you not consider having Príncipe Julio drag de la Vega before the Aragothic Sacred Hundred? Threatening him might have caused him to pause."

"In the confusion of the moment, that ruse did not occur to me," Isabelle said, "but even if it had, I doubt that would have slowed him down. His passions were enflamed."

"That does not excuse you from being equally hot-tempered. You exceeded your authority."

"I did not exercise my authority or claim to act in l'Empire's name."

"Nevertheless you were my ambassadress, and your actions reflected on me."

The "were" lanced Isabelle like an arrow through her breastbone; she was already condemned.

"And are you not merciful?" Isabelle asked. "Hysia Dominguez was horrified by her master's death and bullied into confessing his murder. She was about to be a human sacrifice, and everyone seems to think that's acceptable because she's just a soulless clayborn. I can't speak to souls, for those are the Builder's province, but if justice doesn't work for the weak then it doesn't work for anybody, and we are nothing more than barbarians with shinier buttons."

"Strange, I was under the impression that you had studied history," Grand Leon said. "If you had, surely you would know about the tens of thousands that I have sacrificed, sent onto impossible marches and shoveled into the mouths of the enemies' guns, just to bring l'Empire this much peace, this much space in which to negotiate a more permanent armistice. I did not spend those lives so that you could fritter this chance away on the vanity of your pristine virtues."

Grand Leon's brows drew down, and his bloodshadow rolled forward like a wave encroaching on a sandcastle. Isabelle set her teeth and braced for pain. She'd been shadowburned before, so many times she'd lost count, and there was no getting used to it or rising above it.

But Grand Leon's bloodshadow halted an eyelash short of Isabelle's shadow. "If it is justice you wish, then you shall have the rule of law. Tomorrow you shall stand accused of interfering in the affairs of an allied power, and you shall present your defense to the Imperial Parlement. Perhaps their judgment will remind you of the smallness of men."

Isabelle's skin chilled and her breath ran away. The Imperial Parlement existed to judge high nobility indicted of crimes against l'Empire. It was composed of men from the lower orders of nobility and the clayborn gentry who were always happy to condemn their social superiors. Many of them considered Isabelle the Breaker's get and loathed her just for being alive. This wouldn't be a trial, it would be a slaughter.

Yet Grand Leon had given her no choice, offered her no other surrender.

"As you say, Monsieur," she breathed.

Numb, she backed out and wobbled from the room. She stumbled on the stair, overbalanced, and might have fallen save that a strong hand clasped her shoulder and set her back on her balance.

"Steady," said the newcomer in a rumbling voice.

Isabelle turned and found herself nose to nose with a Seelenjäger. Isabelle had never seen one of the shapeshifters in person, but he could be nothing else. His lean face was covered in sleek tawny fur with spots like those of a leopard. His eyes, half-lidded but perfectly alert, were cat-slitted and the color of honey.

He was dressed as a Praetorian guard, one of Grand Leon's personal bodyguard of sorcerers. His black doublet was blazoned with a golden thundercrown: jags of lightning woven into the shape of a coronet. His broad-brimmed black hat bore a triple loop of gold braid for a band.

He descended onto the step with her, which made him a handspan shorter than she. He doffed his hat and swept a bow despite the limited space. "Pardon my lack of a proper introduction. I am Capitaine Erste Ewald Bitterlich, at your service."

He was excessively polite for someone whose job was clearly to remove the rubbish. "Thank you," she said, resisting the urge to spew her bitterness at him. He wasn't at fault for his master.

He extended a courteous elbow. "May I have the honor?"

Usually she would have rejected the offer. She was quite capable of navigating stairs on her own and since losing her right arm she was extremely reluctant to give up custody of her left . . . but just now she needed the stability. The whole world had turned upside down and her thoughts ran in circles like a rat in a barrel. Did Grand Leon really mean to feed her to the eels, or was this part of some greater strategy?

She descended the stairs mechanically, allowing Bitterlich to guide her. She felt strangely weightless and hollow. This must be what it felt like to fall from the sky cliff, falling forever through sky and storm into ever-thickening gloom.

As soon as they were out of earshot of the audience chamber, Bitterlich said, "I for one, applaud your actions. There is no more virtuous act than protecting the weak."

"Thank you," Isabelle said, ingrained politeness serving her well. *The cost was too high,* she wanted to say, except that if she had to do it over again, she would.

Up the stairwell from below wafted a horribly familiar voice, biting and cold as a sharpened icicle. "Do not pretend you know my mind."

That was her father, le Comte des Zephyrs. But what in all the ten thousand Torments was he doing here? When last she'd seen him a year ago on l'Île des Zephyrs, he'd been all but confined to his bed, slowly dying of the red consumption. He was too weak to travel.

Another voice, high and mocking, replied, "I knows ye'd sell blood for coin."

Isabelle emerged from the stairwell and spied two men in a curtained alcove just off the landing. It was the same alcove she'd occupied not half an hour ago awaiting her audience.

The first man was des Zephyrs, though not in his own body. He'd inhabited one of his bloodhollows, a man shadowburned to the verge of death, stripped of his mind but left alive to serve as a vessel for le comte's will. The bloodhollow was nearly transparent, with white bones and ghostly organs visible through skin like glass. The bloodhollow explained how he had come to be here, if not why. Most Sanguinaire nobles kept bloodhollow emissaries at the capital for routine business, though it was considered gauche to appear before le roi in this way.

The other gentleman, if the term could be stretched to fit, was a short, wiry man with a wheat-yellow doublet striped black like a wasp. His narrow jaw ended in a pointed chin that had been furnished with a long, waxed, upcurling goatee. A pointed hat arched forward from his brow, giving his profile the aspect of a crescent moon. The air around him swirled in constant motion, the sorcerous blazon of a Gyrine Windcaller.

His gaze found Isabelle, and his small black eyes glittered. He drank her in from toes to crown, and a lecherous smile grew upon his face. Isabelle felt suddenly greasy.

"What giantesses bestride this land?" he asked, glancing at des Zephyrs. "'Tis one of yours, is she not?"

"She is nothing of mine." Des Zephyrs's voice quavered with hatred, quite unlike his usual controlled sneer. His facial features, pushing out from within the bloodhollow's face, were blurred like soft clay. Pushing himself across the deep sky from his sickbed must be taxing his waning strength. What could have inspired him to make such an effort?

Des Zephyrs said, "If you wish to see the face of a true traitor, look before you. She abandoned her family in our moment of need."

Isabelle's hackles went up, anger flaring amidst the despair in her soul like ghost fires in a bog. "You sold me like chattel before I was even conceived." In point of fact, des Zephyrs hadn't actually fathered her. Isabelle's actual sire was a Fenice named Lorenzo Barbaro, about whom she knew absolutely nothing else, despite putting out subtle inquiries.

Isabelle said, "I wonder what you traded me for." Alas she had no leverage to compel that answer from him. "I imagine it is all spent by now, wasted on spite. My only consolation is that you have no heir save Guillaume, a man who cannot count past ten without dropping his trousers."

Des Zephyrs's face contorted in anger. "Guillaume is my true son and heir, and you are nothing. Your life is dust. The whole city is atwitter with the tale of your stupidity. The bookmakers are giving good odds on your neck in a noose."

Isabelle twisted one corner of her mouth up. "Your true son and heir is the same boy you said had all the wits and spine of a garden slug." And since when had he cared for the opinion of gamblers?

Had he grown so much smaller in the last year, or had she grown so much bigger? She had ascended heights the petty, vindictive comte could not dream of. That was why the precipice before her felt so much dizzier.

Des Zephyrs took a step toward her, raising his hand as if to slap her, but Bitterlich stepped between them. His voice rumbled like a tiger's growl. "I would advise against aggression, Monsieur Comte, if you like all your pieces attached."

Des Zephyrs faltered but said, "I am an invited guest of Grand Leon."

"And I am the man who throws out unruly guests," Bitterlich said.

Des Zephyrs gestured to Isabelle. "And yet she is still here."

That barb stung Isabelle. Her father could not know her predicament, but sometimes a stab in the dark struck true.

Bitterlich's eyes narrowed just a fraction. "Be aware that I shall inform His Majesty that you offered violence to one of his guests."

Des Zephyrs spat on the floor. "*Schwarze Bestie.* Your kind are fit for the yoke and plow. Your word will not stand against a Sanguinaire."

The Gyrine slapped a hand on des Zephyrs's shoulder. "Haul in yer tongue. We're here to work."

Isabelle turned her attention to the aberration that was the Windcaller. Air swirled around him in a constant vortex. His people, the Gyrine, had been declared anathema by the Temple, expelled from the Risen Kingdoms hundreds of years ago. They survived on great clan balloons, prospering by piracy and theft. No one dealt with them openly, and they certainly weren't invited to royal audiences, but here he was.

Isabelle said, "I thought Gyrine made a point of never working."

"'Tis not easy being the lords of the sky," he said. "What with all the tithes to be collected, we leaves simple drudgery to folks more suited for it."

"And how do you propose to collect tithes from Grand Leon?" she asked.

The Windcaller flashed a smile that looked like a badly maintained picket fence. "'Tis a private matter."

A herald appeared from the stairs and said, "His Imperial Majesty, le Roi de Tonner, Leon the Fourteenth, summons le Comte Narcisse des Zephyrs and the Gyrine Windcaller Hailer Dok of the Black Rain Clan."

Isabelle watched des Zephyrs and Dok up the stairs. They were up to no good, whatever they had planned, and her father's behavior was more than strange . . . but Grand Leon had made it utterly plain that he no longer valued her opinion. He could take care of himself.

Bitterlich waited until they were out of earshot, then said, "I congratulate you on overcoming your heritage."

Isabelle snorted. "It is not hard to escape that which is trying to expel you. All you have to do is not resist."

Bitterlich escorted Isabelle into the foyer beyond the landing. Bronze doors bearing images of Grand Leon in his glory boomed shut behind them. Around the room snaked a long queue of people awaiting their chance for a word with le roi. The length of the wait for an audience was legendary and most were turned away at the gate, but still the line persisted. Some of the waiters prayed and schemed to obtain a favorable nod from the one man who could smite their foes or elevate them above their rivals. Others earned their keep merely by being part of the line, watching and counting, and reporting back to their masters who had gained access to the inner sanctum. What would they make of Isabelle?

Isabelle detached herself from Bitterlich. "Thank you, Capitaine, but I can find my way from here."

"If I may," Bitterlich said sotto voce. "There is still a blizzard outside, and I know a place where you may shelter safely for the night."

Isabelle allowed herself to be led. She wouldn't make it down the Rivencrag in this blow.

Bitterlich guided her through lamp-lit wooden corridors, many of which were built at odd angles, sloped, or curved, up and around and down again. The spires themselves were filled with the remnants of a vast and intricate structure, like the internal organs of some immense mechanical beast. Mere mortals, even mighty ones like Grand Leon, were compelled to build around these immovable obstacles, claiming the space but never dominating it. The strange construction made the place a maze.

Fortunately Bitterlich seemed to know his way around.

He said, "If it is not too much of a burden, may I ask you about your father?"

"I have no burdens left," Isabelle said, her bitterness sloshing over the rim of her cup. "What do you want to know?"

"He has a reputation for being shrewd and cagey, not trustworthy by any stretch, but not . . . reckless."

Isabelle had spent a lot of the last year not thinking about Narcisse des Zephyrs. He wasn't her problem anymore, but Bitterlich was right; le Comte wasn't up to his old standard.

She said, "The red consumption wastes the mind as well as the body. I am given to understand that raving dementia is amongst its final stages."

"How advanced is his disease?"

"By all rights he should have been dead years ago, but he's too wicked to die."

Bitterlich snorted. "Men who know they are bound for Torment cling to the gates of the graveyard."

Isabelle arched her eyebrow at this heresy. It happened to be one she shared, but caution was in order when discussing such things. She said, "Saintborn are automatically acquitted. Our Souls cleansed of sin and sent straight to Paradise Everlasting."

Bitterlich shrugged. "If a man has lived his whole life outside the Builder's directives of reason, compassion, and mercy, it is fair to imagine that he does not believe in salvation, either. Torment, though, such people understand; they have already built a gateway to it in their hearts."

"I like your theology," she said, which won her a brief bright glance from those gorgeous golden eyes. She'd seen people with mouth smiles that didn't reach their eyes. Bitterlich did it the other way around.

They fetched up on a landing before a curtained doorway flanked by two Thunderguard and a doorman in royal livery.

"What can I do for you, Capitaine?" asked the doorman.

Bitterlich said, "Please inform the comtesse that Princess Isabelle is here to see her."

The doorman nodded and ducked inside.

"Comtesse who?" Isabelle asked, alarmed. She'd been anticipating a quiet bed someplace she could fall over for the night, not an introduction to a member of the court.

"Coquetta," Bitterlich said.

Isabelle's eyes rounded. "Are you mad? She's one of the Trefoil." The Lace Trefoil were Grand Leon's three permanent mistresses. They formed Grand Leon's innermost circle, and it was to them most of l'Empire's daily business had devolved. Coquetta was the youngest, though still old enough to be Isabelle's mother. She arranged Grand Leon's social schedule, and was chief shepherd of the capital gossip.

Bitterlich said, "I suspect you will find her nothing but compassionate."

The doorman returned and on his heels came a gorgeous plush woman with a round face and an infectious smile.

The doorman said, "Princess Isabelle, be known to Comtesse Coquetta."

Coquetta glided over and clasped Isabelle's one hand between both of hers. Coquetta's fingers were cool and trembled, but her manner was all welcome. "Princess Isabelle. What a delight it is to meet you at last. My, you are a tall one. Come in."

"It's a pleasure meet you, too," Isabelle said automatically.

Coquetta swept her into a receiving room done up in pale blue and subtle silver, unusual colors for a Sanguinaire, who usually insisted on white for everything in order to show their bloodshadows to best effect. Coquetta, though, had one of the weakest bloodshadows Isabelle had ever seen, barely a pink stain where it was cast. Yet even a little sorcery was better than none in the eyes of the Temple and the law.

Coquetta's face was pale and the brief whirl of activity left her breathing heavily, yet pointing that out, even to offer sympathy, would have been the height of rudeness. Célestial women were always perfectly healthy, thank you very much, never mind that boiling fever or the sucking chest wound. It was akin to the way Aragoths felt about suicides.

"I've heard so much about your adventures," Coquetta said, getting her breath back. "Is it really true that you stabbed Mad Queen Margareta in the bum?"

"I was trying to make an important point," Isabelle said. "Madame Comtesse, before I say anything else I must inform you that Grand Leon has decided to try me before the Parlement."

"Over that kerfuffle with Consul de la Vega," Coquetta said, without a hint of surprise. "That is unfortunate, but my boudoir is hardly his court, and I will entertain who I wish."

"Won't you harboring me make him angry?" Isabelle had no desire to cause trouble for anyone else.

"Of course not. You should evict from your head the notion that Leon ever acts on impulse or out of anger. Every move is calculated to serve his political purpose. He wants to keep the Grand Peace alive, don't you?"

"Of course, but—"

Coquetta continued. "Several of Consul de la Vega's personal family members are amongst the staunchest opponents of the Grand Peace. They have spent the last several hours howling for justice before the law, demanding satisfaction. Why would they do that, given that Grand Leon has backed you to the hilt on every move you've made in the last year, given that all of society has taken to calling you *le cousin imperial*? Surely they must expect Monsieur to defend you now as he has before."

Coquetta said nothing and Isabelle forced herself to work it through. "Because while de la Vega might want my guts made into sausage, his allies couldn't care less. I imagine all of their howling is aimed at their own people, 'Look how untrustworthy the Célestials are, and so forth.'"

"Exactly," Coquetta said. "Grand Leon will let them work themselves into a fine frenzy, accusing l'Empire of betraying its commitment to the treaty, and then discredit their argument completely."

"By giving them my head in a kettle and calling it soup," Isabelle said. She was in no mood to praise Grand Leon's political acumen. She was sure to be convicted, and what then? What if Parlement decided her good deed was a capital crime? Should she appeal to Grand Leon and throw herself on the mercy of a man who stood to profit by showing her none?

Coquetta made a grim smile. "The only reason this ploy will work is that the enemies of the Grand Peace know how valuable you are to Grand Leon. But Leon never destroys anything of value. It may be that someday a different sort of opportunity will be placed before you."

Isabelle looked away. "I think that I will not wait for crumbs." The next time she saw Julio, she would say "yes" to his proposal . . . if this mess did not disqualify her.

"As well you shouldn't," Coquetta agreed. She cast a glance at Bitterlich. "Is there something else you need, Capitaine?"

Bitterlich, standing patiently just inside the door, said, "A matter of my duty, though Mademoiselle des Zephyrs may find it of interest as well. Can you tell me what business Comte Narcisse des Zephyrs has with le roi? I was under the impression that Monsieur was not taking unsolicited audiences this month."

Coquetta frowned and said, "He isn't, but there are some protocols that must be obeyed. Monsieur des Zephyrs called in his death wish."

Surprise lifted Isabelle out of her wallow. Every Sanguinaire was entitled to a hearing before Grand Leon as a dying wish. It was ever and always a last request, for if the Sanguinaire for some reason failed to expire, he or she would nevertheless be treated as dead thereafter. These requests usually involved the imminent disposition of the soon-to-be-deceased's estate.

"That doesn't make any sense," she said. "There's no question at all about who will inherit l'Île des Zephyrs, unless something has happened to Guillaume."

Coquetta dabbed her sweating face with a kerchief. "I don't think so. If memory serves, he came with your sister-in-law for her confinement."

Isabelle said, "I'd heard Arnette was pregnant, but I can't imagine my father letting Guillaume out of his sight, much less off the skyland."

"They're staying in your family's townhome," Coquetta said.

"I didn't even know my family had a townhome in Rocher Royale. My father always called the capital a den of thieves and flatterers. He never left l'Île des Zephyrs in all the time I was growing up, more's the pity."

"The property was a wedding gift from your mother's parents to encourage the young couple to visit. It doesn't seem to have worked."

Why was Guillaume here? As much as his father kept him on a leash, Guillaume had no particular desire to escape. The entire purpose and focus of his life had been waiting for his father to die so that he might inherit the countship. He had so far been stymied by his sire's stubborn refusal to expire . . . until now. The death wish would render Narcisse des Zephyrs legally dead, clearing the breach for Guillaume.

"Do you have any idea what my father's death wish is?"

Coquetta shook her head slowly as if trying to stir up some elusive memory. "He actually put in the petition several months ago, but the death wish is a confidential affair, and I had no reason to pry."

Bitterlich said, "Narcisse brought a Gyrine Windcaller named Hailer Dok with him to the death wish audience. I don't suppose your minions have told you anything about him."

Coquetta huffed a hopeless laugh. "A Gyrine? Really? I'll keep an ear out, but with all the nobility flooding in for Grand Leon's birthday party, my friendly gossips are having a hard time just keeping a finger on the biggest troublemakers and the most lurid scandals."

"An open ear is all I ask," Bitterlich said. "And now I must take my leave. Madame Comtesse, Mademoiselle des Zephyrs, should either of you hear anything about Windcaller Dok, please let me know. Builder keep." He bowed himself out with an elegant flourish.

"Savior come." Isabelle was sad to see him go.

Coquetta said, "Quite a handsome fellow, our Bitterlich."

"Hmmm . . . I hadn't really noticed." *Except his eyes.* He had the most delightful eyes.

Coquetta gave her a sideways look. "Most Seelenjäger are so bestial. The ones with the boars' tusks or bear heads are bad enough, but at least you know which end you're talking to. We had one emissary last year from Öberholz who had a shell like a crackback. Introducing him at parties was a chore, 'Isn't his carapace such a lovely shade of olive drab, and I'm given to understand that eyestalks are very useful.'"

Isabelle laughed. It felt raw, like scraping her soul with a rasp.

Coquetta retired to a chair and a servant appeared with a wine service. The comtesse's color had not improved. She glistened with sweat despite the dry tepid air. Isabelle accepted a cup of wine and let the maidservant fill it all the way up.

Coquetta took a pull at her drink and said, "I understand your Julio is quite a fine fellow."

Alert for an interrogation, Isabelle said, "Príncipe Julio is a very honorable man. He sets himself very high standards."

Coquetta tilted her head and regarded her quizzically. "High standards are all well and good, but how does he make you feel?"

The question caught Isabelle flat-footed. When she was around Julio she usually felt ready to get on with the day's business. How else should she feel?

"No one has ever asked me that question before," she said.

"Not even Jean-Claude? For shame. I will have to have words with that man. He sometimes forgets that nurturing someone means their heart as well as their head."

"I don't think . . . Wait. You know Jean-Claude?" Of course, he was a King's Own Musketeer and therefore familiar with the court, but she could not recall that he'd ever mentioned Coquetta.

Coquetta laughed. "Has he ever told you how he became King's Own Musketeer?"

Isabelle's pulse quickened with anticipation. "He always dodges that question."

"In that case, I shan't break confidence except to say I was there. Those were fine times." She looked wistful and added, "I taught him all he knows about the ways of men and women. He was a most excellent student."

No amount of cool breathing could keep the flame from Isabelle's cheeks. She had never thought of Jean-Claude as prone to lust. Her mind had simply omitted that possibility. It was an odd oversight to mentally emasculate him so, and distinctly unfair. Surely he'd had lady friends, but if so, he'd kept the relationships discreet.

"But . . ." Isabelle groped for a delicate way to state the obvious problem. She didn't find one. "You're a Sanguinaire and he's not." The only worse sin, in the eyes of the Temple, were liaisons between sorcerers from different breeds, as the mixing of multiple sorceries could produce abominations, off-spring with twisted powers they could neither contain nor control.

Isabelle herself was the end result of a thousand years of interbreeding by a madman who'd been trying to create the Savior. The only ill effects she'd so far suffered from her unique admixture of blood were a deformed hand and the expression of a sorcery that had been absent from the world since the Saintstime. Many of her great aunts and uncles had not been so fortunate. Kantelvar, the master breeder, had killed any creation that did not meet his expectations, preserving only the bloodlines he deemed fruitful. Her family tree was a twisted, wounded thing watered in its own blood.

Coquetta tilted an eyebrow at her. "Does our liaison bother you?"

"Not even a little," Isabelle said. "But I'm not the one you'd have to worry about."

"The Temple prohibition did make it feel rather scandalous at the time. It added a certain piquancy," Coquetta mused. "But given that a Temple carnifex was hunting us with a death warrant, we hardly worried about earning further opprobrium. And after that particular taboo fell, we just never picked it up again."

"Does le roi know this?" Surely Jean-Claude had not been . . . cuckolding would be the wrong word . . . poaching Grand Leon's nesting hens?

"Oh yes. It was before my appointment to the royal service. A prelude if you will; Jean-Claude introduced me to Leon."

Isabelle's eyes nearly crossed at the thought of Jean-Claude as royal procurer. Jean-Claude specialized in getting people what they wanted, but this . . . this had apparently worked out amicably for all parties involved, so who was she to complain?

Coquetta was thankfully quick to retire, thus releasing Isabelle to do the same. She was shown to a bed, and helped to undress by an un-chatty handmaid. She wished Marie were here. She knew what to make of her friend's silences and her toneless speech. Other people's not so much.

Her mind seethed with the emotions of the day: anger, outrage, humiliation, and fear. She could not wish death and destruction on Grand Leon, for as his fortunes rose and fell, so did l'Empire's, but she would spit on de la Vega did she get the chance. Damn Aragoths and their superstitions. They were nothing more than a way to excuse themselves from the requirements of reason.

A soft rapping came at the arch of the curtainway that set off her bedchamber from the rest of the suite. It was followed by an equally soft whisper. "Mademoiselle des Zephyrs."

"Yes," Isabelle said. "I'm awake."

One of Coquetta's handmaids let herself in. "There's an Imperial courier here, Sir Corbin of the Swift, with a message for you."

Corbin and his riders had served Isabelle well during the negotiations for the Grand Peace, but they were no longer hers to command. No doubt whatever message he had brought her should be diverted to her replacement, probably Ambassador Modeste. Still, Corbin deserved to hear that from her in person. Unfortunately, though her sleeping gown was perfectly modest it was not suitable for receiving visitors.

"Send him up to the curtain," she said, and clambered out of bed to meet him across that barrier.

Boots clomped up to the curtain and she could imagine Corbin's bow-legged gait.

"Mademoiselle des Zephyrs." It was definitely his voice. "I hear they've handed you the sack."

"Yes." The story must be spreading like the plague through the tightly packed populace.

"Damn cruelty that is," he said. "Must say I had my doubts at first, but no one's worked harder or been fairer than you. The lads will not be happy."

Isabelle's throat grew tight, grief welling up at his kindness. "Thank you, that means a great deal to me. I shall never forget your service or your loyalty. Yours or the lads." She was glad now for the curtain; it hid the water standing in her eyes.

"I have a message for ye, just came in this morning."

Isabelle took a breath to ease the spasm in her throat and said, "All official correspondence should be diverted to Ambassador Modeste." He was a good man. He could close out the negotiations well enough.

"Aye, that's already done, but I reckon this one is for you personally. It's addressed to Princess Isabelle des Zephyrs. That's you and no one else." Through the split in the curtains Corbin pushed a thick leather scroll tube. It was tooled in a feather pattern and decorated with bronze studs. Around it was wrapped a black ribbon and a black wax seal: a notice of death.

Whose death? She did not recognize the heraldry on the seal: two feather quills crossed over a braided circle.

Isabelle accepted the tube. "Do you know who sent it?"

"Nay, it was left at the station, but I suppose you could open it and find out."

"Yes, of course," Isabelle said.

"Do you need me to wait?" Corbin asked.

"No, but thank you. Builder keep."

Corbin left and Isabelle sat down on the bed. She turned up the light in her alchemical lantern and studied the tooling on the leather. Her mind was too dull right now to make anything more of it than a beautiful design.

She pulled off the end cap and extracted a roll of thick charcoal-gray paper and a message written in silver ink.

The first line read:

To my dearest sister Princess Isabelle des Zephyrs ni Barbaro, Sorceress de l'Étincelle:

Isabelle's breath caught. She had recently learned Lorenzo Barbaro was . . . well, not her father—that honor she granted to Jean-Claude—but he was the Fenice sorcerer who had cuckolded Narcisse des Zephyrs and gotten Isabelle on his Comtesse Vedetta.

Six months ago, when Isabelle had been sending out requests for information concerning the Grand Peace, she'd slipped in a few private inquiries of her own in the form of, "If anyone knows the whereabouts of Lorenzo Barbaro, please contact this office . . ."

She had not really expected a response.

Yet now she had someone claiming to be her sister and using the correct patronym. She had imagined someday meeting Lorenzo, but somehow she had failed to consider the possibility of his having other children.

Of course, the greatest possibility was that this was some kind of cruel deception.

Isabelle read on.

First, I apologize for not revealing myself to you sooner, but to do so would have been a great danger. Our father was slain by enemies determined to exterminate his line. Those foes believe their work complete. I pray that remains the case. If they become aware that any of his children survived, they will stop at nothing to destroy us.

Now that you have discovered your heritage (for why else would you have released Lorenzo's name into the world?) there is no longer any safety for either of us in ignorance. I imagine you have many questions about our family and our father's life and death, but I will not try to anticipate them here.

I will be attending your emperor's seventy-fifth birthday celebration. If you wish to meet, I will await you in Conqueror's Square at the statue of the brothers over the noon hour each day of the fortnight.

As I imagine you find this letter both incredible and shocking, I invite you to take whatever precautions you deem necessary. Remember, however, that the name Lorenzo Barbaro is not a safe one.

Builder keep you safe from harm,
Your Sister—B

Isabelle's thoughts whirled, excitement and wariness blending in an oil-and-water sort of way. Incredible was an understatement. The letter practically dripped mystery. Not even within her intimate circle had anyone ever named her sorcery l'Étincelle without her explaining it first. Indeed the legal fiction about her spark-arm was that it was a byproduct of the Primal Clay with which the stump of her arm had been healed, something tacked on and not intrinsic to her in the way sorcery was. Still, that did not preclude some especially avid antiquarian from guessing what powers she really had.

Yet who could have concocted the story about Isabelle having a sister? Isabelle had told not a soul but Marie and Jean-Claude that Lorenzo was her sire. So whoever had written this must have the knowledge from Lorenzo's side of the equation.

Even as she goggled at the message, the silver ink bubbled, hissed, and steamed away with a whiff of salt and iodine. How had it known when to evaporate? Thick dark paper, tightly rolled in a scroll tube. Dark in there. She glanced at the alchemical lantern. Was it sensitive to the light?

Unfortunately, stuffing the letter back in the tube didn't halt the alchemical processes. Within seconds, all of the writing was gone. Yet the message remained firmly embedded in her mind. "I have a sister." Or at least someone claiming to be her sister; right now she was not sure which would be more complicated.

CHAPTER

Five

Jean-Claude stood by Lady Niñon's side, holding her hand and telling her absurd anecdotes to distract her from the horror of her situation. He even got her to laugh once or twice. He hadn't released her from the table, figuring that the less moving around she did with her scalp held on by his cravat the better.

He hoped Gretl could make the trek through the raging blizzard, or if she could not proceed, that at least she found safety. Sergeant reported the streets empty. Even Screaming Hall had taken in a dozen would-be revelers who could find no better shelter, and they'd brought Jean-Claude's horse inside. Here in the surgery with its hot-burning alchemical lanterns, fingers of frost worked their way under the rattling shutters as the storm tried to claw its way in.

Niñon's face grew increasingly pale and haggard as time wore on and her strength faded. Jean-Claude had ordered the monks to bring blankets, and they'd covered her from the neck down, but she still shivered.

"I am mad, you know," she said, in a tone of flat resignation.

"What does that feel like?" Jean-Claude asked.

Niñon started to laugh but it turned into a cough. "You may be the only adult who's ever asked me that question. It's horrible. It's like being trapped between two worlds, one of which only I can see. It's much more real than the common world, and everything in it terrible."

"What sort of things do you witness?"

She squeezed her eyes shut. "Nightmare things. Cacodemons. People I know, only different, changed. Things without names. Everything vile."

The memories she was trying to describe agitated her.

"Shh. Shh. I didn't mean to cause upset," Jean-Claude said, though he'd be damned for his curiosity.

She took several deep breaths as if to settle her nerves, then whispered, "It's not that. It's just. Just. I feel a fit coming on." She gasped as if someone was throttling her. "It's going to be bad."

Alarm quickened Jean-Claude's pulse. "Is there anything I can do?"

"S-s-stay," she sputtered as flecks of spittle lashed from her tongue. Her whole body arched against her bonds so hard that the leather creaked and the rivets squealed. Her mouth opened, her lips distending as if something huge was trying to get out. Fresh blood oozed from the seam where her scalp had been cut. She squeezed Jean-Claude's hand so tightly he thought she must grind his bones to powder. She screamed out mindless cries of pain and fury that made Jean-Claude's stout blood run cold and thin. What in the names of all the Torments must she be enduring inside her head?

Jean-Claude had no idea how long the fit lasted. It seemed like hours before she lapsed into true unconsciousness and went limp. She was pale as a ghost, and only by the bubbling of the foam on her lips could Jean-Claude tell she was breathing.

A commotion from the stairwell caught his attention. He turned in time to see Gretl, her face ruddy from the cold and still shaking snow from her mantle, march into the room. She was a small stout woman, both deaf and mute, with the intense stare of a hawk.

She gazed up at Jean-Claude, and her expression grew cross. She made a quick series of gestures that amounted to, "Guard said you hurt!"

"Not me. Her." Jean-Claude pointed at Niñon.

Gretl turned her gaze to Niñon. An appalled look spread across her face. She brushed by Jean-Claude, lifted the makeshift bandage, and sucked in breath through her teeth. She whirled and gestured to Jean-Claude. "You, out." Then she gestured to her assistant, Darcy, a wiry woman with a long face and spidery fingers. "Come. Set up."

Darcy, shivering, dragged in a large snow-caked trunk and opened it up to reveal a whole suite of surgical instruments: vials of liquid, tins of powder, and Builder only knew what else. Jean-Claude was hardly content, but if anyone could salvage this medical mess, it was Gretl.

By the baseboard next to the door lay Ingle's galvanic rod, just a glass cylinder really. Jean-Claude knelt and retrieved it. Ingle had been about to use it to stimulate Niñon's brain through the hole in her skull.

There had been a glass rod in the back room at the Golden Swain. Jean-Claude imagined someone rubbing that rod with felt and then prodding Orem's brain and setting him off like a cannon. Fire in the hole. The very idea made him shudder.

Jean-Claude sought out Sergeant, who had taken up a station near the front doors, out of the snow that crept in under the door but still subject to the chill that stole through the gaps.

Sergeant muttered, "Goat-bothering son of a sow," to no one in particular.

"Have any of the monks tried to leave?" Jean-Claude asked.

"In this weather?" Sergeant asked, incredulous. "There's no way out in back, and no one wants to get close to the door."

"And where did you put Brother Houlen?"

"In one of the cells. This way." Sergeant moved with the jaw-first posture of a man on his way to inflict pain.

Houlen sat on the floor of a bare, bar-fronted cell with nothing but the tattered remains of a straw-filled mat to cushion his backside. He looked up sullenly at Jean-Claude's approach.

"Here's the spineless, boy-buggering slug," Sergeant said.

Jean-Claude leaned, hipshot, against the corner of the cell. "Looks like you've wedged yourself in a tight crack, Brother Houlen."

"I am unjustly accused," he said tremulously, obviously a line he'd been rehearsing. He stood and dusted off bits of straw and rat droppings. "I've done nothing wrong."

Jean-Claude said, "So you deny the accusation?"

"Of course!" Houlen said.

"I see. Unfortunately for you, no one has accused you of anything."

Bafflement, surprise, and suspicion flickered across Houlen's face in rapid succession. "Then why am I detained?"

"For your own protection."

"Protection against what?"

Jean-Claude bared his teeth in a most unfriendly way. "Me. I have this strange urge to break every bone in your body. And because no one has accused you of anything, I'm going to have Sergeant here unlock this cage. Then there will be nothing between me and you, unless of course you want to give me a reason to keep the door locked."

Houlen backed up against the opposite end of the cell. "You're mad!"

"Then it would seem I have come to the right place," Jean-Claude said, making a gesture that encompassed the whole Agonesium. "There's a wrought-iron fence outside. Once I've broken both your arms and legs, I'm going to weave you into it and let you hang there."

"It wasn't me!" Houlen cried. "It was Ingle. He's the one you want. He told us to bring patients to him for treatment."

"And carry out the bodies," Jean-Claude said.

"He said they were already gone, their souls departed to Paradise Everlasting."

Jean-Claude slammed the heel of his palm against the bars with a great bang. Houlen jumped back.

"He cut up their brains while they were still alive," Jean-Claude growled. "Now Ingle is dead, but I still have you. Once I hang you on that fence, I'm going to slit your belly open and sic a pack of hungry curs on you."

"Oh please, I'm just his clerk!" Houlen went down on both knees.

"Then where did he keep his records?"

"They're in his private chambers. I'll show you. Just please don't hurt me."

Jean-Claude had Sergeant let Houlen out. The skittering monk led them into the room next to the surgery. The floor was covered in thick woven carpets of a Skaladin design. The walls hung thick with tapestries. A massive writing desk of some dark wood took up most of one wall. Houlen pointed to a wall-sized bookshelf stacked with paper. "Here they are. Here!"

Jean-Claude hated reading. He especially hated sifting through mountains of documents. People were easier. They could be charmed, bribed, threatened, or even occasionally seduced. They were more than the sum of their parts. Writing was just letters, the dark, inky droppings left behind by long departed thoughts.

"I want two to start with," he said. "Mademoiselle Niñon du Grace and a vagrant named Orem."

Houlen scuttled over to the shelves and started riffling through sheaves of paper with nervous fingers. He returned in a moment with a stack of papers. "This is the woman's." Then he returned to his business.

Glumly, Jean-Claude adjusted his spectacles, picked up the top sheet of the stack, and started working his way through it, mouthing out the longer words with all their damned unpronounceable syllables. Isabelle would have enjoyed this part. She had a way of stringing her net to let the small fry out and snare the bigger fish.

After a moment he said, "It says here that she was committed at the request of her family. Who was her family?"

Houlen paused in his gathering. "I don't know."

"You were there," Jean-Claude said. "You wrote it down."

"That doesn't mean I remember it," he squeaked. "That's why we write things down."

"Broken bones. Iron fence. Split belly. Dogs," Jean-Claude reminded him.

"I don't know." Houlen crept over and examined the paper himself. He pointed to a mark shaped like an omnioculus in the margin. "There. That means she was brought in by the Temple. This mark that looks like a circle and an X, that's the mark of *Infelix Patrueles.*"

"Unfortunate Cousins," Jean-Claude muttered, for he knew that term. Kantelvar, the nigh-immortal madman who had cut off Isabelle's arm, had secretly bred together generation upon generation of sorcerers in an attempt to produce the Savior. That breeding program had many offshoots, and created many half-blood abominations that the madman destroyed to cover his tracks. His euphemism for those doomed souls was *Infelix Patrueles.*

"He's almost a year dead and still making trouble," Jean-Claude muttered.

Ingle had said he was investigating the Builder's gifts. Sorcery. Taking in Kantelvar's culls would have given him a steady supply of victims. "How many more of these Unfortunate Cousins do you have? Was Orem one of them?"

"I . . . I'll have to check."

It took Houlen several minutes, but he came back with a new stack of papers, this one much larger than the first. "These are Orem's. He seems to be an ordinary madman. No, wait. Someone changed the notation. Oh dear . . ." All the color drained from his face and he pushed the file away as if it had tried to bite him.

Jean-Claude snatched up the paper and searched it for lethal phrasing. His own heart dropped into his stomach as he read a recent notation at the bottom: *Unhallowed, unclaimed, le roi's bastard. Mother unknown.*

Jean-Claude felt a little light-headed. He had never fainted, but he wondered what it might be like. It must be preferable to the other truth hammering at his brain.

He'd shot Grand Leon's son.

Jean-Claude closed up the file. "I'll just keep this safe, shall I?" *And then what?* His first instinct was to drop the thing in a fire pit and pretend he'd never seen it.

Grand Leon had many bastards. Indeed, between his children and grandchildren, many of whom were of marriageable age, it had become difficult in the upper echelons of society to find a mate to whom one was not closely related. Yet le roi acknowledged all his progeny without fail. To know that one had fallen through the cracks, and had landed here, broken and battered as a shipwreck, would not please him.

Grand Leon would probably acknowledge that Jean-Claude had no choice, and had taken the only course of action available to him. There would be no official repercussions, but that pale abused ghost would always linger between them.

Before he brought this to Grand Leon's attention he must make damned sure this note was correct.

Jean-Claude said, "How did Monsieur Orem depart your fine establishment? Did he escape? Was he given over to someone else's custody?"

"He was given over, just two days ago. A man took him. I don't know his real name . . . I swear I don't, but he called himself the Harvest King."

"Ah," Jean-Claude said, a small gleeful thrill tugging at the corners of his mouth as he found one thread he'd been looking for. Orem had babbled that name. "Tell me, Brother, what did this Harvest King look like?"

Houlen's expression grew optimistic. "Oh yes, he was an older man, gray beard down to here, sucked on his words when he talked."

Jean-Claude's smile faded. "So he looks like any other old man in Rocher Royale."

Houlen went on hurriedly. "But he wasn't alone. He had a bone queen with him."

Jean-Claude had wondered when the bone queen was going to come back into this. L'École Royale des Spécialistes had provided him with stellar training in combating sorcerers, and their sage advice on bone queens, the combined wisdom of their collective experience came down to a single word: don't.

Young Fenice, fledglings as they were called, received a vitera from their parents soon after they came into their feathers. This symbiotic creature passed a copy of its progenitor's memories and personality to its recipient, an injection of the skills and knowledge of all the lifetimes that had gone before it. This combined with their formidable physical prowess made them a danger in every arena of life. Even the young ones were as strong as an ox, and they could sheath themselves in close-fitting feathers that were lighter than thistledown yet stronger than the best alchemical steel.

As the Fenice got older, the vitera slowly replaced the human host with stronger stuff. By the time a Fenice's feathers turned white and they became a bone king or queen, they could shatter stone with their fists and shrug cannonballs off their hide. Notable instances of defeating them in combat included shooting down the skyship the Fenice was standing on and dropping the side of a mountain on one with a controlled detonation.

The good news was that when the vitera was finally done supplanting its host, the bone queen became a husk, dry and dead. The bad news was that the last thing to go was the brain, which meant they grew more powerful right up to the point their sorcery killed them, almost always in the midst of degenerating madness. Jean-Claude might be trying to deal with an ancient, superhuman, nigh-indestructible madwoman.

"Did this bone queen have a name?" Jean-Claude asked.

"Immacolata," Houlen said. "I imagine she was probably named after the barren saint."

The name meant nothing to Jean-Claude. Indeed the pieces he'd gathered told only the most garbled story. It seemed likely that this Immacolata had delivered Orem to the Golden Swain, lit his fuse, and barred the door on her way out. But why? Was there a meaningful link between Ingle's hideous experiments and Mistwaithe's damaging news about des Zephyrs? And why choose Orem as a weapon? If someone had told him yesterday morning that he'd have a fistful of names in a scandal involving Isabelle's family, he'd have thought he had the problem by the short hairs.

"What else do you know of the Harvest King?" Jean-Claude asked. And if that part of Orem's mumbling had been rooted in experience, how much of the rest might be as well?

"Nothing," Houlen said, and then decided he'd better elaborate. "I mean, I never spoke to him. He was always Prior Ingle's guest. They never let me in."

"How frequently was the Harvest King a guest here?"

"Two . . . no, three times."

"And you never overheard a word they said?"

"No . . . I mean, yes, but I didn't understand any of it. They talked about the Neverborn Kings, and a new paradigm. I looked it up in the *Instructions* because I thought it might have something to do with the Firstborn Kings, but I couldn't find anything. From the way Ingle talked it was some kind of group, like a cult."

The creation of the Firstborn Kings was the root of all Temple doctrine. The Risen Saints had emerged from the Vault of Ages to rebuild the world after the great sundering. The Firstborn Kings and Queens were their progeny of saints from within their own number, but those numbers were tiny. The Firstborn Kings had therefore taken clayborn women, the Blessed Queens, to wife and from them got the Secondborn Kings from whom all modern sorcerers descended, and who were supposed to nurture the broken world until the Savior came.

"Did the Harvest King ever take anyone else away?"

"Just Orem."

"Did Ingle keep any record of these meetings?"

"Not that he told . . . no, wait . . . he kept a personal journal." He scurried to the writing desk and rattled through its drawers. "He never told me what was in it, though. Ah. Here it is." He fished out and handed to Jean-Claude a large, leather-clad tome, tooled with a pious scene of Saint Isaac drawing the agony out of a madman.

Jean-Claude opened the book on the desktop. It was clearly some kind of medical treatise, given all the annotated illustrations of vivisected brains, but the blocky workmanlike text wasn't written in le Langue or in Saintstongue, or any other language he could recognize. Even the letters were strange.

"What does this say?" he said, jabbing his finger at the text.

Houlen glanced at the writing and his face fell in dismay. "I've never seen this before. Maybe it's a code."

"Of course it's a code, you lout," Jean-Claude said. "The question is, where is the key?"

Houlen didn't know. The number of things of which the mendicant was unaware grew like weeds in an untamed field. Jean-Claude spent some time searching the desk, and then all but dismantling it, looking for some secret stash where the journal's key might be hidden, to no avail. Chances were, the only copy had been in Ingle's now slowly rotting brain.

Jean-Claude took a turn at the text itself, but really had no idea where to begin. He needed to get this thing to Isabelle. If there was anyone who could pull sense out of the spatter it was she.

~

Jean-Claude was still accumulating stacks of paper when Sergeant, at his post by the door, stiffened up and said, "Builder's Bollocks!"

And then a woman's voice, soft and hollow, drifted in. "I am looking for Monsieur Jean-Claude."

"Let her in, Sergeant," Jean-Claude said, rising from his seat.

Sergeant goggled as Marie passed by him into the study. As always in dim light, she glowed like Bruma, the winter moon. It made her look cold. Did she feel cold? She'd just come in from a blizzard. Jean-Claude still had twinges of guilt, more painful than his game leg, when he remembered the day Isabelle's father had hollowed her out. He hadn't seen it coming and had been powerless to save her.

"Greetings, mademoiselle. What brings you out in this storm?" When last he'd seen her—saints, was it only this morning?—she'd been on her way with Isabelle to put the last few shims in to level out the Grand Peace. He'd hoped she and Isabelle were snugged tight in Rowan House for this storm.

Marie said, "We should speak in private."

Jean-Claude didn't like the sound of that. "Keep watch," he said to Sergeant, and led Marie down the hall to an unused sitting room.

"What's happened?" he asked, worried that things had gone wrong in his absence. Marie didn't look worried, but then she never looked anything but blank and masklike. "Where is Isabelle?"

"When I left her, she was on her way to report a diplomatic faux pas to le roi."

"What sort of faux pas?" Jean-Claude said, his nerves awash with trepidation.

"She interrupted an execution," Marie said, and then proceeded to relay the event in great detail, word for word in many cases, right down to de la Vega's swearing of revenge.

Jean-Claude rubbed his face in dismay. Saints, he was proud of Isabelle's character, but what a mess. Grand Leon would be furious. Jean-Claude paced the floor, his restless desire to race to Isabelle's aid at odds with the blizzard outside and the sure knowledge that whatever had transpired in le Ville Céleste was beyond his ability to avert.

He asked Marie, "But if she is up there, what are you doing here?"

"You needed to be told what transpired," Marie said. "I followed you to the Lowmarket but you had already gone. I asked around and found out you had come here."

Jean-Claude doffed his hat and ran his hand through his thinning hair. "As soon as the weather permits, I need to go to le Ville Céleste." He had to argue on Isabelle's behalf. The Harvest King, the Fenice, Kantelvar's *Infelix Patrueles,* and the whole business with Mistwaithe could wait. Isabelle was brave and resourceful, but she spent too much time in her own head, and deep down she expected people to behave rationally.

"Tell me what happened in the Lowmarket," Marie said. "Isabelle will want to know, and if you miss her at le Ville Céleste I may see her before you do."

Jean-Claude frowned. He'd always made a point of keeping Isabelle apprised of threats and gossip about her so she could be part of her own defense, but he'd always avoided speaking in front of Marie. As a soulless bloodhollow, she'd been a spy for Isabelle's father. But she was free now, her own person, and she had a good point.

"Very well." He told a somewhat expurgated version of his day's meandering trek, from seeking Mistwaithe to the present moment.

Marie absorbed this without reaction, staring straight ahead across what landscape of thought Jean-Claude could not guess.

"I will help you defend Isabelle," Marie said.

"Of course you will," he said. "You're her handmaid."

"I mean I will be her bodyguard, just as you are."

The proclamation befuddled Jean-Claude. "Eh. No." Had she lost her mind?

"I will help," Marie repeated, a statement of fact rather than a request. "There is too much for one person to do."

"I have handled Isabelle's security for years," Jean-Claude said, his pride fluffing up.

"Yes, while she was living on a remote skyland where the biggest threat to her was her own family. This is more complex. I have already been helping, getting between her and enemies, but I need training. You will take me as an apprentice."

"Absolutely not!" Jean-Claude declared, appalled. "You're one of the people I'm supposed to be protecting. Besides, much of what I do is disgusting, vile, and dangerous, totally inappropriate for a woman."

Marie slowly tilted her head to one side, like a great snowy owl observing a mouse. "Do you really think women live in a different world from men, a world without violence, pain, deceit, blood, and treachery? I was made a bloodhollow at age thirteen out of pure spite. I spent the next twelve years in living death, a tool of oppression against my heart's dear friend, the sister of my soul."

A hint of fervor in Marie's echoing voice rattled Jean-Claude's heart. How hard must it have been for her to conjure even that much outward expression? "Don't you think you've suffered enough? You deserve a normal life."

"Then I deserve less than I want," Marie said. "Isabelle has promised me many times that I may have anything within her power to bestow me. Will you not hold good her word?"

"Isabelle would not approve invoking her name for such a request."

"Would she not? I know her as well as you do, possibly better."

Jean-Claude waved his hand as if trying to swat away some persistent fly. Unfortunately, Isabelle would probably side with Marie. "This is a moot point. Musketeers don't take apprentices. We send tyros to the academy, and they would not matriculate you, no matter what Isabelle might allow."

"I do not wish to be a musketeer. I wish to be Isabelle's bodyguard. I am perfectly suited to the task. I am nearly always by her side, I have a perfect memory, I am in good health, strong and sturdy."

"You are not as strong as a man," Jean-Claude pointed out, pulling himself up to his full height, to tower over her physically when towering over her mentally wasn't working.

"No, but I am just as quick, and no man is more powerful than a bullet. Furthermore, I have no shadow, which means I am immune to Sanguinaire sorcery."

"Eh." Jean-Claude paused in wonder. "You are?"

"Whenever a bloodshadow crosses yours, you feel it like a thousand maggots crawling on your skin, even if the bloodshadow isn't doing anything to you. Since my recovery, I have trod on several bloodshadows. I felt nothing.

They are no more to me than a stain on the cobbles. A bloodshadow needs a victim's shadow to grip."

"Fascinating," Jean-Claude said, his mind sprouting ideas of how such an immunity might come in useful. Many of Isabelle's enemies were likely to be Sanguinaires . . .

"No. No," he caught himself. "It can't work."

Marie continued her relentless appeal. "Queen Xaviera of Aragoth is a notable fencer, strategist, and general officer who held her family's keep for a year against a Skaladin host."

"Queen Xaviera is a virago," he said, which Her Majesty had considered a compliment when he had swept his hat to her after she worsted him in their first fencing match.

"And I am a freak," Marie said. "There are only two choices for a freak: hide from your freakishness or make it your strength."

"There are other ways to be strong."

She shifted her stance to stare him directly in the eyes. White lashes framed ivory orbs with pearl irises, like some ancient alabaster goddess. "I want to be like you."

"Me." Jean-Claude laughed almost manically. "Girl, I am no one to emulate. I am vulgar, violent—"

"—vexatious, vagrant, vafrous, vigorous—" she said.

"Stop that!" he spat. The alliteration game had always belonged to him and Isabelle. Though now that he looked back, Marie had been there when they invented the game. It was the same day she'd been turned into a bloodhollow. The day he failed her. Marie never had a chance to join in the game. It had grown up without her. The whole world had left her behind.

"I am also ventose," he said rather sheepishly. "Especially after too many beans."

"Verily," she said, and then she got down on her knees and said softly, "Please."

Jean-Claude's grizzled heart ached. He groped for words, for reasons to deny her, and they presented themselves in plenty. Pain, failure, despair, and death—bugbears he had long-since conquered in his own heart—rose afresh when he placed Marie beside him instead of behind him. He could not fail her again.

Except all paths risked failure. Danger would seek her out whether she was ready for it or not. Training her would likely give him nightmares, but nightmares were meant for facing, walls for climbing, foes for vanquishing. Shouldn't Marie be allowed to choose how to face her perils?

He drummed his fingers on his thigh. "So you want to be a frantic, half-mad, blood-soaked lunatic. I suppose you already have the nightmares for the job, and I can't say it'll turn your hair white. Maybe it will all fall out."

"There are wigs for that," Marie said, without a trace of irony.

Jean-Claude leaned back and saw an icon of Saint Isaac staring down at him from the lintel, a dozen faces on one body. Patron saint of madness. This was a bad idea, but all the best things in his life had been idiotic decisions at the time, so maybe he wasn't the best one to judge.

"One caveat," he said, holding up the requisite finger. "Isabelle must be informed and must release you from service as her handmaid. Until then, you are provisional."

"Done," Marie said. "I will ask the next time I see her."

"By Saint Isaac's good favor, then. Rise, Provisional Apprentice Marie Du-Bois." And then he considered the room full of documents just down the hall and her perfect memory, and he grinned. "Your first assignment awaits."

CHAPTER

Six

Jean-Claude slept on the cold hard floor of Ingle's study and woke up with a crick that ran from his neck to his knees. This must be what it felt like to be laid out on a mortuary slab, another good reason to not die.

Creaking like an old house in a high wind, he levered himself to his feet and paced the Agonesium's upstairs hallway, trying to work some life back into his limbs. The wind outside seemed to have stopped, so he risked a peek through the shutters at the end of the hall. The blizzard had blown itself out. The day had dawned bright and clear, the sky so pale that it seemed almost colorless. Doubtless Grand Leon's birthday party would start on schedule. Opening the celebration during a blizzard would have seemed cruel, but if anyone froze to death in the sunshine, well, they simply weren't trying hard enough.

Jean-Claude yearned to ride immediately to le Ville Céleste and find out what had happened to Isabelle, but haste was frequently the enemy of speed. First he must find out if Lady Niñon had survived the night, speak with her if he could, and discover what, if anything, she knew about Ingle's operation.

He returned to Ingle's study. The desk was piled with books, scrolls, and loose leaves of paper. Sergeant had taken Houlen back to his cell late last night, and Marie was curled up, catlike, in an oversized armchair. Her wooden expression had relaxed and her white hair was tousled in sleep. She looked more human, more vulnerable than usual.

Jean-Claude's stomach tightened in renewed fear and uncertainty for the bargain he'd struck with her. Backing out was not an option. Such a trust, once broken, would never heal.

He shook her by the shoulder and growled, in best drill sergeant fashion, "Wake up, apprentice!"

Her eyes snapped open, and her impassive mask settled into place without any sleep-yearning or even yawning. She stood and produced two ornate dueling pistols and a powder horn from the cushion crack behind her. She tucked the pistols in her belt and slung the horn over her shoulder.

"Where did you get those?" Jean-Claude pointed to the guns.

Marie said, "I found them in Ingle's prayer alcove under the altar. I decided that if I am going to be a bodyguard, even a provisional apprentice, I should be armed."

"Are they loaded?" Jean-Claude asked, with no small trepidation.

"They would be useless otherwise."

"How . . . no, wait. You were there when I taught Isabelle how to load a pistol." And Marie never forgot anything. "Do you know how to shoot?"

"Your exact words were, 'Don't, but if you must, point the barrel at whatever you want to destroy, squeeze the trigger, and don't flinch.'"

Jean-Claude let out a long-suffering breath. "Yes, that does sound like me." And she'd been storing up every dumb thing he'd said for the last twelve years to be deployed at need, saints help him. "Well, there's a bit more to it than that, a lot more if you want to be any good at it, which you do." Jean-Claude was really not the best person to teach her the awful art of combat. Fortunately he knew someone who was.

Marie asked, "What is our plan today?"

"That depends; what did you find out?" he asked. Ingle's encoded tome had been as impenetrable to her as it was to him, so he'd put her in charge of Houlen and set her to sifting through the Agonesium's records.

"There were no mentions of the Harvest King or of Immacolata," Marie said. "References to the *Infelix Patrueles* go back twelve years. There are fifteen mentions in all. Eight of them were delivered in the last three years. Lady Niñon was the most recent, delivered twelve months ago."

Jean-Claude lifted his hat to rub his forehead. He was more than used to human cruelty, but the thought of Lady Niñon being kept in this dire pit, chained up like an animal for a whole year, and then being vivisected made his heart sick. Saints forgive him, but he should have kept Prior Ingle alive if for no other reason than to kill him more slowly.

"Are any of the rest of them still alive?" Jean-Claude asked.

"None who were delivered here," Marie said.

When he posed no further questions, she began her limbering exercises, the same ones she had performed every day for twelve years as a bloodhollow under Isabelle's care. The difference was, unless Jean-Claude was mistaken, she was quietly pushing herself well beyond her former limits of flexibility. She did a forward bend that didn't end until her whole upper body was behind her knees. Just observing her made Jean-Claude's back ache.

It was quiet, this pitting of herself against herself, all the physical ambition of an adolescent boy without any of the boasting. Did she have the same yearning for recognition burning somewhere under the still, deep snow of her expression?

She asked to be your apprentice, didn't she?

A huge thump shook the room like a mortar shell, knocked books from shelves and dust from the ceiling. The wall plaster cracked and the floor jumped like a skyship hitting turbulence. Jean-Claude fell hard. Marie sprawled on the floor next to him.

Fear hammered Jean-Claude's heart. A shadow passed behind the window shutters, and a tremendous blow blasted them from their hinges. Splinters flew and a massive shape rammed itself through the opening, wide shoulders cracking the wooden frame like matchsticks.

Jean-Claude grabbed one of the heavy chairs and hauled himself up as the monster finished dragging itself into the room. It was the size of a bear, with the shape of a bulldog, a ridge of thick scales along its back, and curved claws on every toe. It surveyed the room through deep-set, bloodshot eyes with sagging lids. Its gaze fixed on Jean-Claude.

"A King's Own Musketeer, one of Grand Leon's own personal maggots. Corrupt from feasting on the flesh of the corrupt."

Jean-Claude found himself absurdly grateful that the thing could speak, and in a Rocher Royale accent. It was a Seelenjäger surely, and not some horror that had clambered up out of the Gloom. If it could speak it could think, and that meant its head was already full of lies for Jean-Claude to use. He squared his shoulders and assumed an air of unconcern.

"Indeed I am a King's Own Musketeer, wielder of le roi's law, instrument of his will, his eyes and ears in all the dark places of his realm," he said, his jaunty voice so practiced that it passed on none of the quaver in his belly. "If you're looking for Prior Ingle, I'm afraid he's gone to visit some old friends, but if you'd care to leave a name, I'll be sure to pass it on, Monsieur Seelenjäger."

"Ingle is dead," the Seelenjäger said, not contradicting Jean-Claude's assertion, "slain by one too feeble to endure the light of his vision. You may think of me as the first prince of the Neverborn, and I have a message for your roi. You may tell him his days are numbered. This decadent festival of his will end with the crowning of a new roi, and the rise of a new order in the world. Now be gone, maggot. Become a fly and buzz in your master's ear, or stay and be slain, I care not which."

Outrage burned in Jean-Claude's blood but he kept it hidden behind his smile. The first one to lose his temper was the first to lose his life. Marie had come to stand by Jean-Claude's side, which wasn't the best place for her, but that was a lesson for later, if there was a later.

Jean-Claude gestured for Marie to get out of the room.

He said to the Seelenjäger, "Could you be more specific? Grand Leon gets general threats every day, and I'd hate to waste his time with one he's already heard, or perhaps you could come with me and tell him yourself. If you turn witness against your coconspirators, perhaps he'll keep you on as a hunting dog."

The Seelenjäger growled, a noise to turn a man's guts to water. "You dare mock me? Your roi's doom is all around him, even amongst his most intimates, and there is nothing he can do about it. Tell him that, musketeer, and mayhap I will keep you as a body slave."

Could there be any truth to the Seelenjäger's claims that there was a traitor amongst Grand Leon's inner circle, or was the beast just hoping to start a witch hunt and sow discord in a moment where unity was needed?

"I don't imagine you came all the way up here just to tell me things I already know," Jean-Claude said. "Grand Leon surrounds himself with traitors. It makes them so much easier to keep track of."

Marie had almost made it to the door when the Seelenjäger sprang, an immense blur that soared by Jean-Claude and barred the door. The force of its passing nearly pushed Jean-Claude off his feet.

The Seelenjäger growled at Marie, "Not you, Breaker's get. Only le roi's rat may leave." Marie scurried away from the massive jaws.

The Seelenjäger swung its head slowly, searching the rest of the room for something. His gaze came to light on Ingle's journal resting on the table.

"Surely you don't expect me to stand idle and let you slay an innocent girl," Jean-Claude said.

"You don't have a choice. You only live because you have use, and because it will feel good to break your spirit, and show Leon's minions for the weaklings they are. Mind you, it will feel just as good to slay you and let your corpse deliver my message for me."

"Your message, or the Harvest King's?" This was a leap, but not much of one.

The Seelenjäger's gaze shifted back to Jean-Claude. "A clever rat, then."

"Clever?" Jean-Claude asked, and in a nerve-racking display of nonchalance, he did the most foolish thing he could think of. He casually turned his back to the Seelenjäger and strolled toward the table, gesturing like an actor delivering a soliloquy in the round. "I've just been following the trail your master laid out for me . . . but I don't suppose your master tells you all his plans. I doubt he's even told you why he wants this book."

He picked up Ingle's journal and held it up for the Seelenjäger's inspection. "Which means you have no idea how upset he'll be when he doesn't get it." He tossed the book into the fireplace, to land upon the freshly stoked logs.

The Seelenjäger's eyes rounded and it lunged after the book.

"Run!" Jean-Claude shouted at Marie. He drew his rapier and pistol and hurried toward the door. Marie threw the door open but pelted into Darcy and Gretl, who were just coming the other way.

The Seelenjäger hooked the book with its claws and flung it from the fireplace, along with a paw full of burning coals. Jean-Claude aimed his pistol at the massive barrel chest and squeezed the trigger. The gun spat fire, smoke, and lead. The shot struck the monstrous shoulder. Blood spattered, and the beast howled in rage as much as pain.

Jean-Claude kept expecting it to change shape, to throw on a faster form or one better armored, but it merely ducked its head and charged. Jean-Claude sidestepped and thrust his rapier. It opened a shallow cut on the beast's other shoulder. The Seelenjäger slammed into Jean-Claude and knocked him to the ground. The world spun, dark at the edges. Everywhere hurt. He'd lost his sword. He floundered to his side, to roll over and stand. The Seelenjäger stepped on his back, pinning him fast.

"And now, musketeer, I'm going to gut you like a fish, then sit back and watch as you try to stuff your innards back in again."

Jean-Claude still had his main gauche, but the damned thing was pinned beneath him. If he could just get turned over . . . "Won't be much of a show if you go in through the back," Jean-Claude wheezed.

The bang of a gun shook the air. Smoke billowed from the doorway. Bits of blood and bone exploded from the Seelenjäger's head. It screamed and spun, claws raking Jean-Claude's back and arm. Jean-Claude rolled and yanked his main gauche from its scabbard. Another gunshot boomed. Through a pall of smoke stepped Marie, her ghostly whiteness shimmering in the haze.

The Seelenjäger lurched toward her, howling its rage.

Jean-Claude snarled, seized the Seelenjäger by the back leg, and stabbed up into its groin. His blade found soft flesh. Blood sprayed his face and soaked the rug. He twisted the blade, yanked it out and stabbed again, jarring his arms to the shoulder when the blade hit the pelvis.

The Seelenjäger yelped and whirled about, dragging Jean-Claude in a bloody circle. Jean-Claude lost his grip and tumbled away. He rolled to his knees and came on guard, but the Seelenjäger was done. It wobbled toward him, leaking blood in rivers. Half the bulldog face was ruined, one eye gone. Its legs quivered, and it panted in bewilderment, crimson saliva pouring from its mouth.

It fell with a thud and a last rattling wheeze. It shrank, like bacon in the pan, from the size of a bear to the size of a man and regained its human shape except for its bulldog head and neck. His clothes, which had slipped off to wherever a Seelenjäger kept them when they changed, came back in time to be drenched in his dying blood. His doublet and hose were of fine blue fabric, and his tall boots were of the highest quality.

Marie rushed over and helped Jean-Claude to his feet.

"Thank you," he said. "Are you injured?"

"No," she said.

Gretl came in, trailed by Darcy, their aprons as bloody as a butcher's smock. They stomped out burning coals before they did more than singe the rug.

Gretl's expression was thunderous. She locked onto Jean-Claude's gaze and let fly a flurry of hand-speech, too fast for him to catch all of it. "Idiots. Plague-ridden Torments. What happened? Building shakes, now this!"

"You're wounded," Darcy said, circling around Jean-Claude and laying a long finger beside the gash on his arm. "We'd better take care, less it fester."

"In a moment," Jean-Claude said. His leg ached, and the pain in his back and arm was razor fresh. If he sat down just now it might be hours before he stood up again.

To Gretl he said, "This Seelenjäger attacked us. He was working for a man called the Harvest King, who apparently was in touch with your old master." For she had been enslaved by the mad artifex Kantelvar before Isabelle rescued her.

Gretl's face drained of color. "He's dead!" she signed as if demanding of the universe that it be so.

"But his schemes live on, going feral like dogs too long without a master. He brought Niñon here, and trouble for Isabelle departed from here. Did Kantelvar ever mention the Harvest King to you?"

"No," Gretl replied.

Jean-Claude grunted; he supposed he couldn't be that lucky.

Marie faced Gretl. "What about a Fenice sorceress, a bone queen named Immacolata?"

Gretl made a negative gesture. "Imprisoned on a remote skyland. No guests."

Jean-Claude rolled the Seelenjäger over on his back. The sorcerer's deadweight was like heaving around an awkwardly shaped bag of wet sand.

"What are you looking for?" Marie asked.

Jean-Claude shook his head. "Every time I've done battle with a Seelenjäger, it was like trying to fight a whole zoo. They're constantly changing to get an advantage in shape, but this one seemed content with just the one form, even after he was wounded. Plus he spoke with a Célestial high-snob accent, and those bloody rags he's wearing are Rocher Royale's latest fashion."

"There are lots of Seelenjäger living in l'Empire now after the conquest of the Terras Annexes," Marie pointed out.

"Yes," Jean-Claude allowed. It was part of Grand Leon's plan to unify l'Empire's disparate bits into one unified nation.

"But look at the form he took for his erstepelz," Jean-Claude said. That was the Seelenjäger's resting shape. "If there's one thing I know about Seelenjäger, it's that the first kill is the most important. They're going to wear it as a trophy for the rest of their lives, even into death. They take great pains to hunt down the biggest, meanest, toughest animals they can: bears, lions, boars. It's a huge mark of shame to take a domestic animal as a first kill, even something like a bulldog." He toed the corpse's canine head. "And he called himself the prince of the Neverborn."

"He could be a lateborn bastard," Marie said. "Some Seelenjäger's Céles-tial by-blow. He grows up thinking he's clayborn until one day his sorcery comes in and he realizes he's not. He doesn't know anything about being a Seelenjäger, so he does it wrong and here we are."

Jean-Claude grunted. "You're probably right."

Darcy managed to maneuver Jean-Claude onto a footstool and got his tab-ard and doublet off. The thick gambeson and cuir-bouilli corselet he wore under his doublet had saved him from being flayed to the bone, but only just. Darcy and Gretl made short work of cleaning the wounds and he only needed two stitches. Marie, unbidden, sewed up the rent in Jean-Claude's doublet. Gretl applied a salve that was supposed to keep wound rot at bay and a layer of bandages would keep the stitches from tearing. Shirt, corselet, doublet, and tabard went back on.

"Thank you all," he said. "Now I have to go. Gretl, what about Mademoi-selle Niñon?"

Gretl's fists balled up and she shook her head a firm negative. "She hurt long time. Starved. No strength. Many stress. Too many."

Jean-Claude's heart sank, in grief, in failure. If he'd arrived just a few minutes sooner, before Ingle had her skull open. He'd faced such regrets before, endured them when the men he dragged off the battlefield died in the surgeon's tent or just gave up the ghost on the way, but this was worse. Niñon never had a chance. She never even had a weapon, nor a champion until it was far too late.

"What now?" Marie asked.

Jean-Claude looked around at all the stacks of papers and books. "Isabelle is going to want to see all this. Catalogue what you can and take anything that looks important back to Rowan House. Make sure to take Ingle's jour-nal. Take the Seelenjäger's boots while you're at it. That's custom work, and the shoemaker likely knows who they were made for. Also, if a dwarf named Sedgwick shows up to sell information, buy it."

"What are you going to do?" Marie asked.

Jean-Claude rubbed the back of his neck as if that might relieve the ten-sion that had come to dwell there. Something sick and evil was growing here, a stain spreading just under the city's skin. Scores of soul smudges cried out for justice, and if the scribblings on Orem's record were to be believed, one of Grand Leon's sons had somehow slipped through the sieve and been murdered. He didn't understand how Ingle, Immacolata, and the Harvest King all fit together, but he aimed to find out. Yet first he had his own family to look to.

"I'm going to find Isabelle." She needed his help, and as sure as Torment awaited, he needed hers.

⸺

The morning after Isabelle's disastrous audience with Grand Leon, she woke from restless sleep and prepared to present herself to Parlement for trial, but what defense could she make for herself when the law itself was the problem?

Coquetta's page hurried into the foyer and whispered something to Coquetta.

"Send her in," Coquetta said. She was dressed for the day in mourning gray, a sartorial choice that she did not deign to explain to Isabelle. Her face nearly matched the color of her gown. The dark hollows under her eyes looked like shallow graves. Isabelle wished she could offer sympathy or succor, but tradition foiled compassion.

The page disappeared back into the hallway and reappeared in an instant with a royal herald, who announced, "Duchess Sireen Trintignant, First Mistress of the Bedchamber, Foundation Dam of the Second Line, Keeper of the Flame, Hostess of the Autumnal Feast, Order of the Sacred Shadow."

A bloodshadow spilled through the doorway, forming a sanguine pool underneath the foyer's alchemical lantern. Onto this mark stepped a dark-skinned woman in a white silk gown with a birdcage veil over her broad face and wise dark eyes. Two Praetorians stepped in at her sides. Bitterlich was not among them, alas.

Isabelle and all the maidservants curtsied deeply. If Grand Leon ruled l'Empire for the ages, Duchess Sireen kept it going from day to day.

Coquetta said, "A full retinue today. Surely you didn't think I was going to run away?"

Sireen strode across the room and embraced Coquetta like a sister. "No, but I thought you could use an ally today, the steelier the better." Her famous voice carried the resonance of a tune even in such a prosaic statement.

"The damned fool," Coquetta said. "Why couldn't he stay away and be happy?"

Sireen held Coquetta at arm's length. "Some men need anger to feel alive."

Isabelle's mind spun as she realized who they must be talking about. It was perhaps the greatest scandal of Grand Leon's long reign. Grand Leon was famous for having hundreds of children by many different women and equally famous for recognizing and providing for all of them. He might not be a wonderful parent, but he was rightfully admired for being a good provider.

Yet amongst that throng had been one who was his favorite, elevated above all others, Coquetta's first child and only son, Lael. From the day he was born, Lael took after his imperial father in every way, from his looks to his outlook. By the time he was ten, everyone in l'Empire knew he would be named heir.

Alas, he proved to be unhallowed, without the Builder's gift of sorcery, ineligible to hold land or title, much less inherit the crown. Every method benign and cruel had been deployed to encourage his sorcery to manifest, but by the time Lael was fifteen, even Grand Leon conceded that he was bereft.

Isabelle knew exactly how that ordeal must have felt, having endured it herself, the shame and disappointment of having been born flawed and unworthy. There was a darkness in that pit that still fueled her nightmares.

Grand Leon eased Lael out of court life, sending him to l'Académie Militaire Royale to be trained as an officer, as was the fate of most unhallowed sons. That should have ended the tale.

Except Lael refused to be dislodged. He refused to go where he was told, remain where he was sent, or bide silent about his ouster. He named Grand Leon a tyrant and a despot and defied him to the point that even Grand Leon's staunchest allies had pleaded with him to have the boy executed or at least quietly assassinated as anyone else's son would have been for the same crime.

Instead Grand Leon had disowned Lael, deprived him of his name, and expelled him from l'Empire.

Isabelle had barely noticed the scandal when it blossomed, being all of twelve years old, and might never have thought twice about it save that Lael's travels and travails became a legend in their own right. Every so often a new rumor would sprout up that Lael had been spotted seeking out a legendary healing spring in Stehkzima, or smuggling a recently discovered quondam artifact off Craton Riqueza, or robbing the vaults of the Tyrant of Skaladin in the City of Gears. Most of the tales had likely been woven out of whole cloth, or embellished to the point where they might as well be. Yet they persisted and grew.

Isabelle had developed a good deal of sympathy for Lael in her youth. After all, she too had been unhallowed, despised by her wicked parents, condemned to a life of poverty and misery. The ongoing Legend of Lael had been Isabelle's key inspiration when she invented her own nom de plume, Lord Martin DuJournal, the adventuring mathlogician.

Now, fifteen years after he left, Lael the wayward bastard had returned and placed before Parlement a request to be heard on the matter of his heritage, asking that the tradition that precluded the unhallowed from holding land or title be deemed unlawful.

As ambassadress, Isabelle had noted the event and ordered all of her people to steer clear of it. They were far too busy creating the future to relitigate the past.

Yet Coquetta could not have avoided this conflict even if she tried. Fifteen years ago she'd stood by Grand Leon's side as he'd exiled her son. Isabelle could hardly imagine how that must have torn at her.

Coquetta drew back from Sireen, gestured to Isabelle. "Sireen, I make known to you, Mademoiselle Isabelle des Zephyrs."

"Rise," Sireen said, and looked Isabelle in the eye when she complied. "I am pleased to meet you in person. I am sorry that it must be under such dreadful circumstances."

Isabelle summoned what grace she had in reserve. "Thank you, Madame Duchess. I pray that we may meet again under less grave circumstances."

Sireen's expression was as stiff as stone. "If the Builder so provides."

Should Isabelle have asked for her aid, presented her case to the woman who was all but reine? Not if she wanted the woman's good will, she suspected. Sireen was here to aid Coquetta, not Isabelle.

The three of them plus Sireen's retinue set out for the Galerie du Parlement. Isabelle felt both hollow and heavy as if she were some ghost trapped in tar. She had no allies in Parlement, no defense but the truth, which was a wooden coin in the realm of politics.

"Are you ready for this?" Sireen asked, her voice loaded with care.

Isabelle looked up, but Sireen had been talking to Coquetta. Isabelle's fate did not rate a thought much less a word.

"Of course not," Coquetta replied with an air of resignation. "But I'll live. It's not as if I haven't been through this before. He's such a fool boy."

"He was when he left," Sireen said. "Now he's a full-grown fool, and those are harder to forgive. Has he tried to contact you since he arrived?"

"He hasn't tried contacting me in years. Impervia tells me that he's spent most of his time in the city consorting with other unhallowed folk, adventurers, and second sons, listening to their complaints. He must know he's being observed, but he hasn't made any attempt to conceal his actions, nor has he said anything that might be construed as a message to me. It's all very peculiar."

Isabelle had expected the Lace Trefoil to be a hotbed of intrigue and interpersonal rivalry, but these two plus Impervia, the Trefoil's third leaf, had been living cheek by jowl since before Isabelle had been born. From the small sample Isabelle had seen, they seemed more like sisters.

They reached a heavily curtained archway with two posted guards. The rumble of conversation greeted them as they stepped through to a balcony overlooking the Galerie du Parlement.

The meeting place of the judicial body was built within a cylinder that ran through le Ville Céleste's main structure at a slant. A wooden floor had been built across the tunnel and rows of seats ascended from that base in a series of elliptical arcs. To Isabelle's left, in an elevated gallery facing the chamber, sat Grand Leon, his bloodshadow overflowing his throne, his fingers steepled before him, his face cast in shadow and his expression unreadable.

Directly across from Isabelle's perch was another balcony filled with Aragoths. Isabelle was disappointed to see that Julio was not amongst them. No doubt his absence made political sense—the Aragothic crown would not intercede on her behalf—but he might have showed up without his badges of office to support her as an individual. Front and center, wearing the pride of the victor, stood Consul de la Vega.

In the center of the floor stood the dictator's pulpit and the speaker's platform.

On that platform stood Lael. Isabelle had never met him, but there could be no mistaking him for anyone else. He looked more like Grand Leon than le roi himself. This was the man in his prime, with a powerful build and a confident poise. His glossy black hair was tied back in a tail save for one loose curl that danced on his forehead.

He dressed according to his legend, eschewing courtly finery for a leather doublet, riding breeches, and tall boots. His only concession to ceremony was a long crimson cape that he wore covering his left side in the manner of the fabled orators of Om. The fabric rippled in a breeze that had gotten in from somewhere. Such were his poise and bearing that he seemed to fill the space, and it was hard to look away.

His voice was deep but rough, as if he were just recovering from a cold. He seemed to be winding down his speech. "We cannot cleave to the notion that nobility carries with it the prerequisite of sorcery. Being a Sanguinaire does not gift one with the knowledge or grace to be the holder of power or the leader of men. Likewise being born without sorcery does not render one incompetent or ignoble."

The assembled parlementarians, all wearing black cloaks and deep cowls over white masks, shifted and muttered, sounding generally uncomfortable. Isabelle guessed they were moved by his presence if not by his words.

Lael continued, "Consider your choice carefully, my countrymen, for what you decide today will bind not only the present but all future generations, your own sons and grandsons should they be stricken by such foul luck as I have endured. Shall you condemn them for no fault but an imperfection, which the traditions of blood argue they receive from you, their forebears? Shall you repudiate your own kin to be and tell them that they have no souls? Or will you show wisdom and mercy as the Builder commands?"

His words stirred Isabelle's heart. She had spent her whole life counted amongst the damned and considered herself to be in the best company. She loathed the idea that, because she had discovered her sorcery, she might now be bound to Paradise Everlasting whilst leaving Jean-Claude, Marie, and all her friends to suffer in Torment. In the unlikely event that the afterlife played out that way, she swore on whatever soul she possessed that she would storm the Ravenous Gate and break every rattling chain in the Breaker's dungeon.

Lael went on, "I do not ask you to make any new law, nor to reinstate me in my parents' good graces. I merely ask you, by the power you were given for precisely this purpose, to declare that the principle of saintblood primacy is itself in error. Builder keep you."

Lael bowed and left the speaker's stand to wait in the place of the petitioner.

Isabelle looked aside at Coquetta, who took in the closing argument wearing a wooden expression.

Isabelle whispered, "Why did Grand Leon allow this to happen?"

"To put the matter in its grave," Coquetta said.

The dictator of the Parlement, wearing white robes with a black mask, his bloodshadow spread behind him like a cape, called, "Sagax Junker to rebut."

Onto the speaker's platform stepped a Temple sagax dressed in a cloth of gold stole over a white chasuble, both embroidered with the linked gears of the eternal machine, and a conical hat emblazoned with the omnioculus. His mustache bristled like an angry cat across his upper lip and along both cheeks.

"Messieurs of the Parlement," he said, in a thick Öberholzer accent that made even the blandest of greetings sound like a declaration of war. "There is very little to say in rebuttal to this man's argument, because the argument is incoherent on its face. It is possible to utter the words 'The Builder is wrong,' but those words make no sense to any sane and pious mind. So it is with the defendant's wheedling."

He lifted a copy of the *Instructions* from a hook upon his belt and brandished it at the gallery like a bomb with a lit fuse. "The *Instructions* are exceedingly clear on this matter." He opened the book and read, "*So that the Savior may rise, let the saintborn sorcerer be king, each in his own land and according to his powers. Let he who has no sorcery, but is made of soulless clay, be his subject. Let the master rule his subjects as a shepherd tends his flock, to protect and nurture them so that their numbers grow, and to take from them such bounty as he needs. Let the clayborn be obedient and humble. Let the saintborn be generous and merciful. Let each be content in his place and diligent in his work until the coming of the Savior and the remaking of the world.*"

Junker slammed the book shut with a resounding boom. "The Builder has ordered the world. To question His will is to disobey Him. To disobey Him is to invite the Breaker in and ensure your own damnation."

The assembly muttered amongst themselves. Isabelle could not imagine they were happy to be harangued by such bombast, but they would endure much worse ere they did more than whine about the insult. The venal would never vote to erode their own privilege. Sagax Junker left the stand and went to lurk in the shadows in the defense's corner.

The dictator asked for comments from the assembly, received none, and called Lael once more into the speaker's circle. "Monsieur Lael, you have put a petition of law before the Parlement. The Parlement has heard your argument and has and will now render a verdict. Do you understand that this decree is binding for all time and without recourse to any appeal until the Savior comes?"

"Yes, and I also understand that this ruling will be made a matter of public record and any attempt to inveigh against it will be considered treasonable."

Isabelle found it odd that he would bring those points to everyone's attention.

"In that case, let the Parlement vote." The dictator looked past Lael and said, "By a show of hands, who votes to accept this unhallowed man's petition?"

Silence and stillness filled the chamber to a nearly suffocating depth. It seemed to Isabelle that Lael surveyed the hooded noblemen in the same way the capitaine of a lonely outpost would survey an encroaching barbarian horde, but his stoic expression never wavered.

"Anyone," asked the dictator, and the question echoed from the far wall. "Let the record show no votes in favor of the petition. All those against?"

Every hand in the Parlement went up, along with the susurration of a group exhalation. More than a few cast less than covert glances at Grand Leon, looking for reassurance. Grand Leon, still as if carved from stone, gave no indication of having noticed the proceedings at all.

"Let the record show unanimous agreement against the petition," said the dictator. "What say the judges?"

The dictator turned to the bank of judges, black masks and black cowls sitting at the flat edge of the room beneath Grand Leon's balcony. "The verdict favors the defense. Do you stand ready to deliver a judgment?"

The lead judge stood and said, "It is the judgment of this court that the tradition of sorcerous primacy is not a mere habit of the state, but instead a matter of sacred and secular law so obvious that there was no more need to write it down than there would be to inscribe law dictating that the Solar should rise. Let this court therefore make it clear that sorcerous primacy is the law of the land in fact as well as tradition, for all time until the Savior comes. Now go and trouble this court no more."

Lael merely lifted his chin and looked down his nose at the Parlement. "As you wish, messieurs." He turned to face the box where Coquetta stood with Isabelle and Sireen. "My deepest regrets, Mother. Would that we might have been a family again."

Coquetta gripped the balustrade to keep herself from shaking. "I have never denied you, my son."

Lael's voice took on an edge. "Be that as it may, no man can bear to be seated at the common table in his own house."

Colonel Martel Hachette, the commander of the Praetorian Guard, stepped up to the speaker's platform and whispered something in Lael's ear. Lael frowned and said to Coquetta, "May the Builder keep you."

"Until the Savior comes," Coquetta said.

Lael allowed himself to be escorted away. He did not have the look of a man defeated or even disappointed. Had he intended this outcome? Isabelle didn't see how it would benefit him, but then she did not know his mind.

Coquetta turned from the Gallerie and sagged against the doorframe. "Damn that boy's pride." She started shivering like a leaf in a gale.

Sireen and Isabelle hurried to steady her. Isabelle placed her hand on the back of Coquetta's neck. Her skin was all but on fire. Isabelle shot an alarmed look at Sireen.

"I'll have her escorted back to her suite," Sireen said firmly.

"And summon a physician," Isabelle said, taboos be damned.

"I'm f-fine," Coquetta mumbled.

Sireen glowered, but not particularly at Isabelle. "There's no harm in asking someone hypothetical questions," she said to Coquetta.

From below the dictator announced, "The Parlement will now consider the case of Princess Isabelle des Zephyrs. The defendant will approach!"

Isabelle gathered her dignity and descended to the floor.

—

Isabelle stood in the witness circle with her feet planted apart and her hands on her hips. She wore a metal plate on her right hip under her outermost skirt that allowed her to brace her spark-hand without having to concentrate on it.

Across from her, in the questioner's circle, stood a Glasswalker lawyer. His body was back in Aragoth somewhere, no doubt resting comfortably on a couch. His espejismo, cast here through a mirror, was everything he wanted to be: tall, straight, and handsome, with a deep baritone. It was only too bad that the soul-distortion that molded Glasswalkers' espejismos into their perfected physical forms did not likewise improve their morals.

The lawyer had been presenting the Aragothic case against her, which consisted primarily of repeating a set of facts that were not in question. Isabelle could hardly deny, even if she wanted to, that she had stolen Hysia from the gallows, a lynching in reverse, as it were.

"You then spirited the murderer away and are even now concealing her," the lawyer said. "Do you deny it? Yes or no?"

"I stand by my opening statement," Isabelle said, clearly enough to be heard in the back row. It was the only answer she'd given him since he'd started cross-examining her. The tactic had fairly well stymied him. Most nobles were a lot less clever than they thought they were, and couldn't resist sparring with their interlocutors even when they had nothing whatsoever to gain by it. Isabelle, by contrast, had experienced a childhood that included regular bouts of savage torture. It would take more than the feeble provocations of a man who dare not lay a hand on her to get her to contradict herself.

The lawyer said, "Let the record show that the accused refused to answer the question."

The Dictator of Parlement, in his white robes and black mask, stepped forward and said, "Mademoiselle des Zephyrs, if you continue to refuse to answer questions, it will be taken as a sign of your guilt."

That was not technically a question, but Isabelle said, "The prosecution is only allowed one interrogator at a time."

"I am merely enforcing the rules of the Parlement," he said. "You will answer the questions as directed or you will be held in contempt of this court. Do you understand?"

Isabelle said nothing, showed nothing on her face. Holding her in contempt could result in her incarceration, which would only serve to delay the resolution the Aragoths were determined to obtain.

"Answer me," demanded the dictator.

Isabelle said nothing. She had to pee. If they kept this up much longer she would lose the battle of the bladder, which was a humiliation she did not need.

The Aragoth said, "I have no further questions."

The dictator recovered himself. "Do you wish to call any more witnesses?"

"No. I think that avenue has been exhausted."

"Do you wish to make a closing statement?" the dictator asked.

Isabelle said, "I believe you are skipping the part where I get to question my witnesses."

The dictator said, "As you refuse to answer questions, it would be inappropriate to allow you to ask them."

Isabelle said, "I imagine you believe I will appeal a guilty verdict to Grand Leon. I doubt you want me to appeal on the basis of your breach of protocol."

Isabelle couldn't see the dictator's expression behind his mask, but she imagined it was an unnatural shade of purple.

After a moment, he spoke in a voice that sounded like it had been subdued by use of corporeal punishment. "Who, pray, would you question?"

"Him," Isabelle said, gesturing to the lawyer. Lawyers were not immune to the conceit that they were smarter than everyone around them. She had stymied this one, but she wagered he thought he could turn the tables on her if he could get her talking.

Her guess seemed to be confirmed by a lifting of his eyebrows. "I see no harm in letting demoiselle interrogate me, as long as she sticks to the facts of the case."

"Agreed," Isabelle said, and they ceremonially switched places.

"Before I begin," Isabelle said. "For proper frame of reference, under which kingdom's laws am I being tried?"

"Under the law of the Grand Peace treaty, which obligated each kingdom to respect the other's laws on matters that occur within the other's territory," he said.

"So in essence, I am being tried in a Célestial court of crime against Aragothic law," Isabelle said. "Very good. That is all, no further questions."

Both the lawyer and the dictator looked at her as if she'd lost her mind. The lawyer's bafflement turned to suspicion.

The dictator said, "In that case, we should move on to closing statements."

Isabelle stood impassive as the lawyer made his argument. It did not take long. It didn't have to. Even the Aragothic observers looked bored.

Then the dictator called on Isabelle to give her closing statement.

Isabelle stepped up to the podium and faced the faceless parlementarians. What galled her more than anything else about this trial was that neither law nor facts actually mattered. She would be destroyed to entrap the Aragothic opponents of the Grand Peace and so prove that l'Empire would honor the law. If that wasn't irony, then the word had no meaning.

"The facts of this case are not in dispute," Isabelle said. "Yesterday I rescued an innocent woman from being executed for a crime she did not commit. I can prove this beyond any reasonable doubt. Consul de la Vega knows this, and so he has chosen to make it irrelevant by accusing me, by way of the

Grand Peace, of violating Aragothic sovereignty. The consul claims that, as an outsider, I have no business interfering in their miscarriage of justice whether or not I am correct on the facts, or indeed whether my actions are just in the eyes of the Builder."

She paused to gather the assembly with her gaze. "Yet as my interlocutor pointed out, I am being tried under Aragothic law. Under Aragothic law, any saintborn noble may choose to provide aid and council to someone accused of a crime. Consul de la Vega argues that I am not allowed to do so on Hysia Dominguez's behalf because I am not an Aragothic subject. This creates the legally untenable position of proposing to subject me to the penalty of a law while simultaneously denying me the rights afforded under that same law. Either I am eligible for the protections of the Aragothic law, in which case I was duty-bound to act as I did in the defense of an innocent, or I cannot be subject to the law's penalties, in which case Consul de la Vega has no standing to bring charges against me."

The assembled Parlement hardly reacted, but she knew better than to press on. She wished Jean-Claude were here. He would have been clever and convincing, whereas all she could be was logical and honest.

The dictator strode to the podium and flourished his cape. "The arguments have been made, all the evidence has been seen and weighed. Is the Parlement prepared to render a verdict?"

Isabelle girded her heart and set her jaw. Might Grand Leon have pushed in her favor behind the curtains? It was foolish to hope. She had nothing but hope, one dying ember in a blizzard.

The dictator asked for a count of the guilty votes. Like a field of dark grass erupting at the first brush of spring, black gloved hands rose up.

"A majority," declared the seneschal of the Parlement.

"Guilty!" declared the dictator, hammering the podium with his fist like a Temple extoller at the climax of a sermon. There was a rumble of congratulations amongst the visiting Aragoths, men thumping Consul de la Vega on the back. The Parlement began chattering amongst themselves.

"Do you wish to appeal?" the dictator asked, in the tone of a twelve-year-old bully offering a taunt.

Isabelle turned to glance at Grand Leon in his private gallery. He would reject her appeal. The whole point was to let the law run its course, rather like letting a river overflow its bank to wipe out a town. If she held her appeal in reserve, she might someday be able to ask for clemency, if there was a someday.

"No," she said. Nothing now stood between her and the gibbet save the whims of the judges.

The dictator turned to the bank of judges in their cowls. "The verdict favors the prosecution, the defendant is guilty of violating the sovereignty of an allied state, do you stand ready to deliver a judgment?"

The three judges bowed their heads together and nodded as if coming to an accord. The central judge stood. The dim ruddy lights behind him turned his shape into a burnished silhouette, a shadow limned in flame. His voice rolled out like thunder, deep and booming, with echoes that lingered in the dark spaces in the back of Isabelle's mind.

"As the defendant is guilty of contempt for the law, so shall she be denied its succor. Henceforth she shall be outcast, banished from court, stricken from all rank and title, forbidden from holding land or deed, and denied the right of petition. She may not enter binding contracts nor hold a passport. You are hereby ordered to turn over all official papers, stamps, seals, and other paraphernalia of office and vacate the Ambassadorial residence forthwith, and trouble this court nevermore."

Isabelle felt like she'd been hit in the chest with a hammer. This was an invitation to go beg in the streets or starve to death. She couldn't even marry her way out of it because marriage was a legal contract. She'd bet anything the Aragothic delegation had insisted on that codicil for precisely that reason. Isabelle was numb, her whole body as senseless as a lump of clay. They'd made her a child, a permanent infant who could never grow up, a social invalid. What purpose could she have now?

"Mademoiselle." A soft rumbling voice dragged her out of the dark well into which her thoughts had plunged. Capitaine Bitterlich had appeared beside her, his expression somber and his eyes full of concern.

"We should get you out of the line of fire." For the second time in as many days, Bitterlich extended his elbow to Isabelle, and for the second time she took it. Nearly drunk with dismay, she nevertheless checked the square of her shoulders and lifted her chin, only leaning on the gallant capitaine a little as they exited the Gallerie. Jeers and taunts were flung at her from the balcony, as if she were an actress who had muffed her lines. It hardly mattered; the damage was already done, and it was fatal. Any further humiliation would be akin to rats savaging a corpse, disgusting but not particularly painful.

"Are you to be my jailer?" she asked, once they had reached the relative privacy of the hallway.

Bitterlich's voice was low and firm. "I could not bear such a task. What they did to you was butchery. They should be honoring you, not casting you aside."

His affirmation hurt like a needle into bone. Why should being told she was right by this almost stranger hurt more than being told she was wrong by her enemies?

She gripped his arm a little tighter. "Don't be too kind," she breathed, her voice husky on the edge of tears. She'd be damned if she was going to turn into a sobbing puddle person in public. Later, perhaps, when no one was looking.

"Where are you taking me?" she asked.

He said, "To wherever your friends are, to put you in the company of people who will lift you up and who deem you a whole person despite the law."

The thought of her friends, her household was another blow to her heart. "They all depended on me, my incomes, my status. We only had Rowan House because I was the ambassadress." Now they would all be out on the streets in the middle of this festival with a threefold winter coming on.

He placed his hand over hers, comforting rather than capturing. "In that case I will be practical. I know a man who has rooms to let. Private rooms."

"Even with all the crowds? Last I heard rents were up thrice over and inns were stacking people like cordwood."

"He doesn't need the money and he likes his privacy, but he owes me a favor or three."

Isabelle's pride bristled at the thought of accepting charity, but she stuffed that beast back in its cage. Her whole life must depend on charity now. "Thank you," she said. She would take any help she could get and find a way to repay him later.

Isabelle and Bitterlich joined the line of people exiting the quondam spire. The fact that there was only one serviceable entrance and it no wider than a fat man meant queues going both ways. Inbound traffic and outbound alternated through the oddly shaped doorway like two lines of dancers passing through each other.

Isabelle emerged onto the high balcony that served as le Ville Céleste's front stoop and into the clear bright day left behind in the wake of yesterday's storm. Light gleaming off knee-deep snow stung her eyes and the chill wind got behind her veil and scratched her cheeks. She took a deep breath of the snow-scrubbed air, just to feel the living sky in her lungs. She'd completely lost track of time in the alien environment of the spire.

"Might I have a word before we set off?" Bitterlich asked, gesturing to the balcony that ran round the spire.

Isabelle followed numbly. "This isn't going to be another dreadful surprise, I hope."

"No. Not for you, anyway. I wanted to ask you about your father."

"I thought you said it wasn't going to be dreadful." Even her humor was dire at the moment.

Bitterlich chuckled anyway. He took her well around the spire, out of the wind and out of sight and hearing of the courtyard. He brushed snow off the rail and rested his hand on it. "I'm just trying to understand something. You don't have to say anything if you don't want to. Yesterday, after our encounter on the stairs, I became curious about your father's death wish. When someone makes a death wish, Grand Leon usually has a pretty good handle on what they're going to be asking for, to the point that he usually has his answer ready beforehand. Last night, after I left you with Coquetta, I had a chat with the Lord Chamberlain's apprentice who informed me that there had been no documents prepared before or after your father's audience."

Isabelle's curiosity stirred despite all her troubles. "Interesting, but what does that have to do with me?"

"It turns out there was a document prepared for your father's death wish, when he initially made the request several months ago."

Isabelle was flummoxed. "You mean this is his second death wish?"

"His second *attempt*, anyway. The first one never materialized. Apparently he lost his nerve. There was, however, paperwork for that one, and since it never came to fruition, it was a dead letter. I convinced the clerk to let me borrow it."

"What did it say?"

Bitterlich opened a case on his belt and produced a scroll. "Read for yourself."

Isabelle drew on her *gant de acier*, the metal glove she wore on her spark-hand that let her do two-handed things like unroll a scroll. Sparks flew where her otherwise intangible fingers brushed the metal.

"That's amazing," Bitterlich said. "Can you feel with it?"

His enthusiasm was refreshing. Most people looked at her like she was carrying around a live viper. "Most things, it doesn't feel. No heat or cold. I am aware of pressure, though it doesn't have the same quality as skin."

"Hmmm. In the right circumstances, that could be incredibly useful."

"Occasionally," she allowed. She'd used it to kill a madman once.

He cocked his head and said cautiously, "There are some wild rumors about how you acquired it."

That was another thing Isabelle usually didn't talk about, but then she was usually afflicted with people who thought she was the Breaker's get. "I lost my arm in battle," she said. Admittedly it had been a short, one-sided battle, and she'd been hors de combat before the actual surgical severing, but she felt she was owed some consideration for trying.

"Oh," Bitterlich said, looking downcast. "I'm sorry."

"Don't be," she said, though his sympathy warmed her.

She unrolled the scroll. There was the usual legal preamble, seals declaring authenticity and so on and so forth down to the bit that mattered.

Isabelle shivered with a chill that had nothing to do with the icy day. According to this document, her father had asked for Guillaume to be cut out as heir to the des Zephyrs estate in favor of Arnette's as yet unborn child. Additionally, Narcisse des Zephyrs had asked to be made the child's guardian regent.

"That's a bit eerie," she said.

Bitterlich said, "It doesn't make any sense to me at all. I can see him wanting to skip your brother if he's as much a fool as you say, but what sense does it make for him to ask to be the child's guardian if he's going to be dead?"

Isabelle huffed and watched the puff of her breath roll away on the wind. "I can see a path to it making sense. The last time I saw my father, he couldn't even sit up in his chair. His bloodshadow was eating him. It was like watching a sugar lump dissolve into a film of water, only infinitely slower. He had invited into his court a madman named Artifex Kantelvar."

"This Kantelvar is the one that you killed in the royal court of Aragoth," Bitterlich said. "A deed of renown."

"A deed of desperation, from my point of view," Isabelle said. "It's been educational to see how other people romanticize it. The point I'm getting at, though, is that Father was trying to bargain with Kantelvar to shrive his bloodshadow."

Bitterlich's brows lifted and his whiskers bent forward. If he'd had a tail, Isabelle imagined it would be twitching. "That's not supposed to be possible this side of legend."

"Kantelvar was the other side of legend," Isabelle said. "But he said it couldn't be done. More precisely he said, 'Even if I could, I wouldn't,' which now that I think about it sounds a lot like one of his evasions. My father wants more life, and he'd be willing to sacrifice literally anything to get it, even his bloodshadow. But without his bloodshadow, he'd no longer be Sanguinaire. He'd be stripped of all his land and titles. To get around that, he makes this death wish. He'd be legally dead, but he could cling to life, status, and power by becoming his grandchild's guardian and regent."

Bitterlich's expression grew thoughtful. "Do you think it's possible he might have found a way to shrive his bloodshadow?"

"If so, why change his death wish?" Isabelle asked. "Why involve the Gyrine in making a new, presumably different death wish?"

"Perhaps Hailer Dok offered him a better option."

"Better than more life?" Isabelle asked, dragging herself back from the inherent temptation of a mystery. "This speculation is all very interesting, but what is its purpose? If you really want to know what my father is up to you can ask Grand Leon, or that Windcaller. I would like to go . . . back to my people." Not home anymore. "This great shadow oppresses me." She gestured to the spire.

Bitterlich readjusted his cape and then tugged at his cravat to center it properly. "I understand. I'm sorry for detaining you."

"I'm not sorry you did," Isabelle said.

They descended the broad set of stairs into the courtyard.

"Isabelle!" came a shout over the heads of the crowd.

Isabelle's pulse quickened. She looked up as Jean-Claude approached on horseback. She quickened her steps to meet him. "Jean-Claude! Thank the Builder." He wore his long coat over his musketeer's tabard, which was stained dark . . . that couldn't all be blood, could it?

"Thank Marie," he said. "She's the one who sent me up here. Is everything well?"

Pain resurfaced, loss and humiliation like a bruise slowly spreading through her whole being. "Nothing is well," she said. "Oh, Jean-Claude, have you met Capitaine Bitterlich?" she asked automatically, gesturing as the Seelenjäger in question strolled up.

Jean-Claude's eyebrows lifted in surprise. "I can't say that I have. Thank you, Capitaine, for watching over Isabelle. I will take it from here."

"I leave her in your custody." To Isabelle he said, "May I have permission to call on you?"

"Of course," Isabelle said.

Bitterlich tipped his hat and said, "If you find yourself in need of shelter contact Monsieur DeGris on la rue des Chapeliers and mention my name. Builder keep you safe from harm."

"Until the Savior comes to take you home," Isabelle said.

Bitterlich's face flickered like a flame, and there was a sound like crinkling paper as tawny fur became black feathers and golden eyes became black jewels. His whole body collapsed like an empty sack being wadded up, then stretched out into the shape of a great raven. He beat the air with wings of dark iridescent feathers, rowing vigorously until he found a rising wind to carry him away.

Isabelle realized her mouth was hanging open. She knew what Seelenjägers could do, knew that startling transformation was only the barest whiff of his power, but knowing had not prepared her senses for the stunning strangeness of it.

"Oh," she breathed in wonder. "Do that again."

Jean-Claude stared after the retreating raven. "Why would you need to change lodgings?"

"It's a tedious and ugly story," she said.

"When was the last time you had anything to eat?"

"This morning," she said. Just after midnight was technically this morning.

He extended his hand down to her. "All aboard. I know a place where we can get out of the wind, get you some food, and you can tell me what happened."

Jean-Claude pulled her up behind him. The weight of Isabelle's destruction settled on her. Jean-Claude had been assigned as her defender since birth. She could not imagine he would be allowed to continue in that capacity now. She threw her arm around him, clinging tighter than a barnacle, hanging on for dear life.

CHAPTER

Seven

The Monk's Measure, advertised by a sign depicting a supine friar with a flagon perched on his protruding belly, was one of the few permanent buildings atop the barren, windswept royal plateau. It had once been a monastery, but Grand Leon evicted the monks as part of his ongoing dispute with the Temple. Its main building, the former great hall, stood on the precipice of the cliff, above the wine cellar. Its warehouses, stables, blacksmith, and boundary wall extended inland.

The low-ceilinged common room, crowded and noisy, stuttered into an awkward silence when Jean-Claude and Isabelle entered. Isabelle's spark-arm stood out like a firework in a coal mine. Isabelle stiffened at all the stares, but Jean-Claude took her by the elbow and led her down the stairs to a basement alcove with a window that opened to the deep and distant sky.

Isabelle faced out the window, staring into the sky without seeing it. She was gray-faced, her eyes dull and downcast, her normally loose lanky movements heavy and limp. He'd seen her hurt before, but he'd never seen her look so beaten.

"What happened?" Jean-Claude asked, and was there anything he could do about it?

Isabelle shook her head. "I offended Consul de la Vega, I was charged with infringing on the sovereignty of an allied nation. Grand Leon threw me to the Merciful Parlement. They convicted me and declared me outcast." Her voice trembled with rage and frustration.

"Blessed Builder," Jean-Claude said, horror and outrage fighting for supremacy in his mind. "That's lunacy. Why?"

"Because I outlived my usefulness as a negotiator at precisely the same moment I matured as a sacrificial goat," Isabelle said. "Grand Leon found a way to turn my faux pas to his advantage. It's the same logic as sacrificing a legate in a game of thwarts. De la Vega's allies object to the treaty, so they overcommitted to getting rid of me. They reckoned Grand Leon would defend me and therefore discredit l'Empire's commitment to the Grand Peace. Our adversaries got themselves up to a gallop, telling everyone in Aragoth how faithless l'Empire was. Grand Leon tossed me off the cliff and they dove right after me. I imagine Julio and Alejandro are even now presenting this verdict as proof that the enemies of the peace are fools as well as cowards. The Grand Peace is in a stronger position now than when I finished negotiating it yesterday. From Monsieur's point of view, it couldn't have worked out better if he planned it."

"This difference being that you aren't a game chit," Jean-Claude said. He had a vision of punching Grand Leon in his saggy, pest-ridden face. Isabelle had served l'Empire well.

"Player or pawn, I still lost," Isabelle said. "I can't even marry my way out of this. Outcasts can't make contracts. I have to warn the household, help Valérie and Gretl find new patrons." Isabelle's voice started to crack. Tears leaked from her eyes and she scrubbed them away with the same dull determination as buffing rust off a knife.

Jean-Claude wrapped his arm around her shoulders. "Clearly l'Empire doesn't deserve you. What's needed here is some outrageous revenge plot. I know, we'll seize a ship and take up piracy. We will make you Pirate Capitaine Isabelle."

Isabelle laughed, a bleak sound like an owl's hoot on a frozen night. "And you would be sky sick the entire time. Master gunner, lean to the port rail. Fire at will!"

Jean-Claude made convincing retching noises, and Isabelle laughed harder, her tears flowing freely, until she started to hiccough. "Oh *hic* dammit."

He cracked the ice off the top of a water barrel, rummaged around, and filled a cup for her. She drew it down until the spasms stopped, then sagged forward, her elbow on the windowsill and the cup hanging loosely in her hand. After a few more shuddering breaths she asked, "Short of piracy, what do we do next? Everyone was depending on my stipend."

Jean-Claude put his hand on her back. "The first thing that I'm going to do is have a word or three with Grand Leon, and see what can be done about this wretched sentence."

"Are you sure that's wise?" Isabelle asked. Her voice was more weary than afraid. "He might consider you taking my side as treasonous."

"Mayhap," Jean-Claude allowed, "but he never has before."

"And how many times have you defied him?"

"More than is probably wise," Jean-Claude said, "but it has been my observation that good leaders, whether they run a business, an estate, or an empire, always keep close to them advisors and subordinates who are willing, at times of great need, to tell them to stick their head in a bucket of pig shit."

One of Isabelle's eyebrows quirked up. "Is that an exact quote?"

"Conversations with Monsieur are generally considered confidential."

"So that would be a 'Yes,'" Isabelle surmised.

A heavy tread on the stone steps announced the arrival of the proprietor, a barrel-chested ox of a man with legs like stone pilings and sergeant's stripes tattooed on shoulders that had to turn sideways to make it through the door. An old puckered scar circled his neck and he wore a hangman's noose like a cravat. "Who? Here?"

Isabelle started as the man unfolded as much as he could in the narrow space.

Jean-Claude popped up and said, "Sascha. It's good to see you again."

Sascha's eyes glinted and his mouth curved in a huge horse-toothed smile. "Jean-Claude!"

Jean-Claude stepped back and said, "Goodman Sascha, be known to Mademoiselle Isabelle des Zephyrs."

Sascha gurgled and his throat twitched. "Madd'm."

Isabelle overcame her surprise and said, "Thank you for the use of your cellar. It's good to be out of the wind."

"Though we could use two bowls and a bottle of your best," Jean-Claude said.

"*Oui*," he rumbled, and hurried off.

"You know him?" Isabelle asked.

"We served together once, when we were younger. He's a lout, but a good lout. He was in the Iron Fists. Got a girl in trouble and her family strung him up in an old barn."

Isabelle's hand went to her throat in sympathy. "That's horrible."

"I got there in time to cut him down, luckily. The girl, Josephine, testified that she seduced him and they were married on the spot. Last I checked they have two daughters and a grandson that he dotes on."

Isabelle's expression sagged in uncharacteristic melancholy. "I stopped you from having children, didn't I?"

Jean-Claude's heart gave a twinge. There had almost been another child once. It was not a time he cared to think about.

"I'm lucky I found you," he said, recalling that long ago day, holding her close, a squalling newborn surrounded by the enemies that were her family. He'd usurped Grand Leon's authority and named the tiny girl after le roi's mother. Somehow they'd both survived the experience and the twenty-six years since. "It was the best thing I ever did."

Sascha returned with two trenchers and a big bowl of eggs, chickpeas, and a thick white gravy, along with a bottle of something resembling wine. He plunked the food down on an upended barrel and fetched two stools.

Isabelle pulled up her veil and fell on the food like a vulture on a carcass. Jean-Claude suspected she'd been forgetting to eat again. She got so far up in her head that she neglected everything below the neck.

"How are Josephine and the kids?" Jean-Claude asked.

Sascha beamed. "Three. Grand. Children."

"Congratulations!" Jean-Claude said.

"Is. Good," Sascha said, then with a faraway look he added, "Regiment. Called. Up. Every. Body."

It was Jean-Claude's turn to be surprised. "For the parades?"

Sascha nodded. "Been. Twenty. Years. Kids. Never. Seen. Uniform. Proud."

"They should be," Jean-Claude said. "I'll look for you if I'm there for the parade. Give my best to Josephine."

Sascha left. Jean-Claude and Isabelle ate with no more sound than munching and the whistling of the wind outside until Isabelle polished off enough to feed a cavalryman and his horse. Where did she put it all?

At last she subsided. She twirled a bread sop in a last smear of gravy at the bottom of the bowl but showed no sign of putting it in her mouth. Her expression was pensive. "Why did you never tell me about you and Coquetta?"

Jean-Claude twitched away. How in the world . . . but of course, Isabelle had spent the night in le Ville Céleste. "It . . . never seemed appropriate. We were young and—"

"Inappropriate," Isabelle finished for him. "Intimate, indecent, intoxicating, insatiable, inventive, and an inventory of other imperatives initiated with 'I.'"

"Indeed," Jean-Claude said dryly, but his forays into romance were not things he wanted to discuss with Isabelle, though if she was going to find out about his affairs, better she learn about Coquetta than Impervia. He was also relieved to hear her play their alliteration game; however bruised she felt right now, she was not broken.

—

Isabelle pushed the last unfortunate gravy dollop around for another minute. Her hunger was sated, and that stress on her nerves abated, though the meal felt like a lump of plaster in her stomach. Every part of her ached, but Jean-Claude's presence eased her heart. He would always be on her side, assuming he didn't get himself killed.

"You still haven't told me how you managed to get covered in blood," she said. Clearly he'd gotten the better end of whatever fracas he'd been in, but she dreaded the time he wouldn't. He had a tendency to forget that he was no longer a young man when swords were drawn.

"There's a story in that." Jean-Claude put his elbows on the top of the barrel and leaned forward. Isabelle leaned in too until their noses were but a handspan apart.

Jean-Claude said, "You remember I told you about a Goldentongue named Brandon Mistwaithe, recently arrived from l'Île des Zephyrs. Word had it he was going to be auctioning information about a scandal within your father's house. Naturally I decided to attend . . ."

Isabelle listened in rapt fascination and growing horror as Jean-Claude told of the massacre in the Lowmarket, of the lateborn Orem, and the bone queen.

After Jean-Claude had explained his deduction of Mistwaithe's disappearance, Isabelle put her hand on his sleeve to interrupt. "That reminds me.

Yesterday I saw my father on his way to present Grand Leon with his death wish."

Jean-Claude tipped his hat back. "Truly? I never thought that old villain would admit death knew his name, much less invite it in for tea. What was he asking for in return for doing us all the great favor of expiring?"

"I have no idea," Isabelle said. "It turns out this is the second time he's asked."

His look of incredulity grew as she filled him in on the details of the double death wish.

She asked, "Do you think the scandal Mistwaithe was trying to sell had something to do with that?"

Jean-Claude rubbed the back of his neck. "It could be, but how would we know?"

Isabelle exhaled her disappointment, but said, "I don't suppose it matters. My father's misdeeds can hardly disrupt my work or ruin my reputation at this point."

Jean-Claude said, "The tale doesn't end there. After the Lowmarket, I followed Orem's back trail to Screaming Hall . . ." He told her of the deranged prior and the wounded lady, of the Harvest King and the possibility of Orem's parentage.

"His son?" Isabelle breathed. "An unrecognized bastard?"

"Not so much unrecognized as misplaced. I was hoping you could help me confirm his parentage," Jean-Claude said. "Do your blood ciphers work on dead people? I had him put on ice at the city cemetery."

"I don't know," Isabelle said. The blood ciphers were a quondam artifact she'd acquired which could tell if two people were related and to what degree. "I can always try it and see what happens. Even if death is no obstacle, it would only work if the ciphers had sampled some of Grand Leon's blood, and I've never seen his name come up in the cipher's store."

Jean-Claude shook his head. "Do that, please. What concerns me more is how Orem came by his sorcery. He was unhallowed most of his life, but he was a sorcerer when he died. Usually even the oldest lateborn don't manifest much after twenty."

Isabelle leaned back against a stack of crates. "I didn't come into my sorcery until I was twenty-six." Though she was probably not the best counterexample given that her sorcery had been artificially suppressed.

"But think about the timing," Jean-Claude said. "The Harvest King took him out of the Agonesium, and Immacolata delivered him to the Golden Swain at precisely the moment his bloodshadow manifested. How likely is that? There was that hole in his skull and the galvanic rod. What if it was like touching off a cannon? Do you think you could puzzle out Ingle's journal, find out what he knew and how he knew it?"

Isabelle rubbed her temple in sympathy with the trepanned man. "Of course. But if Ingle figured out a way to enliven somnolent sorceries, that's the discovery of the century. That changes the world. What does it mean to be unhallowed if you can suddenly reach in and light the spark? I know how desperate I was to manifest sorcery, if only to make my father stop trying to drag it out of me, and I'm not even the worst case. There are unhallowed people out there, even children, who would gladly cut holes in their heads if they thought there was even a chance it could enliven their sorcery. Think of the eldest son who can't inherit his father's title, the daughter who is ineligible to marry."

Jean-Claude frowned and thumped his fist lightly on the barrel. "They wouldn't be excited if they'd seen what I saw. Orem's bloodshadow was completely out of control. It was like watching someone die of the red consumption in minutes rather than years."

"That wouldn't matter," Isabelle said. "Desperation rarely yields to sense, and besides, all discoveries get refined over time. When Baron Freichester discovered the sympathetic principles, he said the forces he observed were too weak to be useful. Fifty years later we use them to build naval orreries and navigate skyships across the boundless deeps."

"And how will this refinement be carried out?" Jean-Claude asked. "By cutting open more heads? I saw one cabinet full of vivisected brains. I don't need to see any more."

Isabelle paused, checking her own habit of speculation. "I didn't say it should be done, just that it would. Much of the learning may be opportunistic. We have learned much about surgery and medicine owing to war. That doesn't make war good."

Jean-Claude grunted. "And it doesn't tell us anything about the Harvest King and Immacolata or what they mean to do, or what it has to do with Mistwaithe or your family."

This mention of family kicked loose a stuck cog in Isabelle's brain. "Speaking of family, you remember I told you about Lorenzo Barbaro?"

"Your other other father?" Jean-Claude asked. She had three: one of the heart, one of the law, and one of the flesh.

"That one," she said. "A few months ago, I let loose some questions into the world, and they came back last night in the form of a letter. Apparently I have a sister."

Jean-Claude's eyes rounded. "Truly? Can I see the letter?"

"Unfortunately it literally evaporated after I read it. If what it said was true, Lorenzo Barbaro had at least one other daughter, but he was assassinated by someone hoping to end his line for good. His line would include me, if this enemy knew of my paternity."

Jean-Claude's expression grew dark. He asked, "Did she present any evidence to prove her claim?"

"The letter contained things that nobody save Kantelvar or Barbaro could have known. She says she's in town for Grand Leon's party and offered to wait for me in Conqueror's Square if I want to meet her."

"That's the last thing you should do," Jean-Claude said. "If ever there was a setup for an assassination or abduction, that would be it."

"I thought of that, but if she meant to lure me out, why say anything that would make me attend my defenses?"

"Perhaps to scare you into thinking you don't have a choice. If you're in danger, you're going to want to know more about it, who the enemy is, for example. I gather that was not in the letter."

Isabelle frowned. "No."

"So the letter was meant as an enticement."

"That doesn't necessarily mean it was false. I need to contact her to find out the truth, and I need your help."

Jean-Claude pulled off his spectacles and polished them. At last he put them back on and said, "Why is this so important to you?"

Isabelle arched her back to relieve the kinks in it and took a moment to sort her tangled motives out in a way that would make sense to anyone else.

"First, there's the practical reason. Now that I know this person exists, I need to find out who she is and what she wants, especially if she turns out to be a fraud.

"Second is because . . . Lorenzo Barbaro made me. How much of me comes from him?" Did Barbaro know his dalliance with her mother had been part of a madman's plan to breed the Savior? Had he been aware he'd sired a child, or had he just been looking to notch the bedpost of one of the most beautiful women in all the Risen Kingdoms?

Also, what had Isabelle's mother known about her part in that scheme?

Vedetta des Zephyrs had died giving birth to Isabelle's brother Guillaume when Isabelle was two. She'd left no written record of her life or thoughts, just a series of portraits suggesting the only thing that overmatched her pulchritude was her vanity. Barbaro, though, might remember something about her.

"I don't like getting involved with Fenice," he said. "Their vendettas last for centuries, generation on generation trying to wipe each other's children out because that's the only way to make sure that the other fellow never gets reincarnated in some forgotten heir."

"Like me," Isabelle said. "If there is a vendetta out there, we need to know about it."

Jean-Claude grunted. "True, but it shouldn't be you who makes contact. In fact, you should stay as far away from contact as possible. Even if this person is exactly who she says she is, which I doubt, the last thing you want is to be seen together lest someone following her pick up on you."

Isabelle squirmed in the grip of his reason. "What's the point of having a family if you can't ever meet them?"

"Worry about that once we find out if she's telling the truth. What I want you to do is write a letter back to her, no names. I'll deliver it, and see what she has to say."

Isabelle had to admit that made sense.

"Speaking of bad ideas," Jean-Claude said. "Marie petitioned me to become my apprentice bodyguard."

"Really," Isabelle said, a thrill of delight surging through her breast like a single Solar ray on a gloomy day. "That's perfect."

"Not the word I would have chosen."

"But it is the path she chose for herself. I'm happy for her. Marie missed out on a lot of life, and she's trying to catch up. She needs serious challenges. She's making a leap, trying her strength. She's fearless and protective and she loves pushing herself. Did I mention she jumped between me and several armed men yesterday? She'll defend whoever needs defending whether she has training or not. She should therefore have training."

"This is not a path to be set upon recklessly."

"Marie is the opposite of reckless. If she wants to do this you can bet she's thought it through. I trust you will bring her up to scratch," she said with an emphasis on the "trust."

Jean-Claude put his hand over his heart. "I will make her a force to be reckoned with. Saints help me."

One of Isabelle's greatest fears crept up on her. "But what if Grand Leon reassigns you? As an outcast, surely I don't warrant a King's Own Musketeer as a protector."

"Then I will resign my commission, take my pension, and carry on as I always have. After thirty years, l'Empire owes me a farm, if it comes to that."

Relief washed up on Isabelle's shores, bringing with it a flotsam of guilt. She did not want to cost Jean-Claude his hard-won station. "I can't picture you as a farmer."

"Why not?" he asked. "I grew up as one. As far as I can tell, the gentle art of tilling dirt and shoveling shit hasn't changed that much."

"And you've never stopped shoveling shit," Isabelle said. "You'd be bored out of your mind with nothing more vicious to contend with than village gossip."

Jean-Claude said, "You've never been around village gossip, have you? No one holds a grudge like a toothless old aunt. They hand feuds down like family heirlooms and build monuments to wounded pride, some of them can last out the threefold winter sustained by nothing more than half a bag of rotten feelings and a pint of bitterness."

CHAPTER

Eight

Jean-Claude delivered Isabelle back to the stables to collect her horse and the guardsmen to escort her back down the Pilgrims' Road to Rocher Royale. He leaned on the cold stone of the gatehouse walls and watched her wade through crowds of clayborn festivalgoers. The crowds bumped along toward the stadium across the plateau. From that great edifice rose the faint brassy voices of trumpets, tattered bits of their clarion call reaching Jean-Claude's ears even through the ever-whistling wind.

Jean-Claude tried to remember if he had ever been so eager to slap his gaze on royalty, but couldn't find an echo of the urge. Yes, Grand Leon ran l'Empire well. He built roads, mills, aqueducts, and schools instead of palaces. He kept his nobles from ruining the common folk, but by all ten thousand Torments he was a fiend when it came to getting his way. Just now, Jean-Claude thought he might spit on le roi's bloodshadow for sacrificing Isabelle without so much as a thank-you for her service.

When at last Isabelle disappeared over a rise, Jean-Claude climbed the steps to the quondam spire. He needed to talk to Coquetta about Orem. Plus, she just might have heard the names Immacolata and the Harvest King.

Otherwise he'd have to talk to Impervia, and that thought left the taste of ashes in his mouth. There were some sins one could not atone for.

Jean-Claude had to pause to rest going up the stairs inside. Why was the air up here so damned thin? On the landing before Coquetta's suite waited an entry warden Jean-Claude didn't recognize. Time was he had known all the Trefoil's servitors by sight and by name, but he'd been away for so long that even the style of uniform had changed. Now they were on to waistcoats and cravats.

Women's muffled voices came from beyond the curtainway.

"He left us, Mother. We didn't leave him," said one, who sounded cranky.

"Of course, dear, but that doesn't make it hurt any less. I pray your children never give you such trouble."

A wave of nostalgia made Jean-Claude dizzy. He would recognize Coquetta's voice anywhere, even after all these years. They had been so close once, partners in bed and in adventure, but she had chosen ambition over him, and he could not say she was wrong.

"That would require me to have children," said the cranky voice.

"And when are you going to get around to that?" Coquetta asked, her voice a tease.

The entry warden challenged Jean-Claude for his identification, read his papers, and then stepped inside to inform Coquetta. The curtain pulled back and Coquetta rushed out. "Jean-Claude!"

A sharp pain nicked Jean-Claude's heart at the sight of her. How well he remembered her youth, her round soft flesh, her bright eyes and her lusty vitality, but now she looked ill. Her gray skin glistened with an unhealthy sweat, and her red velvet bloodshadow had gone as thin and pink as the drippings from a roast.

The strong-boned, stiff-necked, conservatively dressed woman who followed her out was clearly one of her daughters.

Jean-Claude swept off his hat and made a bow. "Madame Comtesse Coquetta. It's a pleasure to see you again."

Coquetta's small mouth split into a wide grin, and she took his thick hand in hers. Her skin was both hot and clammy. "After Princess Isabelle came by, I thought I'd be seeing you. I'm delighted to be proven correct." He gaze caught on his clothes. "Saints, is all that blood? What happened?"

"I cut myself shaving," Jean-Claude said.

Coquetta gave his humor the eye-roll-head-shake it deserved. "I assume it's mostly someone else's. Come in. I'll have someone fetch you a new tabard."

"Not just yet," Jean-Claude said. "I need to see Grand Leon and I need to make the right impression. Covered in blood in l'Empire's service just about ties a bow on it."

"Well, come in, anyway."

The warden held the curtain aside. Jean-Claude entered a powder-blue receiving room. Coquetta called for wine and gestured to her companion. "Jean-Claude, I don't believe you've met my daughter, Princess Josette."

"Mademoiselle Princess." Jean-Claude bowed. "Your mother writes glowingly of you." She was Coquetta's middle daughter, about Isabelle's age, and one of Grand Leon's many recognized bastards. She had le roi's wide chin and high-bridged nose. According to Coquetta's letters, she was the only one of Coquetta's several adult progeny who remained unmarried and had no major scandals attached to her name.

Josette dipped in return, her bloodshadow fanning out behind her like a peacock's tail. "I've heard a great deal about you, too, monsieur."

"None of it accurate, I hope."

That won a glint from her eye. "Much of it contradictory," she allowed.

Coquetta led Jean-Claude through another curtainway into a withdrawing room furnished with comfortable chairs and a daybed. "If you wouldn't mind, Josette. Jean-Claude and I have a great deal of catching up to do."

Josette cast her mother a worried look, but allowed herself to be excluded. Coquetta sipped her wine, smiled in an old familiar way, and said, "I don't suppose I could tempt you into an hour of fond remembrances?" She traced a finger along his bestubbled cheek. Her touch raised the hanged man from the dead. Some of it was surely memory, but mostly it was because Coquetta remained one of the most attractive women he'd ever met. She didn't have the sort of incandescent beauty Isabelle's mother had once possessed, but she projected a kindness and warmth that Vedetta never could.

Yet Coquetta was playing with him. She had to be. She looked far too ill to be in the mood for bed games. Besides, Jean-Claude doubted the memories in question would last an hour . . . or even a quarter.

Reluctantly, he drew his thoughts away from remembered tumbles. He cleared his throat to make absolutely sure he wouldn't squeak. "Unfortunately, I have business to attend, and I have need of your *other* services."

Coquetta pouted. "You always were so serious."

"That's because you always were doing your best to get us both killed, one mad thing after another, leaping from bridges into river scows, disguising ourselves as clerics in the middle of the Feast of Saint Cynessus."

"Hah," she said. "At least half of those mad ideas were yours."

"Bad ideas," Jean-Claude said. "I said they were bad ideas and you took it as a challenge."

"Hmmm . . . Well, it seems you've found yourself another girl to keep you from dying of boredom. Your Isabelle is quite the young lady."

"She is," Jean-Claude said. "Unfortunately, l'Empire does not agree with us."

"I know exactly how you feel," Coquetta said, and Jean-Claude knew it well. Her ordeal with her son's exile had been harrowing. The difference was, Lael had only been evicted after being given every opportunity not to be, precisely the opposite of Isabelle's predicament, but expelled was expelled from a parent's point of view.

Coquetta said, "But what of you? I've heard the most amazing tales of your recent exploits. Is it true what they say about your adventure at the Lowmarket?"

Jean-Claude recognized Coquetta's working cadence—talking to people was even more her job than it was his—but he did not mind. "Probably not, given the way tales twist like smoke in the wind, but it is what I wanted to talk to you about. Yesterday morning, I was forced to put down a mad Sanguinaire."

"Was it anyone I know?"

"That's what I'm hoping to find out. The problem is that this touches on affairs of state."

Coquetta's eyes brightened, probably because this sounded salacious. "Go on."

"The Sanguinaire in question was lateborn. He only manifested his blood-shadow a few moments before he died. Before that, he had been a resident of the Royal Agonesium for the Deranged. Before that he was a mad beggar."

"A Sanguinaire beggar, how horrid. Had he no family?"

"That's the tricky bit," Jean-Claude said. "When I investigated his records at the Agonesium I found a notation that may indicate the highest of parentage."

Coquetta looked horror-struck and she whispered, "One of Monsieur's?"

"That's what the notation seems to say. But is it real?"

Coquetta looked into her wine cup as if divining an answer from the dark liquid. "Do you know how old he was? We keep a register of our lord and master's bedroom conquests. It's less unsightly than carving notches in the bedposts, and it helps keep track of women making paternity claims."

"It was hard to say. Orem was a grown man."

"That hardly narrows it down, now does it?"

"I'll look at his records again," Jean-Claude said. "Better yet, I'll have Isabelle look at his paperwork. If there's anything there, she'll root it up." Isabelle interrogated books the way he interrogated reluctant adversaries, ruthlessly and creatively. "I am mostly interested in a pair of names, the Harvest King and Immacolata."

Coquetta's hand trembled, and she set her goblet down to avoid spilling it. Alas, she would not discuss her frailty with him, and it would be unconscionably rude of him to ask about it.

She said, "*The Harvest King*? It's a play. There's a troupe of traveling players who have been putting it on, a morality piece based on the old pagan heresies about a god who dies and is reborn. They do it at parties, all out in the crowd. It's very risqué."

Jean-Claude was flummoxed. "A play. Have you seen this thing?"

"Twice," she said. "The Temple's been complaining about it, because it's all about impulse, debauchery, and primal urges, but that only makes people more excited to see it. The audience can become very involved in the fantasy, if you take my meaning. But what does this have to do with your beggared scion?"

"Because Harvest King was the name of the man who took the poor blighter out of Screaming Hall." He did not see how that act intersected with a bawdy play, but he couldn't imagine it was a coincidence. "Do you have any idea where this troupe of players is performing next?"

Coquetta looked at him. Her pupils were but pinpricks, and she wobbled on her feet. "No? Until now I wha nee flooo." Her face went slack, her eyes rolled up in her head, and she slumped to the ground, her whole body thrashing like a landed fish.

"Coquetta!" Jean-Claude dropped to her side and caught her head before she could smash it on the furniture. "Help!"

Coquetta's bloodshadow twitched. It caught Jean-Claude's shadow and hurled him across the room. He crashed into the wall. His spectacles flew from his face and stars spun before his vision. He scrabbled at the floor for purchase, but only ended up bunching the rug. Josette hurtled into the room but stopped short, her face a mask of horror when she saw her mother's convulsions.

"Don't let her hit her head!" Jean-Claude pushed himself up on wobbly knees.

Josette's bloodshadow slicked across the floor and grappled Coquetta's, quickly wrestling her to a standstill.

"Get out," she snarled at Jean-Claude.

Jean-Claude retreated, but only to retrieve his glasses and button the curtains against a bevy of encroaching servants. Coquetta continued to shiver for a few minutes before slumping into unconsciousness.

Rarely had Jean-Claude felt so weak and helpless. What sort of malady was this?

Josette released her grip and stood back. "I would that you had not witnessed that." She strode to the curtains and unbuttoned them. A team of very worried-looking handmaids came silently in and began tending their mistress.

"Come," Josette said. "They will put her to bed."

Jean-Claude followed Josette to the receiving room but looked back in time to see the handmaids hoisting Coquetta onto the daybed. Her bloodshadow seemed to catch in the fibers of the rug. The edge of it tore off, leaving ragged scraps of crimson in the white carpet while the rest of the shadow recoiled, visibly diminished. The bits of bloodshadow trapped in the rug evaporated and dispersed into nothing.

Cold and shaken, Jean-Claude backed into the main hall, where Josette faced him with crossed arms and a twitching bloodshadow.

"Her bloodshadow is dying," Jean-Claude said.

Josette's shadow licked forward and brushed against Jean-Claude's gray umbra. The merest touch of the crimson sheen sent ripples of prickling numbness along the length of his limbs.

"Does that please you, clayborn? Does it bring you pleasure to see a saintborn brought low?" For all Josette's venom, there was fear in her voice.

Jean-Claude chose his next words carefully. "Your mother has always been a great woman, and my friend. I would not see her fall."

Josette twitched as if she wanted to attack and to flee at the same time. In a very hushed voice she asked, "Did you ever love my mother?"

Jean-Claude said, "I gave her what she wanted, which wasn't me."

After a terrible moment, Josette nodded acceptance. She withdrew her bloodshadow and Jean-Claude's knees almost gave out from the relief.

She said, "Promise me you will never speak of what you've seen."

"I will keep her confidence, of course," said Jean-Claude. "It would be my privilege even if it was not my duty, but this isn't going to stay a secret."

With the will of one defying gravity, Josette said, "It can. It must. I'm going to move her out of this damned fiendish tuning fork"—she gestured at the quondam spire around them—"and take her to her own lands where she'll have a chance to recover in peace."

"Does she have the black cankers?" Jean-Claude asked. The skin was the organ of power for the Sanguinaire, and sorcerers only lost their gifts when the gifted organ failed. Such calamity nearly always led to death. Worse, it was widely believed to be a mark of corruption, a loss of the Builder's favor that let the Breaker in.

Josette made a sign against sickness. "No. Nor the slug fever, nor any other malady that I can name. Just these fits."

"How long has this been going on?"

"I don't know. She never mentioned she was feeling ill, and I only caught on two days ago. Having made the catch, I realized she's been hiding something for at least a week." Her hands clenched in frustration. "'I'm as strong as an ox,' she says."

Jean-Claude grimaced in sympathy. "I shall make a discreet inquiry with a physician friend of mine who has great knowledge of strange illnesses."

Josette shot him a warning look, but at least didn't sic the bloodshadow on him again. "I will not have her exposed to slander and gossip."

"I understand," Jean-Claude said.

With a physical effort, Josette took hold of her temper and called her shadow to heel. "She has spurned every physician I have put in her path."

"That's because she hasn't met Gretl yet," Jean-Claude said. "That's a battle of wills I would pay to watch."

"This is not a matter for your amusement," Josette said.

"I make jokes when I'm terrified," Jean-Claude said. "It's a terrible habit I can't seem to shake. Let me bring in my friend. She has experience with strange maladies, and given that she's mute, I guarantee she won't talk."

Josette folded her arms and bowed her head. "Bring your friend."

⌒

The Solar, having seen enough of Grand Leon's self-congratulatory festival, had begun its shallow winter descent. Between the northward drift and the clockwise spin of the Craton Massif, the Solar seemed to be lancing into the tail end of the Hoarteeth mountains. The air was damp from snow and chilled the wind until it gnawed Jean-Claude's bones.

Jean-Claude gathered his horse from the military stable. He had to fetch Gretl and send her up to Coquetta. Then he had to find out where *The Harvest King* was being performed. But first he had to talk to Grand Leon.

He swung into the saddle, waiting for his game leg to stop trying to seize, then set a straight course through the tent city that had sprung up around the stadium. To his left, a temporary clearing opened as two teams of burly men rounded it up in a bout of tower-jousting. Screaming spectators waved betting tokens while two pairs of men, each with one sitting on the other's shoulders, clubbed at each other with quarterstaves and truncheons. In other circumstances, Jean-Claude would have stayed and placed a bet.

Farther on, troubadours and acrobats plied their trade. Jean-Claude didn't see Sedgwick's dwarf troupe anywhere, alas. Hawkers sold everything from beer to baguettes. Fortune-tellers sold the future while mediums sold the past and whores rented out the present in small increments. There was even a "blind leper" hawking the "Reliquary of St. Martin," which seemed to be made of cow's teeth. Jean-Claude declined to point out to his customers that, if the reliquary worked as promised, he'd be neither blind nor a leper. There were some kinds of gullible you just couldn't cure.

Beyond the stadium stood the bivouacs of several famous regiments that had been brought in to pay tribute to Grand Leon. There were the Ice Brigade, who had fought with Grand Leon through the famous winter campaign in the Forest of Sorrows, and the Flying Huns whom he had led to improbable victory at the Battle of Tallhill. Such men, at least, Grand Leon honored, and they loved him for it.

Grand Leon had made sure to invite regiments from the Terras Annexes as well as from the most fractious of his border barons. This both gave the regiments a sense of honor and kept them where Grand Leon could see them, not making mischief back in their home territories.

Jean-Claude made it to the front of the royal pavilion watched over by another queue of guards in blue-and-gold livery emblazoned with the twined lightning bolts of the thundercrown. The guard-capitaine demanded to see his papers and actually read them carefully before taking his weapons and permitting him to a tent filled with other would-be supplicants to the crown.

Most of the baker's dozen petitioners-in-waiting were Célestial nobles of varying ranks, but there were a few exotics as well. Wreathed in a freezing mist, a Volshebnik from far-off Stehkzima had one corner all to himself. Along the opposite wall, a fat man with skin the color of rust, wearing a kaftan and a turban, sat cross-legged on a tasseled pillow. He played a card-and-token game of thwarts against a shriveled rind of a man with a clean but well-worn doublet and boots that seemed to be made entirely of cracked mud.

Next to the entrance stood a grim-looking Fenice with olive skin and a fan of red and orange feathers where his hair should be. His close feathers were not deployed, so he looked otherwise normal, at least if one discounted eyes as cold as a lizard's. Was he here with Immacolata, some kind of handler? Or was he her foe? The most likely scenario was that he was here on entirely unrelated business.

The Volshebnik unfolded from his seat on a block of ice he had apparently conjured for a chair and strode toward Jean-Claude. He wore a sleeveless jerkin of dark leather and a long thick cloak made from the hide of a snow bear. His body seemed to be made of ice, the aspect of the substance he had chosen to master with his sorcery. His winter-starved face looked to have been chiseled from a glacier and pale gray eyes gleamed sharp as poniards.

"You man of the Emperor, his knife."

"I am Grand Leon's servant," Jean-Claude admitted.

"Then you ask him, Ustina? Where? She went to his court. Is gone now."

Jean-Claude put on his best slack-wit expression. He knew nothing about this man, this was not his problem, and he was not about to bugger whatever plans le roi had for this petitioner by becoming involved in them.

He said, "I'm afraid I haven't seen her."

"You look? Anyone look?" The chill in his breath froze Jean-Claude's cheeks and conjured hoarfrost on his whiskers. "Days waiting. Ustina is lost. Could be kidnapped or dead."

"Perhaps you should ask the city watch," Jean-Claude said.

"City watch go to Breaker's Torment!" the Volshebnik snapped. "Is Daughter of Boyar Pyotor Ruus, ambassadress to Empire, my wife!"

Jean-Claude's focus sharpened. "And who are you?"

"Boyar Volody Aisken, Magister of First Council, and tired of being made to wait like dog for bone."

Jean-Claude's brow furrowed. On the one hand, this seemed like the sort of problem for which Grand Leon might clear a slot on his agenda. On the other hand, women went missing all the time, sometimes for good reasons. Even a Volshebnik sorceress might flee a disagreeable marriage, for instance. An ambassadress, though, was a woman bearing a responsibility that was not given lightly, and Volody seemed more concerned for her welfare than for his own proprietary interest. On balance, he found Volody credible.

"Is Ustina Volshebnik?" Jean-Claude asked, just to be sure.

Volody gave Jean-Claude a scornful look. "Of course. Very powerful sorceress. Matrix of fire." In his agitation, the temperature fell. Jean-Claude's breath fogged.

"I will bring this to le roi's attention and remind him of your need," Jean-Claude said.

Volody looked like he was ready to spend hours emphasizing the importance of his demands, but Jean-Claude was rescued by the bong of a bass chime announcing a new arrival. Everyone looked up to see a distinguished lady enter.

Duchess Sireen, High Steward of the Realm, the Ebon Nightingale, Grand Leon's first and favorite concubine, wore an exquisite gown of the traditional white, with just enough ivory and silver in the brocade to suggest hidden imagery conducting clandestine metaphors behind the seams. At fifty-two, she was the oldest of the Lace Trefoil, and had been at le roi's side for more than thirty years.

Jean-Claude could not see her eyes through her lace veil, but he could feel her gaze.

"Monsieur Musketeer," she said in her famous voice. No matter how ordinary her words, she always seemed to be singing. "If you will come with me."

Jean-Claude swept her a deep formal bow. "Yes, Madame Duchess." He brushed the ice off his coat and tabard and followed her out the opposite end of the tent, beyond into the maze of fabric alleys. Sireen slowed her pace and fetched her bloodshadow out of the way as an invitation to walk beside her. He did not know her as well as he knew the other two leaves of the Trefoil. She was always ceaselessly busy, even whilst standing still. She was the axle around which Grand Leon's empire spun.

"I would point out that your vestments are in need of incineration," she said. "In case you hadn't noticed."

"I was nearly disemboweled from behind this morning," he said. "How may I serve you?" He did not imagine it was her habit to fetch every petitioner to the crown personally.

"I have heard very disturbing reports from the Royal Agonesium for the Deranged. I am told you murdered Prior Ingle."

"I shot a man trying to escape arrest," Jean-Claude said. "Was he a friend of yours?" Saints, he hoped not.

"The Agonesium is run by the Ordo Passionum, but the building itself is a grant from the Imperial Demesne; that makes it my purview. Now the Temple is calling for your head. Shall I give it to them?"

Jean-Claude's jaw tightened. "I caught Ingle bloody-handed in the midst of crime that would have shocked the conscience of any reasonable person. I intended to turn him over to Grand Leon. Unfortunately, he resisted."

"What crime?" Sireen asked.

"He was vivisecting his patients."

Sireen looked up at him through her veil. "Is that all?"

"Is that not enough?" Jean-Claude growled. "He strapped helpless people to a table, cut through their skulls, and chopped their brains to pieces while they were still alive."

"So he was performing legitimate empirical experiments on undesirables."

Jean-Claude nearly tripped over a guy-wire pegged in the fabric alley. With effort he regained his poise. "Undesirable to whom? I am sure they had some value to themselves."

Sireen came to a halt at a marginally wider intersection between four supply tents. She held up her umber-skinned hand in a gesture of restraint. "I am presenting you with the arguments your detractors are certain to hurl at you. How shall I defend you? I can use my authority to quash them, of course, but that power grows stronger the less it is used. Now give me a reason I can give to the Temple to make them eat their own tongues."

Jean-Claude had a go at settling his temper, but what would dissuade the Temple from complaining about the death of one of their own? Even if they knew full well everything he'd been doing they'd still cry for vengeance as a matter of political course. "Tell them the victims were saintborn."

Sireen's mouth opened in a silent O before she said, "What in all the saints' names were saintborn doing in the Agonesium?"

"Being erased," Jean-Claude said. "They were the culls from what I can only describe as a sorcerous breeding program. They were given to Ingle to be disposed of anonymously. I imagine Ingle was thrilled to find himself with a steady supply of saintborn on whom to perform his experiments, trying to winkle out the Builder's secrets from their living flesh. Given that the Temple's proscriptions against clayborn spilling saintborn blood, I should think they would have little choice but to repudiate Ingle."

"That should be sufficient to deter them, yes," Sireen said. "I assume you have evidence to support this claim."

"You can tell them I'll publish it in the newspaper if they like." It was an easy bluff; the Temple was even less inclined to want such information released than he was to release it.

"I would appreciate it greatly if you did not," Sireen said. "You like to ruffle feathers, but it's my job to smooth them flat again."

She led him to another tent. "What shall I tell Monsieur is the business for which you saw fit to interrupt his celebration? I warn you he will not be pleased if you challenge him about your ward's disgrace."

"Nothing she did was disgraceful," Jean-Claude said. "And he will not be pleased with any of the news I bring him. Lurking in the bowels of the friar's abattoir I discovered a plot against the crown. These wounds I have sustained are its direct result."

"As you wish," she said. "Builder keep you."

"Until the Savior comes," he replied, and entered the tent. It was stacked around the sides with heavy crates, and in the center was an artfully constructed box, upholstered in leather with a hole in the top. The royal privy.

Jean-Claude made a circuit of the room. Being out of the wind was better than being in it, but he still needed to keep his blood moving. He wished he had more to tell Grand Leon about the Harvest King. The more useful Grand Leon thought him, the more leeway he had to push for Isabelle's benefit.

Outside in the stadium, the trumpets blew a halt to the festivities, and shortly thereafter a procession approached the privy tent. Half a dozen nobles trailed along with Grand Leon, prideful Sanguinaires vying for an opportunity to wash the imperial arse. Such were royal favors sought and even occasionally won.

First into the tent stepped a Sanguinaire Praetorian Jean-Claude didn't know. He examined Jean-Claude's papers, then pulled the tent flap back and admitted Grand Leon. He moved spryly for a man of his years, and his royal couture masked a host of sins. His bloodshadow was still thick as oil, but there was no hiding the age on his face, sagging jowls, baggy eyes, and liverspots on papery skin like battlefields marked on an ancient map.

Jean-Claude doffed his hat and bent his knee. His leg gave a spasm of pain that drew a grunt from his lips. The Praetorian closed the flap and pushed back the would-be privy council.

Grand Leon walked by Jean-Claude on his way to the box, and unfastened his trousers. "Jean-Claude, I expected a visit from you. It is good to know some old things are still reliable. I understand that you have news for me."

Jean-Claude knew better than to waste time. "I have uncovered a credible plot against l'Empire."

"One of many no doubt brewing in the capital just now," Grand Leon said to the accompaniment of a heavy stream into a metal bucket. "I seem to recall it is your duty to dispense of such troubles, not complain about them to me."

"The chief architect of this one has devised a way to wake the somnolent gifts of the unhallowed." Jean-Claude let that hang in the air along with the growing fume. Grand-Leon said nothing, but the fountain continued to flow.

At long last Monsieur asked, "You are sure?"

"Yes," Jean-Claude said. He told Grand Leon of Ingle, the Harvest King, and the bone queen. He wished he could bring up Orem's paternity, but he wasn't going to touch off that powder until he was damned sure it was dry and tight. "The process is not perfect. The unleashed power is wild and out of control, but the fact that it can be done at all is . . . troubling."

Grand Leon huffed. "I would not have thought Jean-Claude, the man of a thousand impertinences, as capable of understatement. Do you know how many unhallowed saintborn there are? Thousands. Almost one in four saintborn children has no sorcery."

"That many?" Jean-Claude said. "I'd always had the impression it was only a few."

"Only a few ever get noticed," Grand Leon said. "The rest get covered up by their families, ignored and never talked about out of shame, but I am called upon to matriculate cadets into the Académie Militaire Royale and half of them are unhallowed. Now imagine what would happen if all those people suddenly discovered they could claim the Builder's gift and prove they had a worthy soul. Then imagine all the people who would stand to lose if suddenly their uncontested claims to land, title, and other inheritance became contested. I do not need another civil war at my age. You will dismantle this conspiracy and bring me the pieces. Intact, if you don't mind. If my reports are true, you seem to have lost the knack for taking prisoners alive."

Jean-Claude couldn't resist the moment. "It would help if l'Empire were not so determined to be rid of my most capable and loyal partners."

"You are of course referring to Mademoiselle Isabelle," Grand Leon said, in the sort of lying-in-wait tone that warned of a line about to be crossed.

Jean-Claude had considered the various approaches to this ambush. A personal appeal was out of the question; Grand Leon's loyalty was entirely to his project. "She served l'Empire well," he said.

"She still does," Grand Leon said, readjusting his trousers. "Her punishment demonstrates that l'Empire is committed to the rule of law. It is not the purpose I would have chosen for her, but it is the path she took."

"Horseshit," Jean-Claude said. "If she committed a crime, who is the victim? She harmed no one, took nothing of value."

"She attacked the very notion of the rule of law," Grand Leon said.

"She saved a woman from being murdered."

"She is not being punished for that. She is being punished for interfering in the internal affairs of a foreign government. That the noble act is inextricable from the illegal one is a cruelty of fate. It is not fair, but laws are not meant to be fair. They are meant to be final."

Jean-Claude's anger boiled. His fists clenched. He wanted to rip off his bloodstained tabard by way of announcing his resignation, to spit in the old man's eye and knock his yellow teeth through the back of his head . . . but none of that would help Isabelle. He needed something that mattered to le roi.

"I thought you intended to make l'Empire a haven and a home for all the different breeds of sorcerers. Are you really going to destroy the only l'Étincelle sorceress the world has seen since the Saintstime?"

"Rest assured, Mademoiselle Isabelle's uniqueness will not be wasted," Grand Leon said, an unmistakable note of finality in his voice. "If my word is insufficient to allay your fears, you may turn in that impressively bloody tabard and collect the deed to your farm."

Jean-Claude's jaw clenched, but quitting would not help Isabelle. "I am but a servant of l'Empire."

"Rise," Grand Leon said, and Jean-Claude levered himself up. His leg, having bent, did not want to straighten again.

Grand Leon said, "Tell Impervia what you have learned of this Harvest King and bone queen. If anyone can help you track them down, it is she."

This command made Jean-Claude blanch. There was no one in l'Empire he wanted less to talk to than the third petal of the Lace Trefoil, Grand

Leon's spymaster. Jean-Claude was not generally haunted by his past—mistakes and failures were a part of life—but sometimes shame left a stain that wouldn't come out.

Jean-Claude rubbed his throat. "That may not be the best idea. Impervia and I had a falling out. I have no wish to reopen old wounds."

Grand Leon waved this away. "A lovers' spat is no excuse to avoid your duty."

Jean-Claude recalled drunken commiseration and sex for all the wrong reasons, Impervia's pregnancy, a desperate attempt to hide both from Coquetta and Grand Leon. Consequences spun out of all control. Impervia miscarried. He still remembered the relief, the utter shameful joy he'd felt at escaping the trap of fatherhood two years before Isabelle was born. That joy shamed him still, a canker in his soul that had never stopped oozing.

Jean-Claude's understanding of the situation finally caught up to the present day, and the blood drained from his face. "You knew about that?" How much of that did he know?

Grand Leon arched his eyebrow at Jean-Claude. "Do you imagine I would take offense when my concubines take other lovers? Such hypocrisy would be a great burden on the mind. Now go."

Jean-Claude stumbled from the tent opposite the side with the waiting courtiers. The only observation that gave him any hope at all was that Grand Leon had not countermanded the order to protect Isabelle. Perhaps he'd forgotten it, such a small command given decades ago, insignificant to Monsieur, but everything to Jean-Claude.

It did not help that he was now compelled to seek out and enlist Impervia. He and Coquetta had been friends and lovers. He and Impervia had been more like flint and steel, striking hot sparks in a dark night. Of course they'd gotten burned.

CHAPTER

Nine

Isabelle and the guards, Marc and DuPont, plodded slowly across the high plateau around le Ville Céleste, careful so as not to trample any of the festivalgoers. The bitter breeze tossed up spirals of dry snow and chased them through the crowd.

Isabelle juggled everything Jean-Claude had told her about the Harvest King. It was certainly easier to think about than her own future.

What under the great sky above did the Harvest King want with Mistwaithe? Was the Harvest King somehow caught up in her family's mysterious scandal? Did the scandal have to do with her father's death wish? Why was Orem chosen for a weapon? Using the bloodshadow destroyed most of the evidence that might have been left at the Golden Swain. It would have destroyed Orem too, leaving the entire massacre a complete mystery to those who followed if Jean-Claude hadn't shot him first. Conversely, Orem's murder might have been an act of vengeance against Grand Leon. Only the Breaker knew how many enemies le roi had in this world and the next.

Isabelle's small cavalcade joined the endless line of people getting ready to descend the zigzag path down the face of the Rivencrag. The chill wind tugged her wig and scratched her cheeks, and the pale sky stung her eyes even through her heavy veil. She gazed down from the cliff edge. Rocher Royale looked like a model in miniature. The skyships swooping in and taking off again were like insects.

She drew a deep breath of cold air infused with the faint coppery tang of the sky and took a moment to envy the sailors on those vessels. Any day on a ship was better than one on land. With the wind in the rigging and the pitch of the deck, the whole world seemed to sing.

"Mademoiselle des Zephyrs!" hailed a deep hoarse voice.

Isabelle looked over her shoulder to find Lael the Effaced on horseback trotting along behind her group. He'd traded out his red speaker's cloak for a crimson riding cape, also draped over his left arm. He halted just beyond Marc and DuPont who turned their horses to block him. The guards' hands rested on their sword hilts.

"May I join you, mademoiselle?" Lael rasped. He sounded even worse than he had in Parlement.

Isabelle's curiosity peeked its head up over the battlements of her personal gloom. What might Lael want with her, and did she really want to find out? Scraping him off would be the wise thing to do, but she sympathized with his plight, and besides, he was the man who had inspired her nom de plume.

"Let him pass," Isabelle said.

DuPont nodded, and Marc shifted out of the way. Lael maneuvered his mount to ride beside her. He was not an overly large man, though his poise and his presence made him seem more substantial than his horse. The wind picked up, but could not entirely dispel the scent of liniment and camphor that hung about him. Probably a salve for his throat.

He bowed to her from the saddle, and she cued her mount to resume its steady plodding. Marc took up a position at the front of the line. DuPont rode the rearguard.

"What can I do for you?" she asked.

He coughed into his hand and winced as if in pain. "I saw you standing on the balcony with my mother. She did not look well. I pray that this ordeal has not overwhelmed her."

Isabelle frowned, for this felt like he was casting his net for rotten fish. "Why don't you ask her yourself?" She nose-pointed in the direction of the spires.

"I was refused re-admittance," he said. "I was only allowed to make my petition in the first place because it suited my father's needs, 'to resolve an outstanding legal issue.' I suspect I shall soon be encouraged to leave the city altogether."

"Comtesse Coquetta is as well as one might expect under the circumstances," Isabelle said, a nonanswer if ever there was one.

"None of this preposterous sideshow is her fault," Lael said. "She defended me to my father when my curse became apparent. In the end she was forced to accede to his demands for the sake of my younger sisters. When next you see her, please let her know I bear her no ill will no matter what damned fool things I may have said all those years ago."

Lael seemed forthright, but Isabelle knew better than to become a go-between in a game of palace intrigues. "I was exiled from court. You'll have to write her a letter."

Isabelle's cavalcade passed under the triumphal arch that straddled the road at the edge of the plateau. The stone carving depicted Grand Leon's conquest of the Terras Annexes and the assimilation of those provinces into l'Empire.

They tromped onto the Skyfall Chasm bridge, a ribbon of rope and wood that spanned a great rent in the Rivencrag separating the royal plateau from the surrounding peaks. The wooden planks vibrated and creaked. The wind made banners of every loose flap of cloth and strand of hair.

"I heard what they did to you," he said. "Shameful. L'Empire does seem determined to be rid of its most capable advocates. We are Grand Leon's best son and his favorite cousin, the two most famous unhallowed scions in all the Risen Kingdoms. Of course, it seems you have been successful in reclaiming you heritage"—he gestured to her spark-arm—"l'Étincelle, if I am not mistaken, the sorcery of Saint Céleste herself."

Isabelle's heart thumped up into her throat. "Not many people recognize it." So few, in fact, that its name had been forgotten, and it was not included in the Temple's canon of sorceries.

He produced a smile that could be used to light bonfires. "I have spent nearly two decades scouring every corner of the Risen Kingdoms and beyond for knowledge of sorcery. I've scaled the *Gor'kiy Rog* in Stehkzima, and sweated through the *Bosque de Serpientes* on the Craton Riqueza."

Their horses clomped off the bridge onto the shelf road, a sheer cliff face on one side and a two kilometer drop on the other. It amazed Isabelle to think that many people made this ascent and descent every day for years on end.

Lael said, "There is not a wizened hermit between here and legend that I have not roused from his mountain cave, and not an archive I have left uncopied. There are only ten sorceries recognized by the Temple today, and three of them are extinct, but there were dozens in the Saintstime, and I know all their names."

"Have you records of all of this adventuring?" Isabelle asked, curious in spite of herself. "Empirical evidence and testimony? Such a body of knowledge compiled into a coherent treatise could greatly expand our knowledge of sorcery, give us new questions to ask."

Lael considered that. "I could let you have a look at my research, and you could tell me what you think."

Isabelle clamped her lips down on an immediate "Yes!" If what he said was true, this was an amazing chance . . . but then there was the matter of Grand Leon's enmity. She had no reason to love le roi just now, but neither did she desire to incur any more of his wrath, and then there was the unanswered question of Lael's motive.

"Why did you come back?" she asked. "You didn't actually expect Parlement to vote in your favor."

He laughed and then coughed as if he was trying to dislodge a burr from his throat. When at last he'd recovered his breath, he said, "Never in the history of humanity has a body of privilege given that privilege up willingly. Never have they deprived themselves of some perquisite because it was moral, logical, or even entirely necessary. People cling to privilege more tightly than their lives."

"Then why present your case?" Isabelle asked. "Just to annoy your father?"

"If my father chooses to be annoyed that is up to him. I wanted to make an implicit assumption of culture into an explicit declaration of law. As a matter of general belief, an argument from the Instructions, or just age-old tradition, the primacy of sorcerers can never be challenged. It's taken as an axiom. But if it becomes a matter of law, explicit and bounded, it can be subjected to inquiry, confronted with evidence, eroded and ultimately overturned."

"Ah," Isabelle said. The idea had some merit. "You lured the badger out of its hole to fight it in the open."

"More to the point, where the Parlement cannot avoid it. Did you not hear what they said, the absurdity of it? The Parlement was very clear that their ruling was eternal, for all of time until the coming of the Savior, as if the opinions of a gaggle of hooded geese, too afraid to show their faces, must be respected and revered by generations not only unborn but undreamt of. It's madness. I guarantee there will come a day probably sooner than they imagine, when they wish to exempt themselves from that law, and then one way or another, the wretched thing will break."

"That's quite a guarantee," Isabelle said.

Lael shrugged and readjusted his cloak. "The deck of fate only has so many cards in it. Eventually someone must draw the Tormentor. The first time one of them is left without an heir because his only son is unhallowed, they will be hoist by their own petard. They must either suffer by their own rules or change the rules to favor the disadvantaged."

"In my experience, those in high places simply pretend the law does not exist when it proves inconvenient. My case being the exception that proves the rule."

"Your case is a moral travesty," Lael said. "But I have something that—"

"Look out! Stop him!"

Isabelle's gaze snapped forward. Marc desperately wheeled his horse around, scattering pilgrims in pursuit of a man in a ragged cape who had stepped out of the upward marching line. Strapped to his chest was a mortar shell, and he held a slow match. He tottered toward Isabelle and Lael as if seeking them in the dark.

"Bomb!" yelled DuPont from the rear. He tried to surge around Isabelle and Lael but only ended up scattering pedestrians and jamming the path.

"Stop!" Lael shouted, reaching for his sword.

A powerful gust of wind kicked up and whipped the petardier's hood from his head. The skin of his face was translucent as glass, revealing his skull beneath. He was a bloodhollow! His burning wick dipped toward the mortar shell's fuse hole.

Isabelle's pulse thundered. She kicked her horse into a gallop and careened into the bloodhollow. He flopped backward, the wick flying from his hand.

Isabelle's horse slipped on the slick, slushy footing. Down it went. A half ton of terrified horse slammed full tilt into the wooden side rail. Braces broke, splinters flew. Isabelle leapt free of the saddle—too late!

She, her horse, and the bloodhollow hurtled into open space. Isabelle stretched back for the road, grabbed for the shattered uprights. Lael's sword fell from his hand as he reached for her. She grabbed him . . . and her sparkhand passed right through his fingers.

For an endless instant, Isabelle seemed to float, staring at the catch that wasn't and feeling absurdly, profoundly foolish. Then momentum and gravity carried her away and turned her over. Birds wheeled below her.

She screamed. The wind tore at her face and terror turned her blood to ice. She flipped head down, her skirt dragging up her legs. The Rivencrag rushed by, hopelessly out of reach, moving far too fast. She flailed and kicked like a child learning to swim. She reached out with her legs and her one good arm to make herself big like a sail. Off balance, she tumbled. Ground. Cliff. Sky. Solar. All whirled through her vision. Over and over.

No. No. No! Memories flashed before her: Marie, Julio, and Jean-Claude most of all. She had to think—had to live—but the world had rules. Gravity. Ground. Cliff. Sky. Shadow.

Shadow?

Something huge rushed alongside her, a sleek black body. Long eagle-talons snapped shut like manacles around her ankles. Great wings unfurled and stretched and stretched some more, creaking like a mainsail in a gale, catching the wind and jerking her body straight. The spiked brass dome of a Temple streaked by meters from her head. She rose, floated. The creature juggled her, shifting its grip. It tossed her and flipped her right side up. Talons became monkeylike feet that caught her under the armpits. She and her bestial savior arced over a row of trees and then settled lightly on the ground. Isabelle touched down with feet planted, but her legs refused to hold her, and she slumped like a mud statue.

All around her spread rows and rows of grave markers. They'd landed in a graveyard. Only the beast kept her from falling flat on her face.

The creature was the size of a horse, black as soot with a head like a raven. It had wings of stretched skin like a bat's edged with long quills like a falcon's. Yet even as her mind tried to define the shape, it changed. Fur, skin, and feathers rippled, wrung, turned inside out until golden-furred Capitaine Bitterlich knelt in the snow beside her.

"Mademoiselle?" he said gently, his slitted golden eyes full of concern. She clutched his arm. He pulled her in. She curled up in his embrace and wept in sheer reaction, taking long ragged breaths and shuddering until at last the screaming in her head died down. She wasn't falling. The ground was solid. Bitterlich was here.

"Thank you," she croaked, when at last she had enough wit to form words. She had the strangest urge to kiss him because words weren't enough, but that was just the residual drunkenness of fear talking. Better than terror, though. Saints but his embrace was warm.

"You are most welcome. Even in Rocher Royale it's not every day that it rains princesses."

Isabelle laughed, a madwoman's cackle. "Didn't anybody warn you? I tend to stumble in front of runaway assassination plots."

"Noted. I shall be sure to add dashing rescues to my agenda."

"I don't even know who this one was aimed at," Isabelle said. She wished her damned knees would stop shaking. Not that Bitterlich wasn't fun to lean on, but this was embarrassing.

Bitterlich grew thoughtful. "I had assumed that one was aimed at your conversational partner. Is there anyone besides the Aragothic consul who might have a killing grudge against you?"

Isabelle managed to push away from him, but not let go. If she locked her knees and kept a death grip on his doublet she wouldn't necessarily look like she was clinging to him.

"The list is not short. Anyone who felt they were loser in the Grand Peace. Fanatics who want to kill me for being the Breaker's get. Anyone in my immediate family. I suspect this one was a Célestial, a Sanguinaire or at least someone who could afford to hire a Sanguinaire. The petardier was a blood-hollow. Where is he?" She swiveled her head, which was a bad idea as it made the world want to turn upside down again.

"Softly, mademoiselle," Bitterlich said.

"Isabelle," she said. A firm decision. "From now on, you call me Isabelle."

"I'm not sure that's quite proper," he said.

Asserting herself in the world was like sunlight on the fog in her brain. She gestured at him with her spark-hand, throwing off glimmers in shades of rose. "I hereby initiate you, Capitaine Bitterlich, into the Sacred Order of People Who Are Encouraged to Call Me by My Chosen Name."

Bitterlich's whiskers twitched. "Well, as long as it's official, it would be my honor."

He was one of the very few people Isabelle had ever met who could make the word *honor* sound like something to be aspired to rather than as a synonym for "willful pride" or "indefensible privilege."

Isabelle reached up reflexively to adjust her veil, but she'd lost it along with her powdered wig and her poor horse during the fall. Somehow she still had her messenger bag.

"How is it you happened to arrive at precisely the moment I needed you most?" she asked, pulling a few stray wig pins out of her knuckle-length hair. Saints, she must be a sight.

"Actually, I was there from the beginning, tailing Lael to see if he made any interesting contacts or said anything treasonous." At Isabelle's appalled look he added, "Your part of the conversation, while fascinating in its own right, was entirely innocent of even the barest hint of sedition. An owl's hearing is superb. I only hope you can forgive me for eavesdropping."

As much as Isabelle didn't like being spied on, she could hardly fault Bitterlich for watching Lael. "You were only doing your job. Did anybody else fall?"

"I don't think so." He looked up and his head warped, fur stretching into feathers. His eyes grew huge, mouth and nose reshaping into a raptor's beak, until his whole head was like a hawk's. His head twitched minutely side to side, and then his gaze fixed on a point as if pinned there.

"Lael is gone," Bitterlich said in a cawing voice. "There he is. He's riding down the trail. Your guards seem distraught."

"You can tell from here?" She carefully leaned back to look up at the cliff. She could not pinpoint the spot from which she'd fallen.

"I can see a mouse moving the grass from a thousand meters," he said. His head returned to its resting shape: his erstepelz.

"That is so fascinating," she said. "What does it feel like to change like that? It's like watching a flower folding and unfolding very quickly."

He gave her the most peculiar look, as if he couldn't quite decide what to make of her reaction. "Watching me shift makes most people's skin crawl."

"I'm not most people," Isabelle said.

He brushed the brim of his hat in a salute-like gesture. "Indeed. I think we may need a word for someone on the far side of unique."

Isabelle turned pink at that compliment. It was a compliment. His tone made it so.

A group of men in workmen's clothing approached cautiously. "Monsieur. Mademoiselle," said the first amongst them, a thick-bodied man in a leather jerkin carrying a shovel. "Are yeh hurt?"

Isabelle said, "No. I mean, I seem to have fallen as far as I'm going to. I'll be fine. Nothing broken."

Bitterlich said, "Mademoiselle des Zephyrs could use a place to sit. Do you gentlemen have a fire or stove?"

"There's a stove in the shed, but it's no fit for a fine lady."

Isabelle said, "I'll be fine."

"I'd like to escort you the rest of the way home, but first I need to fly up and let your men know that you aren't dead," Bitterlich said.

Isabelle weighed this against her state of nerves. "Can I watch you change again? Then I'll go sit."

"I see now the negotiator who managed to talk the belligerent nobles of two kingdoms into not killing each other for a change. Very well."

Isabelle watched avidly, saw a crease, a crinkle, a rustle, and a fanning of dark feathers as he twisted into his raven form. It was like paper folding with an extra set of planes. Was that even possible? What would happen if one integrated a geometric shape past the power of three?

"Fascinating," she breathed. She wished she had her chalkboard, a scrap of paper, and something to write or sketch with.

Bitterlich the raven cawed, "Please rest. I'll be back."

Isabelle turned to the workmen. "Lead on, monsieur . . ."

"Foreman Jillette," he said. He reluctantly led Isabelle to a hut built of crudely dressed stone and furnished with stone benches and a stone table. Much of the available space was filled with crates and barrels. There were a few tattered blankets and some secondhand tankards.

"I'm sorry it's not up to standards," Jillette said, wringing his hat in meaty hands.

Isabelle plopped unceremoniously on the stone bench next to a thrumming alchemical stove. The heat of it should have been enough to bake her black, but just now she couldn't get enough warmth.

"It's perfect. Thank you, foreman. This will do nicely." Once Isabelle had finally stopped moving, talking, and thinking, another round of reactions set in. Her whole body quivered and she broke out in a cold sweat. Her breath came quick and ragged and her stomach wanted to give back everything she'd ever eaten. She bent forward, elbow braced on one knee, and concentrated on breathing, just breathing until the nausea finally passed and the trembling dissipated.

Saints but she hated feeling this weak. She hoped Bitterlich hadn't taken her manic humor as a sign of feeblemindedness or madness.

When the heat from the stove finally became uncomfortable, she unfolded herself, stood, and peeked out the doorway. One of the workmen stood guard, defending her nonexistent honor.

So who was behind the attempt? Bloodhollows generally made poor assassins being both slow and clumsy. The addition of the mortar shell obviated both of those problems. So where had the mortar shell come from? The thing probably had a maker's mark on it.

Feeling a bit more collected, she stepped outside and called to Jillette, "Someone besides me fell, a bloodhollow. He should have landed close to where I landed."

"Ah, aye. There was another, but he blew off over toward Jumper's Landing." He jabbed a thumb over his shoulder. "Sometimes folks come over in pairs, young folks specially, thinking they gonna be together forever. Usually don't even stay together until they hit the ground. Wind carries 'em apart, you see?"

Isabelle was appalled. "How often does this happen?"

He shrugged lanky shoulders. "Sometimes one a month, sometimes in bunches. More people just fall than jump or get pushed. Worst ones sort of bounce and scrape along the cliff on the way down."

Isabelle looked up at the Pilgrims' Road, and up some more at the precipice so far away that its edge was a blur. "That's why you put the graveyard right at the base of the cliff; people fall off." It was all appallingly obvious, logical, and efficient. Isabelle put it atop the pile of things she wished she'd never thought about.

"Yep, and animals. Can't put up a house where you might have an ox cart come through the roof. Had summat similar happen last week. Sanguinaire lady jumped off the very top, flew all the way out past the graveyard. After that it's nothing but streets and buildings. Landed bang on top of a warehouse. Slate roof though. She cracked it but didn't go through."

"I . . . how did you know she was a Sanguinaire . . . after that?"

"Clothes and wig was white before they were bloody. No one ever came to claim her, though."

"That's sad," Isabelle said.

"Chances are, she weren't from around here, what with people coming in for le roi's birthday."

"So her family may never find out what happened to her."

"Maybe what she wanted," Jillette opined. It was as good a guess as any without any actual evidence.

"Take me to the bloodhollow," Isabelle said.

The gravedigger's expression slackened. "It's not a proper sight—"

"Don't," Isabelle said, "presume to tell me what is proper for a lady."

The bloodhollow had landed on a stele and . . . burst. The stench and sight of the poor man's body splattered over several square meters brought up her gorge. She got upwind of the carnage and took a steadying breath, and then another. The foreman and his gang were collecting the pieces and . . . mopping up was not an inaccurate description. She was surprised at just how much there was inside a person, yards and yards of glistening slippery intestines. Red blood. White bone. Corpses should not come with a large splatter radius.

Isabelle passed the edge of the mess and stepped gingerly toward the approximate middle. She wished she had her work apron and gloves. The best she could do was hike up her skirt and bunch it under her arm when she squatted to look for the mortar shell.

"How do you contact next of kin?" Isabelle asked. "I want to talk to whoever comes to claim him." Though unless Jean-Claude came back with good news, even such trivial arrangements for the future might no longer be hers to make.

"We post a notice," Jillette said. "Usually someone comes to claim them pretty quick if it's an accident, but . . . well, he's a bloodhollow. Their folks already think of them as dead."

A shadow passed overhead, and Bitterlich swooped in for a landing. He'd taken a form with a scaled body, huge composite leather-and-feather wings, a hawklike head, and a long serpentine tail. In his grip hung Marc, pale-faced and trembling. The young guard fell to his knees and proceeded to void his stomach.

Bitterlich melted back into his standard shape and fixed the angle of his hat. Where did his hat and clothes go when he changed?

"Mademoiselle Isabelle," Bitterlich said, in what she was beginning to recognize as his officer-of-the-crown voice. "I am happy to report there were no further casualties. Guardsman DuPont has been dispatched to inform your musketeer that you are safe, hopefully before he receives word of your death. Guardsman Marc is here to receive your reprimand for failing to stop the assassin before he could try for you. I am informed that your riding partner departed in distress. If he doesn't get himself killed in his haste, he should be down in a few hours."

Marc stepped forward looking both green at the gills and utterly shame-faced. He had a naturally long face to begin with and his distress made him look as if he was melting.

Isabelle frowned, though not at Marc. He had not failed because he was being inattentive, or because he was bad at his job, but because the attack had come from a novel direction. Still, some form of discipline would be expected, though damned if she saw what he could have done differently. Punishing people for not living up to impossible standards was a zealot's way of thinking.

"Guardsman, what do you have to say for yourself?" she said as sternly as possible. Since her trial and conviction, she had no authority over anyone, but Marc was clearly in need of someone to assign him penance.

Marc dropped to his knees and bowed his head. "I make no excuses. The villain slipped past me all unawares."

The villain had been kilometers away, probably sipping wine and watching the whole debacle through the bloodhollow's eyes.

"Can you think of anything you could have done better?" Isabelle asked.

Marc looked stupefied. "I don't . . . I mean, he didn't make any wrong moves."

Bitterlich regarded her curiously, his head slightly tilted.

"How about you, Capitaine?" she asked of Bitterlich. "Is there anything Marc could have done differently? As far as anyone could see, it was just a man in a cloak. No weapons showing at all until he tried to light the mortar shell."

"Not that I can think of," Bitterlich said. "Although if I had been closer I might have snatched the match cord from the bloodhollow's hand."

"And I was the one who slid us off the cliff. There's plenty of blame to go around," Isabelle said. She returned her attention to Marc. "As Jean-Claude says, sometimes you just get beat. Now get on to Rowan House and fill the staff in on what has happened. Builder keep."

"Thank you, mademoiselle, you are most merciful. Savior come." Marc bowed himself out and hurried off so fast that he nearly tripped over a tombstone.

Bitterlich tipped his hat to her. "In addition to being merciful, you are wise."

"Or possibly just softhearted," Isabelle said.

Isabelle turned her attention back to the cadaver at hand. She rooted around with her spark-arm through the poor bloodhollow's pulped remains, and extracted the bomb.

"This is newly made," she said. "Feel how sharp that mold line is. Let this bump up against a bunch of others just like it and that edge would be blunted in a hurry."

"Someone could have taken it directly from the foundry," Bitterlich said. "I recognize the maker's mark. I'll swoop by later and ask them if they've had any go missing."

Isabelle wished she could swoop. Being able to shapeshift opened up one's range of actions considerably.

Nothing else about the corpse gave any clue to its identity. He'd been stripped of any personal effects he might have been carrying, and his clothing was not particularly distinctive.

"It isn't much to go on," Bitterlich said.

"His face is intact," Isabelle said. "I'll do a sketch of what he looked like when he was alive. That might make it easier to identify him especially if he was recently hollowed out."

"Good idea," Bitterlich said. "I didn't know you were an artist."

"Painting helps me think," she said.

"I should get you back to your paintbrushes then," Bitterlich said. "We need all the thinking we can get."

Isabelle drew stood and approached Foreman Jillette. "Thank you, monsieur. I give you back the body, I would like you to preserve the head so that we may come back to identify it."

"Of course, thank you, mademoiselle," said Jillette. "Will that be all?"

"Unfortunately, no," Isabelle said, recalled to her other duties. "I believe you have another body I need to inspect."

Jillette looked puzzled asked. "No one else fell."

"He's a man named Orem, he should have been brought in by the city guard yesterday."

"Oh yes," Jillette said. "Poor bugger. They brought him in, but he's gone now."

"Gone how?" Isabelle asked.

"A monk from Screaming Hall picked him up yesterday just after the snow started. Said he'd give him special rites for St. Isaac's children, keep his ghost from being restless." He made a sign to ward off the Breaker's Torments.

Jean-Claude had been at the Agonesium last night and had reported no such thing. He certainly hadn't sent some monk to fetch the body. The only logical conclusion was that someone had stolen Orem's corpse, which implied there was something to be learned from it. Isabelle looked out over the city as if she might see a man in a monk's habit leaping from rooftop to rooftop with a cadaver in hand.

"Damn," she said, a weak epithet, but a strong one would have served no better.

"Was this Orem a friend of yours?" Bitterlich asked cautiously.

Isabelle weighed her response. She had already said things to Bitterlich that could cause her grief if he proved less a gentleman than he seemed, but the problem of Orem's sorcery and his alleged paternity were a higher order of trouble, and not necessarily hers to divulge. On the other hand, Bitterlich was exactly the sort of person she would have brought this information to if she didn't have Jean-Claude. Bitterlich could be very helpful to have amongst her counselors. He might be able to identify the Seelenjäger who had attacked Jean-Claude this morning.

"I never met Orem," Isabelle said, quietly enough that the gravediggers wouldn't be able to overhear. She was more comfortable with dangerous truths than any sort of lie. "He was born a madman, lived his life as a beggar, but died a sorcerer. He was the man in the middle of the Lowmarket massacre yesterday."

"Ah," Bitterlich said, looking enlightened. "And presumably whoever absconded with his corpse is complicit in that act."

"Would you like to help us catch them?"

"It would be both a duty and a pleasure, Mademoiselle Isabelle," he purred.

"Then we have one more stop to make before Rowan House. I will explain on the way."

CHAPTER

Ten

Jean-Claude took no shame in being clayborn, but rarely had he felt so much like mud, cold and thick, as he was admitted into Impervia's receiving room. The place was spare to the point of looking unfinished. It held a straight-backed chair and a small round table in a room with bare walls all painted white.

Impervia awaited him. She was a slight woman, even shorter than Marie and trimmed of extra flesh, as if some new breed of sculptor had pared a woman down to the mere suggestion of femininity, daring the viewer to conjure curves out of sharp edges. She wore the whites of a Sanguinaire, though of a severe cut, expensive in its tailoring and fabric if not elaborate in its ornament. Her bloodshadow, dark and glossy as wine, swirled in a gyre around her feet. Her eyes gleamed like polished onyx.

Jean-Claude did his best to meet her gaze without feeling like her stare was stabbing straight through his brain, but being in the same room with her made old memories stir and shake off the cobwebs that had for decades obscured their shape.

"Jean-Claude," Impervia said coolly. "I never expected you to darken my door again. The world retains its capacity to surprise."

"I'm only here on business," he said. In a time gone by he would have taken her sarcasm as an excuse to spar with her—she was fun to fence with—but he'd lost that right when he rejoiced in her miscarriage. "I need to know—"

"Before we get to that, tell me about your Isabelle," she said, cool and clipped.

Jean-Claude took a step back, nonplussed. "She has nothing to do with what happened between us."

"I never said she did," Impervia said.

"Then why bring her up?"

Her eyes narrowed and her tone turned to winter. "From what I understand, you brag to everyone else about her, why not me? Am I not worthy of the story, or do you think I would harm her? Even if I wanted revenge on you, which I don't, I wouldn't take it out on a third party."

Jean-Claude didn't understand what Impervia wanted, but he owed her something, some penance he didn't know how to pay. "Isabelle is amazing. I can't really put it better than that. She's kind and she's brilliant, Builder's Breath is she brilliant. And she's loyal, and she's tough, and as a reward for her virtue she's been shat on by l'Empire, so unless you can help me rectify that, I'd prefer to stick to business."

Impervia ignored this complaint and asked, "What made you claim her when she was a newborn? I've heard the story, but not from you."

Jean-Claude made a helpless gesture. "She was there, this tiny person, and there was no one in all the world to help her. She needed me." An old warmth rose up in his chest at the memory of bright blue eyes and a pudgy hand gripping his finger.

Impervia regarded him for a moment. Without apparently moving she slipped into a more relaxed posture. "I think you would have been a good father to our child. If it had quickened, despite everything you said at the time."

Jean-Claude winced. "I was a jackass."

"Yes," Impervia said, "but that's your problem to deal with."

Jean-Claude didn't feel like he'd been let off the fishhook so much as he'd been mocked for hanging on to it so long.

"So why are you interested in Isabelle?" he asked. "Assuming you wanted to do more than just wind me up."

Her lips curved in a thin smile. "The look on your face when I asked about her was too much to pass up." Her smile faded again. "The matter I intended to address before you presented that irresistible target is that I am surprised Leon tossed Mademoiselle des Zephyrs aside so forcefully, and without consulting anyone in the Trefoil about it, or even explaining his motives after the fact."

"You think he had some ulterior ulterior motive beyond the politics?" Jean-Claude had been too angry to think about it, but the idea didn't shock him.

"I've seen him get as high as four ulteriors," Impervia said. "Though that one may have just been claiming credit for a happy coincidence."

Jean-Claude reviewed his own conversation with le roi. "He said she wouldn't be wasted, but that was all." He didn't like it any more now than he had then.

Impervia's eyes narrowed in thought. "He always told me that he was looking forward to having Isabelle married into the Aragothic royal family."

"A spy the Aragoths couldn't get rid of," Jean-Claude said. "That's exactly what the Sacred Hundred fear about her."

"Less a spy ferreting out secrets and more of an honest observer."

"But an honest observer is the last thing a dishonest actor wants."

"But you are here on business," Impervia said, cutting off that line of conversation. She made a come-along gesture.

He followed her into a much more workmanlike room with a large round table in the center, some pale wood inlaid with darker wood making a large map of the Craton Massif. The walls were floor to ceiling with shelves and cabinets holding all manner of books, bottles, and mechanisms, the purposes of which he could not guess.

Two wine goblets had been set out. Impervia took one and Jean-Claude the other.

Impervia took a slow sip of her drink. "Why did Grand Leon send you to me, aside from a small but noticeable streak of mischief?"

Jean-Claude took a sip to be polite and set the goblet down. "I'm trying to find a man called the Harvest King . . ." The story was getting smoother with practice, if no more satisfying. By the time Jean-Claude got around to describing the charnel house at the Agonesium and his guess about the source of Orem's power, Impervia's face had become a taut mask.

"I am given to understand, that the man behind all this, the Harvest King, is a graybeard with an eye patch who shares a name with a risqué play that's being performed in various noble houses."

"Risqué is an understatement," Impervia said. "What with all the imbibing of sacred wine and the deflowering of various and sundry nymphs."

"So, something of a wandering orgy."

"You'll fit right in . . . so to speak." The glint in her eye was sharp as a needle.

Jean-Claude decided to ignore the jab. "Do you know anything else about this debauched spectacle? Does it have any shadowy patrons or involve any known enemies?"

"Aside from Coquetta's account . . ." She drummed her fingers on her goblet. "Sireen would probably know more than I do."

"Really? Somehow I didn't see her as taking part in that sort of revelry."

That earned him a glare. "She's made a study of ancient stories and legends. In addition to being the name of the play, the Harvest King is an old heathen legend about a dying and rising demigod. As I recall, he tried to steal power from the father-gods."

Jean-Claude said, "You mean like giving people the Builder's sorcery."

"The parallel does make itself obvious. I'll find out where the next one is going to be and send you a message. I'm more interested in that coded book you found. I don't suppose you brought it with you."

"I wanted Isabelle to have a look at it," he said. "If she can't untangle a logical thing, it probably wasn't logical to begin with. I will let you know what she finds."

Impervia's lips quirked up in the direction of a bemused smile. "If the opportunity presents itself, I'd like to meet her."

The very idea made Jean-Claude squirm inside his skin. There was absolutely no reason Isabelle should not meet Impervia, but . . .

"To judge by your squirming, you haven't told her our sad sordid tale," Impervia said.

"How would that have made her life any better?" Jean-Claude asked. "How many mistakes have you not told your children about?"

Impervia's expression grew a few degrees colder. "Was it a mistake?"

Jean-Claude stepped back, flummoxed at this chill. Of course it was a mistake. It had made both of them miserable. "I . . ." he began without any real idea where he was going. Her stare suggested that there was probably no adequate answer to her question. A familiar voice came from the curtainway outside the suite. "I was given to understand the musketeer Jean-Claude had come this way."

That was DuPont, Isabelle's guard. What was he doing here?

Impervia gestured toward the outer room in an as-you-will sort of way. Jean-Claude touched the brim of his hat and brushed through the curtainway to find DuPont, stocky and sweating, at loggerheads with one of Impervia's guards.

DuPont's face briefly lit up when he saw Jean-Claude. "Monsieur, Builder bless, but I've been all about looking for you."

"Why?" Jean-Claude asked. "You're supposed to be guarding Isabelle."

DuPont's face fell so far it might have bounced on the floor. "Well, the good news is, she's not hurt, and she's safe now."

Jean-Claude growled, "That suggests this right and proper state of affairs was at some point in doubt. What happened?"

"You see, there was this bloodhollow carrying a bomb. It came out of the crowd at us. And I couldn't get to it and Marc couldn't get to it, but Mademoiselle des Zephyrs charged it with her horse before it could light the fuse. Good idea, I thought, but then the horse slipped, and they all went over the cliff."

Jean-Claude's heart felt like it had been crushed with a sledgehammer. "Over the cliff!" Only because he needed answers from DuPont did Jean-Claude refrain from throttling him.

"Yes, but she's safe now," DuPont said. "The Seelenjäger caught her. He's taking her back to Rowan House."

Safe, Jean-Claude reminded himself. Still he could hardly think around the calamity. She must have fallen some time ago. The idea that he might rush out and save her was plainly ridiculous, but he could not stand still, either.

"Wait here," he said, and limped to Impervia's map room, but she wasn't there. Jean-Claude winced, but the message was clear. The interview was over, he'd fouled up the end, and he was going to be left wondering why. He hadn't wanted to hurt her the first time, and now he'd done it again.

He bade the guard give Impervia his regrets, and hurried away.

⸺

Isabelle and Bitterlich arrived inside the Agonesium to find it abuzz with activity. Someone had hung the ceiling with a dozen mismatched alchemical lights, chasing the shadows into the cracks in the walls. Mendicant monks herded men in tattered clothes, some in shackles and some with leather masks on to keep them from biting, in a long queue around the great hall. More folk with mops and buckets were scrubbing the place down, teams of women were patching or sewing gray inmate robes. Long tables had been set up where hot soup was being served. The scent of the broth and the soap clashed with the smell of old stone and unwashed men.

Gretl stood as the nexus of this hive, acting as its queen. Pink faced and glowering, she sat one of the residents down on a table and efficiently checked his skin, his mouth, his ears, and eyes. She pointed out details of interest to Darcy, who jotted everything down in a large journal. Gretl had turned the whole place into a machine, taking in grubby neglected men at one end and putting out grubby well-fed and better-clothed men at the other.

Bitterlich stopped and gazed about. "This is . . . unexpected."

"Only if you don't know Gretl," Isabelle said. Since Isabelle had induced her to rebel against Kantelvar, she'd been gaining confidence and assertiveness by leaps and bounds. Clearly she'd found the Agonesium appalling and took direct action to rectify the situation, and woe betide anyone who balked at her silent orders.

Marie stood on a low table, watching over all the industry, a brace of pistols tucked in her belt sash.

"Marie!" Isabelle called, striding toward her.

Her expression still as stone, Marie's hollow voice drifted out like smoke from a chimney. "What happened to you?"

With her wig and veil missing, her blouse torn, and bloody patches on the hem of her dress, Isabelle imagined she looked a mess.

"I fell off the Rivencrag," Isabelle said. "It's a long story." She wanted a good long talk with Marie, soon, but she still had business to attend.

Isabelle gestured from Bitterlich to Marie. "Capitaine Bitterlich, be known to Mademoiselle Marie DuBois, my best and oldest friend." She didn't count Jean-Claude there. He had his own special category. "Marie, be known to Praetorian Capitaine Erste Ewald Bitterlich, who caught me before I made a crater."

Marie said to Bitterlich, "A pleasure to meet you, Capitaine. Thank you for getting between Isabelle and the ground. I should warn you that she is attracted to danger."

Bitterlich doffed his hat to Marie. "The pleasure is mine, and I appreciate the warning. Any friend of Isabelle's must be a special person, indeed."

Marie shifted her gaze to Isabelle and intoned, "Speaking of danger: he's useful, gorgeous, and charming. Julio will be jealous."

Isabelle glowered at her. "Capitaine Bitterlich has been nothing but a gentleman to me." To cut off any further commentary Marie might make in that direction, she said, "Jean-Claude told me about what happened here last night. I need your report on what has happened since, and I need the book."

Marie hopped off the table and hefted a haversack that had been stashed on the other side. She drew out a large journal with a tooled leather cover and handed it to Isabelle. "All of the patients' documents are still upstairs. Did Jean-Claude pass along my request?"

It took a moment for Isabelle to locate the relevant fragment of memory. Marie wanted to be Isabelle's bodyguard. "Yes, and my answer is 'Yes.' You have my full support, I'm happy for you." Though she really wanted to have a talk about that, too, if ever again they had a moment of privacy.

"I can see I will have my hands full fending off dashingly handsome Praetorians."

"He does not need fending off," Isabelle said. Then realizing how that might be taken, added, "He fends himself," which was arguably worse. "Did anyone from here go and fetch Orem's body from the graveyard yesterday?"

"No," Marie said. "Why?"

"Somebody claiming to be from here stole his corpse."

"It wasn't us, and we accounted for all the monks," Marie said. "You should ask Gretl about Mademoiselle Niñon's body, though."

Isabelle approached the examination station. Gretl had laid one of the patients flat on the table. She had two bigger fellows hold him down while she packed a suppurating wound with some astringent-smelling ointment. Gretl was her own kind of warlord, marshalling her medicines and surgical skills against the forces of death.

Isabelle interrupted the next in line and got Gretl's attention. Gretl blinked up at her, her sunken expression beyond weariness. How long had it been since she slept? She washed her hands in a tepid bowl and then signed, "Where have you been?"

Isabelle signed back, "Long story. You do good work here. Marie said you had something to tell me."

Marie turned her attention to Darcy. "Take over. You know your business."

Darcy, who looked equally exhausted, yawned and called the next man up. Gretl grabbed a lamp from a hook and led Isabelle and Bitterlich down to the basement, along a long narrow corridor, and into a cold-room. The casement windows were open to the outside world, letting in the winter. Ice rimed the edges of stone and rafters. On the stone floor lay three long lumps, covered up. Gretl hung her lamp on a hook. Its pale circle of light only made the shadows around it look deeper. She pulled back the sheet covering the nearest lump to reveal a thin woman with blond, bloodstained hair. There was a large shaved patch over her left temple. At its center was a stitched-up wound.

"The mademoiselle," Gretl signed, her dark eyes glittering with equal parts pain and anger. "Underfed, overtaxed. One who cut her open had no plan to put her back together. Wound was dirty, brain cover gone."

"You did everything you could," Isabelle replied.

"Got her stitched up and warmed up, and then gone."

"What's she saying?" Bitterlich asked.

"Describing this woman's death," Isabelle said. To Gretl she signed, "Marie said you'd found something interesting about her body."

"Strange, yes." Gretl pulled out a tool that looked halfway between scissors and pliers and began whisking the stitches from Niñon's head. She peeled open the unhealed wound and pulled back a flap of skin to reveal the hole in her skull. She gestured to a pale purple protrusion on Niñon's brain. The feature was ridged like an earthworm, with no distinct beginning or end. It blended in perfectly, yet seemed utterly foreign.

"Is it a tumor?" Isabelle asked. She'd seen such on sick animals, though admittedly never under the skull.

Gretl's gestures were tight and edgy with fatigue. "Wrong texture for a tumor. Wrong shape. Blended into surrounding tissues, nothing displaced."

"So it's a thing she's always had?" Isabelle asked.

"For a long time at least," Gretl replied.

Bitterlich tugged on Isabelle's sleeve and she translated for him.

Had Orem possessed such a blemish? Was this . . . node . . . the thing that Immacolata had sparked with a galvanic rod to enliven his gift? Every different type of sorcery had its own organ in the body. For Sanguinaire it was the skin, Glasswalkers the eyes, Seelenjäger the liver and so on. Yet the brain controlled the body, the mind directed sorcery as a voluntary act. Could this sub-organ be the source of that control? Mademoiselle Niñon had been culled from Kantelvar's breeding program, which meant she must have been a sorceress or at least unhallowed like Orem.

And how many more unfortunate cousins were out there, trapped in places like this? Were there any left to be saved?

Gretl pulled the sheet back over Niñon and moved to the next corpse. She uncovered the bulldog-faced Seelenjäger Jean-Claude had told her about. Bitterlich twitched at the sight of him.

"Anyone you know?" Isabelle asked. "Jean-Claude said he spoke like a Célestial."

"No one I've ever seen before," Bitterlich said, "and I thought I knew all the assimilated Seelenjäger in Rocher Royale. There are only about ten of us."

A sizable chunk of the canine face was missing, bone and muscle showing through, but Gretl had cleaned up what was there. She pointed to a bald spot over his right temple. "Got curious. Shaved this off. See the scar?"

Over his temple, in a roughly analogous spot to Niñon's, there was a semicircular scar, red and raised.

"So he's had this procedure done and survived it," Isabelle said. "I think we need to cut open his skull and see what's in there."

"Just waiting for you."

Watching Gretl cut into the dead man's head made Isabelle feel like she had ants under her skin, but she refused to look away. Gretl peeled back the dermis to expose a bone that had been cut and healed.

"It's not completely mended." Gretl pointed to the edges of the cut. "Three maybe four weeks." She chiseled a hole and pulled the cap off to reveal a different sort of brain lump. This one was gray with red bumps on it.

"Different patterns for different species of sorcery?" Bitterlich speculated, rubbing his temple.

Isabelle caught herself doing the same thing. She and Bitterlich met each other's gaze and lowered their hands.

"Strange to think I have something like that inside me," Isabelle said.

"I imagine yours is very intricate and subtle, and it probably glimmers," Bitterlich said.

Isabelle snorted. "Yours is tidy and decorous and spends a great deal of time picking out lace for cuffs."

They exchanged an eye-smile. It went on longer than was strictly decorous, but he had such luxurious irises.

Gretl thumped Isabelle on the leg to get her attention. "One more thing: the prior didn't do this."

"How do you know?" Isabelle asked.

"The patient lived," Gretl signed. "Incision was different. Wound was taken care of. A different surgeon is like a different artist. Different style."

After getting the translation, Bitterlich said, "That means there's still someone out there who knows how to do this. A protégé perhaps."

Isabelle knelt and peered closely at the Seelenjäger's nodule, and tried to make sense of it. When Orem's power had been awakened, his bloodshadow had gone berserk. It would have killed him if Jean-Claude had not. Perhaps Orem's madness had prevented him from taking control of his bloodshadow, or perhaps something more subtle had been done to this fellow.

"He called himself a prince of the Neverborn," she said. "He would never have come into his sorcery without this procedure." By itself, that was not a wicked thing. What unhallowed person wouldn't want their sorcery awakened? It was the Builder's gift. One just had to overlook the horrors that had been done to discover it in the first place.

"Is there any way to tell what was done to him after they cut through his skull?" Bitterlich asked.

"Don't know what it looked like before, or what it is supposed to look like," Gretl signed. "I'll have to do dissection." She yawned hugely and blinked.

"You need to get some sleep before you fall over," Isabelle said.

They returned to the great hall, where the human processing continued apace. Bitterlich gazed across the room with a thoughtful expression on his face. To Isabelle he said, "Can you tell your friend, I think she's done an amazing bit of work here today. There's a reason they call this place Screaming Hall."

"You can tell her yourself. She can read your speech if you face her directly and make eye contact."

"Ah," Bitterlich said, and proceeded to do so. Gretl nodded and made a "thank-you" sign.

Marie had obtained a stack of files, which she presented to Isabelle. "These are the *Infelix Patrueles* files." She also presented her with a pair of boots. "And these belong to the Seelenjäger."

Bitterlich glanced at the boots and his eyes rounded in surprise. "Blessed Builder, those are Monsieur Clotaire's."

"So you know who the Seelenjäger is?" Isabelle asked, delighted.

"Ah, no," Bitterlich said. "Monsieur Clotaire is the man who makes those boots. Note the shape of the heel and the detail around the buttons. There's no mistaking his stitching, either. He's very exclusive. Better yet, since every pair is made to order, he can likely tell us who he made these for."

"Perfect." Isabelle beamed at him and handed over the boots. "Let us know what you find out."

Marie said, "Better keep him away from Valérie or they'll spend all day nattering about fashion."

Bitterlich said, "Mademoiselle, I do not natter. I simply deploy an educated vocabulary about a complex and subtle topic."

"Nattering," Marie said.

"Enough, you two," Isabelle said. "We still have work to do."

Isabelle's party had barely left the Agonesium when a clatter of hooves and a "Make way! Make way!" sounded up the street. Isabelle lifted her chin to see over people's heads. Príncipe Julio and two of his guards forged up the crowded street on horseback. Julio's face was pale and his expression grim.

"Julio! Over here!" Isabelle cried, waving her spark-arm, reflexively relieved to see him despite his absence at her trial. But what would he say to her now that the law had abolished their chance at marriage?

The flash of her arm caught his eye, and he wheeled toward her, relief washing over his visage and making his silver eyes shine. The three horsemen formed a protective semicircle around Isabelle's party, walling off the street traffic.

"Thank the Builder you're safe!" Julio said, dismounting before her and taking her hand in a shaking grip. "When your guardsman showed up at Rowan House, babbling that insane story about you falling off the Rivencrag, I didn't know what to think."

His terror on her behalf was oddly gratifying; he did care about her, if not always enough. "I think you should thank Capitaine Bitterlich; he's the one who caught me after I slid off the Pilgrims' Road. I owe him my life."

Julio looked stunned. "So that was true. And the bloodhollow bomber?"

"Also true, I'm afraid," Isabelle said.

Julio shook his head in bewilderment, then said to Bitterlich, "Capitaine, you have my gratitude, both as Isabelle's betrothed and as príncipe of Aragoth."

Bitterlich doffed his hat and made a slight bow. "All in a day's work, I assure you."

"Are we still betrothed?" Isabelle asked, hardly daring to imagine it.

"It's a matter we must discuss in private," Julio said. "And we need to get you back to your dressing room to recover your dignity."

Isabelle considered her state of disarray and decided she lacked the energy to care about it just now. If society wanted to despise her for being poorly dressed after being so thoroughly dressed down, then society could go choke on a chicken bone.

Julio remounted and reached down to swing Isabelle up behind him. Bitterlich knelt to give her a leg up, and for once she did not decline the assistance.

"Thank you again, Capitaine," Isabelle said.

Bitterlich said, "You are most welcome. If you feel you are in good hands, I shall go make the inquiries we discussed. Builder keep you safe from harm."

A flicker of dismay touched Isabelle's heart as he excused himself; she enjoyed his company.

She said, "Until the Savior comes to take you home."

Another guard swung Marie up behind him. Julio wheeled his horse. Isabelle glanced over her shoulder to see Bitterlich twist around like a twirled cloak and emerge as a raven taking wing. Yes, that was definitely geometry she could spend hours immersed in.

Eleven

Rowan House, Isabelle's ambassadorial residence, was carved into the cliff face, one of a dozen stacked along a shelf road like so many books crammed into a bookcase with more rows above and below. The neighborhood had been built into a natural cleft in the Rivencrag. Each dwelling looked across a void some hundred meters wide onto another vertical grid of houses on the opposite face. Isabelle appreciated Rowan House's location near the mouth of the rift, for it provided a view of both the deep sky to her left, and a gorgeous waterfall at the narrow end of the cleft to her right.

The two pillars that fronted Rowan House's arched portico were carved in the shape of rowan trees. Two potted evergreen shrubs did their very best, in the face of impossible odds, to liven up the stone face. An enclosed set of stairs led to a landing. Luc, the youngest of her small troop of guardsmen, stood watch before the door.

Isabelle and Julio dismounted. He handed the reins of his horse to one of his men and escorted her inside. Every step was like a march to the gallows, but she clung to the hope that Julio might offer her a way to slip the noose from her neck.

"You should rest," Julio said. "And then we can talk."

"Talk first and then rest," Isabelle said; too much depended on what they had to say.

Valérie, Isabelle's faithful secretary, met them at the door with her week-old son swaddled in her arms. "Mademoiselle! Thank the saints. We were so worried."

"Thank you, but I'm perfectly fine," Isabelle said. With an incident like falling off the Rivencrag, there wasn't much daylight between fully intact and widely distributed. "We could use some wine and some privacy."

"And how is your son?" Julio asked.

Valérie beamed up at him. "Healthy as can be."

Isabelle tickled little Vincent's chin and Valérie ushered them into the library, plied them with wine and a pungent green cheese, and bustled out again.

Several of Isabelle's recent paintings hung in the library; all of the older ones had been destroyed in a fire. She eschewed the grandiose saint-motif portraiture that was the modern style in favor of a looser hand and pastoral, architectural, or astronomical subjects. More importantly, each contained steganographical equations, proofs, or demonstrations of mathematical principles.

Julio's espejismo could neither eat nor drink, but he picked up a cup out of pure habit and faced her with a worried look. "Are you sure you're not hurt?"

Isabelle's bitterness rose like bile. "Of course I'm hurt. I was condemned for doing the right and noble thing with compassion aforethought, humiliated before the nobility of two kingdoms, and expelled from society. Do you have any idea what that means?"

"It means we cannot be married," Julio said, skewering the salient point and lifting it from the stew.

Isabelle had been circling that point all day like a doomed moth spiraling in on a flame. Hearing the words from his lips nearly made her choke. "Then why did you tell the capitaine we are still betrothed?"

"Because we are, and will be until this curse can be lifted," he said. "I swore I would ask you to marry me, and so I will. I cannot bring you into my house, but I could have you given into the custody of a minor baron, to be a servant in his household. I would pay for your upkeep and your actions would be as unrestricted as possible."

"What do you mean, 'as possible'?" Isabelle asked

"It would be better if you refrained from some of your more controversial pastimes. Your art is fine, but your interest in empirical philosophy should be kept quiet. The sooner you convince people of your contrition—"

"Contrition!" Isabelle wasn't sure whether to slug her wine or throw it in his face. The visage splattering option had a slight lead. "And what have I done to be contrite about?"

"Endangering the Grand Peace for one."

"De la Vega tried to murder an innocent woman. All I did was stop him. Everything else is his doing, and everyone is taking his side. Even you!"

"I'm sorry you feel that way, but—"

"Hysia!" Isabelle called, for she had no doubt that every servant in the household was standing just outside the door.

The door opened a crack and several sets of hands urged Hysia into the room. Pale and terrified, she curtsied and mumbled, "Highness."

"There she is," Isabelle said. "Not a law. Not a concept. A real human being. Now go ahead and tell her I ought to have let her be murdered because it would be convenient!"

Julio blanched and backed away from Isabelle's wrath. "This isn't about convenience."

"Oh yes, it is," Isabelle said, advancing in pursuit. "To accuse Consul de la Vega of attempted murder would have been difficult and costly and worth more than the life of a clayborn in the eyes of men who treat them like cattle. It would have upset his allies. It would have embarrassed his family. It's much simpler to go after me. If I am made to go away, then the accusation against de la Vega goes away as well. My conviction justifies his crime without ever addressing it. And now you want to throw me in an attic and forget about me, because that will be easier than securing my pardon."

Julio held his hands up as if to ward off blows. "Aragoth owes you a debt. More than that, I owe. I will never stop fighting to exonerate you. But it will be much easier if people believe you are repentant."

Isabelle shook her head. "Repentant for what? If I'd married you months ago, I would have been within my rights, indeed I would have been morally obligated to stand up for Hysia."

"But you weren't," Julio said.

Isabelle's heart ached with frustration. Perhaps she should have jumped into marriage right away, but she had chosen to push the Grand Peace because it was important, and she had allowed Julio a year of courtship to get to know him. In that time she had found nothing objectionable. He was honorable, considerate, and trustworthy. What more could she want?

Land and income. Her own place to stand. Her own rights as a voting member of the Sacred Hundred. A place at the table, not just serving up dinner.

Julio said this was just a setback. The problem was if you set something back far enough it might as well be never. "It's just politics," she said.

"Yes," Julio said. "I'm glad you understand."

"Except politics are permanent," she said. "When it was first proposed, our marriage was supposed to solve an intractable problem for Aragoth. You needed a fertile queen. Now that Xaviera has regained her fecundity, that problem no longer exists. Then our marriage was supposed to be a method of binding our kingdoms together, but for that we have the Grand Peace. Again I find myself made redundant. Lastly it was supposed to be a reward for all that I've done for Aragoth, to be elevated as an equal, and that is the one thing your people will never let me have. So what's left?"

"You can still have it," Julio protested. "It's just going to take more work."

Isabelle had no doubt he meant what he said, but she also had no doubt that his efforts to reclaim her legal personhood would be weighed against political cost, and his enemies would see to it there was always a political cost. Julio would never stop, but like the hero in the famous paradox chasing the turtle, he would move slower and slower over time, never catching the beast or crossing the finish line.

"And what do you get out of it?" That was the question she should have been asking all along. Did he find her any more than simply unobjectionable?

Julio looked taken aback. "Aragoth gets you to go on doing what you do, poking holes in everybody's assumptions, asking hard questions and refusing to accept lies."

"Not Aragoth. You. Distinct from Aragoth?"

"There is no me distinct from Aragoth," he said. "My kingdom is my purpose, and I am proud to uphold its honor as my father did."

Isabelle turned to look out the window, to drink in the distance of the deep sky and all the ships adrift thereon. Like Isabelle, Julio had not been sired by the man he called his father. Unlike Isabelle, Julio had loved his cuckolded father. Learning the truth at the hands of his great enemy had hurt Julio worse than any wound to his flesh. Worse, Julio's father died before that injury could be mended, and Julio had been scourged by self-doubt ever since.

He'd raised an idol to his father in his mind and worshipped it with all the fervor of a fanatic. Isabelle had been promised a marriage and so he would give her one . . . because that's what his father would have wanted. It was the honorable thing to do.

"I release you from your vow," she said, feeling a knot untie as she did so. It felt like falling. "I release you and your kingdom from your promise to me." She needed this marriage. She needed the money. He owed her . . . but not as much as she owed herself. She owed herself not to be kept, not to be held to the standards of her enemies' choosing.

"There's no need to do that. We can beat this."

"Possibly," she said. "But it's a battle we'll have to fight over and over again, and how many times will it take before your honor starts weighing like a millstone around your neck?"

"I don't think of you that way."

"But neither am I the object of your desire, the mate to your soul, the soppy metaphor of your choice. I'm just a person to whom your father made a promise under false pretenses and considerable duress. I will not be married under those conditions."

Julio held his hands open as if trying to grasp her meaning. "This is everything you fought for."

Isabelle shrugged. She'd never said she wouldn't marry him, only that she'd released him from his promise. If he really wanted her for any reason at all, he'd have to figure that out and ask again, on his own, without compulsion, without owing her.

Julio's expression was bewildered, as shapeless as a flag ripped away from its moorings by an unexpected gale. "As you will it," he said at last. He started to turn, paused, and produced a silk pouch the color of wine. He opened it and turned out a perfectly spherical mirrored bead.

"I call this an argent pontillius. It's made of the stuff of the mirror realm, a new technique I've been working on."

Isabelle examined it with genuine interest. "I didn't think anything from the mirror realm could survive in the unreflected world."

"That's one of the things that makes it special. There's a lot of theory behind it. The important thing, though, is what it does. Press it to a mirror and it will chime in the Argentwash, and I will sense it. Use it if you ever need to summon me. I still owe you."

Isabelle accepted the gift and gave him a brittle smile. "Thank you." She extended her hand in the gesture of the dome. "May the Builder keep you safe from harm."

He reciprocated in the gesture of the cup. "Until the Savior comes to take you home." With that, he turned and stepped through the pane of the traveler's mirror as easily as she might walk through a doorway. He glanced back at her and then flickered away. Isabelle locked the gate behind him, then brushed once at either eye to whisk away the treacherous tears lurking there before they could send for reinforcements.

Valérie appeared in the doorway. "Mademoiselle . . ." Her face was ghostly gray from eavesdropping.

Isabelle gathered her poise and said, "Summon the household. I have an announcement to make."

Isabelle gathered her household in the receiving room. The wood-clad space with its parquetry floors and wood mosaic walls, designed for receiving diplomatic visitors, had taken on the air of a tomb. It had taken Isabelle all day to get here, and she wanted nothing more in this instant than to run away. Unfortunately, the worst duty of the day still remained to her, the part where she had to explain to her people how she had failed them.

Gretl and Darcy remained at the Agonesium, but the rest of the household, from Valérie through the guards, the cooks, the maids, and all the way down to the scullion watched her with the stiff waxen expression of people expecting to hear bad news. How had she ended up responsible for so many people? She gathered them with her gaze trying to exude confidence and ask forgiveness at the same time.

"I don't know how much you have heard." She had to begin somewhere. "I don't know what rumors have rained down from le Ville Céleste in the last few hours, but my personal circumstances have changed . . ."

Isabelle choked up several times, but managed not to blubber. The staff were not so restrained, clinging to each other and weeping as if this was a funeral.

When Isabelle had finished her confession, she told Valérie about the rooms for let on la rue des Chapeliers. Valérie took over and began ordering the house's evacuation. The household had moved several times in the last few months, so the packing was routine in its form if not its function.

Isabelle stumped upstairs to begin putting her room in boxes. In the doorway, she paused and looked around at the accumulated paraphernalia of her life. She'd never had many baubles compared to other people of her station, but what she did have was precious, the books and philosophical instruments, the pigments and the inks. They were more than mere objects, they were tools of the mind. They helped shape her thoughts and extend her senses into realms otherwise impenetrable.

She sat on the stool at her drafting table. Most of its surface was taken up by miniature buildings made of paper and basswood, an architectural model of the university she had hoped to create in Aragoth. She'd spend countless hours developing the plan in her head, and on paper and here as a mock-up. She was going to have lecture halls designed with modern sensibilities in classical proportions surrounding a plaza laid out in a perfect ellipse. In the middle was a fountain surrounded by a pool surrounded in turn by a botanic garden. If one knew what to look for, one could find in these concentric not-quite-circles a scale map of Caelum and its three moons, Kore, Bruma, and Threin.

It was to have been the project of her life, never to be fully completed any more than the turning of the seasons should be finished. It was to have been her living gift to the world.

Not anymore.

There was a scroop of silk as Marie came in and stood beside her.

"This isn't your fault," Marie said, slipping her arms around Isabelle in a comforting hug that unleashed a flood of tears from her eyes like someone had squeezed a sponge. She returned Marie's embrace and let herself weep. She didn't care whose fault her downfall was, it hurt just the same either way, but thank the Builder for Marie and Jean-Claude, Valérie and Gretl, and everyone who stood with her when the stones started flying.

She feared she might cry all night, that she might not be able to stop, but the clock on the wall said it only took her a few minutes to dry out and find a space to rest. She'd been through worse and for less reason and with fewer ways to fight back. When her father had turned Marie into a bloodhollow, that had been the lowest point in her life. She wasn't going to wallow in this lesser defeat. If people wanted to fling mud at her they were going to have to kneel in the muck to scoop it up themselves.

She released Marie and backed up half a step to blot her eyes and wipe her nose. "Thank you," she said.

"You need to get some sleep," Marie said. "Get cleaned up."

"I still have letters to write," Isabelle said. "And Ingle's journal needs translating."

"Let me rephrase that," Marie said. "Take one of Gretl's soporifics and go to bed or I will club you with a fireplace poker. Trust the rest of us not to burn the house down overnight." She pressed a pair of small, green waxy resin spheres into Isabelle's hand.

"The house is carved out of stone," Isabelle pointed out.

"Now you're just being difficult. Go. We'll take care of everything."

The drugs were bitter on her tongue, and it took several swallows of wine to get the taste out. She lay down obediently, but didn't feel sleepy. She still had so many questions. Had Jean-Claude been able to talk to Grand Leon? Had he found a way out for her?

How had Ingle managed to wake up dormant sorceries in the unhallowed? The fact that it was possible upset the whole order of society.

What was Father doing here with a Gyrine Windcaller and a mysterious death wish? And what was Guillaume doing in Rocher Royale? Perhaps Father had kicked him off l'Île des Zephyrs to prevent him from interfering in whatever scheme he and Dok were brewing.

Who had sent the bloodhollow assassin? At whom had he been aimed? And what did it say about her expectations that nearly being killed wasn't near the top of her list of worries?

—

It was well past dark when Jean-Claude wearily stumped up the steps to Rowan House and into a scene of great industry, with servants of all stripes sorting, stacking, and packing all the household goods for decampment, all in relative quiet.

Madame Supreme Arch General Valérie directed the operation with infant Vincent firmly latched to her breast. She espied Jean-Claude and said, "Welcome back, monsieur. Isabelle is asleep, so is Marie, please don't wake them. Food is in the kitchen."

Jean-Claude snapped off a smart salute. "Understood, madame." Isabelle was alive, and that was all that mattered for now. He still had to resist the urge to sneak upstairs and check. Instead he limped into the kitchen, fished up a bowl of soup from the common pot, grabbed a day-old hunk of bread, and looked for someplace to sit where he wouldn't be trampled to death.

He made his way to the back of the house where all the permanent furniture was staying. It was there on a cloth-covered chair that a dusky woman with red-brown hair sat weeping, her face in the palm of her hands.

"Señora Hysia Dominguez, I presume," Jean-Claude said. He hated to see anyone suffer.

Hysia popped out of the seat as if she'd been stabbed in the bum and gave Jean-Claude a terrified look. "I'm sorry, monsieur, I didn't mean to. I . . . I . . ."

Jean-Claude found a place to sit on one of the dust-cloth-covered chairs. "Have you had anything to eat? There's plenty of something resembling pea soup."

Hysia looked at him dumbly. "No, monsieur. I mean yes. I've eaten."

"Pardon me for sitting," he said. "It's been a long day. My name is Jean-Claude. I'm a friend of Mademoiselle des Zephyrs. What's troubling you?"

Hysia clenched her hands in her apron. "This . . . this is all my fault."

Jean-Claude grunted. "No." He dipped his bread and took a bite. The ghost of bacon haunted the heavy pottage. "Please sit."

Hysia sat with crisp precision, as if she was being tested on her posture. She fixed her gaze to her knees.

"I'm sorry for your loss," Jean-Claude said, and left it there waiting.

"My loss?" Hysia asked, sounding bewildered.

"If my intelligence is correct, you were Ambassador Cubilla's maid," Jean-Claude said. "It must have been a great blow to you when he died."

"I didn't kill him," she said.

"No one thinks you did. Not even the people who convicted you think you did. They were trying to preserve the ambassador's reputation. In my opinion, that's not worth your life."

Like a turtle peeking out of its shell Hysia raised her gaze enough that she could see Jean-Claude's expression. "He was always kind to me."

"He was happy with his job?" Jean-Claude asked. He discovered an onion in his soup and a crispy bit of pork belly.

"*Si*, he loved his work. He was very happy with it," she said, taking another breath as if she wanted to say something, and then deciding against it.

"Except something was wrong," Jean-Claude said.

Hysia closed her eyes and turned her head away, a flinch from remembered pain. "He . . . was not himself. Two weeks ago, he started turning away visitors, spending all his time in his rooms. By last week he wasn't even letting us in to clean. He stopped taking meals."

"And nobody noticed this?" Jean-Claude asked.

"He forbade us to speak of his personal business to anyone. We made excuses for him. We even turned away his lady love."

"What is her name?" Jean-Claude said.

"Madame Veva," she said, "a clayborn, to everyone's great scandal."

"Was she good for him or bad?"

"I liked her," Hysia said, "but it was all very improper, which made it better somehow, though it shouldn't have."

Jean-Claude made a note to inquire after a Madame Veva. The haste of Hysia's conviction and sentencing reeked of deeper troubles in the Aragothic delegation. Cubilla's lady love might know something about that.

"What happened after he stopped taking meals?"

"The last night," Hysia said, her voice becoming tight. "The last night I went to his door to offer him food, and I heard him sobbing. I called out to him, but he did not respond. Later I heard crashing and smashing. He'd . . . I saw later that he'd broken his mirror."

Jean-Claude put his soup aside to give her his undivided attention. In Aragoth, land of the Glasswalkers, breaking a mirror was a capital crime, tantamount to murder. "Why would he do that?"

"I . . ." she began, and stopped as if she'd seen a ghost. Jean-Claude waited for the pregnant pause to give birth. Hysia said, "I heard the shot and I ran in to see what had happened. The broken glass was everywhere. He was lying on the floor next to his chair. And there was the pistol. I could not believe it. I went down on my knees to look in his face. He was gone. His eyes were gone."

"What do you mean, gone? Did someone pluck them out?"

"No," she said. "The silver was gone. His eyes were brown, like a clayborn." A chill settled on Jean-Claude's soul. "He lost his sorcery."

"*Sí.*"

Just like Coquetta.

Hysia scrunched up as if she was either trying to vomit or trying *not* to. "Do you think it could be that he fell in love with a clayborn woman that caused him to lose his silver?"

Jean-Claude gave no credit to the idea that sorcery was the outward sign of a divine soul, but most of the Enlightened faithful did. To lose sorcery was a sign of corruption and moral decay. It was the greatest terror a devout saintborn could face. Clearly Ambassador Cubilla couldn't face it. Just as clearly, Consul de la Vega didn't want word getting out, so he'd tried to eliminate the only witness, which explained much about that trial and made Isabelle's ruination that much more cynical.

"Love is never corrupt," Jean-Claude said. Coquetta had certainly loved him, if not in a keeping sort of way.

There was no particular reason to suspect that the ambassador's loss of sorcery was in any way related to Coquetta's. The types of diseases that robbed sorcerers of their gifts didn't tend to be catchy, but it was a coincidence he didn't like.

"Did Ambassador Cubilla have any other symptoms, aches, or pains, aside from losing his silver?"

Hysia's expression was washed out and devoid of emotion, like a gully after the torrent had run through. "No . . . Maybe. Sometimes he had trouble speaking. His words came out wrong, garbled as if they had lost their meaning."

"Anything else?" Jean-Claude asked.

"No," she said. "I didn't see anything."

Jean-Claude picked up his bowl and stood. Two saintborn losing their gift was probably just a coincidence . . . if there were only two.

"Come," he said to Hysia, "let's make sure Valérie knows you're not to be left behind with the dirty rugs."

—

Isabelle detested sunrises generally; whenever she witnessed them it meant that she was awake at the time of morning dedicated to the divinely ordained punishment of people with hangovers, and she always seemed to obtain one by proxy. Worse were these winter sunrises, which got about their business with all the speed and efficiency of a three-legged turtle.

Just now the light outside her window was bright enough to see by but dim enough to suggest it thought it had better things to do. In a few more weeks, as this slice of Craton Massif turned north and the planet tilted away from the Solar, that glow would withdraw from its duties entirely and leave this part of the world cloaked in night.

With a heavy heart, Isabelle finished signing and sealing the last of her letters of recommendation for her servants, bestowing flowing praise and personal details all around. What good the letters might do, being penned by the hand of a notorious criminal, she could not guess. She arched her back and stretched her shoulders, then tugged the bellpull to summon Valérie to have the words whisked away. That was one shovelful of the mountain out of her way.

She pulled out another sheet of paper and considered the words she would write to her supposed sister. She wanted to meet this stranger, to find out if she was real, to see if they had anything in common. Jean-Claude was right to advise caution, of course.

It took Isabelle several drafts to write.

> *Dear B:*
>
> *Thank you for contacting me in reference to our mutual acquaintance. I look forward to meeting you soon. In your letter you asked me to take whatever precautions I deem necessary to protect myself and to ascertain the truth of your claims.*
>
> *The messenger who brings you this will be carrying a small cylindrical device. Press the round end of the device to a bit of exposed skin, and it will draw a tiny sample of blood. This will sting. With this sample, I will be able to determine if you are who you say.*
>
> *If you agree to this I will meet you at a time and place of my choosing. If not, then I decline.*
>
> *Builder keep you.*
> *—I*

She was still not entirely satisfied with it, but was not sure another attempt would improve it. She opened her sky trunk and reached through the bottom with her spark-arm, unhitching a latch only she could reach, and opened the secret compartment.

Even amongst her most precious things, some were more valuable than others. In the compartment were several quondam artifacts that she'd looted from Kantelvar's stronghold, irreplaceable machines created in the Builder's workshops before the Breaking of the World. The fact that they still functioned after thousands of years of abuse and neglect was a tribute to the Builder's power and craft.

She withdrew a single blood cipher and closed the compartment just as there came a rapping at her door.

"May I come in?" Jean-Claude's voice.

Isabelle's heart lifted at the sound of his voice. She said, "I was just about to send for you."

Jean-Claude had cleaned up and donned an undamaged shirt and a laundered musketeer's tabard, though he was favoring his arm now as well as his leg.

"*Bonjour,* my bright one. You were asleep when I got back last night." He gave her a paternal hug as he came in, as he had since she was a child.

"And you were asleep when I woke up this morning," she said.

He pushed back to arm's length and looked up at her with worry. "Do you have any idea who tried to kill you?"

"No," Isabelle said. "There wasn't much left of the assassin's bloodhollow after he hit the ground, and I don't even know if I was the target. Whoever it was might have been aiming for Lael."

"Lael?" Jean-Claude asked. "You mean the banished bastard? What was he doing there?"

"Talking to me," Isabelle said. "Feeling me out, I think. He tried to talk me into being a go-between for him and his mother. I declined. He told me about his political project, and he recognized my l'Étincelle. That was about as far as we got before the assassin interrupted."

"Count him as one more person to avoid," Jean-Claude said.

Isabelle tilted her head. "Any particular reason why, or just as a general precaution?"

Jean-Claude took a moment to compose his thoughts and said, "Coquetta used to write to me about him, but not like she'd write about her daughters. The letters about the girls were always about what they'd done, or which boy had broken their heart, or something they'd learned. With Lael it was never that way. It was always, he's angry about the way his servants were treated, or he's furious about the insult comte du jour leveled at his father, or incensed about the way his sister was treated by her cousins. No matter what the matter was, he was always angry about it. Coquetta used to say, 'He just wants justice.'"

"Is that such a bad thing?" Isabelle asked. Her life had been noticeably absent actual justice recently.

"One man's justice is another man's vengeance. From what I understand he was never satisfied with reparation or conciliation, he always demanded retribution, often wildly out of proportion to the crime."

"Sounds like a lot of noblemen I've dealt with lately."

"I have a thought about that," Jean-Claude said. "I think I know why Consul de la Vega was so determined to murder Señora Dominguez, and so desperate to discredit you after the fact."

"Do tell," Isabelle said. Making sense of de la Vega's actions wouldn't suddenly reverse her fortunes, but she still wanted clarity.

"The ambassador killed himself because he lost the Builder's gift," Jean-Claude said. "De la Vega was trying to get rid of the only witness to that fact."

Isabelle felt sick to her heart. "Do you think he'll come after Hysia?"

"He might. We'll have to keep watch, but he has to assume she's already told someone. The secret is exposed, and stirring up trouble will only make it more likely to be revealed."

"Damn de la Vega," Isabelle said. "How many people have to suffer for his pride?"

"There's another thing," Jean-Claude said, and he rubbed the back of his neck. "Coquetta's bloodshadow is dying."

Isabelle's hand flew to her breast. "Oh no." She would not see that grand lady suffer, and losing her bloodshadow would cost the comtesse everything, even if it somehow spared her life. "Are you sure?"

"Her shadow used to be thick and opaque. Yesterday it was thin and pink and I saw pieces of it tear off and boil away. I've never seen anything like that in my life."

"Are you thinking these two events might be related?" Isabelle asked.

"I have no evidence, not even really a suspicion. If it doesn't happen to anyone else, then it's just seemed an odd coincidence. In the meanwhile, I'm going to take Gretl up to le Ville Céleste to see if there's anything to be done for Coquetta."

"She and Darcy are still at the Agonesium, cleaning up the neglect," Isabelle said. "Did you get to talk to Grand Leon?"

From the way Jean-Claude's expression sagged, he had, and he hadn't received good news. She should have known that from the fact that he hadn't woken her up last night to tell her.

Jean-Claude took off his hat and thumped it on the side of his leg. "He said your uniqueness would not be wasted, which tells us exactly nothing. Then he told me to get on with my business and find the Harvest King. I wanted to spit in his eye, for all the good that would have done. I should have resigned my commission. I would have if I thought it would have moved him."

Isabelle's heart felt like it was filled with lead, but she had not expected any better. Not so soon after her expulsion.

Jean-Claude said, "The thing I don't understand is why. There has to have been another way to salvage the Grand Peace without tossing your guts to the gulls."

Isabelle had been avoiding thinking about it because thinking about it hurt like an ice pick to the temple. "Maybe salvaging the Grand Peace wasn't the point. He was trying to accomplish something else."

"That's very close to what Impervia said," Jean-Claude said. "She didn't have a guess, either."

Isabelle had no speculation to give him, and the conversation wilted. She picked up the letter from her writing desk and handed it to him. "As we discussed, I have composed my response to B."

He put his spectacles on and read through it.

"Are you sure you want to get involved with this given all our other troubles?"

Isabelle said, "I don't see what I have to lose." She was, in a sense, freer than she ever had been, devoid of legal responsibilities.

"You'll be exposing your blood ciphers."

Isabelle stared at the cipher in her hand. The thing was heavier than any ordinary metal. "It's the only way to absolutely confirm or deny our relationship. Also, it has occurred to me that if this woman is somehow a bone queen in disguise, the blood cipher won't work. It requires blood to work and bone queens are dry as dust. Even when you manage to cut one, they don't bleed."

"Good point." Jean-Claude accepted the blood cipher from her. "I'm going to take Marie with me, her first day of apprenticing. Do you want her to help you get dressed first?"

"Yes," Isabelle said, though the announcement tugged at Isabelle's heart. Hardly a day had gone by in the last twenty years where Marie had not been at her side. Her absence would be like missing part of her own mind.

"Do you need her for anything else?"

Yes. "No." Better to set her loose cleanly. "I'm planning on working on Ingle's journal. That's something she can't really help with."

"Any idea how long it will take?"

"It depends on how clever he was with his code. If he wanted to be able to write it and read it quickly, it can't be that complex." Or so she fervently hoped. It might hold the answer to so many of the questions they'd been asking.

—

"So why do you want to be a bodyguard?" Isabelle asked, holding on to the bedpost as Marie cinched up her corset. It was a question she hadn't the chance to ask yesterday. *Why do you want to leave me?*

Marie tied off the knots in the back and moved around to adjust the front. "Because you forget to watch your back sometimes."

"This can't just be for my benefit," Isabelle said, for as much as she hated to part from Marie, she didn't want to be the only star Marie steered by.

"It isn't," Marie said. "I want to learn to fight. I've always liked physical things. Running, riding, swimming. When we were in Aragoth, I saw Reina Xaviera dueling, and I wanted to go out there and do that. I kept thinking. Me. Me. Me. The same when we went to the challenge courts here. I know it's not normal—"

"You were never normal. You were never afraid of my wormfinger." Isabelle waggled her spark-fingers, making a cloud of light. She'd been born with only a single malformed digit on her right hand. The spark-hand was a definite improvement despite its odd limitations. "You were never afraid at all."

"So you don't mind?" Marie asked.

"I said 'yes,'" Isabelle said.

"Because you believe in being fair," Marie said.

"I think you'll be good at it," Isabelle said.

Marie reached up to adjust the black lace cravat at Isabelle's throat. "Still not answering the question."

"I'm . . . uneasy," Isabelle said. "This feels like a parting of the ways."

"I'm doing this to be your bodyguard," Marie said. "Which rather requires that I stay with you."

"I didn't say it made sense," Isabelle said. "It's just how I feel. I understand you helped kill that bulldog Seelenjäger."

Marie said, "He was going to kill Jean-Claude."

"How did it make you feel?"

After another thoughtful stillness, Marie said, "Strange. I was scared, and I was angry, and the whole world shrank down to one moment, and I was calm in the middle of it. After he died, I felt elated, and then sick. For a long time I couldn't think what to do with my hands. My guns were empty but I couldn't bear to put them down. It didn't feel over."

"Battle nerves," Isabelle said. "I felt like that after I fell off the Pilgrims' Way. From what I understand, it's a fairly typical reaction to that level of danger."

CHAPTER
Twelve

The wind raced through the crowd in Conqueror's Square like a pickpocket, stealing people's breath away and smearing the deep sounding of the noonday bells into a hollow groan.

Jean-Claude's nerves stretched like sails before the wind. He and Marie rode their horses at a leisurely amble across the cobbles, scanning the crowd for a Fenice. This was about like sending a toddler into the woods to look for a bear, but how else was he going to teach her?

"Do you think this person could be who she says she is?" Marie asked.

"A better question is, 'Does it matter?'" Jean-Claude said. "Family doesn't necessarily mean friendly. You and I are more family to Isabelle than some long-lost sibling could ever be. Family is who is there for you when you need them. It's who you go back to."

The elliptical plaza was lined at its edges by a dozen military statues. Some of them were gifts donated by nobles seeking favor, some were commissioned to commemorate specific victories, still others were prizes shipped back from the city centers of lands Grand Leon had conquered.

Chief amongst this latter group was the colossus of the twins, Maximus

Primus and Maximus Secundus, Fenice brothers who had once united all the Risen Kingdoms. Under a single banner, they had set out from Om, chief of the Vecci city states, the ancestral home of the Fenice, and invaded the heretical Tyranny of Skaladin, intent on seizing the fabled City of Gears.

The legendary campaign had ended in disaster with the Great Betrayal; Gyrine Windcallers scattered and shattered the grand armada that had been assembled to ferry supplies up the coast, leaving the Kindly Crusade's ground forces stranded in the Ashlands along the Smoldering Coast. The entire invasion force had been lost, and the Risen Kingdoms left exposed to a Skaladin counterinvasion.

The statue itself was magnificent bronze depicting the Maximi, shoulder to shoulder in full classical regalia, Primus pointing his sword toward the City of Gears, and Secundus raising his flag to signal a charge. The sculptor had left no detail unattended. Their crest feathers swept back from their foreheads like great headdresses. Their faces, etched with close feathers, were stern and commanding.

Jean-Claude let his gaze fall to the plinth at the base of the statue looking for the woman claiming to be Isabelle's sister. Lorenzo had been a Fenice, but it was a trait Isabelle had not inherited. Sorcerous blood was strange that way. It didn't always breed true, even amongst the purest of the saintbloods. This B person was most likely a Fenice, but she might also be unhallowed. Certainly no one around the base of the plinth was decked out in feathers.

"Penny for a poor woman?" asked a beggar hunched up against the plinth, so shrouded in rags that she might have been mistaken for a heap of dirty laundry. Yet her voice was smooth and refined.

Jean-Claude reined in. "Before I give you my charity, let me see your face."

The beggar chuckled warmly, and unfolded herself from the ground. She cast off a top layer of rags and blankets and revealed beneath a tall slim figure in a woodsman's tunic, trousers, boots, and gloves. A deep cowl shadowed her face. Jean-Claude would not have guessed she was a woman save for the voice.

She pulled back her hood just far enough to see her face. "Greetings, Monsieur Musketeer, I assume you are here on my sister's behalf."

Jean-Claude's breath caught. She had Isabelle's exceptional height and narrow frame, the same long lean face, deeply hooded eyes, and high-bridged nose. Her skin was darker, olive in its hue and her lips fuller, and she was close to Isabelle's age. Even Jean-Claude was forced to concede a certain family resemblance.

Yet she was definitely Fenice, for where her hairline should be were rows and rows of feathers, the base of a crest now pressed flat by her voluminous hood. The little bits he could see were jewel tones of blue and green, colors shifting in the light ripples on a pond. Her eyes were the color of emeralds.

Jean-Claude huffed and said, "You have me at a disadvantage, I'm afraid."

"My name is Barbaro Brunela, and I apologize for the circumlocution. As I said in my letter, I have enemies, and I'd rather not share them with your charge. I'll show you where we can talk in private."

This turned out to be a tea vendor's tent set up near the edge of the square. The proprietor provided them old cushions on which to sit and chipped porcelain cups from which to sip a variety of infusions that all tasted like tree bark.

Brunela said, "I know you by reputation, and I've given you my name, but who is your companion?"

"This is Mademoiselle Marie," Jean-Claude said, and that was all she needed to know.

Brunela tilted her head like an owl as she scrutinized Marie. "In all my lifetimes, I've never seen anyone who didn't have a shadow. How does that feel?"

Marie did not start, but she hesitated long enough that Jean-Claude could tell she was thinking it over. "Light feels a little colder than it used to," she said, something Jean-Claude hadn't known. He'd been around her for so long he took her peculiarities for granted.

To Brunela he said, "What is it you want from Isabelle?"

"I want her to stop spreading our sire's name around. There are dangerous people who will begin to wonder why she is interested in a dead Vecci vagabond and come asking questions. If they do, they are sure to notice a certain family resemblance, and Fenice vendettas being what they are, they will kill her out of pure precaution."

Jean-Claude grunted. "So if I impress upon her the importance of her silence, you'll be satisfied and leave her alone."

"If that's what she wants," Brunela said. "Is it?"

Jean-Claude was tempted to say "Yes," and leave it at that, but he couldn't trust Marie not to rat him out. Besides, as much as he wanted to shield

Isabelle from the world's dangers, it was not his place to choose her path for her.

"Not necessarily," he said. He pulled Isabelle's letter from his pouch. "Her own words."

Brunela took the letter, broke the wax seal, and read over the rim of her cup as she sipped her tea. Her eyes rounded slightly and she put the paper down. "She actually has a set of blood ciphers? And she knows how to use them?"

"Do you know what they are?" Jean-Claude asked.

"Child, in my first life I helped oversee the construction of Om, the building of the Prime Temple, the excavation of the three harbors, the collection of antiquities into the first quondarium, and I know family tales that go all the way back to the Annihilation of Rüul. There are many wonderful and terrible things in this world, some that would give you nightmares just to imagine. The blood ciphers, by contrast, are relatively benign, if anything that can unlock secrets can be so described. They can not only tell if people are related, but what sort of sorcery they possess, and if they have any diseases that run in families."

"May I ask a question, in return for the question you asked about me?" Marie asked.

"Usually such tit-for-tat exchanges are agreed upon in advance," Brunela said, "but in this case, go ahead."

"How can you stand having all of those memories?"

Brunela put on a thoughtful face. "It's a bit disorienting at first, remembering things you know you've never done, places you know you've never been, but of course you still forget things. My very oldest memories are little more than impressions, or a sense of recognition, as if from childhood. The ones you want to hold on to you have to make a pearl out of."

"Lucky," Marie said. Her own perfect memory was frequently as much of a burden to her as an asset. It wasn't so much the ability to remember, as the inability to forget.

"Who are the enemies of which you speak?" he asked.

Brunela said, "I will not give you information you might easily use against me, nor will I insult your intelligence by giving you a false trail to chase. Suffice it to say that those enemies are deadly and persistent, and the best hope of defeating them is simply to avoid their notice until it turns elsewhere. That's what I intend to do."

Jean-Claude sipped the tree-bark soup. "Is Immacolata one of these hunters?"

Brunela's eyes narrowed. "So you've heard of her. I pray you have not seen fit to draw her attention."

"I would rather not," Jean-Claude said, "but circumstances make it impossible for me to ignore her presence. It might help me avoid a confrontation if you had some idea what she is doing in Rocher Royale."

Brunela's mouth quirked at one corner, alive to his sally. "She does not include me in her councils."

Jean-Claude took another sip and let the silence stretch. No matter how many lives the Fenice had lived, she had to make it through each hour one second at a time like everybody else. Patience was a skill each generation had to learn anew, and this version of Barbaro seemed no older than Isabelle.

He was beginning to think he might have to finish the whole cup of tea when Brunela said, "May I have the blood cipher?"

Jean-Claude drew forth the quondam cylinder. The purple tint of the metal seemed to run deeper than the surface, as if it was thicker than its dimensions implied. For something that was hardly bigger than his finger, it had quite a heft. He continued to slurp his tea in a manner he was sure Coquetta would not approve of. Brunela was the one who had made contact; she wanted something from Isabelle, and though her gaze did not fix on the blood cipher it kept drifting in that direction.

"Please don't make me order another cup of whatever this is," Jean-Claude said.

"Please don't make me listen to him drink it," Marie added, unnecessarily.

"I know two things about Immacolata," Brunela said. "The first is that she is very near death. The rate of a bone queen's solidification increases as she approaches the end of her life. The second is that the closer to death she gets the more dangerous she becomes."

Jean-Claude's eyes narrowed as his suspicions sharpened. "Is she here hunting Isabelle?"

"If she were, Isabelle would already be dead."

Brunela's disregard of Isabelle's defenders was irksome, but hardly unexpected. Jean-Claude went to some lengths to ensure Isabelle's enemies underestimated him. "What will you do when these old enemies move on to new threats?"

She shrugged. "The world is a bigger place than it used to be. There's a whole new craton to be exploited. I even have some opportunities for investment that Isabelle might be interested in. I understand her fortunes have recently fallen."

The Craton Riqueza drifted in the southern hemisphere. It had been colonized by the Aragoths a generation ago, but Jean-Claude supposed, from Brunela's perspective, that was practically yesterday. "What sort of investments?"

"That's family business," she said.

"I am her man of business," Jean-Claude said. At least this business.

"If she wants to let you listen in on our discussion, that will be her choice at that time."

"Is the Harvest King after you as well?" he asked. There was some danger in speaking that name. Any question you asked told the other person where the gaps in your knowledge were, but he had so few leads that he had little choice.

Brunela's feathery eyebrows lifted. "That obscene play?"

"The man running the show. His name crops up in association with Immacolata's," Jean-Claude said.

Brunela leaned back and tilted her face up as if watching the clouds through the roof of the tent. "It's not surprising that she has allies. For all her power she can only be in one place at a time. She needs spies, scouts, and lookouts to make sure it's the right place at the precise moment. In return she can offer the ability to magically transform enemies into corpses."

Jean-Claude grunted at this entirely reasonable yet unhelpful response.

Brunela extended a gloved hand. "May I have the blood cipher? Or are you hoping I won't give a sample?"

Jean-Claude weighed his options, but she'd already given him several bits of information he had no way to verify. Adding more wouldn't help. He handed over the cipher. This at least would provide reliable information.

Brunela rolled the device between her fingers, then pressed it to her lips in a gentle kiss. With a metallic snap, the needle struck. A bead of blood flowed onto the bulb and was swiftly absorbed. Brunela licked the blood from her lip and handed the cipher back to Jean-Claude.

"Thank you," Jean-Claude said.

"Since you already have proof," Brunela said, "please give this to Isabelle as a gift." From her pouch she produced a locket and presented it to Jean-Claude. There was another locket around Brunela's throat. A twin to this one, or some more important memory?

He flipped the oval open. Inside one half was a tiny portrait of Isabelle's mother. As old and abused as this picture was, there was no doubt of its subject. Isabelle's mother, Vedetta des Zephyrs, had large liquid eyes and skin like porcelain. Her whole face had been constructed entirely of superlatives. The man on the other half must be Barbaro Lorenzo, his green crest feathers tall and proud. His long face could easily have been the precursor to Isabelle's own.

"A very comely couple," Jean-Claude said. He handed the locket off to Marie, who glanced at it and snapped it shut.

"Yes, for all that her beauty was entirely superficial, and she wasn't even that good in bed." At Jean-Claude's look of inquiry Brunela tapped the side of her skull. "I have my father's memories, and his mother's and so on. I've been man and woman, sired children and given birth. There's almost nothing I haven't tried."

That was more information than Jean-Claude really wanted. As old and tired as his body had become, he couldn't imagine having a different one, much less five or ten.

"If you need to contact me and I'm not here, you can leave a message at the Smoking Bucket on Rockfall Street," Brunela said.

Jean-Claude made his farewell, left his tea unfinished, and retreated with Marie.

"So what do you think of her?" Marie asked once they had remounted.

"She's slipperier than a greased eel," Jean-Claude said. "Everything she said had at least two meanings or less than none."

"Listen to what they say, not what you think they meant to say," Marie said. "That's what you used to tell Isabelle."

"And that's what I'm telling you, too. Most of this business isn't fighting or sneaking, though you'll have to learn that, too. Most of it is talking to people and paying attention."

Marie considered that for a moment. "Isabelle always says that it's the simple things that are hard, because you can't break them down into smaller steps."

"Something like that," Jean-Claude said.

"Do you think she really is Isabelle's sister?"

"Probably," Jean-Claude said. "At least by blood." He handed the cipher to Marie, "I need you to take this back to Isabelle. I'll collect Gretl and introduce her to Comtesse Coquetta." He craned his neck to gaze up the towering cliff face and the narrow road threading its way upward. "Then we need to find out where the *Harvest King* will be performed."

"Do you think the Harvest King will actually be there?"

"No, but I'm sure the players will know something, even if they don't know what they know. I doubt we'll be back until tomorrow."

—

It hadn't taken Isabelle long at all to puzzle out Ingle's cipher, which was actually somewhat disappointing. She'd been hoping for a more worthy adversary. She'd been helped by the fact that all of the illustrations were annotated, and she knew what some of them referred to already, which quickly boiled down into a working key.

The inside of the book was filled with meticulous if gruesome drawings of his vivisections. Isabelle was both fascinated and repulsed, and repulsed by her own fascination. She'd always had a taste for the grotesque, but if there was one thing murder by cruel torture should not be, it was fascinating. Yet the drawings were so detailed and observant that she found herself paging through the book and being intrigued by the deeper structures of human anatomy revealed in its images.

Human anatomy. Victims.

She chided herself for becoming lost in the work for its own sake. Clearly the Harvest King was interested in this tome, else why send the bulldog Seelenjäger to fetch it? What didn't he want them to find?

Ingle's writing had the tone of a self-obsessed manifesto, the useful information teased through long paragraphs of self-adulation. Isabelle rechecked her most recent translation, then rechecked it again, then reminded herself that not everything Ingle wrote was necessarily true:

> The presence of multiple Builder's nodes in the transverse cleft
> has so far presented itself in only two specimens, both of which
> displayed blazons and produced active phenomena consistent
> with the manifestation of multiple sorceries.
>
> One of the bi-nodal specimens displayed symptoms of common madness, hearing voices in its head, and being prone to

fits of babbling. The other was coherent and displayed no sign of mental degeneration.

Contained experiments with galvanic shock on bi-nodal specimen number two produced startling effects. With the application of a continuous flow the subject was induced to draw images from a mirror in such a way that had elements in common with both Glasswalking and Goldentongue glamours according to the Temple inquest's Standards of Canonical Confirmation.

After all the useful data from that experiment was documented, I excised the leftmost of the bi-node nodules. Its color, texture, mass, smell, and taste were not dissimilar of other nodules.

The specimen lapsed into a comatose state. I have noticed in past trials that even comatose specimens can occasionally be induced to manifest their sorcerous phenomena, so I applied an increasing flow of galvanic fluid to the remaining nodule until it became clear the specimen had expired. The brain, at that point being somewhat charred, was removed for further dissection . . .

Isabelle examined her fingers for wet ink before resting her face in her palm. She'd only translated a few pages so far, each one a horror show of cruelty and insight. It hurt her soul to read it, but she could hardly look away.

A knock at her door startled her.

"Mademoiselle Isabelle," Hysia called. "There are two Praetorians here. They demand to see you."

A jolt of nerves tightened Isabelle's heart at the mention of Praetorians . . . but that might not be so bad. "Is one of them Capitaine Bitterlich?"

"The feline fellow? No."

Isabelle cursed under her breath. She closed the journal and slotted it into her bookshelf between two necessary but tedious books of logarithm and trigonometric tables. She pulled on her hat and skin hand glove, adjusted her veil, and trooped downstairs to see what was the matter.

The Praetorians who stood in her receiving room, amidst all the baggage waiting to be transported, were the same ones who had escorted her father to his death wish audience. One Praetorian was taller than she, with dark hair and a lean face, his mustache and goatee as thin and sharp as three points on a compass rose. The other was shorter and fairer, though his nose canted off at an angle like a ship with a stuck rudder fan. It made the sound of his breath hover at the edge of a whistle. Both wore the lieutenant's rank, and both were Sanguinaire.

Isabelle's mind raced to catch up with her pulse. These men must have heard her father's death wish. Could they be induced to tell her about it? But why were they here?

She said, "Messieurs, welcome. May I ask who I am receiving?"

The shorter one bowed and swept off his black hat. "I am Roland Probaneux, and my companion is Serge du Moule."

"Mademoiselle," Serge said, his voice deep enough to travel underground. He tipped his hat and studied her with an unblinking stare.

Roland said, "We've been sent to inspect the premises, catalogue the goods, make sure nothing leaves with you that didn't come in with you."

"Contraband," Serge rumbled. "Diplomatic papers."

Isabelle did not trust this explanation as far as she could spit, but it wasn't as if she could stop them if they chose to force the issue, and being banned from court she could not even complain about it later.

"Capitaine Bitterlich examined all the diplomatic papers last night," she said, praying he would forgive her for usurping his name's authority.

Roland said, "I'm afraid Capitaine Bitterlich has been reassigned. Littlepaws has never been trusted with, shall we say, delicate tasks."

"Littlepaws?" Isabelle asked, disliking his tone.

"Everyone calls him that," Serge rumbled. "It's a pet name."

"Not that he has that many friends." Roland's nasal whistle added a note of contempt to his assertion. "He doesn't make friends, doesn't know how to get along. Seelenjäger, you see. More beast than man. Serge and I, on the other hand, we have many friends. We can get things done."

"Do you have a warrant?" Isabelle asked.

Serge pointed to his badge of office. "This one. Official."

Roland said, "Now that all the niceties have been observed, mademoiselle, please stand aside. We don't like to hurt girls."

"Much," Serge amended.

Isabelle tried a different tack. "You can tell my father and his Gyrine friend that they have no business sending people to paw through my underpinnings."

"Le Comte des Zephyrs is a fool's own fool," Roland said. "The Wind-caller's tale is a full-throated lie. There's never been a Gyrine shat from his mother's bowels that could tell the truth, even on the Breaker's rack."

"Thieves and pirates," Serge agreed.

"Serge and I, we'll be keeping our feet on the ground."

"Solid rock," Serge echoed like a particularly lugubrious parrot. His blood-shadow teased the edge of Isabelle's shadow and it felt like ants crawling under her skin. Isabelle's stomach was a cold knot.

"Stop that," Isabelle said. She clenched her spark-hand and it flared, sending out firefly motes of lavender light. She couldn't actually hurt him with it, but he didn't know that.

Serge's shadow drew back a bare handspan.

"No need to be so touchy," Roland said airily. "I'd hate to think that a convicted criminal would interfere with two honest soldiers carrying out their lawful orders. Imagine what could happen if we felt threatened. Self-defense can get very messy."

"Filthy," Serge said.

Their bloodshadows rolled forward at the slow, inevitable pace of a funeral march. Isabelle didn't like bloodshadows. They were well enough when Sanguinaire kept them to themselves—after all, sorcery was not a choice; at least it didn't used to be—but being threatened with one turned her bones to suet. Too many times had her brother cornered her with his shadow, slowly constricting her space until she either broke down and begged for mercy, or until he caught her shadow and burned her until she wept.

Isabelle withdrew toward the stairs to her room. If they were after papers, that probably meant they were after Ingle's journal, which meant they must be working for the Harvest King, for who else knew the thing existed?

Serge's bloodshadow whipped out and hooked Isabelle by her shadow. Pain flared through her like a fire through dry tinder. Serge shook her paralyzed body like a terrier worrying a rat and then tossed her into the kitchen. Control of her body came back just in time for her to slam into the stout leg of the kitchen table.

"No interfering," Serge said.

—

"I still don't see why this is necessary," Coquetta protested, as Gretl spread her fingers and examined her hand over a bright light. "I'm perfectly healthy, just a touch of the cold and fatigue."

She looked even more pale and wan since the last time Jean-Claude had seen her, and the trembling in her hand had become a constant. Fear lurked like a feral rat behind her soft brown eyes. Josette, standing by, bit her lower lip and folded her arms as if finding herself party to something unconscionable.

Jean-Claude took Coquetta's other hand and sat beside her. Two alchemical heaters turned her chambers into an oven, but her flesh was still cold and moist as a frozen slug.

"Did you have a chance to check Grand Leon's engagement calendar?" he asked, as much to distract Coquetta from the medical investigation as any hope of finding an answer.

A spark came back into Coquetta's eyes. "You know I did. I thought, 'What if we knew this woman was pregnant but she never presented us with a child?' I found several records like that but discreet inquires revealed that all but two were miscarriages. Of the two remaining, one died of the galfesters before coming to term. The last one died of childbirth, but there's no record of the child dying."

"That's interesting," Jean-Claude said. "But that doesn't prove anything about Orem."

"Not by itself," Coquetta said, "but the family lives in Rocher Royale, so I had Josette call upon the woman's brother. What did you find out, dear?"

Josette's expression darkened. "The Travers family is part of a purity cult. They are convinced they are all direct descendents of Saint Guyot le Sanguinaire, particularly chosen as the vessels of pure blood through which the Savior will be reborn. They are equally convinced that Grand Leon is not one of the chosen few."

Jean-Claude winced. "Let me guess, a family tree with no branches."

"He would not admit to incest," Josette said, "but his contempt for outbreeders implied it. He was not at all displeased to tell me that his sister had in fact delivered an impure bastard and they had left the newborn on the steps of the Chapterhouse of the Order of Saint Orem."

"Patron saint of the forgotten," Coquetta said. "It's still not proof that your lateborn Sanguinaire was that same child, but I rather suspect it's just a matter of tucking in the corners."

Jean-Claude lifted his hat and rubbed his forehead in dismay. "Grand Leon will not be pleased."

Coquetta said, "It should not be too hard for you to direct his wrath at the Travers."

Coquetta's hands trembled more violently, and Josette stepped in. "Mother, you're about to have another fit. The rest of you. Back off."

Gretl and Darcy stepped back in a hurry.

Coquetta's eyes became unfocused. "Am I, well that's no goolllmm."

No sooner did she start to convulse than Josette's bloodshadow snaked in, surrounding Coquetta's shadow and compressing it, holding her still, but not rigid.

Jean-Claude stepped back. Gretl and Darcy engaged in a rapid exchange of hand speech.

Jean-Claude's heart sickened to see Coquetta so reduced. When Josette relaxed her grip, bits of Coquetta's bloodshadow came away like a maple shedding its leaves for winter.

Jean-Claude waved to get Gretl's attention and asked, "Any ideas?"

Gretl's hands made signs Jean-Claude hadn't seen before. Darcy translated, "She thinks she might be able to do something about the seizures."

"What about her bloodshadow?" Josette asked.

Darcy made a helpless gesture. "We can only speculate. It's usually a problem in the brain that causes seizures, the old texts are clear on that. Given that her sorcery is withering it might be the Builder's node."

"What are you talking about?" Josette asked

Darcy said, "We think sorcerers' brains are different from clayborn. You seem to have an extra feature, and our guess is that it allows you to work your sorcery."

"How do we fix it?" Josette asked. "I'll get you anything you need."

Darcy shook her head. "We can't cure her. The best we can do is alleviate some of the symptoms."

Josette's jaw set. "Do what you can."

While Darcy rattled off a list of ingredients, Jean-Claude knelt at Coquetta's side. She was ambitious, ruthless in her own way, and yet also kind and compassionate. She made the world a better place. She didn't deserve this.

Yet Coquetta wouldn't be the first sorcerer to lose the Builder's gift this week. To Josette he said, "Mademoiselle Princess, have you or your mother's gossips lately heard of anyone else suffering a similar malady?"

Josette opened her mouth as if to reply, but paused halfway there. A thoughtful expression spread across her face. "Why do you ask?"

"Because Ambassador Cubilla also lost his gift. We think that's why he committed suicide. As far as I know, there's no connection between the two events; Cubilla might have gone blind drinking wood spirits, but it's still unnerving."

Josette's brows pinched and she rubbed her thumbs on forefingers. "I have not heard any such rumors, but then again we have not been listening for them. I shall have our people make discreet inquiries."

"Thank you," Jean-Claude said. "How long until Madame Comtesse wakes up?" Coquetta didn't really look asleep right now. She looked absent, as if her mind had gone somewhere else.

"She comes around in about a quarter hour," Josette said. "She barely remembers anything for about an hour after that."

Jean-Claude creaked to his feet. "In that case, I'll be back."

Josette asked, "Where are you going?"

"To talk to Impervia," he said. "Saints help me."

~

Jean-Claude made his way through the maze of le Ville Céleste's central spire as if he was walking through knee-deep mud, every step an exhausting effort of will. Between the huge bustle of the festival crowd and the demands of social function, almost no one in the upper echelons of Grand Leon's government was keeping regular hours. There were ceremonies to be attended, awards to be given, ribbons to be cut, and events to be dignified. Perhaps Impervia would be gone and he'd be forced to leave a message. Not that he could convey any part of what he needed to say through a messenger.

It wasn't that he didn't want to talk to her. It was just that he didn't want to make a mess of it again, and for some reason that didn't seem to apply to anyone else, he couldn't seem to avoid putting his foot in it.

He finally caught up with her in a ballroom in the main spire at a ceremony honoring the Gray Spiders: soldiers' widows who had taken up arms in a protracted guerilla war against Öberholzer raiders and rebels during Wolfgang's rebellion. Their unit had been created in desperation, but after the war its charter had not been renewed. Jean-Claude reckoned that had been a mistake. None of the few remaining widows were under fifty, and the eldest was older than Grand Leon, but he could think of no force more ruthless or intractable than a regiment of well-armed, well-trained grandmothers with grandchildren to protect and with no illusions whatsoever about honor or glory. He stood in the back of the crowd in attendance, mostly made up of those same young relatives, all beaming and bouncing as Impervia hung silver medallions over their grandmammas' necks.

Impervia wore a confection of white lace and silver that left her shoulders bare. Her heavy veil obscured her eyes but revealed lips painted white, giving them the stage all to themselves. Jean-Claude could not help but remember the fire in those lips. It stirred embers in his loins.

Impervia praised the Gray Spiders for their bravery and their loyalty and bestowed upon them each the official version of the ranks they had worn unofficially all those years ago.

As flinty as those venerable dames might be, their bent backs straightened and their eyes glistered with pride.

After the ceremony's tasteful conclusion of old women being mobbed by several generations of progeny, Impervia pulled him aside and escorted him into a sitting room he hadn't visited before, a wood-paneled semicircle. The curved wall was built with inset shelves, some of them loaded with trinkets, others with books. Near the apex of the curved wall stood an old-fashioned mechanical orrery, the kind driven by springs and kept in line by gears. Isabelle would have loved it.

Paintings hung on the straight wall, one of Grand Leon and the Trefoil together and others of each individually. Here was Impervia as a younger woman. She had aged into the severity of her expression. Her features growing sharper with time, like a good cheese. Once he would have made that joke to her face. She might have laughed.

In the painting, she was surrounded by her four children, all regal and poised, even the youngest who must have been five at the time of the sitting. The artist had painted in grave lilies into the background for the ones she'd lost. Two miscarriages and a stillbirth. How different might that painting be if she hadn't miscarried his child? A lump of regret weighed in his soul, which made no damned sense. What then would have happened to Isabelle?

"The last time we talked, I offended you," Jean-Claude said.

She shrugged. "You're a congenital oaf and a seasoned dullard. I'd forgotten that."

It was another statement that once would have provoked a spirited verbal tussle. A dozen tart responses came to mind. He swallowed them all and absorbed the insult, letting it drip down into the cellar of his soul.

Impervia frowned. He wanted to say she looked disappointed, but he didn't trust his own mind with her.

He turned to less fraught topics and gestured to the painting. "I hope your children are well."

One corner of her mouth quirked up. "Amazing. Of course I've had my tragedies, but those misfortunes were ultimately very contained." She cupped her hands together. "Their ghosts are small. My living children are expansive, and now I have grandchildren to spoil." She opened her hands and splayed her fingers as if spreading her offspring on the wind. "Joy doesn't negate sorrow, but shows it at its proper scale."

On that, Jean-Claude wholeheartedly agreed.

"I assume you're here on business," she said. "Did your Isabelle manage to translate Ingle's journal?"

"She'd only gotten started when I left, but we have learned, by way of examining Ingle's victims, that in addition to the known organs of power, sorcerers have a node in their brains that allows them to work their sorcery. We guess, and it's only a guess, that it's a defect in that node that makes some saintborn unhallowed. We also think that the Harvest King knows how to spark life into the node. What we don't know yet is how he does it, or who he is. I was hoping you might have found out where the play is next to be performed."

Impervia shook her head. "Don't worry, I haven't sneaked off to see it without you, though given how reluctant you are to endure my presence, I suspect the inverse would not have proven true had the opportunity presented itself to you."

"I was not aware that you had any desire to participate in such lewd debauchery," Jean-Claude said. "That's why you have minions."

Impervia waved this off. "Minions extend my senses, not replace them, but you didn't climb all the way up the Rivencrag just to ask me that."

"True," Jean-Claude said. "There is more, and I fear worse. The first artificial sorcerer I killed in the Lowmarket, the madman named Orem who was taken from the Agonesium by the Harvest King and delivered to the Golden Swain by Immacolata, was one of our master's plentiful progeny, a stray as it were."

Impervia's lips pressed into a flat line, as if keeping some invective from escaping.

Jean-Claude said, "Notes I found at the Agonesium suggest the Harvest King was aware that he was kidnapping Grand Leon's son, which sounds to me like a personal vendetta."

"That hardly narrows the field," Impervia said. "And if this was supposed to be a blow struck at Grand Leon's heart, then it should have come with some sort of message. If Orem had been consumed by his bloodshadow, you would never have found out who he was."

"Nothing about this fits together," Jean-Claude said.

"So what makes the least sense?" Impervia asked. "That's likely where the hole is."

Jean-Claude had been picking at the tangle for three days now. "I wish I knew . . ." he said. "I wish I knew what Immacolata wanted from Mistwaithe." He'd started with that question and followed the strings back toward their beginning, but those ends were frayed, spreading out and getting lost. He needed to go the other way, to find out where and how they all knotted together.

"Did you ask Mistwaithe's partner?" Impervia asked. "Goldentongues almost always travel in pairs."

Jean-Claude would have kicked himself if he had two good legs. He was a cursed fool. Impervia was right. Goldentongues who wanted to pass without notice needed to cover up their sorcerous blazon, their glorioles, but they couldn't cover their own, so they traveled in pairs, each covering the other so they could pass for clayborn. How could he have forgotten that? Most likely because he'd been too busy following up on Orem and all the horrors that entailed. "Breaker take my balls."

"Like paying with an empty purse," Impervia said dryly.

Jean-Claude bit down on a retort. There had been a time when that sort of insult hadn't been an insult, but a game, a challenge, a fierce seduction. His groin certainly hadn't forgotten, but he'd lost the right to entertain such desires with her even if their energies weren't needed elsewhere.

"Yes," he said wearily, surrendering the field without a shot fired.

Impervia frowned and assumed a more professional tone, cool and distant. "Do you have any idea who his partner might be?"

"I have a pretty damned good idea," Jean-Claude said. "I'm going to have words with that squeaky little bastard."

Thirteen

Isabelle stormed about her room in a fury of frustration. Her soul still ached from being shadowburned and there was an immense bruise spreading across her shoulders. She'd waited in the kitchen with her terrified staff, the heavy table barricading the door until Serge and Roland were well and truly gone. She'd emerged to find her room ransacked, her instruments cast aside and half of them broken. Her scale model university had been flipped over and flattened, her clothes strewn everywhere. Worst of all, the villains had stolen her books, every single one of them, and all her papers, even her unfinished manuscripts and notes. They'd looted the warehouse of her mind and pillaged her life's work.

Of course they'd also taken Ingle's journal, the only thread she had to the Harvest King and the murder of all those people in the Lowmarket.

She spent some time cursing to vent her rage, because it was either that or cry, and she was done with crying. She began triaging her empirical instruments: working, broken, and beyond repair. They'd smashed her aetherscope and her pulse refractor, delicate things that she had no hope of replacing.

She stacked and sorted and invented all sorts of unlikely comeuppance for the two Praetorians.

There came a knock on her doorframe. She whirled, ready to tear someone's face off, but it was Marie, looking blank as ever.

"What happened?" Marie asked.

Isabelle gestured at the room, the empty shelves. "Praetorians. Serge and Roland." Isabelle groped for complete sentences and found only invective. "Illiterate, monkey-buggering dog spawn!"

"Bitterlich's friends?" Marie asked

"No. They said he'd been reassigned. Which means he was assigned to me." It meant he'd been following her and not Lael up on the Pilgrims' Road. He hadn't been nice to her because he liked her, but because she was his job. Saints but she was a fool.

"Or they were lying," Marie said.

"Maybe," Isabelle allowed; it was an idea she was willing to entertain, but Bitterlich had better have a good answer for her, or . . . what, she'd just be more furious? What a useless way to be.

"Where's Jean-Claude?" she asked.

"Up at le Ville Céleste with Gretl and Darcy," Marie said. "Did the Praetorians have a warrant?"

"Of course not," Isabelle said.

"Who sent them," Marie asked, "or do you know?"

"The Harvest King," Isabelle said. "Unless someone else knew about the journal." It could be someone they'd overlooked completely. "I saw these two the other day with my father. They escorted him into his death wish audience. I thought they might be working for him, but they called him a fool. They didn't believe the Windcaller's tale."

"What tale?" Marie asked.

"They didn't bother to explain," Isabelle said, her voice finally losing its brittle edge as she ran out of fury. Here was a question she could grapple with. "All they said was that they planned to keep their feet on the ground." She glowered into the distance. "That means my father's death wish involves not keeping their feet on the ground. It means flying, going somewhere, but where would he go, and why would he need Grand Leon's sanction to do it?"

Marie said, "Somewhere he thinks he can be cured of the red consumption?"

Isabelle shook her head. Doing so hurt. "There are any number of fabled places of healing, sacred springs, mystical groves, and so on, but Father has never been to any of them. He doesn't believe in magic."

"Maybe he's desperate enough to try," Marie said.

"Even if he is, that doesn't explain why he'd need Grand Leon's permission," Isabelle said. "More to the point, what can Grand Leon get my father that he can't get any other way, and how does he benefit from being legally dead?"

"Maybe it's because dead people don't pay taxes," Marie said.

Isabelle snorted. "If Grand Leon could put an occupancy tax on graves he would."

Marie opened her trunk. "They took my books, too."

"Don't you have them filed away?" Isabelle asked, tapping the side of her head. Books were the one thing she wished she could memorize.

"It's not the same thing as rereading them," Marie said. "I remember what my senses tell me, but I don't remember things I only imagine. Books take me out of myself. It's amazing that the same words are different stories every time."

"Oh," Isabelle said, ashamed that she hadn't known this. "I'm sorry."

"At least my books were relatively inexpensive."

"You mean cheap and lewd," Isabelle said wryly. Marie had a fondness for skirt-lifting romances.

"I sometime read your books . . . when I can't get to sleep any other way."

Isabelle snorted. "What about you. Did you find B?"

"Her name is Brunela," Marie said, and handed over the blood cipher. "She knew what this was, and she agreed to your test. Plus there was a certain family resemblance."

Isabelle examined the cipher. "She even knows how to use the cipher, she's already set her name in the matrix." Isabelle reached into her sky chest. "At least Serge and Roland didn't find the compartment. I should have put the journal in here."

"You didn't know what they were after," Marie said.

Isabelle came up with a whole box of blood ciphers. "I still wish I'd thought of it." Such was the utility of hindsight.

She tipped the box out onto her writing desk like some heretical oracle casting bones. She twisted the clamp end of Brunela's cylinder and set it down amongst its peers. With a sound like whetstone gliding over the edge of a knife, fissures opened in the formerly unbroken faces. The carapace unfolded into four thin, insectlike legs, and the ciphers scuttled together in a softly clicking swarm. They crawled all over each other for a few seconds, then one of them raised itself to the vertical. All the others climbed up, forming two branches, then four, eight, sixteen, and at last thirty-two, a diverging tree of parents, grandparents, and so on through five generations. Isabelle bent to peer at the names pressing out from the skin of the barrel. "Lorenzo Barbaro, Fenice," she said, "same sire I have." She twisted a ring on that one and the whole family shrub shifted slightly. One cipher bug crawled down from the top to join Brunela branching off Lorenzo at the bottom. "Isabelle des Zephyrs, l'Étincelle."

"They're the Breaker's own toothpicks," Marie said.

"But they work." This confirmed beyond any doubt that Brunela was her sister. The certainty made her feel slightly disoriented. What would it be like to meet her? Would there be some connection? Isabelle twisted another ring and the whole tree collapsed in a rattling pile. Isabelle swept them back into their box.

Marie produced the locket and presented it to Isabelle. "She said this was a gift for you."

Isabelle opened the locket and her eyes rounded slightly as she took in the images. "Hello, Mother, Father. I guess now we know where I got this nose from." She traced Lorenzo's face, then blew out her breath and closed the locket. "What is she like?"

"Slippery," Marie said. "Manipulative. Jean-Claude doesn't trust her and I don't either. Aside from being your blood relation, we still don't know who she is."

Isabelle put the blood ciphers back in the trunk. "Did you find out anything else?" Who was this person with whom she shared a sire?

"She says she knows of Immacolata, but doesn't know why she's in Rocher Royale," Marie said. "She also says she's lying low and waiting for your father's enemies to become interested in other things, and she wants to meet you."

"Brunela," Isabelle said. "I want to meet her too." A sister in potential was one thing, but in the flesh was entirely something else.

A *rap rap rap* startled Isabelle. She whirled to find a fluffed-up raven perched on the sill outside her ice-glazed window. It bowed to her and swept a wing as if doffing a hat.

"We have a visitor," Marie observed.

Isabelle swallowed her heart down from her throat and jerked the window open.

"Bitterlich, what do you think you are doing here?"

"Trying to get in," he cawed.

"This is my bedroom," she said. "What do you imagine people will think?"

"That you are a slightly crazy person who yells at innocent birds?" Bitterlich ventured.

"I have a front door." She did not slam the window, but only because she feared breaking the glass. A dollop of snow splatted on Bitterlich's head. He shook himself off, gathered his epic dignity, and dropped toward the front of the townhome.

Isabelle had time to don her glove and tug her dress back into shape before bootsteps sounded on the landing outside her door. There came a very ravenlike *rap rap rap* on the door.

Isabelle opened the door and found Bitterlich there in his human-feline erstepelz, hat in hand, and looking so prim that she grinned at him despite her current misgivings. Had he been assigned to her? If so, for what purpose?

"Capitaine Bitterlich," she said. "What a pleasant surprise. Do come in."

Bitterlich arched an eyebrow at her. "What a difference a door makes." He stepped inside but did not shut the door, very proper. "What happened here?" he asked, a worried look crossing his face as he took in the general disarray.

"We received a visit from your subordinates, Roland and Serge."

Bitterlich's mouth opened and his whiskers drooped in horror. "Those villains? They didn't lay a hand on you, did they?"

"Serge shadowburned me and bashed me into a table," she said. "Then they locked me in the kitchen and robbed me of every book, pamphlet, and scroll in the house on the pretense that I might be attempting to abscond with privileged diplomatic material."

"That's horrible," Bitterlich said. "I assure you they are not my subordinates. I am generally on detached duty. They report to Capitaine Sabot, when they can be bothered to report at all. Their footprints all have grave-markers on them."

"They said you'd been reassigned," Isabelle said.

"No," Bitterlich said, and then paused as if it had occurred to him that he'd just caught his foot on a trip wire.

"So you were assigned to me," Isabelle said, disappointed more than anything. She had been a fool to think someone of his rank and position would have expended such effort on her behalf without an ulterior motive. "Does Grand Leon think so little of me that he has sent you to ensure I do not turn traitor?"

Bitterlich backed off a step and placed his hat over his heart. His whiskers drooped and he managed to give her a wet cat look without actually being soaked. "No, mademoiselle. His exact words to me were, 'Keep her safe.'"

"Why?" Isabelle wanted to believe him, a state of mind that called for extra caution. Grand Leon had thrown her off the proverbial cliff to the proverbial wolves beyond the proverbial pale.

"I do not pretend to know the twists and turns of his mind," Bitterlich said. "But he has often expressed a fondness and admiration for you. After spending yesterday in your company, I can see why. If I had to guess, I would say he fears your enemies, yet unsatisfied with your official punishment, would attempt to extract some personal revenge."

Isabelle settled into a bone-deep confusion. How could she be mad at someone for being ordered to protect her? If he had not been so instructed, she would be dead. Had he really enjoyed spending the day with her? Did it matter?

"Why didn't you tell me about your orders on that first day, on the way out of my audience? Did you imagine I would prefer the sense that you were stalking me?" That came out more harshly than she intended, but she did not want to be a fool.

"I . . . no. That first day, you were so upset. I didn't know anything about you. I didn't know how levelheaded you are. I was afraid you might lash out at any instruction that came from Grand Leon."

"What about the next day? When I asked what you were doing there, you said you were following Lael, not me." That was the lie that bothered her.

Still gripping his hat like a shield, he said, "I have no excuse for that except habit. I am used to working alone, keeping my own counsel, being a spy, not a bodyguard. Usually the people I'm assigned to are my enemies and it behooves me to conceal my orders. I apologize for not making my purpose and sanction plain."

Marie said, "If you are a spy, why were you assigned to be Isabelle's bodyguard?"

"Monsieur did not say," Bitterlich said, "nor have I figured it out on my own."

Isabelle folded her arms, careful not to let her spark-arm drift through her flesh arm, and tried to flush her emotions away. They were only confusing things. She had never been under any illusions that Bitterlich wouldn't report her actions back to Grand Leon. Making that understanding explicit changed nothing, and if she somehow forced him out, le roi would just send another. As Jean-Claude liked to say, "Better the spy you know," and Bitterlich was very useful. She just had to be careful not to let him inside her defenses.

At last she said, "I'm assuming you had a good reason for showing up on my windowsill."

Bitterlich brightened slightly at this change of subject. "Yes. As it turns out I had some success yesterday. I spoke to Monsieur Clotaire about the boots, and he told me he sold them to a Monsieur Elliot Odson, the son of a wealthy wool merchant."

"His family are clayborn?" Isabelle asked.

"Yes, and apparently he looked very much like his father before he took his rather unfortunate erstepelz, so not some noble's by-blow. The most interesting thing about him, from my point of view, was that he was a grumbler. According to his parents, he was unhappy that his family was snubbed in society, woolmongers being ineligible for titles."

"Just the sort of person who might have been tempted by the chance to obtain sorcery, but as far as Ingle's notes have been able to tell us, those techniques only work on the unhallowed. You actually have to have a Builder's node."

Bitterlich said, "I wondered about that, too, but who says being unhallowed only lasts one generation? One of his parents could have been an unhallowed by-blow and handed it on to him like their odd heirloom on your crazy aunt's mantel that turns out to be worth a fortune."

Isabelle considered that from a mathematical point of view and shuddered. "If that's the case, second- or third-generation unhallowed people are everywhere, which makes the consequences of this discovery even messier."

"Sorcerers do spring up among the masses from time to time," Bitterlich said. "They call them Blessedborn if they can't figure out who the noble father is. It could be they're manifesting ancestral traits, like snakes with legs."

"There are snakes with legs?" Isabelle asked, curious in spite of herself. She'd never heard of such a thing.

"It's rare," Bitterlich said. "I've seen pickled specimens. The *Instructions* tell us all creatures change over time. The legged snake is just the Builder's way of reminding us that things never completely forget what they were."

Isabelle asked, "Did Odson's parents know about the awakening of his gift?"

"No, and the last time they actually saw him was weeks ago. They said he'd taken to spending his time with the sort of people he claimed he didn't want the family name associated with."

"Señora . . . mademoiselle." Hysia had appeared just outside the doorway. She curtsied and said, "I beg your pardon, but there is a Monsieur Lael to see you."

Surprise lifted Isabelle's pulse up a notch. She hadn't invited Lael, but then their conversation yesterday had been rather abruptly interrupted.

Bitterlich's eyes rounded. To Isabelle he said, "A word, please, first."

Isabelle said to Hysia, "Have Lael wait in the library."

After Hysia took herself out, Bitterlich spoke in a low, fast whisper. "Isabelle, if I may. I know I have no right to impose on you, but this presents an opportunity. Lael's circle has been impossible for us to penetrate, but he seems very interested in you. If you could engage him—"

"And how much trouble am I going to get in for that?" Isabelle asked. "For someone as disgraced as I am, being seen in Lael's company will surely raise suspicions of sedition and treason. The noose may have slipped off my neck last time, but it left rope burns."

Bitterlich already had his hat in his hands, so he went down on one knee. "If you help with this, on my honor, I will obtain the proper sanction."

Was not the question of his honor part of the problem? Truly the lie he'd told her was small. It would have been insignificant except that the other side of the equation loomed so large.

"What precisely do you want me to do?" she asked, by way of testing the winds.

Bitterlich stood. "Find out what he wants from you. Don't try to be anything you're not, and don't commit to anything he asks, just be open to consideration."

Isabelle considered her options. What he was asking was no more than she had done in a day's work as ambassadress, and Jean-Claude's warning about Lael's character stuck with her. If Lael was a danger to l'Empire, it was her duty to discover it. Plus, a little bit of sanction could stretch a long way.

Moreover, she was curious what Lael wanted, and why in the world he wanted it from her.

"Very well," she said. "But I expect that sanction promptly."

"Yes," he said. "And take me with you."

Isabelle's brows knitted, perplexed. "How?"

Bitterlich put two fingers down on her writing desk and started walking them across the surface. Then with a sound like crinkling paper his whole body slid up along itself, as if he were pulling off a shirt, and flowed down into his hand, which did a swift pirouette and emerged as a bipedal mouse.

Isabelle all but gasped. She knelt down to observe him at mouse level. "That's incredible, though I think you would look quite a bit more dashing with a tiny hat."

Bitterlich bowed and swept an imaginary hat to her, with enough flourishes that she had to bite her finger not to laugh. *Caution*, she reminded herself, not that her back brain seemed to be listening.

In a very high, small squeaky voice, he said, "If you could drop me off just outside the room, I should prefer to witness unobserved."

Isabelle cupped her hand for him and he hopped into her palm, tiny claws tickling her skin. She lifted him up to eyeball level. "How do you get all of you in there?"

"Cheek pouches," he squeaked, puffing out his cheeks.

Isabelle rolled her eyes and went downstairs with Marie at her side. She set Bitter-mouse down in the hall. His form rippled again and his colors shifted so that he blended perfectly with the molding.

Isabelle shook off the amazed shiver she always felt at his transformations and strolled into the library. The window had been cracked open and a brisk breeze swirled like an excitable puppy around the legs of the man standing within. Up close and off his horse, Isabelle finally got a good impression of his stature. He was no taller than she but he possessed the sort of physique that attracted words like *paragon*. He was still dressed in what she could not help but think of as adventuring kit, leather and other durable fabrics in a variety of styles collected from far-flung places, well-maintained but worn from the road, and festooned with ornaments, each of which hinted at a story. He did not so much occupy the space as grace it. The scent of camphor lingered about him, giving him a somewhat medicinal air.

Isabelle, well aware that wickedness often wore the best clothes, blinked to dispel the impression of grandeur that clung to him. It didn't help.

Lael had pulled the cloth off Isabelle's painting of the great harbor at San Augustus and was gazing at it intently. Her pulse spiked a little at the idea that a man who had spent so many years solving puzzles might instantly recognize mathematical equations implied by her layout. And what would she do if he did?

"Monsieur Lael," she said.

Lael turned and bowed to her, the crimson cape covering his left arm rippling in the breeze. "Mademoiselle, I am tremendously relieved to see you alive and unharmed. I thought I had grabbed you and . . . I hadn't."

Isabelle said, "I recall feeling rather foolish at that moment myself. Fortunately I have other protectors."

"Builder be praised for good fortune," he said.

Isabelle said, "Allow me to introduce my friend, Mademoiselle Marie DuBois. Marie, Monsieur Lael."

"It's my pleasure," Lael said.

"Charmed," Marie said, in a voice so dry it could have parched a cactus.

Lael said, "I'm sorry I did not seek you out immediately, but the nature of the attack required I warn my people to attend their defenses."

It had not occurred to Isabelle to wonder precisely where Lael had gone after she'd fallen. "Do you have any idea who might have carried out the attack, or indeed at whom it was aimed?"

"No," he said. "I have more enemies than I care to enumerate, and any number of them could have conceived that atrocity. I've had dozens of attempts made on my life over the years, and the unfortunate fact is, unless whoever it was tries again, we may never know who they are or which one of us they are after."

Hysia came in bearing wine cups she must have just unpacked for the purpose. Everybody took one and wet their lips.

Marie said, "Is there anyone who hates you both?"

"Even if there were," Isabelle said, "that person would have no way of knowing we'd be riding together at just that moment."

Lael said, "I would rather look for common allies than common enemies. The former are more valuable than the latter. To which end I would like to invite you to a soirée I am hosting tomorrow."

"What sort of soirée?" Isabelle asked, for this was precisely the sort of thing she imagined Bitterlich would be interested in.

"A meeting of other like-minded people, the freethinkers, empiricists, and others unfairly outcast and derided. I intend for it to be a marketplace of new ideas, a living portrait of what society could look like were it not dead at the root."

"Dangerous ideas for outcasts to have," Isabelle pointed out. The soirée sounded fascinating on its face, except for the questionable motives of the host.

"All ideas are dangerous when they are first conceived," Lael said. "Imagine the first savage who put one stone upon another, wondering if his gods would punish him for upsetting the way of the world. In a hundred years his people might be building stone temples to the gods or raising obelisks in their names. You were unjustly humiliated and ostracized for trespassing on a ridiculous superstition. You must feel as if the whole world has turned against you, but you will find there are people who are sympathetic to your plight, people who have suffered similar rebukes for equally fatuous reasons."

"Such as being rejected for being unhallowed," Isabelle said.

"Or for being secondborn, or born a woman. Do you imagine that the Parlement or even the Aragoths would have been so harsh on you if you were a man? They did not have to think twice about tipping you into the gutter because they felt in their deepest hearts that a mere woman should not have had high stature to begin with."

Lael's observation struck Isabelle like a snowball to the chest, leaving a dripping cold bitterness that ran into her veins. "It was a Parlement of fools," she said, but she was not here to relitigate that humiliation.

Lael put his drink down and produced from one of several belt pouches a small, tightly wound scroll, bound with a red ribbon and sealed with a stamp. "The invitation stands. If the disaffected do not have each other, they have no one."

Isabelle accepted the scroll without comment. His fingers, brushing hers, were hot to the touch as if he had a fever, though he showed no other sign of it.

"It's taking place at the chapterhouse of the Esoteric Brotherhood of the Azure Flame."

Isabelle recalled the name. "Aren't they the ones who refuse to speak in statements?"

"Yes. They believe that questions come closer to the truth than answers do," he said. "A strange but harmless practice. Also, I'll let you examine my finds as they relate to l'Étincelle sorcery. I would have brought them with me but some are fragile and all are irreplaceable."

Isabelle's heart thrilled: now that was a temptation. She'd had almost no luck finding useful information about her sorcery. "Thank you."

He nodded. "You are welcome. I will warn you it's not much, bits of things mostly, sometimes without any context. You'll have to tell me if you learn anything useful from them."

"I will," she said. "Most definitely."

"In that case, I shall take my leave." He let his gaze take in the packed-up room. "I can see you have work to do, but I hope you can spare some time for my soirée."

"I have your invitation. Builder keep you safe from harm."

"Until the Savior brings you home," Lael said, completing the gesture. He bowed and took himself out.

As soon as the outer door shut, Bitterlich bloomed up from behind the chair. He tugged at his doublet and adjusted the angle of his hat. "That's quite an offer he made you, very personal and slightly mysterious, just the kind of thing a spy gives when he's trying to tempt a prospect over a line."

Isabelle was puzzled. "Are you saying I shouldn't examine his collection?"

"No," Bitterlich said. "It's just that's the way you turn someone. You start with a legitimate give, and work your way up through several levels of questionable offers until taking the last step into treason. Most people actually stop before they get to that point, but the spy doesn't care; he's usually playing several marks at a time, and all he needs is one."

"I take it you speak from experience," Isabelle said.

"Not like you might think. I've been recruited into treasonous plots several times now. For some reason people think a lone Seelenjäger in a court full of Sanguinaires must lead a miserable second-class existence and therefore be an easy mark. I just tell Comtesse Impervia what I'm doing and let myself get sucked into the enemy plan, then disappear right before the Thunderguard knock down the door."

Isabelle laughed. "That sounds remarkably like the sort of thing Jean-Claude would do."

His expression became grim. "Do you know what the bastards usually offer me to try to get me on their side?"

"Personal and mysterious," Isabelle said. "A new skin?"

He smiled thinly. "I applaud you. Yes. They offer me some exotic specimen, some amazing creature from a far-off land, just so I can kill it and take its skin. Some poor scared beast that's been locked in a cage ever since it left that far-off land. I try to give them to the royal zoological park, but sometimes there's nothing I can do but put the wretched things down. I do not take those skins."

Isabelle said, "I beg your pardon if this question is out of line, but clearly you have a lot of skins. How do you choose which ones to . . . put on?"

Bitterlich stared into some memory. "Seelenjäger custom demands we pick animals with a great deal of fight in them. The more of a fight they put up, the stronger the spirit. The whole point of the wild hunt is to get the beast to express itself to the fullest."

"You turned into a mouse," Marie said.

"It was a very lively mouse," Bitterlich said.

Reluctantly, Isabelle dragged the conversation back toward its original topic. "Did you notice that Lael has a bad arm? He never uses his left for anything."

"I hadn't noticed. That's a good catch," Bitterlich said.

Isabelle shrugged her full arm and her stump. "I've only ever had one working hand. I know what it's like to try to hide it. I twigged to it when he had to set down his wine to give me his invitation. After that it was obvious."

"Impervia will be interested to know that," Bitterlich said. "She asked me to say she'd like to meet you."

"Why?" Isabelle asked. What would Spymaster Impervia, the thief of secrets, want with Isabelle?

"That was apparently not information I needed to know."

Marie said, "Are you working for Impervia or Grand Leon?"

"I work for l'Empire," Bitterlich said. "The Praetorian charter is to protect and preserve the rightful monarch and ensure the peaceful transition of power to his designated heir. I answer to Grand Leon as his subject unless that obedience is overruled by my duty."

Incredulous, Isabelle asked, "And Grand Leon puts up with that?"

"Considering he wrote the charter, yes. He styles himself as an absolute monarch, but there's a problem with having all power concentrated in one individual. When that person dies, all power is suddenly cut loose. It's like a money bag burst over the Lowmarket; everyone in reach scrambles to gather as much as they can. That's not what Grand Leon wants."

Isabelle took another pull at her wine, recalling an old conversation. "He once told me that men must die, but an empire can live forever."

Bitterlich nodded. "Since I was made a Praetorian, I've noticed him investing quite a lot of his power in other people, establishing independent institutions that are chartered to l'Empire and not to him. He appoints people to the institutions and gives them certain types of authority, molds their traditions and culture, but he's set them up to exist without him. Whoever gets l'Empire from him is going to find themselves hemmed in on all sides."

"Thus allowing him to rule from beyond the grave," Isabelle said. "That's both forward thinking and utterly devious."

"So what's to stop the next roi from dismantling these institutions?" Marie asked.

Bitterlich said, "They could, I suppose, but that would mean shuttering the chancery, purging the admiralty, disbanding Parlement and a dozen other institutions that are needed to make l'Empire work." He plucked invisible institutions out of the air and tossed them aside. "He'd have to reduce l'Empire to a shadow of itself. Mind you, the world has produced such fools in the past, but Grand Leon is unlikely to pick such an heir."

"He's shown a distinct reluctance to pick anyone," Isabelle said, a fact that made every reasonable person in l'Empire nervous. "Civil war will dismantle l'Empire just as quickly as an incompetent leader."

"In Lael's case," Marie said, clinging to her point. "Who are you working for?"

"I am working *with* the Trefoil," Bitterlich said. "The problem being that Grand Leon has something of a blind spot when it comes to Lael."

"Likely to forgive him anything short of outright treason?" Isabelle asked.

"Say rather that Grand Leon tends to forgive him piecemeal. He forgives an infringement here, an insult there. Nothing ever accumulates."

"So the Trefoil would like to build a substantial case against him before presenting it to Grand Leon."

"If there is a case to be built," Bitterlich said. "Lael has been remarkably well behaved, which of course makes the Trefoil suspicious."

"And you?"

"It's my job to be suspicious, but . . . yes. I ought to have some sense of why he's here and why he insisted on a trial before Parlement, and why he didn't make more of an effort to win."

"His argument sounded superior to its rebuttal," Isabelle pointed out.

"That's not how you win an argument before Parlement. You do that before you ever set foot in the chamber, through bribes and blackmail, and all the usual tools of politics. Lael is surely aware of that, and yet he made no effort to swing any member of Parlement to his side."

"Exactly like I didn't," Isabelle said ruefully.

"Err . . . it's not as if you were given a chance to prepare."

Isabelle waved this off. "So Lael played exactly by the written rules, and not the unwritten rules. As if he was trying to show the process is corrupt, perhaps?"

"If it was political theater, who was the audience?" Bitterlich asked. "I wish I knew."

"And you think that audience might be present at his soirée, so you're dying to go."

"I was not the one invited," he pointed out.

Isabelle put on her innocent face. "Weren't you? He said I could bring a friend. He didn't specify which one, unless you want to go as a mouse."

"A mouse is good when I want to listen to people, not when I want to talk to them."

"In that case," Isabelle said, "you can come with me, and Marie can go as a mouse."

"Jokes like that are why you don't have more friends," Marie said. "I expect you two will want to huddle together and discuss your plans. Meanwhile, I have a mess to clean up." She walked out without a backward glance.

Bitterlich looked after her. "Is she always so—"

"Sarcastic," Isabelle said. "Yes." She was acutely aware that Marie had left her alone in private with an attractive unmarried man without a chaperone. A week ago this might have been scandalous. Right now ruining her reputation would be like trying to chisel graffiti into gravel. "So what is our plan tomorrow?"

"Circulation and conversation," he said. "I suggest you play the part of the disaffected diplomat, see what he's trying to sell. I'll be . . . I could either be the equally disenfranchised outcast, or I could be the hardcase loyalist there to keep you in line. It will depend on who else is present. I don't want to get my roles too tangled."

"Any idea who else is invited?" Isabelle asked. She had spent so much time working with foreign diplomats that she was woefully uninformed on local politics.

"The people he's had more than casual contact with are mostly clayborn merchants, lower gentry, unhallowed scions, and empirical philosophers.

Some are political grumblers. Some are radical thinkers. Some are social climbers. There's no single thread that ties them all together that I can see. He's also been very adept at avoiding any of Impervia's informants."

"Any sorcerers?" Isabelle asked.

"A few. Mostly landless scions. He's been generally avoiding the upper crust. The only message he's been peddling is the same one he brought up in Parlement."

"You mean the one that actually makes sense?" Isabelle asked. "Do you know what really bothers me? Most of my friends, my heart's dearest family, are clayborn. Now that Lael has gone and made a cogent argument in their favor, if he does turn out to be up to something nefarious and l'Empire puts a stop to him, then he will be the example every hidebound traditionalist points to when they are trying to rile up fear of the future. No one will ever want to be on the side of the villain Lael. It will kill any hope the clayborn might have of obtaining the rights the saintborn take for granted. Grand Leon has long discouraged his Sanguinaire from slaughtering clayborn to feed their bloodshadows, but he's never had the power to ban it outright. What if the next roi is less merciful?"

Bitterlich tugged at his cuffs in what Isabelle was beginning to recognize as one of his thinking gestures. "If the traditionalists don't choose Lael as their Breaker's prophet, they'll choose someone else."

"But it won't be Grand Leon's son. Not Monsieur's bastard. He becomes a repudiation of everything Grand Leon has done." Isabelle gazed out on Rocher Royale, a city on a cliff, a place that should not exist. "History will claim that Grand Leon conjured this place into existence in an act of sheer political will, but it's clayborn who figured out how to make it work. Commoners chipped the city from the stone, channeled the water, built the terraces and the greenhouses, navigated the turbulent airs, and did every other thing to actually bring civilization here to dwell on the edge of oblivion."

Bitterlich came to stand beside her. "You know it's fascinating just listening to you think out loud."

Isabelle discovered the futility of trying not to blush at Bitterlich's compliment. She supposed having an easy companionable manner and silk tongue were useful skills for a spy, but where were cold-water thoughts when she needed them?

Bitterlich said, "You're right. People will use Lael as example to stifle progress, but there isn't anything we can do about that, except keep fighting for the future and winning. It's been my experience that in any contest one-third will be for, one-third will be against, and the middle third will wait to see who is winning before jumping in on that side and pretending they were there all along. People want to be on the victorious side, even if they don't gain anything themselves."

"Pretending your way to victory," Isabelle grumbled. "This is why I prefer mathematics," she said, and then cursed herself for forgetting she wasn't supposed to understand mathematics. "I mean, reading about it. Proofs and all." Saints but she sounded like a dimwit.

Bitterlich's purr was unperturbed. "I liken empirical philosophers to people climbing an endless cliff. You must prove every new hold before you commit to it. Such discipline instills a strength of reason and a power of foresight that the winds of emotion find harder to shift. You published Monsieur Martin DuJournal, a clayborn mathematician, did you not?"

"I was his first publisher, yes," Isabelle said. After her nom de plume had become popular amongst the intelligentsia, she'd arranged for a publisher in Rocher Royale to handle his subsequent works to avoid drawing any attention back to her.

"Have you read him?" She asked.

"Of course," Bitterlich said. "I admit my comprehension of mathematics becomes confounded once the alphabet gets involved, but DuJournal makes the principles plain enough that I can hum along even when I don't know the words."

I could help you understand, Isabelle wanted to say, but as sophisticated as she had become, an understanding of the empirical sciences was still forbidden by her gender.

Bitterlich went on, "So you publish other clayborn thinkers: Deerbond and his processes of derivation. Berger and his alternate alchemical matrix. The saintborn have no advantage over the clayborn in the advances of empirical philosophy. Show me ten famous symphonies and I will show you nine clayborn composers and a thousand clayborn musicians. The same goes for painting and dance. The very fashions we flaunt"—he fluffed his black cravat for emphasis—"are designed by those who often cannot by law wear them."

"And you think I'm fun to listen to," Isabelle said. She could listen to him rumble on all day in that vein. Alas for caution. Now that the professional exchange was over, she ought to turn him out. Keeping him around for company only amounted to deluding herself about his intentions.

He picked up the painting Lael had been looking at and set it on a chair to better examine it. "This is your work?"

"Yes," Isabelle said, reflexively preparing to receive incoming criticism.

"It's beautiful," he said. "And it's laid out like a conch shell." He drew a spiral in the air with his finger.

A geometer's spiral. Isabelle did not say aloud. He was the first person to notice it.

"I've never met anyone with so many talents," he said. "You're astounding."

"I dabble," she replied. Short answers were best. She was less likely to trip over her own tongue, or babble. She ought to move him along.

"Tomorrow," she said. "The soirée. Don't forget to bring me my sanction first."

"Of course," he said. "If I may also suggest that you might be allotted a working budget commensurate with the responsibility of the duty."

"You mean a working woman's wage," Isabelle said wryly. "Yes, actually, I shall insist on that." Most women of her class would have been horrified at the idea of accepting grub money, but to Isabelle a coin was just a number and addition was commutative.

"Considerably more than a laundress's pay, I should think," Bitterlich said. "If we must value work with coin, danger and intrigue must fetch a premium."

Isabelle looked sideways at him. "Usually, the employer's agent tries to bargain the cost of services down."

"Which is why I'm not a man of business," Bitterlich said. "My priorities are all askew."

"One more thing," Isabelle said. "Given the way Grand Leon thinks, if he didn't want you to save me *from* something, he wanted you to save me *for* something. I'd like to know what." She'd spent the last year being a servant of le roi's purpose. She wouldn't go back to being a mere pawn.

Bitterlich's eyes narrowed. "I will see what I can do. Builder keep you, Isabelle."

"Until the Savior comes," she said.

When he'd gone, she returned to the painting, feeling light-headed and more than a little silly. Yes, he was a spy, but everyone in Rocher Royale was a spy for someone else. And he had saved her life. He'd been perfectly polite and professional, and somehow she'd turned into a jumpy twit. Imagine what would happen if he actually tried to seduce her.

On second thought, don't imagine that. Just think cold thoughts, or better yet do something. She blew out a long breath and then climbed the stairs to help Marie pack.

CHAPTER

Fourteen

By the time Jean-Claude arrived in the Lowmarket, the Solar had begun to dissolve into the upper haze of the deep sky horizon. At this point in the craton's spin, the Solar set would be well antiwise of Rocher Royale, nearly parallel to the Towering Coast, its slanting rays delivering only a beggar's share of light and warmth to the stony city.

Jean-Claude set out to find Sedgwick. There was no guarantee the dwarf would have lingered around the Lowmarket, but there had to be a reason he and Mistwaithe had chosen that area for their auction in the first place. Likely it was where they knew best and where their friends were.

The market was, if possible, even more crowded than it had been two days ago when the bloodshadow slaughter had occurred. Even the Golden Swain was open for business despite the calamity that had taken place there, because what choice did the proprietor have?

Jean-Claude began canvassing the shop owners who were generally keenest on gossip, but was getting nowhere until a dwarf child ran up beside him.

"Monsieur, Monsieur! A message for you!"

"Eh? From whom?" Jean-Claude said. He hoped it might be Sedgwick, but that was not actually implied by this selection of messenger.

"Earl Mistwaithe, come on," chirped the young one, and hurried off into the crowd.

Hope leapt up in Jean-Claude's breast, but he stuffed it back in its barrel. It would be amazing to find the Goldentongue alive, too amazing by half for Jean-Claude's taste. He cued his mount to follow the urchin at a brisk walk but checked his weapons in their sheaths and kept a chary eye on the crowd and the rooftops. Yet his escort waited for him at each corner and did not lead him down any narrow side streets or blind alleys.

The urchin seemed immune to the normal impediments of city movement, bobbing and swimming through traffic as if it wasn't there. It was only after he stepped in a puddle and didn't make a splash that Jean-Claude twigged to the trick. Goldentongue indeed; the urchin was an illusion. Could anyone else see the child, or was this all in his head? The idea that this deception was actually evidence the message was not a lie made his head hurt.

The urchin led him at last to a small square that existed primarily to contain one of the city's many fountains. In one corner was parked the dwarf acrobats' wagon. The dwarves themselves milled about mundane tasks like fetching buckets from the well for the two bored-looking mules hitched to the front of the wallowing, bow-sided wagon.

The dwarf child skipped to the back of the wagon, opened the narrow door, and hopped inside. None of the adults paid him any mind. Could they not see him, or were they illusions, too?

"Ho the wagon," Jean-Claude said, approaching cautiously, though what good it would do to remain alert when anything he saw, including the ground beneath his feet, might prove false was hard to judge.

A dwarf acrobat looked up from the business of braiding a rope, regarded Jean-Claude with sullen eyes, and jerked his nose toward the back of the cart.

Jean-Claude dismounted, approached the wagon, and knocked.

"Come in, Monsieur Shenanigans," came a familiar sardonic voice. Sedgwick, or else an illusory imitation. Yet who else would name him that?

Jean-Claude peered into the wagon. There was a narrow corridor down the center and stowage on either side, crates lashed down as they would be on a ship, an alchemical stove in one corner and netting above holding bundles of clothes, bags of beans and rice, and other supplies. There were tools for working wood and leather and even spare timbers for wagon repair. There was only one bench here where people might sit, and it looked like it might fold out into a bed. Across the very front of the wagon a curtain had been drawn. The illusory dwarf child had vanished.

Jean-Claude considered the logistics that the wagon implied, assuming it wasn't all fakery. He squeezed inside, wincing as his wounded arm scraped the door post. "I'm here. Show yourself."

"As you command." The curtain drew back theatrically. Sitting on the far side was Sedgwick, though not as Jean-Claude had first met him. His doublet was clean and mended, all the details picked out in thread of gold. Every pure-gold button gleamed. His twisted spine was straightened, and his off-centered eyes were leveled out. His skin was flawless and his hair a mass of golden curls. What's more, the wagon changed without changing. All the wood was polished, the beat-up leather seats mended and soft, and the air light and fresh. Yet when Jean-Claude took his eyes off Sedgwick to examine the refurbished structure, it all went back to being shabby and worn.

"Gahh, stop that," Jean-Claude said, closing his eyes and rubbing them.

"Can't, gov," Sedgwick said. "It's the gloriole, I can't snuff it any more than a Sanguinaire can dye their shadow black. Fact of the matter is, I can't even see it myself, so I have no idea what it looks like to you."

Jean-Claude opened his eyes, and regarded Sedgwick directly. The effect was disconcerting. His brain knew it was being lied to but couldn't bring itself not to believe. Jean-Claude paused for a moment, putting things together. A good interrogator, like a good lawyer, rarely asked questions. "So your partner is dead," Jean-Claude said. "He was still alive when we were working over the Golden Swain because you still looked like a clayborn."

Pain gouged deep furrows in Sedgwick's face. "Yes. He's . . . he wouldn't have dropped the veil from me if he was still alive."

Jean-Claude softened his voice. "I'm sorry."

Sedgwick didn't look convinced. "So what do you want now?"

Jean-Claude said, "I need to know why the Harvest King wanted to kill him."

"First, let us discuss payment," Sedgwick said. "I am currently without a source of income and am in need of funds to buy skyship passage for a whole wagon and a set of mules."

Jean-Claude's eyebrows went up. "You're asking me to pay you to help me bring your partner's killer to justice."

Sedgwick shrugged. "Brandon always said, if you need revenge on someone it is because they have already cost you something. Do not pay twice for it. Besides, Monsieur Shenanigans, by helping you I am working in the interest of your roi, am I not? And I would hate to think his largesse is overstated."

Jean-Claude settled. "Of course. Passage I can get you, to any port you care to travel, assuming you can find a ship that's going there. Dare I ask if there's anything else you want?"

Sedgwick's smile became strained. "Not unless you can raise the dead."

"So tell me about the Harvest King. Start at the beginning."

Sedgwick leaned back on his bench that had become a throne in Jean-Claude's eyes. "A lot of what we did, Brandon and I, was brokering deals for other people, most of it's even legal if you squint right. We were in Port Luthon in Brathon, when a man calling himself the Harvest King approached us about making a deal with le Comte des Zephyrs. We were to offer le comte a cure for his disease in return for his wife's bride price. The price was right, the risk seemed low, so off we sailed to l'Île des Zephyrs. Brandon got an audience with des Zephyrs. Le comte heard the bargain and accepted it."

"What was the bride price?" Jean-Claude asked.

"No idea. It was something that le comte was supposed to understand."

"You weren't even curious?"

"We were being paid not to be. Besides most people's secrets aren't all that interesting to anyone but themselves."

Jean-Claude grunted acknowledgment of this truism, but it didn't help him now. The story he'd always heard was that Vedetta had basically been willed to Narcisse by her father. She couldn't have been happy about that; the most comely woman in all the Risen Kingdoms, foisted off on a poor comte on a remote skyland, and yet she had gone.

She and every other player in that game had been Kantelvar's pawns, but the clockwork artifex's favorite method of manipulation was to make deals with people. Might he have offered something to Vedetta to get her to play her part, to marry Narcisse or perhaps to bear Isabelle? But what could he have given her that the Harvest King might know and want to claim nearly thirty years later?

"So was des Zephyrs cured of the red consumption?" Jean-Claude imagined word of that miracle would have spread to the farthest winds by now.

"Not as far as I know," Sedgwick said. "A few days later, des Zephyrs sent us a message, said the deal was off, and ejected Brandon from l'Île des Zephyrs."

"Any idea why le comte went back on his word?" Jean-Claude asked, closing his eyes to get away from the damned gloriole. He could not imagine Narcisse des Zephyrs turning down a cure for his red consumption at any price . . . assuming he thought the cure was real.

"You mean other than being a two-headed snake?" Sedgwick said. "Brandon couldn't stay, and the first ship leaving was coming here, but I stayed behind to see if I could figure out what was what. I couldn't gain access to the château, and after a week I was about to give it up as a bad job, but that's when the Harvest King showed up on a Gyrine clan balloon, which is odd, because the Gyrine don't take passengers."

Jean-Claude leaned back against the ribs of the wagon. "Not unless they have an irresistible reason. Which clan?"

"Seven Thunders," Sedgwick said. "The balloon looked like it had been chewed on by a great fetch."

"What happened next?"

"I told the Harvest King what had transpired. He wasn't pleased, but he didn't seem angry at us, didn't even ask for his commission back. He just thanked me for our service and disappeared. I got on the next ship bound for Rocher Royale."

Jean-Claude pinched his nose. "So what was the scandal Brandon was trying to sell the day he was taken?"

Sedgwick sniffed. "A bit of spite. Small change, I think, compared to the rest. Catch."

Jean-Claude opened his eyes to see a silver disk tumbling through the air in his general direction. He started and very luckily caught it before it bounced off his nose.

As his skin touched the metal, the world faded away and he found himself standing in a narrow space, looking through a crack in a slightly open door. Beyond was a bedroom, one bed and two occupants. One of them was Isabelle's sister-in-law, Arnette, vastly pregnant and naked as the day she was whelped. She was scooted all the way down to the end of the bed, her ankles up on a skinny man's shoulders. Definitely not her husband. He churned her like a butter tub, while she made little gasping noises.

At least he can't get her any more pregnant. Was she already carrying his child?

Despite his best intentions, Jean-Claude's own groin stirred. Did he have to add voyeur to his list of sins, now? Pretty soon he'd have the complete set.

The skinny man drizzled a handful of coins over Arnette's stomach. The disks bounced and tumbled off her taut belly. Arnette gathered a handful of them to her bosom, laughing as if she'd won some wager. Some of them spilled on the floor.

Jean-Claude closed his eyes and forced himself to drop the coin. When he opened them again, the wagon had returned and the coin spun to a stop on the floorboards. It was certainly enough to ruin Arnette and cast doubt on the paternity of her child. If Grand Leon declared the whelp a bastard, it would be ineligible to inherit the countship. Jean-Claude knew better than to wish ill on a child for the sake of harming its parents, but the coin would have been quite a prize for someone wanting to put the screws to Arnette and Guillaume.

"Was that a true seeing?" he asked.

"Yes," Sedgwick said. "I picked the coin up off the floor on my way out. It touched both of them and it remembers."

"Where was it, and who was the billy goat?"

"At des Zephyrs's townhome. The man is a Gyrine Windcaller named Hailer Dok. He came in with des Zephyrs's boy and his wife about a week ago."

"Dok?" Jean-Claude asked. "Was he from the Seven Thunders clan?"

"Aye."

Jean-Claude's thoughts spun as the whole sticky conundrum shifted to revolve around a new center. Hailer Dok had sailed with the Harvest King, he'd accompanied Narcisse des Zephyrs to his death wish, and he clearly had some hold over Guillaume and Arnette. This was a man Jean-Claude needed to talk to.

"Do you know the Harvest King's real name?" he asked.

"No, nor what he really looks like; he was wearing a glamour charm."

Jean-Claude's eyebrows went up. "You can tell?"

"Not just by looking, but I pushed at him with my sorcery and encountered resistance. He hadn't offended me at the time, so I didn't push any harder."

Jean-Claude pulled on a leather glove and picked up the coin. It was tarnished almost beyond recognition. Almost, but what he did see made him very slightly dizzy. Above what looked to be the tips of a crown of feathers was part of a phrase: *ericordiam per—*

Jean-Claude was neither a collector of coins nor a scholar of history, but he hadn't suffered through Monsieur Soneaux's military history class without learning about *Misericordiam Peregrines,* the Kindly Crusade. If this was what he thought it was—but first he had to finish his business with Sedgwick.

"This gives me much to think on," Jean-Claude said, pocketing the coin. Had all the coins Dok drizzled on Arnette come from the same source? "But I don't see how this gets me any closer to finding your lover's killer."

Sedgwick stiffened slightly, and his voice came out strangled. "How did you . . ."

"You've only got one bed," Jean-Claude said. "You speak his name like a benediction. Your whole manner speaks of greater pain than anger. Or call it a lucky guess."

Sedgwick's eyes narrowed, but he said, "He was, yes."

Jean-Claude said, "You brought me here to help catch his killer. There must be something else you want me to know."

Sedgwick said, "The only thing I want right now is off this damned ledge before winter sets in."

Jean-Claude imagined Sedgwick probably had a hole card, but he wouldn't play it until he had passage in hand.

Jean-Claude said, "I don't have the money to hand you for a passage, but if you follow me down to the docks I'll give you a roi's mission. You get transport, the capitaine gets paid. Good enough?"

They were well into the clear cold hours of the night by the time Jean-Claude found a capitaine heading to Brathon and dragged him out of a losing game of hangman's bones. Jean-Claude had a scribe write out a listing for Sedgwick as le roi's messenger which any ship that wanted to dock in l'Empire was obliged to accept. Most capitaines actually liked them, for they paid a generous price.

"Satisfied?" Jean-Claude asked, handing over the passport and boarding papers.

Sedgwick slowly folded the paper and put them in his portfolio, then rested the leather case on his lap. "Indeed I am, musketeer."

"So why are you leaving in such a hurry, without even waiting to see how your revenge plays out?" Jean-Claude asked.

Sedgwick drummed his fingers on the leather case. "There are three names you should look into: Gustav Delacroix, Justine Leroy, and Hans Schmidt, three people with nothing in common other than being sorcerers who are occasional contacts of ours . . . mine."

"And what can they tell me that you can't?" Jean-Claude said.

"Where they are, for a start," Sedgwick said. "Gustav likes to haunt the Cock and Bull, but no one has seen him in a week."

"I know Gustav," Jean-Claude said, playing the Breaker's counsel. Gustav was the destitute fifth son of a minor family. "Never met a barrel he didn't want to see the bottom of. Most likely hiding from his creditors."

"But I know where he hides," Sedgwick said. "He wasn't there. Justine spends a great deal of her time draining the purses of her various paramours, but none of them know where she is."

"Maybe she found a new provider for the duration of the festival."

Sedgwick shrugged. "Anything is possible, but her rose hasn't bloomed for many winters. Most of her special friends are in it for the comfort rather than the adventure. Hans sent me a note that he was in town, but when I checked his lodgings, he'd disappeared without paying up. That's something he might do, but if he was going to scamper, he wouldn't have left his kit."

"So you think someone has a list of sorcerers, and your name might be on it."

"You're not as slow as people say you are. I have a rule about going missing. Always do it on your own terms, preferably before anybody realizes you were there in the first place."

Unease crept up Jean-Claude's spine and shivered against his neck. In a city like Rocher Royale, in a throng such as had gathered for Grand Leon's birthday, three missing people were less than a drop in a rainstorm. Three missing sorcerers, on top of one missing and known to be dead, was more disturbing. Jean-Claude had met sorcerers so insolvent that they even had to borrow begging bowls, but even the most destitute sorcerer had a place in the world. No clayborn could deny them succor under penalty of law. There was only so far they could fall, and not through the cracks, not for long anyway.

Yet, if there was someone preying on sorcerers, this festival made the perfect hunting ground. Everyone's routine was disrupted, and a person might go missing for weeks without anyone noticing.

Jean-Claude eased himself to the wagon door and opened it. "One more question, though, just for my curiosity. Is there a real Earl Mistwaithe?"

Sedgwick snorted and pointed to himself. "Or I would be if my family hadn't disowned me. I didn't measure up, you see." His grimace betrayed an old pain. "Brandon always looked the part, so I let him play it. I figured the title was mine to dispose of in any case." He deflated a little bit then and his gloriole washed the wagon with shades of melancholy.

"My condolences for your loss," Jean-Claude said. "May the wound heal cleanly."

—

Isabelle sat alone at a table in the corner of a shop selling kafe, a syrupy beverage that smelled like paradise, tasted like old boots, and made her teeth buzz. It was like a revenge drama in liquid form, bitter but exciting.

Isabelle had found herself surplus to needs in the process of getting her reduced household moved and settled in at la rue des Chapeliers. Restless, she'd commandeered Marie and Gaston and went to seek out Brunela. She was the only one in her small inner circle who hadn't met her sister yet, and she had so many questions.

She'd sent Marie up to the Smoking Bucket a few streets over to inquire if Brunela was in. If so, and if she deemed it safe, Marie would lead her back here. Otherwise, she would leave a message. Gaston was her lookout, and would bring word to Isabelle if anything went wrong at that end. She ought to have at least one more lookout, but Gaston was the only guard who'd thrown in his lot with the household after Isabelle's disgrace.

She was on her second tiny glass of the kafe when Marie drifted in with a hooded woman in tow. Isabelle came alert. The newcomer was tall and narrow like Isabelle with a dark green gown trimmed with white fur. Isabelle rose to meet her, and the newcomer lifted her cowl far enough that Isabelle could see her face.

Isabelle's breath caught, for although she had seen paintings of Fenice before, they did not do the Vecci sorcerers justice. Her face, long and lean like Isabelle's, wore a mask of feathers so close and fine that they might have been painted on. Jewel tones of blue and green shifted in the light, like ripples on a pond. Her eyes all but glowed green.

"Brunela," Isabelle said.

"Isabelle," Brunela said, and they both smiled slowly, as if some gleeful secret had been exchanged between them.

I have a sister. Isabelle had to break eye contact before she did something embarrassing, like giggle.

In hand speech, she asked Marie, "Anything suspicious?"

"Everything suspicious," Marie replied in kind. "But here we are." She took herself off to stand watch from a distance.

"Would you care to sit?" Isabelle asked.

They sat and Brunela said, "I'm sorry to hear about your ostracization. Alas that the appeasement of fools is a sure sign of a kingdom in decay."

"I'll survive," Isabelle said. "What brought you to Rocher Royale, or what kept you here after delivering your warning?"

Brunela made a noncommittal gesture. "Like you, I will survive. It's what I do. I'm here because my current patron is here, an individual who requires my discretion, which is the one resource I have in abundance."

"Can you say what sort of work?" Isabelle asked.

"I keep my employer alive," Brunela said.

"Bodyguard?" Isabelle asked.

"Something like that," Brunela said. She accepted a cup of the kafe from the vendor. With a soft sound like silk being dragged through a ring she withdrew her close feathers, the blue-green scales collapsing into hairs and slipping back under her skin quick as a frog's tongue. Given that her face looked perfectly normal afterward, Isabelle deduced the feathers must go to the same sort of sideways space that Bitterlich's other forms did.

"What can you tell me about our parents, about how we came to be?"

"Our parents hardly knew each other," Brunela said. "Which is to say, I hardly knew your mother at all beyond the few days we spent together ensuring your conception."

"Ah," Isabelle said, not at all sure how to digest the fact that the woman sitting across from her was, at some level, both her sister and her father. It had uncomfortable undertones of incest.

Brunela sipped the kafe. "You know, if you really want to know me and everything I know, I can give you my vitera."

Isabelle was stunned. "Your ancestral memories? I'm not a Fenice. No feathers."

"Children of two Fenice parents generally come into their feathers about the same time they achieve puberty, but cuckoos like you and me frequently do not express our sorcery until we receive a vitera-memoria. Lorenzo was counting on that to keep us safe, but now if I give you my vitera, you would have my memories, and our father's, and our grandmother's, and so on. You would know everything there is to know and it would be as if you'd known it all along. We'd be more like twins than anything else."

The very idea gave Isabelle chills. "I think I like my mind the way it is."

Brunela tilted her head quizzically. "Are you sure? I was told you are a seeker of knowledge. I have whole lifetimes to give you."

"That's not quite right," Isabelle said. "I'm a seeker of what comes next, of the unknown. A head full of other people's post-conceived notions would hardly be conducive to clear thinking."

"Your ancestor's memories, the everdream, are more like really vivid dreams than anything else," Brunela said. "You can enter them and experience the past as they did."

"I was under the impression you could only hand vitera down to your children."

Brunela laughed. "But you are my child, as well as my sister. And just think, you'd get to pass on what you learn to your children, if the Builder grants them to you, an instant education, and if your children don't have to spend twenty or thirty years relearning what you already know, then think what new vistas they could conquer. That's always been the problem with humanity. Every generation has to start over, but not the Fenice. We get to move forward onto new battles and fresh glory."

Isabelle had to admit, after the initial shock wore off, that the idea had a certain appeal, as did any dream of immortality. What could she do with a thousand years? Of course they wouldn't all be her years, they would be her children's if she was ever so lucky as to have any. Given her inability to enter into a marriage contract, she was most likely doomed to remain a spinster. And would she even want to impose on her hypothetical offspring that way, following them around and shepherding them their whole lives?

"To be clear, it's just your memories you pass on, not your personality or will. Yes?"

"The personalities are still there, to an extent, and your experiences flow back to them, so in a sense they have awareness. I guess you could say that being part of the everdream is like falling asleep and dreaming the future."

Isabelle tried to get her head around this. "So Lorenzo is there, listening to us."

"On the edge of wakefulness, hmmm, in a sense."

"Can you talk to them?" Isabelle asked.

"Not as such, but if you take an idea into the everdream you will certainly get their opinions."

Isabelle's curiosity tugged at the bit, but she pulled back hard on it. Caution was called for here. "If you gave me your vitera, I'd become a Fenice, feathers and all."

Brunela extruded her facial feathers again, a mask of shimmering green and blue. "Would that be such a bad thing?"

A little thrill raced up Isabelle's spine, for Brunela was certainly beautiful, and powerful. Even young Fenice were as strong as a dozen men, or so it was said. "But that's not the point. I'm already a sorceress"—she cast motes of light from her spark-hand—"and having two sorceries makes one an abomination."

"Or so the Temple claims," Brunela said. "The saints themselves felt differently."

"Do you remember the Saintstime?" Isabelle asked. That would make her possibly the second oldest person Isabelle had ever met.

"Sadly not, but I remember people who claimed to have been alive at the time of the Annihilation of Rüul, but even since my first birth, the Temple has become more rigid in its way of thinking. It clings to power, turning to faith as more and more of its hoarded knowledge is rediscovered elsewhere or rendered obsolete."

"When was your first life?" Isabelle asked.

"It was during the founding of Om. I was a foundling. Nobody knew who my parents were. Nobody even knew I was a Fenice until my feathers came in. I had no patron, so I worked for the temple for several generations, right up until the Kindly Crusade."

"Were you there for that?" Isabelle asked. History had a few generally agreed upon turning points, but few were as emphatic as the Kindly Crusade.

"Everyone was there for that."

The proprietor arrived and set down two more cups of nervous energy.

"Tell me about it, as one who was there," Isabelle said.

Brunela took a sip of the scalding liquid. "Before you can understand the Great Betrayal, you have to understand the politics of the hegemony. The Maximi had united all the Risen Kingdoms by force, but the coalition was fractious and unstable. They needed something to unify the people, a common victory for all to share and to form the seed of a new unity."

"So they decided to invade Skaladin," Isabelle said.

"That's where the historians start to go wrong. They look at consequences and presume incorrectly that they were intended. What really happened was that a Skaladin raiding party attacked a border outpost, wiped it out, and carried off a few sorcerers. Now this was nothing new. The Skaladin have been culling the saintborn ever since the Eldest Circle banished them into the Ashlands. But this time one of the people that got carried off was some nobleman's only son and heir. The nobleman didn't have the resources to recapture his progeny, so he turned to the Temple.

"The Temple didn't want to pay for an expedition, so they put out a call for a crusade. They whipped their followers into a great frenzy. The very idea of soulless heretics treating sacred sorcerers like so much livestock induced apoplectic hysteria like nothing I had ever seen.

"The populace rose up and demanded a crusade to liberate the cullborn, and who else to lead it but the Maximi? I remember at the time thinking that the Temple would have loved to see the Maximi march out into the Ashlands never to be seen again. What they were less happy about was an expedition that would drain their coffers and depopulate the lands around Om. Yet that's exactly what happened.

"The Maximi were made dictators by acclaim. They swore to march to the City of Gears, reclaim the treasures stolen by the Skaladin, throw down the tyrant, subjugate the populace, and rescue the cullborn from captivity. Loyal regiments were summoned from all over the goodlands, and the faithful swelled the ranks. They plundered the Temple's troves and carried off the wealth of ages. They were locusts upon their own land, but anyone who dared speak out against the Kindly Crusade was suspected of heresy."

"Did you take part?" Isabelle asked, fascinated.

"Of course. I marched in the vanguard all the way from Om. It was a chance for glory and conquest. Honor would be earned, legends born, fortunes won. I would go down in history, and being somewhat immortal I would live to bathe in the adulation of generations to come."

Brunela stared across the distant vista of her deep memory, the gleam in her eyes recalling passion, or perhaps rekindling it. "Pity the warrior who never faces a great enemy. Heroes need monsters to slay, and what monster was bigger than the Tyrant of Skaladin."

After a reflective moment, she deflated and went on, "Of course it didn't work out like that. The Gyrine betrayed us all at the Treacher's Coast, scattered the Vecci armada, destroyed our supplies, cost us our only chance to annihilate the Tyrant. Without the fleet, we had no hope of going forward, so we turned back and convinced ourselves that extracting ourselves from that mess would be seen as victory. Needless to say, we failed at that, too."

"You survived," Isabelle said.

"I was the exception. I was there the day Maximus Primus died. We'd been quick marching toward the city of Bladestone, which we'd sacked on the way in. If we could hold out there . . . well, we never found out. We were ambushed in the Spinehills. Primus was slain by a cullborn Sanguinaire, reduced to a soul smudge and left to burn up in the desert. I barely escaped, and by the time I returned to Om, the hegemony was already fracturing. Of course, you could know all this, this and dozens of lifetimes as if they were your own."

Isabelle shrank from this suggestion. She didn't like the idea of sharing her skull with anyone. "People already think I'm the Breaker's get. I have a Writ of Exception from the Omnifex that justifies my l'Étincelle, but it wouldn't protect me from being an abomination."

Brunela leaned back and withdrew her feathers. "Take some time and think on it. Our family's memories are your birthright, and no law or custom can keep you from claiming them."

Isabelle was glad to change the subject. "I will, and I thank you for the opportunity. For now, what happened to you, to Lorenzo? You don't remember dying, do you?"

"No, the vitera I inherited came out of Lorenzo's head before he died, and it only has his memories up to the point it was dropped. How much do you know about Lorenzo's death?"

"Only that he was murdered by Immacolata."

Brunela asked, "Do you know how a Fenice becomes a bone queen?"

"It happens when you get older. Your feathers turn to bone."

Brunela said, "Not precisely. The vitera symbiote will do literally anything to keep its host alive. If the human part of you suffers damage you cannot heal, the symbiote replaces whatever tissue cannot mend with much stronger stuff. You become less human and more Fenice. Sometimes the damage is caused by aging. Just as often it is caused by violence. In Immacolata's case, it was done to her with cold malice, by torture.

"In every war there must be soldiers sent forth to fight and die for the cause with no expectation of getting them back. Immacolata was chosen to be a weapon. To maximize her efficiency as an engine of death, her controllers gave her to the flensing worms."

"I don't even like the sound of that," Isabelle said.

"You shouldn't." Brunela paused for a moment as if deciding how to continue. "There is a ritual involved. The subject is bound fast and cut deep. The worms are introduced into the open wounds. They burrow quickly and multiply rapidly. They can strip a human carcass to the bone in just a few days. In the case of a fledgling Fenice, the symbiote replaces human tissue with Fenice thews and armor, turning her into a bone queen more or less overnight."

Isabelle's stomach soured in revulsion. "That's horrible."

"Thoroughly horrible. The practice is frowned upon even amongst the Fenice and only the most cruel and desperate dare perform it. They did it to Immacolata and then set her to kill Lorenzo and end his line."

Isabelle leaned back in her chair, as if that might get her farther from the hideous idea. "Why in all the Torments would she obey them after they did that to her?"

"Because the Fenice aren't gravebound like other mortals. There's no reason for us to ever really die. Before they turned Immacolata into a bone queen, they took her vitera, pulled it out of her, and stuck it in a jar somewhere. She'd do anything to get it back, to pass it on to some relative in order to be reborn."

"So if Immacolata was trying to eradicate Lorenzo's family, why didn't she come after you or me?" Isabelle asked.

"She doesn't know we exist. You were being born on l'Île des Zephyrs, and I was coming of age in Vecci, both anonymous cuckoos in unlooked-for nests."

"Then how did you find out about Lorenzo?"

Brunela said, "This is the part of the story you may find hard to countenance. In this life, I was an orphan growing up. I was told my parents had been lost when their skyship went down to sabotage. When I came of age I was approached by a man, a monk who told me of my lineage and my father's true fate. He told me Lorenzo had made a bargain with him, and he'd held on to Lorenzo's vitera until one of his children was ready to receive it."

A horrible understanding filled Isabelle's mind. "This monk, what did he look like?"

"He's been through the exaltation ritual. He was mostly made of gears and springs. He'd had both legs and an arm replaced with quondam prostheses, and one of his eyes," Brunela said.

"I knew him under a different guise," Isabelle said. "He's the one who cut off my arm." She rubbed the silver stump. He'd mended her wound with Primal Clay, leftover dregs of the stuff from which the Breaker had crafted the clayborn before the Breaking of the World. "I killed him about a year ago." And yet here he echoed back from a deeper time to make trouble again.

Brunela's eyes narrowed. "That was when you stopped the Aragoths from going to war. Was he involved in that?"

"It was all his doing," Isabelle said. "But you must have taken the vitera from him."

"Oh yes." Brunela tapped her head. "Lorenzo and all of our ancestors are in here. The unbroken chain is what the Fenice are. It's what we do. Denying it would be worse than suicide. It would be like killing our whole family."

"So you must have gotten the rest of the story from Lorenzo."

Brunela sipped her kafe again. Isabelle's had gotten cold, which was probably just as well because it was making her eyeballs rattle.

Brunela said, "The monk, or one of his predecessors, approached Lorenzo with a deal he couldn't refuse. Lorenzo knew he was going to die. He was alone against an implacable foe. His only chance was to make Immacolata feel she'd succeeded. So Lorenzo was to bed a certain Sanguinaire comtesse and get a child on her, in exchange for the monk holding the vitera in safekeeping. His enemies didn't know about his children, and if he died, the hunters would stop searching. He went to his death in order to protect us, and to carry on his legacy."

Isabelle took all this in. It certainly sounded like one of Kantelvar's twisty bargains. He always kept his word, exactly to the letter, and in such a way that the people he bargained with ended up worse off than they had started.

"So if Immacolata thinks Lorenzo's line is extinct, why is she still here?"

"Lorenzo planned to take her with him when he died. Clearly that didn't happen. My guess is she managed to catch him by surprise. She would have checked his corpse and found the vitera's nest empty." She put her hand inside her cowl and rubbed the back of her neck. "Once you've plucked your vitera, it takes a while to generate a new one. Immacolata would have guessed he'd tried to pass the vitera on somehow. She has to stick around long enough to be sure that didn't happen."

"So what evidence would convince her that we exist?" Isabelle asked. "I released nothing but those letters. If they don't touch off her powder, what would?"

"Another witness," Brunela said. "Some old rumor of our parents' liaison and the possibility of progeny therefrom."

Isabelle slowly turned the cup of now-cold kafe on its saucer. "Where did the deed take place and who were the witnesses?"

"When I, Lorenzo, was introduced to your mother, avoiding witnesses was my top priority. I met Vedetta here, in Rocher Royale. She was recovering from her previous miscarriage, which I have cause to believe was arranged by the exalted monk. She was waiting for the craton's spin to be right before returning to her husband."

Sorrow and loathing surged in Isabelle's heart at the idea that some other child had been slain to ensure Isabelle's conception. "So my father, I mean Narcisse, didn't know."

"Not unless Vedetta told him."

"Do you think she would have?" Isabelle asked.

"She agreed to keep it secret, but who can say how well that promise kept her? She had the Breaker's own vanity and a sharpish tongue."

~

Jean-Claude entered the navy yard that took up the best and most sheltered end of what passed for Rocher Royale's harbor and asked for Lord Commodore Jerome. He found him in the officers' drawing room at the naval chateau. Jerome had lost an eye and gained a head full of gray hair since the last time Jean-Claude had seen him, back when he'd been a mere capitaine. Though creeping up on fifty, he was still trim and fit, far more so than Jean-Claude.

Jerome and a half-dozen senior officers had crowded around a circular dice table, taking their turn at a game called Thrice.

"Lord Commodore, greetings," Jean-Claude boomed.

Everyone at the table looked up. Jerome's initial look of confusion bloomed into recognition and thence to delight. "Jean-Claude, saints be kind! How long has it been? Twenty years. Come come, join in . . . unless this is official business." He looked more wary than thrilled at this prospect.

"Official, I'm afraid, and private."

Jerome, being the senior man amongst his fellow officers, made a polite motion of dismissal, and all of his contemporaries gathered their money and decamped.

Jerome regarded Jean-Claude quizzically and said, "I heard you were involved in some kind of fracas down in Lowmarket, scores dead, and Prior Ingle at the Agonesium."

Jean-Claude snorted. "Nothing to do with today's visit." Or so he fervently hoped. "What I have for you today is an opportunity."

Jerome laughed. "Oh no. I know all about your opportunities. You're always at your best when you're selling a man his own boots. I think I shall decline the opportunity."

"You haven't even heard it yet."

"Correct. It's safer that way."

"It comes down from Grand Leon."

Jerome deflated. "So it's a mandatory opportunity, is it?"

"I suppose you could refuse. It'd be fun to watch."

Jerome grumbled, "Well, spit it out. It's been too long since I've had the deck swabbed of your vomit."

"Fortunately, this will not require either of us to set foot on a ship."

Jerome looked at him skeptically. "What, no mysterious cargo to be transported?"

"I'm afraid not," Jean-Claude said.

"No need to hijack one of our own ships? No suicidal run through an enemy fleet in the dead of night?"

Jean-Claude said, "If you're looking for danger, I suppose you might get a paper cut."

Jerome's remaining eye narrowed. "What are you playing at?"

"I just need some information about fleet operations, particularly operations that may have begun sometime in the last two days. Something unofficial."

Jerome rubbed his face. "Oh saints, this is some sort of corruption investigation, isn't it? I'd rather have the suicidal run through an enemy fleet."

"It was not suicidal; I'd paid off the lookouts."

"You didn't tell me that at the time," Jerome growled.

"I wanted to keep you focused," Jean-Claude said. "Has anyone started shifting a great deal of freight around in the last few days?"

"It's a naval base," Jerome said. "Shipping and unshipping supplies is what we do. Right now with all the birthday traffic we've got our hands full just keeping the picket ships and the outlying sentries up and running." He paused, as if struck by a thought. "Though come to think of it, Capitaine Cowe just got promoted to commodore, and he's pulled the tarps off the *Thunderclap*."

"Would you like to explain that in landlubberese?"

"The *Thunderclap* is a new type of frigate, and by new I mean experimental, new aetherkeel, new orrery, new guns. It's been moored under tarps since last year for lack of funding. Cowe showed up with his freshly inked promotion yesterday and whipped the tarps off. His family's rich as cream and honey, so I figured he'd bought his promotion the old-fashioned way by paying for the ship."

Jean-Claude said, "That may be all there is to it. On the other hand it may not. I'd be interested in knowing more about Cowe's project, like where in Torment's teeth is it going?"

"Nowhere for the next few months. Even if he managed to get her rigged and ready to sail, we're about to turn face on into a threefold winter. In three weeks' time, every ship in port is going to be lashed down tight until we swing around out of the Twilight Circle."

Jean-Claude picked up the dice on the table and gave them an absent toss. "Surely the weather won't be bad every day of the winter."

"No, but even if you could sail, there's no place to go that you wouldn't get to faster and safer by waiting for the craton to bring you down into warmer skies."

"What if you wanted to go somewhere in the Twilight Circle?" Jean-Claude asked.

"Where?" Jerome threw up his hands. "There's nothing there but ice and more ice."

Jean-Claude pulled out the coin. It had taken him some time to buff and polish the silver so that it might be easily read. "I'd handle this with gloves on if I were you." The memory charm had shown no sign of wearing off.

Jerome put on gloves and his monocle and examined the piece. "What's so—" Then his confusion turned into wide-eyed disbelief. "The *Conquest*."

"I see you haven't forgotten your Saintstongue. *Misericordiam Peregrinus*, the Kindly Crusade. Unless I miss my guess, that's from the pay chest on the flagship *Conquest*." When people talked of lost treasures, the pay chest of the *Conquest* was the one they imagined, the wealth of a century in a single hoard. The way Jean-Claude figured it, Dok had found the treasure, but he needed le Comte des Zephyrs help to get at it. Des Zephyrs had used his death wish to get a warship for Dok, but what had Dok given him in return? Had he promised a cure for the red consumption? Jean-Claude would find the man and question him.

"You're joking. You've got to be. This is a hoax, another one of your damned fooleries."

"I'm not, and it isn't," Jean-Claude said. "Or if it is, the joke's on me. If I'm right, the man who dropped that coin is ultimately behind the sudden urgency in that ship being completed. So I want you to find out where it's going." He held out his hand.

Jerome handed him back the coin, his hand still trembling. "Yes, I can see that you would."

⁓

The stars were bright on the black inky night by the time Isabelle arrived at the quarters Valérie had rented from Monsieur de Gris. The place was cramped but clean. Despite the fact that there were only two rooms, Isabelle had to veto the assumption that she would get one all to herself. Rank had its privileges, but geometry had its limits. By her decree, all the ladies would sleep in one room, the two gentlemen and all the luggage would be packed into the other. Such privacy as might be required would be arranged by curtains and a certain level of selective deafness. Given that le Ville Céleste was known for having comtes and ducs sleeping in the closets, this inset was a luxury. Bless Bitterlich for the recommendation.

Gretl and Darcy had arrived just before she did. They filled her in on Coquetta's deteriorating condition and their helplessness against it. That was the damned thing about disease. It was an invisible intangible assassin. It couldn't be tricked, arrested, or killed. The Builder withdrew his protection and the Breaker took her due, and neither clayborn nor saintborn nor Temple sworn could appeal that judgment.

Weary but not sleepy, Isabelle lay on her cot, trying to clear her head. Her mind kept drifting back to her conversation with Brunela. The initial fizz of discovery had worn off, but the sense of connection had not. They'd ended up talking for the better part of an hour, just about life, and Brunela had such a great deal of life to talk about, dozens of lives braided together into one greater life, an anticipation not of old age and death but of rebirth.

Isabelle was generally suspicious of unverifiable claims, such as threats of Torment and the promise of Paradise Everlasting, but the Fenice lived what everyone else merely imagined, picking up the next life where the current one left off. According to Brunela, it never really became tedious, for the world kept changing.

There came a pounding at the door. Isabelle got up from the cot. She didn't know who to anticipate here. It could be Bitterlich or Jean-Claude, or it might be an enemy. The one real problem with these rooms was that, being cut into the rock, there was only one way out.

"Who's there?" Gaston shouted, approaching the door with his knife out.

"I am, you thunderous lout," came Jean-Claude's reply. Gaston sheathed his knife and Isabelle's nervousness transformed to delight. The insult was actually a necessary part of the exchange. If he'd been overly polite, it would have signaled trouble had come with him.

Gaston opened the door and Jean-Claude stumped in, looking bone weary, and rubbing his sore arm. Isabelle stepped up and hugged him. "I'm glad you found us."

He squeezed her, and she winced for the bruise on her back. He let go and looked around. "I knew which street it was on, and it's not a very long street." He eyed the rooms suspiciously. "Not quite up to the old standards."

"We'll be fine for a few weeks," Isabelle said, and Valérie appeared with wine and pastries that she'd acquired from a street vendor. They sat, Jean-Claude on a stool and Isabelle on the cot. Marie scooted up next to Isabelle. At an eyeball gesture from Isabelle, the rest of the house found other places to be.

Jean-Claude leaned back on one of the woven mats hung on the walls to keep all the heat from bleeding away into the limestone.

"Gretl told us you'd gone looking for Mistwaithe's partner," Isabelle said.

"Sedgwick," Jean-Claude said. "He and Mistwaithe were apparently go-betweens for your father and the Harvest King. The Harvest King offered to cure Narcisse des Zephyrs's sickness in exchange for your mother's bride price."

"What bride price?" Isabelle asked.

"That's what I want to know," Jean-Claude said. "I can't help but think she must have made a deal with Kantelvar, something in exchange for having you."

That thought loosed a puff of cold retroactive dread in Isabelle's mind. If her mother had perhaps been a less horrible person, Isabelle never would have been born.

Isabelle asked, "Did my father get his cure? That might explain why he'd changed his death wish."

"He did not," Jean-Claude said. "In fact, after initially accepting the bargain, he canceled it, which makes no sense."

Isabelle shook her head. "Something must have happened out there to change Father's mind."

"Guillaume might know," Marie said. "Or Arnette."

"They're on the list for tomorrow," Jean-Claude said. "Speaking of which, it seems Hailer Dok is cuckolding your brother."

Isabelle's eyes rounded. "He is?"

"I can produce evidence if required."

The idea was as amusing as it was appalling. "I wonder what Arnette's up to? She always was in charge of that relationship."

"Maybe she's looking to trade for better," Marie said, her ghostly voice drifting in through the cracks in the conversation.

"Better than a countship?" Jean-Claude asked.

"Better than Guillaume," Marie said. "He's about as useful as a doorknob on a tree."

"But Arnette would find it hard to give up land and title," Isabelle said. "She was always grasping."

"Maybe not so hard," Jean-Claude said. "I think I know what Dok is after, and it's possible Arnette's just looking for a bigger share."

"A larger stake," Marie said. "More stuffing for her purse."

Isabelle flushed. "Marie!"

"That was too good to pass up," Marie said.

"Exert yourself," Isabelle said. "Jean-Claude, what is Dok after?"

Jean-Claude showed her a coin. "Look but don't touch. It's got a memory glamour on it."

Isabelle pulled out her jeweler's loupe and examined the coin: a Fenice in profile, crest feathers and close feathers proudly on display. The words around the edge read *Maximus Primus: Misericordiam Peregrinus.*

Isabelle sat back heavily on her cot, Isabelle sat back heavily on her cot. "Brunela and I were just talking about this. Not the *Conquest,* but the crusade."

"You talked to her?" Jean-Claude said, alarmed.

"Yes," Isabelle said. "We took precautions. She was there for the Kindly Crusade, not aboard the *Conquest*, though."

Brunela had only touched upon the subject of the Great Betrayal. The Gyrine Windcallers had cut a deal with the Tyrant of Skaladin for a place in his realm in exchange for dispersing the Vecci Armada. So it was that a Gyrine flotilla ambushed the supply fleet commanded by Maximus Secundus, scattering the fleet to the winds and stranding Maximus Primus in the middle of a desert from which they would never escape.

A thousand legends had been born of that treachery, of the legions who pressed forward into the waste or the legions who fled, of supposed survivors, of curses laid upon the Gyrine for their duplicity. Chief amongst those legends was the one in Isabelle's hand. The entire payroll for the Enlightened army had been carried aboard Secundus's flagship *Conquest*. Special coins stamped just for the invasion, and special medallions for the capitaines and centurions cast from pure arcanite. It was the wealth of a century tipped into the Gloom.

Except there were always stories of treasure surviving, of treasure being spirited away, of treasure maps, and treasure curses. Every few years someone claimed to have found the *Conquest*'s payroll, but the storytellers always turned out to be frauds or fools.

"Is that a true coin or a forgery?" Isabelle asked.

"I'm no minter," Jean-Claude said, eyeing the coin afresh. "But if Dok and your father presented coins like this to Grand Leon as evidence they'd found the *Conquest*, he would have had them checked."

Isabelle handed her loupe to Marie to examine the coin. Isabelle said, "But why would the Gyrine want to involve l'Empire?"

"My guess is the Gyrine already made a try for it, but their clan balloon got chewed up in the process. They need a warship. A friend of mine in the navy tells me one is being made ready."

"Surely Dok doesn't think Grand Leon will let them keep the treasure," Isabelle said. By legend it was enough to pay off l'Empire's debts. Of course legends of that sort were prone to exaggeration.

Jean-Claude put the coin away and adjusted his seat. "I don't know what bargain Dok made with Grand Leon or des Zephyrs, but there is one certainty. Both sides will keep their bargain to the letter, and not a comma further. What interests me more is what did the Harvest King want with the *Conquest*? He was along on the first try. Is he still working with Dok, or did he get what he was after?"

Marie said, "If Dok is cuckolding Guillaume, do you think he's staying at des Zephyrs's townhome?"

"We will check that tomorrow. Tonight you and I are going to follow up some threads Sedgwick gave me and talk to a man who might know a thing or two about Hailer Dok. I want to have ammunition before I sail into hostile skies."

Isabelle watched them out. Between the Harvest King, Immacolata, Dok, and various des Zephyrses, there were too many players for there to be just one plot. The dance partners had all changed at least once, and chances were everyone had their own agenda, each working at cross purposes to the other. No wonder it didn't seem to make any sense. She needed to think about what each one wanted individually and then worry about how they interacted.

She fished her chalk and slate out of her sky chest, scraped all the names across the top. She'd just added in Lael because he was a problem on his own, when Valérie scratched at the door.

"Come in," Isabelle said, putting the slate down and rising to meet her friend.

Valérie, Gretl, Darcy, and Hysia all came in and curtseyed to her. "Mademoiselle, may we have a word."

Isabelle's eyebrows went up in surprise. "What is it you all have to say that you feel the need for this formality?"

Valérie said, "It's because we're coming to you with an official petition on behalf of ourselves and the household. We were planning on bringing this to you anyway, but what happened yesterday accelerates the need. Without your ambassadorial stipend, the household needs money; we have it in mind to start a business. We want you to be part of it."

Isabelle was unsure she'd heard correctly. "What sort of business?" Speaking of people with their own agenda; she should have known Valérie would find a way to save the household if she could.

"Ah." Valérie took a long wooden box from Darcy and opened it. "These."

Isabelle examined the pale wax rods. "Candles?" she asked, and then an old memory broke loose and stumbled to the fore. Not just any candles. "Are you out of your mind? Those things are poison! You know what they did to Xaviera." The smoke from candles such as these had rendered the then Princesa of Aragoth infertile. Her inability to produce an heir had nearly caused her to be pushed aside.

"Not poison," Valérie said. "Xaviera didn't know why she couldn't conceive, so she thought she was barren, but once the candles were removed she got pregnant within the month."

Isabelle clamped her mouth shut and forced herself to think. Just because the candles had been a nightmare for one afflicted by them unwittingly didn't mean they were bad. Fire could kill, but it could also cook. "So who do you think is going to want to buy infertility in candle form?"

Valérie and Darcy exchanged a look. Darcy rolled her eyes and made a surrendering gesture as if she'd just lost a bet.

Valérie nodded and returned her attention to Isabelle. "Any woman who has as many as she can feed already. Any woman who just wants to indulge herself or her gentleman friend."

"Every prostitute, everywhere," Darcy added.

Isabelle said, "How do you even know how to make these things?" They had been one of Kantelvar's special recipes.

Valérie said, "We gave one to Gretl. She figured out what was in them and tried several recipes."

Gretl signed, "It's been working for Darcy."

Isabelle's eyebrows shot up. "Darcy?"

Darcy turned a shade of pink normally reserved for sunburn victims.

"With who?" Isabelle asked, and why hadn't she been privy to the gossip?

"Gaston," Darcy said, lifting her narrow chin defiantly. "It's for research . . . and fun."

Valérie's response was dry. "It was more along the line of, 'Since you're going to be doing this anyway.'"

Darcy turned even redder. "It's so much better than the sheepskin, and my menses has gone for three months now, and that's a relief on its own."

"Really," Isabelle said. That alone would convince her to use the things even if she never got around to trying sex. "And what is it you want me to do as my share?"

"The mathematics," Valérie said.

"You want me to be your accountant," Isabelle said. Truly it was the lowest form of mathematics, consisting of addition, subtraction, and lying to the tax collector.

"It will bring in money," Valérie said. "Enough we don't have to break up the household."

"Money," Isabelle said. Everything came down to that. "Very well. I assume you have some numbers you want me to look at."

Valérie presented her with a thin sheaf of papers, which Isabelle dutifully added to her list of things she needed more time to do. There were hugs all around and the women retreated, leaving Isabelle's heart that much lighter. It was good to know that whatever happened to Isabelle, her people were not helpless or lost.

—

The night had closed in. Low threatening clouds glowed a dull yellow in the reflected light of the city. Jean-Claude and Marie paused beneath a fishwife's awning to slurp down bowls of all-week stew.

Jean-Claude had impressed on Marie the need to make frequent stops in one's ambulations, and not just because he was an old man with a game leg. You had to stop and look behind for anyone who might be following you. You had to stop and watch people and feel the mood of the city. You also had to take it as a duty to be well fed and rested whenever possible because you never knew when it wouldn't be possible.

A night of walking around Rocher Royale, talking to people who knew people who thought they had seen things had left Jean-Claude more tense and restless than he had been when he started. He and Marie had scoured the city for Sedgwick's friends and heard only accounts of missed engagements and late payments.

"What do you think it means?" Marie asked, her head bent next to Jean-Claude's.

"It means a lot of people aren't where they usually are," Jean-Claude said. "Until we actually find one of them, it will be hard to know why."

The wind whipped through the narrow street, bringing with it the fetid smell of the sky docks and the lighting tang of the deep sky.

Jean-Claude put down his bowl and stood. He almost wished someone had been following them, stalking them throughout the day. If they had an enemy, they could lay an ambush and catch a prize but they seemed to be condemned to chasing ghosts.

"What now?" Marie asked.

"One more man to talk to."

They walked through the lower city. Flotillas of alchemical lanterns made Rocher Royale's main thoroughfares a river of orange and yellow light dappled with ever shifting shadows. Every intersection had turned into a small market, with musicians, vendors, celebrants, and pickpockets of every shape and speaking every language. One could not escape the skirl of pipes and the hammer of drums down the whole length of the city.

"Who is this man?" Marie asked

"Jackhand Djordji. He used to be a King's Own Musketeer, now he's an Old Hand."

"Is that a title?" Marie asked.

Jean-Claude snorted. "It's more a term of respect."

"For age and wisdom?"

"Let me put it to you this way, when the imperial treasury sends out its payroll, the Old Hands get their pensions before the generals and the admirals get paid." Their shop talk, long memories, and web of gossip made them the venerated oracles of the military class.

"What do we want from him?" Marie asked.

"Two things. First, Jackhand Djordji used to be Grand Leon's personal champion, the greatest swordsman in all the Risen Kingdoms by some accounts. He's the only clayborn I know of who ever bested a Tidsskygge in single combat." That vanishing breed of sorcerer from the fjords of Stalfjell were so swift they could outrun bullets. "With any luck I can talk him into training you to fight."

"Isn't that supposed to be your job?" Marie asked.

"My job is to make sure you get the best training possible. I know how I fight. Djordji knows how everyone fights. If there's a true seam of talent in you, he'll find it. Just let me make the introduction."

"And the second thing?"

"He's a Gyrine, jumped ship from them when he was a kid. He's never said why and it's best not to ask. He never went back, but he's no stranger to them, either."

"And you think he might know something about Hailer Dok," Marie hazarded.

"Right on the first guess. There may be hope for you after all."

"I choose to interpret that as friendly banter," Marie said, and Jean-Claude was not sure who was winding up whom.

The Kettle Street market stood off the main road leading up from the docks, just before the granite apron of the lower city gave way to the sheer limestone cliffs of the upper. It existed mostly to serve as a catch point for sailors and prevent too many of them from wandering up into the more genteel layers of the city. Two taverns, a gambling hall, and a brothel formed its perimeter while four score and some merchants scrabbled for territory and sales in the open center. It was also the unofficial hub for brawling, dueling, and other forms of rude justice in the lower city.

Jean-Claude and Marie strode under the boundary arch. A single lantern hung from its keystone, its desultory light shivering like a beggar without a blanket. A scuffle broke out amongst the merchant stalls, three toughs setting upon one victim. Marie's attention was riveted to the brawl.

"Don't watch them," Jean-Claude said.

"Why not?" Marie asked.

"Because you never know when a ruckus in one place is a distraction for some quiet skullduggery somewhere else. Be sure to notice a fight, but don't let your mind be part of it, unless you are the main attraction."

A crowd quickly gathered round to watch the show, and Jean-Claude pointed out the pickpockets working the backs of the excited crowd.

"So the man being beaten is an accomplice?" Marie asked.

"Usually. If these folks want to kill someone they catch him in a back alley and stab them in the kidney. No witnesses and less chance of getting hurt. They don't fight in public unless they want to be seen."

"And if you are wrong, and it turns out the man in the middle is innocent?"

No one in this part of town is innocent, Jean-Claude wanted to say, but that wasn't strictly true. Those who stole bread for hungry stomachs or sought refuge in intoxication were merely wretched. True evil nestled in the hearts of those with wealth taking what they did not need from those with little.

Jean-Claude drew his pistol and fired a shot in the air. "Halt, you bastards!"

The crowd scattered like leaves on the wind, combatants, spectators, pickpockets, and even the victim taking to their heels. Within moments nothing was left of the brawl but an empty space with a forgotten hat in it.

Jean-Claude began the process of reloading the pistol. It would be just his luck to actually need the thing.

After a moment, Marie asked, "How much trouble will firing that cause?"

"Not much. When the guards get here and find no bodies and no blood, they'll chalk it up to drunken revelry."

Jean-Claude finished reloading and put the pistol away. He turned his protégé aside from the square into a tavern called the Rusty Nail after the only thing left on its sign post after the plank had been stolen by some miscreant, oh, twenty-six years ago . . . all in good cause, of course.

Cracked stone pillars held up sagging wooden beams, and most of the furniture looked like it had been cobbled together from bits of other furniture that had been tossed from a high cliff onto sharp rocks. Most of the patrons were similarly motley, and every eye in the place swiveled to follow Jean-Claude and Marie as they crossed to the bar. Jean-Claude let his own gaze wander the crowd like a restless urchin, a random pattern never stopping anywhere long enough to be caught. Djordji had been old when Jean-Claude met him, though admittedly his definition of what counted as old had relaxed somewhat since then. Still, it would not have surprised him if the Old Hand had seen his last sunrise, except that no word of it had ever reached Jean-Claude's hairy ears.

At one end of the bar, in a deep-shadowed niche sat an old man with a tattered hat and a weathered coat. He puffed on a burlwood pipe, bright orange embers flaring up like the charcoal in a forge. Thin streams of blue smoke jetted from his nostrils, like the warning breath of some great dragon of old. A knot of uncertainty unwound in Jean-Claude's chest; Jackhand Djordji was still alive and even more eroded than Jean-Claude remembered him.

Jean-Claude leaned on the bar and caught the barkeep's eye. "Ale for me and the girl, and wine for the graybeard at the end of the bar."

"Money up front," the keep grunted.

Jean-Claude slapped a generous sum on the bar. The barkeep wiped it up with his rag and in due course produced two mugs of liquid that looked and smelled a bit like a horse had pissed in his oats, and placed a bottle of wine down in front of Djordji.

Jean-Claude played at sipping his ale, which was certainly better than drinking it, and watched the crowd. Marie did the same though without the pretense of drinking. It might be that Djordji was not receiving petitioners today.

After a few minutes and half a mug of wine Djordji ambled up and slammed the bottle on the bar. "Jean-Claude, is it? I almost doesn't know ye. Looks like you swallowed a fat man." His breath smelled of wine and ashes. "What happens to yar arm?"

"Seelenjäger," Jean-Claude said.

"How many?"

"Just the one."

Djordji spat on the bar in disgust. "One! One! Ye learns nothing what I teaches. Three together should never tickle yer beard much less cut ye shaving. Slit yer own throat in shame before ye sullies my reputation."

Everyone else in the bar edged swiftly away from Djordji, but Jean-Claude said, "Or maybe your lessons weren't as good as you thought."

Djordji stepped away from the bar and pulled back his scuffed and scratched coat to display the gleaming hilt of his rapier, slung for a left-handed draw. "Or maybe you're a spineless wastrel, a mangy cur to be put down."

The crowd's nervousness reached a tipping point and everyone not too drunk to move shuffled for the exit.

Jean-Claude tossed back his own jacket to reveal his sword, the seal of a King's Own Musketeer on both scabbard and pommel. "Feel free to have a go."

The general exit became a rout, complete with a cloud of dust. In moments the Tavern was empty but for the inebriated, the belligerents, and the apprentice. Even the barkeep had cleared out.

The old man and the even older man glared at each other.

"That's one way to obtain privacy," Marie said.

Djordji's gaze flicked briefly to the moonglow woman. "Who's the frill?"

"Mademoiselle Marie DuBois, friend of Isabelle des Zephyrs and my protégé."

Djordji snorted in genuine surprise. "A girl! I hears you go daft. Fool I am nay to listen."

"She's a survivor," Jean-Claude said. "She spent twelve years a blood-hollow before Isabelle restored her humanity."

Djordji studied Marie more closely. "So she's that one, is she. The Sanguinaire call her the Whiteshadow, say she's possessed by one of the Breaker's Torments."

"That's not entirely accurate," Marie said tonelessly. "I have no shadow, not a white one . . . but I like the name."

"And the Torments?"

"Does it matter? They will believe what they want to believe. I plan to spend no time whatsoever appeasing them."

Djordji laughed with a smell like someone emptying an ash bucket. "A healthy attitude."

Jean-Claude said, "She put two bullets in the Seelenjäger."

Djordji elbowed Jean-Claude out of the way to address Marie directly. "How?"

"With pistols," Jean-Claude said.

"Who asked you?" Djordji said. "It's her tale."

"The Seelenjäger came in through the window, Jean-Claude distracted it and told me to run," she said. "I got as far as the door, but when I looked back, the Seelenjäger had knocked Jean-Claude to the ground. It had completely forgotten about me, so I reminded it. I pulled my pistols, aimed, squeezed the trigger and didn't flinch. I hit it once in the chest and once in the head. When it turned to face me, Jean-Claude disemboweled it."

Djordji bestowed Jean-Claude with an annoyed look. "Knocked down, is ye? You doesn't even kills one by yourself." He poked Jean-Claude in the sore shoulder. "You 'prentice drags your lard from the cooker. When's the last time you has serious practice?"

Jean-Claude was not about to waste an hour letting Djordji harangue him about his lack of martial dedication. "The thing is, this was no ordinary Seelenjäger. We think someone has found a way to make sorcerers out of the unhallowed."

Djordji's eyes narrowed, and he blew out a long stream of sweet acrid smoke. "That's the Builder's patch. Best not to fool with the maker of all things."

"Which is why we're trying to find the one responsible, and for that we beg your council," Jean-Claude said.

"A Gyrine then, or why seek me?" Djordji pulled the pipe from his stained lips and jabbed the stem at Jean-Claude. "You ask me to betray my kin."

"I'm asking you to protect your kin and mine," Jean-Claude said. "A Wind-caller named Hailer Dok is in this up to his eyebrows, and he's hooked my Isabelle into it."

Djordji said nothing but pulled out a knife, scraped the bowl of his pipe, stuffed it with dragonweed, tamped it down, and lit it with all the ceremony of a sacred offering. He took a puff, and before long a haze of smoke had accumulated under the battered brim of his hat.

Jean-Claude relaxed into the bar, taking the weight off his game leg and giving Djordji all the time he wanted. Patience was a form of respect.

In due course Djordji said, "Hailer Dok. Whistler Aisling's boy. Seven Thunders clan."

"He claimed to be from the Black Rain clan."

"Ah," said Djordji. "Papa Wisest gives the sky to the Gyrine, tells us to forget the land and all its troubles. No more do we sow or reap but take our tithe from what's cast on the wind. So we scatters like dandelion puffs spin-wise and antiwise and across the deep sky. We sings up the wind, we whistles in the rain. We are kings of the sky. But to every kingdom comes a dragon, so they say."

He blew a ring of smoke and watched it tunnel its way across the empty bar before going on, "Years gone by, just after the time of troubles, Singer Dande of the Spinning Choir clan seeks to challenge the Mother of Storms, what you plowborn calls the Torrid Gyre. Where the winds curl tight they holds treasure in their fist, or so they say." His left hand curled into a claw.

"So the vote is taken, the capitaine appoints, the crew selects, and may the Builder guide you on the way. Weeks they soars, taking the bounty of the sky, they call up the winds to bring the aerofish for their nets and the rain for their barrels, they chases away the miasma, and watches the thunder chase the lightning across skies no other man sees.

"Confident in their songs and their strength, they enters the Mother of Storms, and the great spiral guides them toward her bosom. Around and down they glide, sure there's a skyland at the center.

"One night the stars go out. There's a cloud up above, a veil across the night, but not to worry the Spinning Choir, for their song is mighty and no cloud affrights them.

"Then comes the rain. Rain but not water. It's some foul ichor, black as the Breaker's heart, the blood of Torments gushing up from some terrible spout and falling upon them. Whatever it touches withers and rots. The silken bag frays, the ropes unravel, the wood rots, and the chains rust. Hearty men are aged to graybeards in a trice.

"The Windcallers sing, but the sky does not heed, the clouds do not break, the black rain does not part, the deluge does not stop until all hands are but withered bone, the bag bursts, and the Spinning Choir plunge into the Gloom. All hands lost."

He paused again to refill his pipe, then said, "As I know you plowborn wonder how the tale gets told if all hands be lost, but Windcallers speak to the wind and listen to it too. Before she dies, one of the Spinning Choir calls out to her sister in the Two Skies clan, a warning to all."

"Beware the black rain," Marie said.

Djordji cocked an acknowledging eyebrow at her, then looked at Jean-Claude. "Protégé, eh?"

"She's at least as much trouble as I was," Jean-Claude said.

"Not pissing likely."

"There's one other thing." Jean-Claude pulled out the *Conquest* coin and set it on the bar.

Djordji glanced at the coin, the merest flicker of the eyes. "Where does you find that?"

"Dok dropped it. Be careful of it; it's got a Goldentongue's memory inside it."

"And how does you know the outside's not an illusion, too?"

"No object can have more than one glamour on it," Jean-Claude said.

"Three hundred years that's gone missing," Djordji said. "Ought to stay missing."

"Is there some kind of curse on it?" Marie asked. Her tone was flat but her posture was eager.

"Is greed a curse? Is stupidity? The plowborn calls the wrecking of the Vecci Armada the Great Betrayal. We betrays the Maximi, they says. We betrays the Temple. We betrays the Enlightened, the Risen Saints, and the Builder himself." Djordji spat on the floor and then met Marie's gaze. "Even yer master there believes that, though he shouldn't. I warrant he never once asks why he thinks what he does."

Jean-Claude searched his mind for a reason and found nothing. "It's the only story I was ever told, unless you grace us with another?"

"There's no tale to tell, just one fact everyone forgets." Djordji puffed his pipe. "The Maximi don't unite the Risen Kingdoms in goodwill, they conquers us. Go think on that."

And with that, Jean-Claude concluded the audience was over. "As you say, elder."

Djordji tapped the spent ash from his pipe on his boot heel, then picked up his bottle. "Builder keep."

"Savior come," Jean-Claude said. Once the elder had declared the conversation was over, it was time to go. He and Marie stepped away. Jean-Claude only paused at the door to look back and say, "About that sword practice . . ."

"Challenge courts. Tomorrow morning. Sun up," Djordji said. Jean-Claude tipped his hat to the old hand and slipped out the door.

Once they were safely away, Marie asked, "Does he know the lessons are for me?"

Jean-Claude grinned. "I imagine he'll figure it out when you show up without me."

"Do you think he'll turn me away? Especially if he feels like he's been tricked."

"No, it was a good trick. He'll keep his promise. He will do his damndest to make you quit, but he does that with everybody; you have to prove you're serious. What he won't do is train you wrong, too much pride wrapped up in it."

"Or you could come too, and work on that leg."

"It's just a little stiff in the cold." At his age wounds took longer to heal. That was all there was to it. He wasn't ready for that farm just yet.

"Could you have taken three Seelenjäger without getting shaved?"

Jean-Claude snorted. "There was a time I would have tried. But dancing around with Djordji won't lop off twenty years or twenty kilos."

"It might scrape off ten."

Jean-Claude glowered at her. "I think you have this backward. I'm supposed to be the one haranguing you into better habits."

Marie paid his ire no heed. "Except you don't have to. When you tell me to do something, I do it, as a good apprentice should."

"Are you sure you wouldn't rather be apprenticed to a lawyer?"

"They won't matriculate women in the guild."

Jean-Claude shook his head. "They're afraid you'd take over."

They made their way into the upper city where even the cross streets were wide enough for a mule cart. Marie said, "I'm not sure I understood why the story of the black rain was so important."

Jean-Claude grunted. "The Gyrine are as superstitious as anyone else, only more so, and they pay attention to omens. They don't talk about calamities directly, lest the Torments take notice. The black rain was a voyage of ill omen, a whole clan lost. For Dok to have taken such a name is a sign of either desperation or madness, so what has driven him to that state?"

Fifteen

Isabelle hadn't intended to leave the rooms this evening but two unrelated factors conspired to change her mind. The first was infant Vincent, who had decided to start yowling like the Breaker's own Torments, making any sort of mental work impossible. The second was that Bitterlich had dropped by to update her on his investigations, and the idea of a stroll with him was not without merits of its own. She just had to remember that his allure was a professional façade, superficial and transitory.

They'd found a spot to themselves, out of the wind, in one of the cave markets that had been carved out of the Rivencrag. A forest of columns, each as thick as a house, supported arches that held the immense weight of the rock above. This particular venue held the stone market, high quality marble being one of Rocher Royale's only exportable commodities, and a competitive gallery of stone carvers and sculptors, the art having been refined to its sharpest point in a city of stone and fountains.

Isabelle huddled in her warmest cloak as she sipped from a goblet of hot mulled wine. Bitterlich simply pushed his fur out another knuckle length, which was cheating as far as she was concerned. It also made him look extremely fluffy.

"I have your sanctions and an advance against your expenses," he said, handing her a tightly rolled scroll and small bag of heavy coin. "I also asked Impervia for more information about Lael, so we wouldn't waste any time duplicating her work."

Isabelle opened the coin pouch, saw flashes of gold amongst the silver. Her heart skipped a beat, and she quickly closed the sack and wished she had someplace safer than on her person to hide it. "What did you find out?"

"Impervia has been tracking Lael ever since he left l'Empire. He spent more than a decade seeking the gift he was not given. He isn't the first unhallowed person to be obsessed with obtaining sorcery, but he took his quest farther than most. He delved into the quondarium archives in Om, he sought the city of Rüul, he searched for the Vault of Ages itself.

"Then, a little more than a year ago, l'Empire lost track of him." Bitterlich scooted around to do a better job of blocking the wind for Isabelle. "He'd been doing another round of research in Om, and then poof. Gone. He vanished so completely that Impervia thought he might have been kidnapped or killed. Eventually we got it from a smuggler that he'd left the Goodlands altogether and passed through the Gates of Ash into Skaladin."

Isabelle sucked in a sharp breath. It was heresy for anyone to have any sort of contact with the Skaladin, though for the clayborn that sin tended to be absolved by ritualistically rubbing coin across a cleric's palms. For a saintblood, even an unhallowed one, to trespass in the cursed lands of the first heretics was a mortal offense, even if one discounted the possibility of being ritually murdered by the Skaladin heretics themselves.

"What was he researching before he left?" Isabelle asked.

"Apparently, he'd been delving deeply into the Reaving of St. Skalexes and the founding of Skaladin."

"Why?" Isabelle knew the tale; every Enlightened child grew up with it. The Reaving was the first and greatest schism amongst the saintborn and the only one to have taken place amongst the Risen Saints themselves. Saint Skalexes, brother to Saint Guyot le Sanguinaire, had rejected the Eldest Council's decision to divide the saintborn into ten bloodlines. He and his followers had been banished from the saintly city of Rüul and driven into the Ashlands. As they passed the twin peaks called the Gates of Ash, the Builder had withdrawn his favor and the Breaker had stripped the heretics of their divine sorcery. The stricken people were driven into the desert by a great storm, never to be seen again . . . until Saint Skalexes's descendants resurfaced fifty generations later as the wicked and terrible Tyrants of Skaladin.

Bitterlich shrugged. "This is a man who has spent the last fifteen years digging up lost knowledge of sorcery. I suppose it makes sense that he might also desire knowledge of sorcery lost."

Isabelle frowned. "The Tyrant would love to do l'Empire harm, and nothing would give them greater pleasure than to use Lael as their weapon."

"Correct," Bitterlich said. "A month ago Lael appeared in Rocher Royale. We don't know how he got here, but I am reliably informed that sneaking into a port city in the middle of a huge influx of visitors from every cranny of the world isn't actually all that hard. He made his official appeal to Parlement, then spent a whole month bouncing around as a guest in the houses of the dissatisfied and disaffected while waiting for his trial."

"I didn't get a month to prepare," Isabelle grumbled

"Given that you once overthrew an usurper in a little less than a week, I'm not surprised they wanted to pile on while you were down."

Isabelle snorted, trying to imagine all of Parlement cowering before her reasoned arguments.

Bitterlich went on. "Did Serge and Roland take any of your unfinished manuscripts?"

"They took everything," Isabelle said, fuming. "Even my notes." Only after the words had left her mouth did she realize what she'd admitted to. Damn his purr.

But Bitterlich moved on smoothly. "I did manage to find out where Serge and Roland have been. Some friends of mine spotted them coming out of your family's townhome day before yesterday. That's where your brother is staying. I was hoping you could tell me what they might be doing there. I was under the impression that your father would not involve Guillaume in anything important."

Isabelle was happy to hurry the conversation down this not-about-me path. "He wouldn't, but this may not be about Guillaume. Arnette was staying there as a prelude to her confinement, and I just found out she's been cheating on Guillaume with Hailer Dok, the same Gyrine my father took to his audience. Serge and Roland might have been there with him."

Bitterlich frowned. "That doesn't bode well. Before I came to see you, I took it upon myself to visit the place. I found no living persons within."

A feeling of dread grew in Isabelle's heart. "No living persons implies there were nonliving persons." Not that she had any love for Guillaume or Arnette, but she didn't want them dead. And Hailer Dok was her most direct link to the Harvest King.

"There are three soul smudges," Bitterlich said.

The very notion of soul smudges made Isabelle's skin want to creep away, but she asked, "Who?"

"I have a guess, but I'd like a second opinion. You should probably come have a look."

—

They were met at the door to the townhome by a guard Bitterlich had posted there. No one else had been by or tried to enter. Bitterlich took her through to the kitchen. Three soul smudges oozed through the kitchen floor like blobs of oil soaking through bread. Their mere presence made Isabelle's flesh crawl and she knew from experience that actually touching one would suck all hope from her soul and bring a crushing wave of despair. Did they remember who they were, or could pain exist without knowledge, left behind like spilled blood?

Isabelle considered the context for the cursed remains. "The cook, the maid, and the scullion?"

"That was the same conclusion I came to," Bitterlich said. "Household staff tend to congregate in the kitchen when there's trouble with their masters."

"So what happened to their masters?" Isabelle stepped gingerly over the pathetic remnants and opened the alchemical stove. It was cold. She sparked it to life and left the door open.

"What are you doing?"

Isabelle gestured to the soul smudges. "They're attracted to light and heat, like moths only slower. This will put them out of their misery. I'm surprised you don't know that, living amongst the Sanguinaire."

"This kind of murder doesn't happen very often in Rocher Royale," Bitterlich said. "Grand Leon discourages it rather strenuously, sacred right or no. As for the masters, my first guess is that they were involuntarily removed."

"Not fled?"

"No need to kill the servants if they did that. This was a matter of eliminating witnesses. Also, the one thing Guillaume and Arnette can't do is disappear voluntarily. He has to be present to be made comte, and she has to give birth in the Royale Crèche."

"And Dok expects to be given a warship," Isabelle said, having filled Bitterlich in on that news as well.

Bitterlich said, "Plus, there were more scents in the main hall than could be accounted for by your brother's household, even with Dok as a guest."

"Anyone you recognize?"

"Several, including Serge and Roland, your brother, and Dok. There was also a pregnant woman—your sister-in-law, I assume—and several people I've never met."

"You can smell pregnancy?" Isabelle asked.

"And other bodily functions," Bitterlich said.

Isabelle considered asking him what she smelled like, but decided the answer would likely be mortifying.

"So who could have kidnapped two or more fully capable Sanguinaire?" she asked instead.

"Serge and Roland could, or anyone who could snuff the lights could rob them of access to their bloodshadows. Or someone just holding a gun to the pregnant woman's head, or her belly. We can speculate all day."

"Or we can look for other clues." She stepped out of the kitchen—it would take a while for the smudges to find the oven—and Bitterlich followed her.

Like Rowan House, this townhome had been chiseled out of the cliff face. A corridor ran straight back into the Rivencrag with all the rooms opening up off one side. The walls had once been painted white, but time and grime had left them in need of refinishing.

The dining room held nothing of interest, but the withdrawing room was furnished with family portraits in a neo-Agamanteum style. Modern dress had been replaced with mythical costumes and elaborated with iconography appropriated from the post Rüulic period. The exaggerated style had thankfully gone out of fashion a few years before Isabelle was born. Time and neglect had done an unkindness to the canvases, but the faces were still recognizable. It was her mother's side of the family, people Isabelle had never met. The ones who weren't long dead despised her father almost as much as Isabelle did.

Isabelle's gaze was drawn inexorably past three generations of ducs and duchesses dressed as heroes and heroines of myth, to the very last row of pictures where her mother ought to be, but the woman there . . . was her mother according to the brass plaque.

"But that's not possible," Isabelle said.

Bitterlich cast his gaze about. "Something amiss?"

She pointed at the canvas depicting a very ordinary looking woman who had Isabelle's long chin and eyes so deeply hooded they ought to have their own cult.

Bitterlich read the plaque, then looked at Isabelle. "I see the resemblance."

"But it's wrong," Isabelle said. "She didn't look like that. She looked nothing like me."

"Then she was less fortunate than legend would have it."

"No, I mean she was almost a completely different woman. She was beautiful." She fumbled open the locket Brunela had given her and showed it to him. He looked from the portrait on the locket to the one on the wall.

"I see your point," Bitterlich said. "Could she have, er, changed with age?"

"One's jaw does not generally shrink as one ages," Isabelle said, and if Isabelle had inherited this face, that meant this old grubby painting was Vedetta's true likeness, which meant her mother's visage must have changed somehow. Had she been wearing a glamour charm? Those wore off.

Bitterlich scuffed his boot on the floor and pulled the brim of his hat down as if to shade his eyes. "I'm guessing people used to compare you unfavorably to your mother."

"Used to?" Isabelle snorted, turning her back on the painting. "They still do."

"Could she paint a picture of a harbor in a perfect geometer's spiral?"

"She rather preferred to be the subject of paintings," Isabelle said. *Wait; the last time he'd called it a conch shell.*

"Did she ever step between two armies and stop a war?" Bitterlich asked.

He was trying to make her feel better about herself, but she really didn't feel bad. Her rewards were in results rather than accolades. "Technically I didn't step between two armies, either." It had just been a great hall full of angry sorcerers.

"Would she have stepped up to stop the execution of an innocent woman?"

"No, but—" Isabelle's mother had murdered innocent people every month to feed her bloodshadow.

"Could she have solved Holcomb's conjecture, and explained the proof in such a way that even a mathematical novice could understand the implications?"

Isabelle froze with another denial on her lips. He'd been trying to win her confidence, to make her drop her guard and admit to forbidden knowledge. "I don't know what you're talking about," she said stiffly.

Bitterlich said, "After our conversation, I went and cracked open my copy of DuJournal's *Adventures of a Mathlogician* and—"

"Stop," Isabelle snapped, and found herself shaking. Her nom de plume was one of her oldest secrets. Martin DuJournal was a shelter, a refuge, to which only two other people had the key. "You have no right." Saints, but she sounded like an idiot, or else one accused of some heinous crime. Secrets were all the more terrible for being precious.

Bitterlich's expression sagged and his whiskers drooped. He took a step toward her. She wanted to bolt, but he was between her and the door. He looked up into her eyes. His were the color of honey.

He went down on one knee. "I'm sorry for frightening you. It wasn't my intent even if it was my result. I don't have a good excuse for my curiosity. I don't have any right to your secrets, even the ones I think I know. I just wanted . . . that is, what I meant to say that the world is full of beautiful women, but you . . . you are a flame flickering under snow."

Isabelle's cheeks burned and she felt a little dizzy. A flame under snow. The purr in his voice shivered all up and down her spine. In a good way. Did he really think that? Did he really feel that way? About her?

Bitterlich stood back and recomposed himself, dusting off his impeccably clean sleeves. "As soon as I have you safely home, I'll deliver a report to his Majesty on everything we have and have not found. At that time, I will petition le roi to have me replaced as your bodyguard."

Isabelle blinked, stunned. "What? But you just said—"

"I don't mean to frighten you or make you uncomfortable. You aren't my enemy, and I have no right to any part of you."

Isabelle was flummoxed. She'd been afraid, so he'd seemed frightening. He'd made deductions, so she hid every part of herself that she wanted to share. Everything was backward and it was making her crazy. Jean-Claude said she shouldn't trust him . . . but no one said she had to distrust him either. There had to be a middle ground in there, a laboratory of wait and see where uncertainty was resolved by experiment and evidence.

Flame under snow. Who else had ever said anything like that to her?

She wanted to say something, but her mouth felt glued shut. She'd never felt this way around Julio. Julio was a wet blanket. She'd set Julio free and he'd just left. If he'd wanted to stay, he would have said something.

Say something!

"If you quit," she said, and realized she had no idea where the sentence was supposed to land. "If you withdraw, who will accompany me to Lael's soirée?" All her breath ran out of her at once.

Bitterlich tilted his head. "There's always Marie." His voice was laden with an abominable fae humor. She had a horrible feeling that was his style.

Isabelle lifted her chin and said primly, "Marie can't dance. Besides, the height difference would be absurd." She raised her hand to Marie's head level, which was well below Isabelle's armpit.

Bitterlich paused for a moment and then said, "Well, we must certainly save you from absurdity." He bowed to her again. "If you will permit me to accompany you."

"Yes," she said. In his case, it was a word she could stand to be saying more often. "But for now I need a different favor."

"Whatever you wish."

She led him upstairs to the bedroom, which was more suggestive than she wanted it to be. She pulled the heavy cover off the mirror in the corner, drew out the argent pontillius Julio had given her, and pressed it to the mirror. The reflective bead sank into the surface of the mirror like a drop of water into a still pond, sending out ripples into the glass.

"What is that for?" Bitterlich asked.

"Summoning Julio," she said. "I'm going to have him take me to l'Île des Zephyrs. I need you to guard my body while I'm away. No telling how long it will take him to show up, though."

"Of course. It shall remain safe with me and from me."

"I didn't think you would take advantage," she said. He was far too proper for that sort of behavior. "But I thank you for being explicit."

"What do you hope to find there?" Bitterlich asked.

Isabelle's brows drew down as she considered the notes she'd made about various people and their motives. "Several months ago, several parties landed on l'Île des Zephyrs, each with a different goal in mind. Everyone expected a deal to be made, a scheme to advance, and every single one of them was disappointed. I want to know why."

Pushing through a mirror always felt to Isabelle like squeezing through a wall of gritty mud. The stuff passed through her as she passed through it, seeping in through every orifice and pore, and leeching out again the same way. There ought to be a sucking sound and a loud plop as she finally emerged into the receiving room of le Château des Zephyrs, but the glass didn't even ripple.

She wobbled upright, clasping Julio's hand for support, and took a deep albeit useless breath. Her real body, along with her heart, lungs, and other essential organs, were thousands of kilometers away in the bedroom of her family's townhome. The form her consciousness inhabited now was an espejismo, a mirror image of her true self. The actual geometry of the switch was fascinating enough that she'd drafted a paper on it. There was new math to be had here, if ever she had time to sort it out.

Julio steadied her. Glasswalkers drew vitality from the Argentwash, the space between mirrors, and his espejismo showed it. He was always handsome in a brooding sort of way, but his espejismo was a paragon of physical perfection, strength combined with grace. It was how he expected himself to be. Did he ever find holding such expectations wearisome?

"Are you feeling well?" he asked.

Isabelle only winced on the inside. In Aragoth, people asked such questions all the time, and women were offended if their men didn't fawn over their injuries and illnesses. Even Queen Xaviera, who was the terror of the fencing courts and had led men in battle, had been known to engage in dramatic dizziness when it suited her.

"Just getting my bearings," Isabelle said, waving a hand at the room. It was the wrong hand. Her right arm was flesh and her left arm was spark, and everything in the room looked backward too. It was small but well-appointed with comfortable chairs and tapestries. Across from the mirror, a single stout door, iron-banded and locked from the other side, gave the receiving room a decidedly prisonlike feel, but the presumption was that anyone who could get here through a mirror could get out the same way.

"When you summoned me," Julio said, "I thought you might have changed your mind about coming to Aragoth. Instead you want to go to the one place you've spent your whole life trying to get away from."

"I'm not planning on staying," she said. "I just need to talk to my father."

"The man who tortured you both physically and emotionally," Julio said. "Why?"

"Family business," Isabelle said. She tugged the bellpull. "Thank you for bringing me, and agreeing to wait."

"I don't like sending you in there alone," Julio said. In his displeasure, his scar seemed to slither like a snake under his skin.

"He will say things to me he won't say in your presence."

A small window in the door opened and in peered a pair of eyes surrounded by wrinkles like ripples in a pond. "Monsieur, mademoiselle, welcome to le Château des . . . oh dear saints! Princess Isabelle, is that you?"

"Yes. May I come in, Master Denis?" Clearly news of her downfall had not yet reached l'Île des Zephyrs . . . which was strange, for surely Father would have brought it back with him when he withdrew from his blood-hollow emissary.

"Of course. Of course." The keys rattled, the lock clicked, and the door swung open. The chamberlain bowed them in, nervously double-dipping. Isabelle slid by him into the corridor beyond, scraping off Julio and forcing Denis to keep up.

Isabelle came to a halt at the first intersection. She wanted to turn right to reach the great hall, which meant she ought to turn left instead.

"What business brings you here?" Denis asked, huffing up alongside her.

"I've come to speak with my father."

Denis's eyes rounded, adding another concentric wrinkle to his already remarkable collection. "But he's not here."

Isabelle could not have been more stunned if he told her she'd been chosen as the next Temple Omnifex. "But he has the red consumption. He's bedridden."

"So he was," Denis said. "His long ordeal was a test from the Builder. He endured to the end without despair and just when it seemed he was to be lost to us forever, his body dissolving into his own shadow, he spoke the Builder's prayer in full faith and was granted reprieve, returned to us in full health."

Isabelle had no doubt that Denis was a true Enlightened believer, the sort of man who believed fervently in a deity that agreed with him on all major points, particularly those points that provided him more wealth and status than the fellow standing next to him, but in all her years at Chateau des Zephyrs she had never once heard him wax prophetic.

"How many people witnessed this miracle?" If le comte had enjoyed a recovery it was something of an anti-miracle, but then why use his death wish?

Isabelle and Denis arrived in the le Chateau des Zephyrs's great hall. The worst day of Isabelle's life had taken place here, between the two rows of white marble columns. Le Comte des Zephyrs had sat on the dais in the center aisle and used his bloodshadow to burn Marie's soul down to ash and turn her into a bloodhollow.

"The whole town witnessed it when he rode in procession from the chateau to the docks."

"But did anybody actually witness his recovery from the red consumption, that moment his shadow receded? Temple law says that to actually qualify as a miracle, the event has to be witnessed by someone who can testify before the College of Architects."

Denis looked stumped. "Well . . . I suppose it was Guillaume who was in the room with him. He certainly testified to the truth of it."

Isabelle glanced up at the portrait that stood by the entrance to the Grand Hall. Her father had always kept a painting of himself there, but a picture of Guillaume had been added next to it. Now that she knew what their mother looked like, it was easy to see where Guillaume had gotten the drowsy eyes and the hollow cheeks. It was less easy to understand how the reviled son's portrait had come to occupy a place of honor. What could have changed his status?

Isabelle put the events in order, and a slow drip of horror trickled down her spine. "This miracle. It was after he'd already reached an accord with Earl Mistwaithe to cure him, wasn't it?"

Denis's already stiff visage became waxen. "Yes. Le comte's recovery obviated the bargain."

A growing sick certainty drove Isabelle's reasoning forward.

"And he also canceled the death wish he made with Grand Leon."

"Of course, since he was no longer going to die, requesting a death wish was premature."

Cold as clay, Isabelle fixed Denis with her gaze. "I imagine Guillaume was relieved to find out he was no longer disinherited."

Denis took a step back, as if he knew he'd made some mistake but couldn't figure out what it was. "Well, of course."

Isabelle let out a breath at that last bit of confirmation. "Guillaume never should have known about Father's death wish. Father would have taken pains not to tell him about it. He wouldn't want him to know until the matter was a fait accompli."

Denis's face gave the impression of wanting to retreat and hide behind his head. "Well, you know how your father was, bitter and—"

"Was," Isabelle snapped. Very telling, that slip of the tongue. "Was, past tense."

"Was," Denis scrambled, "before his recovery. Yes. After his recovery he was a changed man. He was touched by the Builder."

"Hollowed out by Guillaume, you mean," Isabelle said, her usual elation at a deduction sucked away by the vortex of stupidity her brother trailed in his wake.

Denis drew himself up. "Mademoiselle, how dare you—"

Isabelle jabbed the finger of her spark-hand in his face. "Don't." Pink and purple sparks flashed and he flinched away, whether more fearful of her powers or her privilege she could not say.

"I will tell you what happened here," she said. "And then I will tell Grand Leon, and unless you want your name to feature prominently in that discussion, you will cooperate with me fully and without hesitation." This was almost as much a bluff as her powers were. She could turn this information over to Jean-Claude or Bitterlich, but none of her testimony would be admissible to the court.

"Several months ago a Goldentongue named Mistwaithe showed up and offered my father a bargain, a cure for the red consumption. He told my father he could be shriven of his bloodshadow. What precisely did he ask for in exchange?"

"Your mother's bride price," Denis said. "I don't know what that is, but your father said he could provide it once the cure was proved."

"And he never said anything else about it?"

"Not in my hearing."

Isabelle cursed her luck, but plowed on. "Then my father made his death wish to bypass Guillaume as heir and make himself the regent of Arnette's soon-to-be child, which would have been quite the coup if he could have pulled it off. Unfortunately for my father, someone told Guillaume about the death wish." The glower she gave Denis could have melted stone.

Denis made gurgling noises but did not attempt to deflect blame.

Isabelle went on. "Guillaume saw the countship, one thing in all the world he had ever wanted, the whole purpose of his existence, about to be stripped away from him forever. Being a hotheaded idiot he exploded, he barged in on my father and attacked him in his madness. No doubt Father fought back, but there wasn't much left of him by that point. The weak man overcame the weaker man, but for whatever reason he didn't finish the job."

"Weak man?" came a petulant voice from a niche behind a curtain near the door. Out of that niche stepped a bloodhollow. Once it had been a young man, now all transparent flesh and misty organs over white bone. It was dressed in the traditional style of an emissary, in a hooded robe with a long mantle white with a crimson trim. Guillaume's visage pressed out from the bloodhollow's face.

He said, "You should thank me, sister. I tore Father's soul to pieces, held him down and shredded him bit by bit while he begged me for mercy. When I was done with him, there was not enough left of him for the Builder to claim or even the Breaker to keep. He will drift forever in oblivion, a sob on the wind."

His venom nauseated Isabelle. She despised her whole family and would shed not a tear for her father, butcher that he had been, but that did not make Guillaume less contemptible.

"What have you gained for your fit of pique?" Isabelle asked, circling to keep both Guillaume and Denis where she could see them. "Not your countship. You have committed patricide, a crime for which there is no excuse. With the testimony Denis will provide, your wife and child will be outcast, and you will end your life starving in a cage overhanging Crows' Feast Square, spat on by the clayborn, and drinking your own piss to quench your thirst."

Denis squeaked in outrage. "I never said such a thing. Monsieur Guillaume—"

"Be silent, you sniveling wretch," Guillaume snapped. From under his robes he produced a pair of pistols. He leered at Isabelle. "These aren't as novel as a walking mortar shell, but they'll suffice to the need of putting down the Breaker's own bitch."

Isabelle stared into his small mad eyes to avoid being enraptured by the guns. She'd heard it said that controlling a bloodhollow was like operating a marionette with mittens on, but a pistol ball didn't have to hit square to be lethal. If he managed to kill her espejismo, she'd dissolve away in a silver mist, and her body lying on a bed back in Rocher Royale would just die. What a horrid shock that would be for Bitterlich.

"I imagine you could do that," she said, "but Arnette's not here to hold your hand. Do you even know where she is or did she stay with that Gyrine goat?"

Guillaume raised the pistols toward her face but his hands quaked with his rage. "Arnette belongs to me, and we are with the Harvest King. Dok and his cursed scheme can die in whatever hole they're hiding in. The world is turning upside down, Izzy. The Harvest King rises and the Tyrant Leon falls. And when the Harvest King is crowned, I will be standing at his side. Do you imagine me a mere comte. I shall be a duc or even a roi under the emperor of the world."

"If you believe that, you're a bigger fool than I thought," Isabelle said. Indeed, why would the Harvest King let an obvious scorpion like Guillaume anywhere near him? He must serve some purpose. "The Harvest King doesn't need you. You're nothing more than a prop, a stalking horse."

"He has the power to bestow sorcery, and to those who are loyal he will give it in abundance."

"You already have sorcery. Unless you mean to become an abomination—" The realization stunned Isabelle even as it fell out of her mouth.

"Why stop at just two?" Guillaume said. "Why not have them all?"

"Do you imagine he gives such gifts for free?" Isabelle asked. "You have nothing with which to earn his favor."

"I am his most trusted and loyal lieutenant," Guillaume said, in the tone of one trying to will a thing into existence. "He has Mother's bride gift."

"Mother had no bride gift," Isabelle said, hoping to goad him into revealing what it was.

"Oh, no. I know you too well, sister. This is my victory, and I'll not have you stealing it. I will have power like the saints themselves, and you will be food for worms." He pressed forward with his pistols outstretched.

Isabelle gritted her teeth, wondering if she'd hear the bang of the gun before a pistol ball tore through her head. Guillaume's grandiosity ran before a breeze of panic. Yet if he was a loose cannon, at least he was aboard the enemy's ship. He'd already betrayed his father and Dok. Maybe she could nudge him into one more act of treachery.

"Victory?" Isabelle asked. "Scapegoat is more like it. He'll toss you like a slops bucket when he's done with you, and what will you do then? I almost feel sorry for you, always on the wrong end of the trade, always following someone else around like a whipped cur. First it was Father, then it was Dok, and now it's the Harvest King. You will never know what it means to be in charge of yourself. Don't look behind you, but I imagine Arnette is already clawing at his codpiece, looking for a more substantial patron, and there's not a cursed thing you can do about it."

Bloodhollows were colorless, but Guillaume's face burned with rage. Perhaps she'd goaded him a bit too hard . . . or a bit too close to home. "You insolent bitch!" He pushed the gun at her and pulled the trigger. The hammer struck. Isabelle ducked hard. The pan smoked but didn't fire.

Guillaume stared at the pistol, appalled. How long had it been since he loaded that gun? How long had it sat in that niche getting damp?

Isabelle surged up and rushed him. She was big for a woman and bloodhollows were weak. He aimed his other gun and squeezed the trigger. She clamped her spark palm over the muzzle. The pan flashed. The gun bucked and backfired, blasting the stock to pieces. Isabelle's spark-hand evaporated to the elbow in a cloud of pink and purple smoke, and a galvanic shock buzzed all the way to her eyeballs.

The bloodhollow toppled backward, limp as a fallen flag. Isabelle clutched her tingling stump with her flesh hand and shook her spark-arm as if trying to put out a fire.

To her immense relief the jangling sensation in her bones finally eased and her spark-hand re-formed. It felt like a limb coming back to life after the circulation had been cut off, all stinging thistle needles.

Denis had fled, an action in keeping with his character. Guillaume had been knocked out of his bloodhollow at the first shock of pain.

Isabelle knelt by the bloodhollow's head. Its face was burnt, black char on glass. Once this had been a human being, somebody's son. Marie's experience told her that a dim afterglow of that person still remained, drifting in an endless void, enduring absolute agony but unable to think, or to know who it had been, or to die.

Marie was the only person Isabelle knew of who had ever been brought back from being a bloodhollow, but even if Isabelle understood fully how it had been done, this wretch would not survive the procedure. Its flesh was withered with neglect, its crystal skin papery.

Isabelle gave herself no time to dither or doubt. She drew her maidenblade with her spark-hand and pulled the bloodhollow's chin up to expose its throat. She stabbed the artery. Her blade met resistance, then pushed through, like biting into the skin of an apple. She leaned back from the spurt and pulled the knife sideways, bumping through the throat's gristle. The clear fluid that passed for its blood spread out in a wide pool.

Finished, Isabelle released the head and then turned away, dry heaving with reaction, her espejismo having no stomach and nothing to put in it in any case. She could not have done any differently, would not leave the blood-hollow to suffer, but saints what a horrible mercy.

When at last her body stopped rebelling, she rolled over and sat with her back to a column. Breathing heavily was as useless as retching in this imagining of a body, but some reflexes ran deep. She looked up once more at the portraits on the wall. There was a whole series devoted to her mother, each one slightly prettier than the last, until they passed some invisible frontier into the ridiculous. No one's eyes were really that big, or mouth that dainty. Isabelle had always assumed that these exaggerations were artifacts of the paintings, but what if they were real?

Kantelvar destroyed people by giving them their heart's desire.

"He made her beautiful," she realized aloud. That was the thing she wanted most. That was why Isabelle had inherited none of her comeliness, because her looks weren't in her blood but had been plastered on after the fact. But how? It wouldn't be a glamour charm . . . but there was another way.

Primal Clay. Isabelle found herself reaching up to stroke her silvery stump. The *Instructions* said Primal Clay was the secret St. Iav the Betrayer had stolen from the Builder and given to the Breaker. It was the stuff of which the clayborn had been made. Only dribs and drabs of it remained unquickened in the world today, but Kantelvar had possessed a reserve. Not only had he used it to cap off Isabelle's stump, but he'd used it to sculpt the face of a whipping boy into an exact likeness of Príncipe Julio's. He could have used it to mold Vedetta the face of her dreams. The fact that she'd kept changing, kept improving herself meant that she must have had a supply of the stuff: her bride price, and Guillaume had given it to the Harvest King.

Isabelle rose, sheathed her maidenblade, and strode from the room. Julio would be waiting, and Bitterlich, and Grand Leon must be told of her brother's perfidy. Would he believe her? Or would he believe that Isabelle was just looking for revenge on her family?

CHAPTER

Sixteen

The sky was bright but the Solar had not yet cracked the ramparts of the Rivencrag when Jean-Claude sat down on a cold stone bench outside a street vendor's stall with a bowl of steaming potluck. It had the consistency of pea soup and tasted brown. Good enough for men looking for energy rather than experience.

Marie was long gone to the challenge courts. Last night, Jean-Claude thought himself clever, sending her to Djordji, but in the light of morning it felt more like cowardice. She was his apprentice. He should be teaching her, but . . . He couldn't use age as an excuse; Djordji was older than he by a generation. Was it that he didn't want to hurt her? Well, that was true, but training bruises were things to be proud of.

Fool. You don't want to embarrass yourself. Five minutes of sparring and he'd be knackered. He wasn't good enough anymore. He'd taken too many shortcuts, relied too much on cleverness. Yes, battle was always a last resort, but he'd let the fortress fall to rubble. His leg was stiff and his mending arm itched madly. Nothing to be done about that, though.

Then there was the matter of Isabelle's brother. Isabelle had sent Capitaine

Bitterlich to report Guillaume's treachery to Grand Leon, but the kin slayer still needed to be caught.

"Monsieur Musketeer." Jean-Claude looked up as Sergeant appeared from the crowd. The city guardsman's protrusive eyebrows twitched like the antennae of some great insect as he homed in on Jean-Claude.

Jean-Claude swallowed another spoonful of the potluck and said, "Well met, Sergeant, what can the awful majesty of the law do for you today?"

Sergeant snorted. "I don't know about any nob-polishing majesty, but since you've seen to grant me so many fine gifts these past few days I have one for you."

"What sort of gift?" Jean-Claude asked, his curiosity piqued.

"I found the lie-mongering whore-straddling Goldentongue you were looking for."

Excitement flared up in Jean-Claude's soul until he remembered Mistwaithe was dead. "Where?"

"Atop a heap of bloody corpses."

"Ah, and how many are in this heap?"

"Depends on how you count the bits."

Jean-Claude sucked down the rest of his meal and wiped his whiskers on his sleeve. "Where are we going?"

"Turvytown," Sergeant said as they set off through the crowd. That was the part of the city that actually clung to the underside of the craton's lip.

The streets were no less congested than they had been for the last week, but unless Jean-Claude was mistaken, the atmosphere was somewhat subdued. The nonstop deluge of music had died to a trickle.

An itinerate Iconate extoller stood on a street corner, prophesying doom for those who did not reject the false light of man's reason for the pure truth of revealed enlightenment. He'd managed to draw a crowd. "Do not pray for le roi's good health, but for his salvation. Saint Yves the Unforgiven but waits to lay his saving hand upon le roi's brow and open unto him the doors to paradise everlasting if only he will yield and submit to divine command!" From the volume of the muttering that followed, Jean-Claude gathered that some raw emotion had been touched.

"Did something happen last night?" Jean-Claude asked. "Some ill news I've not heard?"

Sergeant glanced at the Iconate, spat, and said, "Toothless piss drinkers. Rumors is all. Word's come down le roi is sick."

Jean-Claude's heart near seized up. "Sick how?" Builder forbid he should have contracted the same shadow rot that afflicted Coquetta.

"Depends on which rumor. Could have caught the galfesters. Could have the white fever. More than likely the slack-skinned, limp-dragging old goat just had too much to drink and the rumor spread through the city like a fart in a closed room. Wouldn't let it worry you. We get the same shit-smelling mouth-noise every few months. By tonight they'll have him walking on clouds and slaying dragons with his cock."

Jean-Claude grunted, hardly reassured. The shadow rot attacked the Builder's gift, and that could not happen unless the Builder had withdrawn his mighty hand. So it was that such ailments were seen as a sign of corruption.

That grim thought followed Jean-Claude all the way down to the scuttledocks, which hung in the upside-down world of Turvytown under the lip of the coastline.

The scuttler skiffs, which specialized in hunting nethercobs and crackbacks, docked beneath the overhangs where the craton's rock curled over the edge of the aethercoral reefs like the crust of a pie over the edge of a pan.

Beneath this rim was suspended a vast web of rope bridges, hanging cranes, anchor points, and rope hammocks. Hundreds of scuttlemen serviced their long shallow skiffs, crawling, climbing, and swinging like so many monkeys over the endless drop to unload the day's catch.

Jean-Claude's vision swam and his gut heaved as he contemplated the rope bridge before him and the fatal fall below. Some ways down was the Miasma, a greenish mist that boiled with an internal life and stank of decay. Beneath that, the Galvanosphere wrapped the world in an everlasting thunderstorm. At the very bottom was the Gloom, impenetrably black and unreachable. The Gloom's nature was only ever hinted at by the few scraps of things that ever floated up from its murk: enormous behemoth bones, frigid night scales, jagged blight beaks.

The depths called to Jean-Claude, pulled on him. The platform upon which he stood was held up by nothing except rope anchored by spikes driven into stone. The wood seemed to bend and flow under his feet, tilting him toward the precipice. The creaking ropes threatened to fray and snap. *L'appel du vide* urged him to let go, to slip over the edge and fall forever.

"Musketeer!" Sergeant's voice penetrated the swirl of dizziness.

Jean-Claude blinked and shook his head.

"Doddering, flea-bitten cur, what in all the Torments are you doing?"

Jean-Claude clung to the ropes and tried not to look down. There was no way he was going to make it across the swaying, creaking rope bridge to the hub where the skiffs were tied.

Jean-Claude said, "I don't think there's any point in both of us traipsing out to this skiff if they can just bring it around here."

"Frothing, gut-griping gidgeon," Sergeant grumbled. "I'll see what I can do. Like as not they'll just toss the damn things overboard and to stink with it."

"Not if they want to get paid, they won't," Jean-Claude said.

Still griping, Sergeant crossed the wobbling rope bridge to a large skiff and started gesturing to the occupants, who set about unmooring from their berth. Like most such vessels, the skiff in question had a shallow hull that hung suspended like a bucket under a buoyant keel. Unlike most, it was a bonekeel, fashioned from the rib of a great behemoth.

In the time before alchemical aetherkeels had been developed, the occasional behemoth bone fetched up on the craton's rim had been the only way to make skyships. Their scarcity, odd and irregular shapes, and sometimes fragile qualities had left shipbuilding a primitive art for a very long time. To see one still in use today suggested a business passed down through several generations.

The skiffs generally lacked sails and instead maneuvered around the reef with push poles and grappling hooks like upside-down insects. The vessel in question crossed the inverted harbor with surprising alacrity, even making a few downward leaps. The crew pushed off the ceiling with poles and arced under another vessel before popping back up and catching themselves on the ceiling with their prods.

As was the custom, the skiff was brightly painted and decorated with a stylized mural, in this case depicting a man with a hook for a hand, and a trident fighting off a monstrous crackback with claws the size of a horse.

The skiff's capitaine might have been the man in the mural. His left hand was missing at the wrist and the stump fitted with a hook. Nothing, however, had been put in to replace his missing teeth. As the skiff drove in, he leapt from the gunwale, caught hold of the suspended ropes with hook and hand, swung like a monkey, and flipped onto the platform where Jean-Claude waited.

"Bless me black heart. Old Sergeant said he'd hooked one of le roi's own stickers but I never believed him. Capitaine Flandin of the *Laughing Gull* at your service, monsieur."

Jean-Claude levered himself up and tried to imagine that the world extended no farther than the edge of the platform and that none of it was moving. "Capitaine Flandin, I am Jean-Claude, King's Own Musketeer."

Sergeant heaved himself up much more carefully and said, "Show him your catch."

Flandin's men finished tying off the skiff. Several dead nethercobs were piled amidships, wide flat bodies with hard shells the color of the corals in which they lived, some green, some yellow. Long segmented legs stuck out in all directions, and the blackish ichor that served as their blood dripped from open beaks. By tomorrow morning this catch would be on its way to the kitchens in the high quarter.

Several whole and partial human corpses were laid out on a canvas next to the nethercobs. Using the canvas as a sling, the scuttlers hauled their grisly catch onto the platform. This manhandling released a new cloud of reek that crawled up Jean-Claude's nose and down his throat, making him want to gag. Nevertheless he knelt to have a closer look at the dismembered, decomposing deceased. Alas that he was better at getting stories out of the living than the dead. Isabelle should have been here for this.

Judging by the size and duplication of various parts, he guessed he was looking at five individuals. The first two were just an arm and a rib cage that didn't belong to each other or anybody else. The third was a torso missing everything from the pelvis down. Jean-Claude suspected it had been a woman by its small size and a few strands of long hair clinging to a bit of rotting scalp. Unlike the others, she seemed to have been burned before being discarded. The fourth corpse was more complete and recognizable as a Seelenjäger, owing to the bits of leathery hide and a slightly elongated jaw sporting tusks like a boar.

The fifth and freshest one was a short thin man whose throat had been torn out. Judging by his lack of serious decomposition and the fact that he had not been devoured, he could not have been dead for more than a day or two. He was the only one with enough skin left to describe a face. It was a skinny face, dismayed in death.

"That's him," Sergeant said.

"You can swear to it?" Jean-Claude asked.

"Aye. The white-livered ear-greaser was mincing around the Lowmarket for a few weeks afore the Golden Swain massacre. That's him, all right."

So why had Mistwaithe been murdered? And what did he have to do with these other unfortunates? Were these all the bodies, or were there others still undiscovered?

Mistwaithe had still been alive after the Golden Swain massacre. The fact that his captors had waited to kill him suggested they wanted something else from him first. Had Mistwaithe threatened to expose the Harvest King, or was there something more fundamental behind his murder?

If one corpse was a Goldentongue and another a Seelenjäger, were they all sorcerers? Was someone hunting sorcerers? Given Orem's transformation and Ingle's experiments, was someone taking the saintborn apart to see how they worked?

That idea made him shiver. Grand Leon's birthday party was to last a fortnight, but people had been arriving for months. Who would notice if a few strangers disappeared? Their families. Their . . . husbands.

Jean-Claude surveyed the half-corpse of the woman. A corpse burned, now that he looked more closely, from the inside out. He recalled Boyar Volody describing a sorceress who had mastered the element of fire. He had a sinking feeling that Volody was going to have to wait for Paradise to be reunited with his Ustina.

Then there was the Seelenjäger. Several people had described Sedgwick's contact Hans Schmidt to him, as a man with tusks like a boar.

"Where did you find them?" Jean-Claude asked Flandin.

"Down past Herrow's Maze," Flandin said. "These cobs strung their net over one of the whistling vents, and it caught 'em as they fell."

"Whistling vents?" Jean-Claude asked.

"Cracks that run up into the rock. Aerofish and other beasties fly up in there for shelter or spawning and the nethercobs try to net them on the way out."

Jean-Claude grunted and added giant, armored, web-spinning spider things to his pile of nightmare fuel. "Do people often get caught up in these nets?"

Flandin scratched under his chin. "Not in my memory. They say some of the cracks go all the way up into the caves in the Rivencrag. I wouldn't know. Every few years someone tries to climb up there and doesn't come back. I leaves well enough away."

Sergeant said, "So, musketeer, are you satisfied with the catch of the day?"

Jean-Claude straightened up and conjured his coin purse. "Indeed, gentlemen." He held up enough silver for every man. "I need them put on ice at the city graveyard." He would ask Isabelle or Gretl to look at them.

Flandin shrugged. "As you will it, monsieur."

Jean-Claude doled out the coin, then cleared his throat and said words he imagined he would spend the rest of his life regretting. "And then, Capitaine. I need you to take me to this whistling vent." Somehow he'd have to climb up the vent, Builder only knew how far and—

"Beggin' your pardon, monsieur, but no. Not for le roi's gold or the Builder's grace. Gigging's good at the vents when you can get it, which you usually can't. You never plans to get there, see. You just hopes you're up the right canyon when the mist breaks. Get in and get out. Last night Mother Gloom took a deep breath, sucked the Miasma right down into her rotten lungs. We scuttled through Herrow's Maze like the Breaker was astern, and found this lot at Delver's Hole."

Jean-Claude tried not to feel a surge of cowardly relief at this. "How often do you get this chance?"

"Maybe once or twice in a spin." He gestured to the massive nethercobs in his skiff. "You don't get beauties like this lest they have time to grow."

Jean-Claude pondered the arachnoids, considered the grim reality they represented, and then held up two more coins for Flandin. "And that's to throw the rest of your catch overboard."

Flandin looked at him as if he'd grown a second head. "You're daft."

"Those things have been feasting on saintborn, and I doubt your customers would appreciate committing cannibalism even at one remove."

Jean-Claude climbed up out of the Turvytown slums into the shipyards where the stink of bubbling tar overtook the smell of fish rot in the competition for most offensive odor. This low in the city, the road was less packed than it was higher up, being mostly occupied with those leaving the festivities early or arriving late. The people he passed on the street were hunched more tightly together than even the chill wind required. More than once he heard Grand Leon's name invoked in conjunction with a ward against evil.

Jean-Claude's thoughts lingered on the mortal remains behind him. Why had they been killed? More experimentation? Hopefully Isabelle could tell him more.

He arrived at la rue des Chapeliers to find Gaston standing watch at the top of the stairs that led down to the basement rooms. Jean-Claude didn't like having rooms below street level. They were difficult to defend and impossible to escape, but there hadn't been a choice.

Gaston saluted, which was not technically necessary, but Gaston was the type of man who was happiest when there was a chain of command. "Monsieur."

Jean-Claude returned the salute and said, "Anything to report."

"Mademoiselle Isabelle was called to Madame Faustine's."

"The dressmaker?" Jean-Claude asked.

"Yes, sir. A messenger showed up with an invitation signed by Comtesse Coquetta, but that's not all. We have guests waiting for you. Comtesse Impervia."

Jean-Claude went from feeling vaguely uneasy to positively ill in the space of a heartbeat. What dire business could have brought Impervia here?

Jean-Claude thanked Gaston, straightened his tabard, and limped down the stairs. He rapped on the door and Hysia opened it. The smell of spices and cream wafted out the door, along with the sounds of women laughing.

Hysia slipped through the curtainway to the first room and said, "Monsieur Jean-Claude is here."

Jean-Claude stepped through. Gretl and Darcy were off somewhere, but Impervia and Valérie sat across a table laden with a creamy pot pie, spiced sausages, and greens so fresh they must have come from a hothouse. A bottle of wine and a box of candles also stood to hand.

Valérie, beaming, popped up and said, "Jean-Claude, you never told me you knew Comtesse Impervia personally."

"He doesn't like to admit it," Impervia said. "You'd almost think he was ashamed of me." She wore a gown even more enticing than the one he'd seen her in yesterday, white silk, silver thread sewn with decorative buttons of mother of pearl. The effect was rendered incongruous by the fact that she was currently holding baby Vincent. On the other hand, she was a grandmother.

Jean-Claude decided to overlook her remark. He wasn't ashamed of her, but rather of the way he'd treated her, but this was not the company in which to discuss that. "Madame Comtesse, what brings you here?"

"Business, of course." She stood and handed the baby off to Valérie. "I will definitely be investing in your venture, madame. I will have my seneschal contact you."

"Thank you, Madame Comtesse," Valérie said, beaming. She bustled out, taking Hysia with her.

"Venture?" Jean-Claude asked.

"Women's business," Impervia said. "Sit down."

Jean-Claude couldn't decide if that was an invitation or an order, but he eased himself onto the sky chest that was serving as a chair and waited.

"Eat something," she said. "I imagine it's going to be a long day."

"Why?" Jean-Claude asked, fishing up a spoon. After weeks of mostly street vendor beans and eggs, the creamy spice sauce grabbed his tongue and made him sweat and shiver. He'd almost forgotten what it was like to have food that was actually cooked and not just beaten into submission.

Impervia said, "I've been speaking with Comtesse Coquetta. You didn't tell me about her infirmity."

"That information wasn't mine to give," Jean-Claude said.

Impervia made a gesture as if setting that point aside. "After speaking with her and coordinating with Josette and Sireen, we have discovered no fewer than eight other saintborn who are suffering the same affliction. Worse, the walls of silence are starting to crack, and rumor is flowing freely. Le Comte Gebraux showed up at the Temple in tears this morning, begging for absolution. He tried to give his entire estate to the artifex, which of course did not sit well with his son. They're still yelling about it, and when last I heard they'd got lawyers involved."

Jean-Claude put down his spoon, the excellent food turning to mud in his belly. "Just what we need, a plague with a garnish of lawyers."

Impervia's lips bent in a wry smile. "At least you can execute lawyers."

Damn that smile, barely there, like the edge of a razor. "Yes, but they breed so quickly." He must not get drawn into banter. He cleared his throat and said, "I don't know precisely how this relates, but my sources led me to Mistwaithe's body, and he wasn't alone. There were five or six other corpses there, all sorcerers, including one boar-headed Seelenjäger named Schmidt and a woman who I suspect was a Stehkzima ambassadress."

Impervia leaned back, her expression sickened. "Ustina?"

"You knew her?"

"We met a few times. She was . . . forceful. She could turn into a living flame."

"Could you identify her? I had all the corpses put on ice."

"Possibly, but not just now. Our priority remains finding the Harvest King, to which point you should get a bath and change clothes. I brought a new dress uniform for you. You look like you've been sleeping in a pigsty."

"Dress uniform?" Jean-Claude hated the damned stiff uncomfortable things.

"I need an escort; we're going to watch a performance of the *Harvest King*."

Seventeen

Isabelle stood on a pedestal in the center of Madame Faustine's fitting room, while Madame Faustine herself walked a slow circle around her, her left hand cupping her right elbow while her right index finger tapped her chin. Isabelle felt like she was once again being judged on the dock in Parlement.

Madame Faustine designed clothes for Comtesse Coquetta, and by extension the rest of the Trefoil. She didn't run a business, though money was exchanged, nor did one ask for services. If one received an invitation, as Isabelle had this morning, one showed up at the appointed hour to be draped in art.

Faustine's eye was critical, and her voice was pinched. "Mademoiselle, you dress like someone who has been taught to hate her own reflection. That arm is magnificent, but you treat it like it belongs to someone else."

Isabelle held her spark-arm up for the customary inspection. Everyone had to stare at it. "People see it and say 'Breaker's get.' It's not something I care to emphasize."

Faustine arched an eyebrow at her. "Has hiding it ever worked? Has concealing it ever made someone believe it was not there, or stopped someone pointing it out to insult or shame you? No? I didn't think so. It's yours, it's gorgeous, and you should treat it as such. Then when the small-minded try to shame you, you flaunt it. Win that battle enough times and your arm will become an object of envy rather than scorn."

Isabelle shriveled a little at this advice. Even if she privately reveled in her sorcery, she had no illusions anybody else ever would. "I don't need people staring at me. I need them to listen to me."

"I am conscious of that conundrum, but if you trust not one other word I say, trust me when I say that you must dazzle when you are young so that men will not forget you when your age makes you invisible."

A small army of attendants descended on Isabelle. Faustine declared Isabelle's dress an affront to fashion and ordered her out of it with all the authoritative force of a general commanding her troops to charge. Isabelle submitted without complaint to being groomed like a show pony. Her own staff had trained her not to interfere in these rituals. She had only one arm left and didn't want to be beaten with it.

Over the course of an hour, measurements were taken, swatches compared to skin tone, the densities of various fabric discussed, all while Isabelle endured the role of goose-pimply mannequin.

Faustine eventually settled on black, but not just any black. This was shimmering black shot through with hints of pink and purple that picked up the glow from her spark-arm and set it to play around the creases and curves.

The finished ensemble had a broad-brimmed hat, a long black wig, a birdcage veil, a short-waisted jacket, and a lace cravat over a trim bodice. The most daring innovation was the skirt, soft pleats that fell only to her knees and tall boots rose to meet the hem. Boots with spurs. The whole thing strode beyond the frontier of propriety and claimed a great deal of masculine territory without yielding an iota of the feminine.

What would Bitterlich think of this? The thought popped into her head, unbidden, and she quickly shooed it out like chasing a rat with a broom. Yes, Bitterlich was fascinating to talk to, and quite handsome, and the shapeshifting was amazing, but he was also a Praetorian, and the last thing he needed to be doing was staring at her dress.

At last Faustine let her down off the pedestal.

"Thank you, madame," Isabelle said. "It's delightful."

"It had better be very much more than that," Faustine said. "I am informed you are an outcast. Society recognizes two sorts of outsiders, the contemptible and the powerful. Both are conditions in the minds of those around you. Always strive to give people the impression that you might have something they want or fear. I give you these weapons lest you go into battle unprepared. Use them well."

She stepped out into the waiting room and found Bitterlich missing. No, wait, there was a large cat with stripes and spots very similar to his, curled up on an upholstered chair.

Isabelle cleared her throat. "Capitaine Bitterlich."

The cat's ears twitched and it blinked lazily. It gazed upon her in the insolent way of cats, stood, stretched, and kept right on stretching until Capitaine Bitterlich stood before her. His gaze drank her in and he purred, "Mademoiselle Isabelle, if you don't mind my opinion, I must say you are amazing."

Isabelle warmed to this compliment. "And you are entirely dashing." She chastised herself for this flirting, but the voice of caution was losing. If she'd wanted to get rid of him, she'd had the chance last night.

He extended his elbow for her. She didn't need it for balance this time—it had been almost half a day since anyone had tried to kill her—but she took it anyway, because she liked the feel of him.

She asked, "What did Grand Leon have to say to your report?"

Bitterlich made a huffing noise and assumed an imperious expression. "He said, and I quote, 'Bring him in.' I have a warrant for Guillaume's arrest, but that isn't what worries me. Late last night, Grand Leon collapsed at his ball. Enough people saw it that the rumor started going round that he'd had a stroke. This morning he was up again as if nothing had happened, but he is seventy-five."

Dread filled Isabelle's chest. Grand Leon was the keystone of l'Empire's arch. Without him the whole thing crumbled. His perpetual resistance to naming an heir only made it worse. "How are the High Houses responding?"

Bitterlich shook his head. "Too soon to tell. By the time I left this morning, there were a lot of people actively waiting to see what other people would do. There have been moments like this before. Grand Leon got pneumonia once and by the third day half a dozen different would-be heirs were starting to make public noises 'in case the worst should happen.'"

"Do you think this will convince him to designate an heir?"

"I would like to think so, but I don't have much hope."

"But why not? He told me once that he wanted to create an empire that would outlast him. You would think that picking an heir to follow him would be a necessary step."

"He doesn't think highly of any of the candidates."

"I can see that, but the only option is to let all the people he doesn't like sort it out by force."

"I agree, but not even the Trefoil have been able to convince him of a successor."

"Who do they recommend?"

"They have paraded a variety of candidates before him. He always finds a flaw in them: too greedy, to lazy, too vindictive, too dull. I think he knows he must let go, but he doesn't know how. This choice is the one risk he cannot mitigate by other means, and his hand is frozen to the wheel."

Just what would Isabelle do if Grand Leon died? Escape had always been her plan, to move to Aragoth and marry Julio and just . . . just pretend l'Empire wasn't her problem anymore. That wasn't an option anymore. As Grand Leon's cousin, she would become a target for abduction in the succession war that would surely follow, or be hunted as the Breaker's get and torn apart by the mob.

"What will you do if he dies without naming an heir?" Isabelle asked.

"That will depend on who steps up to replace him," Bitterlich said. "Some of the pretenders would likely try to recruit me. Others would likely try to kill me. The Praetorian Guard helped usher Grand Leon into power, and some of our number feel it is our right to choose his successor. All the Praetorians are second- and third-born sons, which means they all have older brothers, and bumping your older brother into the kingship gives you a leg up when it comes to distributing the lands and titles of the vanquished. It would be messy."

Isabelle's mind snatched one of those facts out of the air. "But you're not a second son. Capitaine Erste Ewald Bitterlich. That Erste means first, doesn't it?"

Bitterlich grimaced and his whiskers turned down. "My parents were Lord and Lady Bitterlich. After they were killed in Wolfgang's uprising, I was brought here and raised in the Imperial Orphanage. My family's estate was disposed of long before I came of age."

"Oh," Isabelle said. She hadn't meant to cause him pain. "I'm sorry."

"The world is full of tragedies," Bitterlich said. "So many that you could not count them all. They are the dark between the stars, but one does not gaze at the sky to see the darkness. Besides, you didn't exactly have an idyllic childhood, either."

"No," Isabelle said. "And yet here we are. So who would you promote to be the next roi?"

"I would probably be fatally excluded from the argument if I tried to voice an opinion. I would much prefer that Grand Leon pick an heir, and get Colonel Hachette to swear to him. Hachette is a hidebound ox but he's honorable, and he could keep the rest in line."

"I mean if you had your pick?" Isabelle asked.

"Is that a question you would want to answer?" he replied.

"I don't know any of them that well."

"For a group of people who have been maneuvering to obtain this appointment their entire lives, the pool of potential heirs is remarkably unprepared to actually perform the duty. It's a bit like asking a condemned man what he doesn't want for his last meal."

——

The spiral ziggurat of the Esoteric Brotherhood of the Azure Flame was one of those buildings everyone marveled at but nobody emulated. It was built of square platforms one atop the other, each one twisted just a few degrees clockwise so that the whole thing made a quarter turn and seemed to be looking over its own shoulder.

The Azure Flame's chapter house, built in the style of a classical shrine, sat at the ziggurat's base. Its grand hall was paneled on all sides with great mosaic murals depicting strange otherworldly landscapes populated by grotesque beasts that seemed to sprout like trees from the ground and melt into rivers flowing down from crooked mountains. Buildings were constructed out of senseless words and the people themselves were disjointed and rearranged so that men walked on their hands or juggled their heads. It was quite the most disconcerting artwork Isabelle had ever seen, and it made for a disturbing venue for a soirée.

Between rows of marble columns carved with even more weird creatures gathered a herd of well-heeled gentry, clayborn but with a few Sanguinaire mixed in. Most were people Isabelle had never met, though they generally seemed familiar with each other and gathered in what looked to be habitual cliques. Amongst them circulated azure-robed servitors handing out drinks and courtesans to ensure nobody drank alone.

From this swirl emerged a pear-shaped Sanguinaire in an ill-fitting white doublet. His face bore the spider's-web veins of a man who spent too much time looking into the bottom of a cup. He strolled ponderously toward Bitterlich, waving with the hand not occupied with his beverage.

"Bonjour, Capitaine Bitterlich, haven't seen you around much lately, and you, mademoiselle."

Bitterlich made an almost inaudible sigh and said, "Monsieur Tristan, allow me to introduce you to Mademoiselle Isabelle des Zephyrs. Isabelle, Monsieur Tristan Hauet."

Tristan looked Isabelle up and down and goggled at her spark-arm. "So you're Grand Leon's Breakerborn, bad luck about those Aragoths. I bet you're not so keen on peace treaties right now."

The greeting on Isabelle's lips died and fell into the sour pit of her stomach. Instead she summoned her reserve and said calmly, "I am not the Breaker's get." She held up her spark-arm. "This is a divine perquisite." Or at least that's what it said on her Writ of Exception.

"I meant no offense," Tristan said with the air of one wounded.

Isabelle's first reflex was the ingrained urge to apologize for defending herself. She stuffed it down and instead gave her anger a bit more lead. "You may not have meant to, but you managed to anyway."

Tristan puffed up defensively. "Mademoiselle, I apologized. There's no need for you—"

Bitterlich clamped his hand down on Tristan's shoulder so hard that the Sanguinaire's knees creaked. "There's no need for Isabelle to do anything." Conversationally he added, "Tristan was two years ahead of me in the Praetorian Academy before he washed out. Now I believe he lives on his parents' sufferance. The last I heard, they'd cut off his allowance owing to gambling debts."

Tristan looked peevish. "I'm not cut off, Littlepaws. I've just developed less expensive hobbies, though if you ever want to apologize—"

"No," Bitterlich growled, his ears and whiskers flat back and his fangs bared. Isabelle had never seen him so much as ruffled before, but the glare in his eyes should have set Tristan's powdered wig on fire. Tristan wilted and retreated, muttering about uppity barbarians and what was society coming to?

Isabelle tilted her head toward the departing lush. "*That* was in the Praetorian Academy?"

Bitterlich smoothed his hackles and adjusted his cravat. "They will let any sorcerous second son matriculate; they are more particular about who they graduate. In all, Tristan is one of life's lesser hemorrhoids. He did manage to resign without disgracing himself, though only barely."

Isabelle considered the man and his context. "Were his failings academic?"

"They were more generalized than that. He lacked the perseverance to obtain mediocrity in any subject. Why do you ask?"

"Because I'm wondering why he was invited to this soirée," Isabelle said. "Why would he be of interest to Lael?"

Bitterlich frowned thoughtfully and surveyed the crowd. "That's an interesting question. Let's circulate."

Isabelle followed Bitterlich around the hall. Twice more, Bitterlich was intercepted by people he already knew. None of them managed to insult Isabelle quite as oafishly as Tristan, but they did seem to be holding an unofficial contest as to which member of any given group could stand farthest from her without actually exiting the conversation. More than once she was sure she heard whispers as people walked away. "Divine perquisite. Who does she think she's fooling?" "Insulted the Aragothic . . ." "If she'd been anyone but le roi's cousin . . ." ". . . ought to be ashamed to show her face . . ."

Isabelle probably could have asked Bitterlich for a complete accounting of the slander, but what would be the point except to make her even more irritated? If only there was some glorious achievement she could point to, some accomplishment that would impress even the flintiest of hearts. Perhaps she could do something outrageous, like saving two whole kingdoms from annihilating each other in a pointless war?

"Ignore them," Bitterlich said.

"I've been ignoring them my whole life," Isabelle said. "It hasn't helped. And if you tell me to smile, I will rip your whiskers out and poke you in the eye with them."

"I believe you would," Bitterlich said.

"Why did that first fellow, Tristan, call you Littlepaws?"

Bitterlich stiffened, and took his time answering. "It was a childhood taunt. I shouldn't let it affect me."

"I'm sorry," Isabelle said, though she remained curious. Whatever had embedded that reaction in his soul had been no mere playground insult. Lit-tlepaws. "The cat," she realized out loud. "The one who has your markings."

"Stop," he snarled, not loud but sharp as fangs. "If I have no rights to your privacy, is not the inverse true?" His glare could have melted lead.

Isabelle seized her curiosity and her good intentions in both hands and drew back a step. "Of course. I'm sorry." Though she was also more curious than ever.

With a visible effort, he relaxed his posture and said, "We have work to do."

Isabelle turned away from him to pay attention to the party. She was sup-posed to be playing the part of the mysterious outsider. Plots ought to be congealing around her like cream. Much of the party's traffic circulated through a library off the great hall wherein were arranged plinths and tables displaying dozens of artifacts, bits of quondam mechanisms, sketches and notes. Each one was accompanied by a card explaining where it had been found and what if anything was known or guessed about its manufacture and function.

A group of men was gathered around a clockwork mechanical arm that stood upright on a plinth. It reminded Isabelle greatly of the quondam-mechanical prosthesis exalted clerics wore, assuming such clerics wanted three elbows and a hand that looked like a metal starfish. On a pedestal nearby lay a curve of yellow crystal in the shape of a horn with a surface that bub-bled as if it was boiling. There were a variety of other fascinating oddments just glimpsed through a forest of people.

Isabelle found herself trying to look everywhere at once while keeping up with Bitterlich. Over there was a clear cylinder that seemed to be filled with an ever-shifting webwork of cracks and fissures, as if it was just looking for exactly the right configuration to shatter. Isabelle wanted to stop and exam-ine any one of these more closely, but they were not the sort of mystery they'd come here to investigate.

Another pass around the party and Bitterlich completed his inventory of the guests. He bent her ear and spoke in a voice that betrayed none of his earlier outrage. "I think I have detected a theme for today's gathering. We seem to be surrounded primarily by the sorts of people who don't get invited to Grand Leon's soirées: second sons and daughters, the nephews and nieces of very important people, and more than a few clayborn gentry, knights, and baronets."

"In other words, people who have spent their whole lives standing on the threshold of the feast and never being let in," Isabelle said. Discontent fomented best not amongst those who were truly downtrodden, but amongst those with the fewest intact necks between themselves and power.

"Mademoiselle des Zephyrs, welcome!" A sonorous bass voice rolled through the gathering. Lael emerged from the crowd and strode toward her, the crowd melting away before him. His right arm spread in greeting. His left arm, still covered by his crimson cloak, hung at his side. The flap of his heavy cape kicked up a puff of air that broke against her ankles.

"Greetings, Lael," she said. "Allow me to introduce my . . . companion, Capitaine Erste Ewald Bitterlich." Her tone was arid and disapproving. They had decided to play reluctant companions, a disgraced woman and her handler.

"Monsieur," Bitterlich said, in an equally quelling tone.

"It's a pleasure to meet you," Lael said. "Be welcome."

Isabelle said to Bitterlich, "If I might have a word with my cousin." As Grand Leon's son, Lael was her second cousin. Given Grand Leon's many offspring, she had a bumper crop of such relations.

Bitterlich regarded her suspiciously. "I have my orders."

"Yes, I know, but this is a party not a melee, and I'm not running off. You can give me a moment of privacy."

Bitterlich gave her a narrow-eyed look, but took himself off.

Lael watched him go. "I see that my father intends to keep close tabs on you after the insult his Parlement delivered."

Isabelle twisted one corner of her mouth up in the barest fraction of a smile. Her degradation before the law still felt red and raw. "Le roi wants to keep me out of trouble," she said. "You said I might find like-minded people here, but so far all I have been met with are a string of insults from the other guests." She gestured broadly to the crowd, her spark-arm leaving a tail like a comet.

Lael cast his gaze upon the partygoers. Many of them were watching this conversation, more or less covertly. Lael said, "Rabble, most of them, but in order to find rubies one must start with the right sort of river and sift a great deal of mud."

"You said you had unearthed some artifacts regarding l'Étincelle," Isabelle said. That was the bait he'd set to draw her in, and it would be a shame not to see what he had to offer.

"Indeed." Lael presented his elbow to escort her, and she reluctantly took it. Through his sleeve, his arm felt feverish. Was he sick? He showed no other sign of infirmity, though the smell of medicinal ointments still lingered about him.

He led her through the library of treasures.

"Are these your discoveries?" Isabelle asked

"Mostly. A few were obtained from diggers, a few others from dealers. Some of them I keep to trade for less ornamental but more informative pieces."

He brought Isabelle into a smaller, quieter room, with a circular table on which were arranged stacks of documents and notebooks. A bright alchemical lantern hung over the table, but the rest of the room was swathed in a thirsty black cloth that drank up the spilled light, making the table and the room's two other occupants appear half real and half shadow.

The first was a balding, thin-faced man in the red-trimmed yellow robes of a Temple sagax. He stood in conversation with a large man in monkish robes, dark brown and roughspun. That one wore a face-covering hood with a bicorn peak that curled back and around like the horns of a mountain ram . . . or was he a Seelenjäger under there?

Their conversation died as Lael and Isabelle approached.

A breeze that had sneaked in from somewhere rippled Isabelle's skirt and tugged at Lael's cape.

Lael said, "Sagax Quill and Hasdrubal, be known to Mademoiselle Isabelle des Zephyrs."

Sagax Quill dipped his head cautiously in Isabelle's direction. "Mademoiselle, I have been following your career with some interest."

It was not at all hard for Isabelle to let bitterness stain her voice. "You'll have to let me know where it ends up, as I seem to have lost track of it."

In a voice that sounded like it had been run through a saw mill, Hasdrubal said, "Neither victory nor defeat are permanent states of affairs."

Lael said, "Quill is an empirical philosopher within the Temple. He should have been made a Savant by now, but his ideas burned too brightly for eyes accustomed to the dark, and so he was deflected into a less troublesome role."

"Not ideas," Quill said. "Observations."

"And what sorts of things have you observed?" Isabelle asked.

Quill glanced at Isabelle's spark-arm and then up to her eyes. "That much of the Temple's understanding of sorcery is wildly mistaken. To a point you might be interested in, there are no such things as the Breaker's get."

That was as heterodox a statement as Isabelle had ever heard from a cleric. "How did you come to that conclusion?"

Quill lifted his goblet to his lips and took the sort of drink that tried to wash away an old bitter memory. "I met a boy, a child no older than twelve, a sorcerer's bastard. He had in his touch the power of healing. He used it to save his brother after the boy's pelvis was crushed by an ox cart. Young and foolish as I was, I reported this miracle to my Temple superiors. Clearly this was a gift from the Builder. The Temple dispatched a quaestor and a carnifex to judge the miracle. After a trial in which I bore witness to the most breathtakingly irrational arguments ever to pass human lips, the boy and his whole family were burned as the Breaker's get."

That story made Isabelle's belly churn with horror, but she kept her voice even. "And what did you do about it?"

"Nothing," Quill said with a grimace. "I was still too enthralled by the idea that the Temple had special knowledge that was not subject to the critique of evidence or reason. I tried to convince myself that their judgment was for the greater good, that the problem was with me. In the end I was unsuccessful."

"And yet you are still part of the Temple," Isabelle said.

"The Omnifex and the artifexes do their best to convince the world that the Temple is an indivisible monolith, but it is a cairn of many stones with many cracks. The Observationalist rebellion nearly shattered it, and there remain those who chafe under the Confirmationist yoke. The Iconates cling to the Traditionalists' cloaks out of fear that the Recentionists will take their shrines away, and so it goes."

Isabelle turned her attention to Hasdrubal. "And what brings you into this fold? Your name is Skaladini."

"I was a slave of the cohort Ild'Sar before Lael rescued me." His voice carried a bray in every vowel. "My life is his."

Isabelle was taken aback. "You were a cullborn?" Might he know something about Lael's doings in that forbidding land, or how he had got from there to here?

"It is much better to be a sorcerer in the land of the Enlightened," he said.

Lael said, "But it's still not perfect, or anywhere near it. The Builder gave it to his saintborn children to improve the world and prepare it for the Savior's coming. Instead, they cling to the familiar, look to the safety of the irretrievable past, and claim to have inherited by right what their ancestors gained by accident, theft, and bloodshed."

To Isabelle, Lael said, "Shouldn't you be allowed to be a comte? Why should being unhallowed disqualify you, or being a woman?"

"The unhallowed are still saintborn," Quill added. "Lack of sorcery notwithstanding."

Isabelle said, "Be that as it may. Truth does not sway men's minds unless it first serves their ambitions. It certainly doesn't explain what you want from me."

Hasdrubal said, "Your voice. Your story. You are your roi's cousin, and unlike Lael you have never defied him, yet see how you have been treated."

Isabelle's pulse picked up to a quick trot, for this was the thread she'd been looking for. In a very flat tone she asked, "You would ask me to inveigh against Grand Leon?"

"Saints forbid," Lael said. "I learned the futility of that when I was young, and proved it again the other day when he rejected my arguments before Parlement."

"Not that Sagax Junker's argument was theologically sound," Quill muttered.

Lael waved this aside. "My father made his decision, and now everyone must live with it. From now until the end of time, only a sorcerer in the full possession of his powers may be considered a noble worthy of title or stewardship over so much as a footprint of land in l'Empire Céleste. All I want you to do is remember that."

A blue-robed Azurite acolyte hurried in and bowed to Lael. He whispered something in Lael's ear. Lael frowned, nodded, and sent the Azurite off again.

"Another matter needs my attention." Lael picked up a slender notebook with a battered face and binding and presented it to Isabelle. "This is the trove you are looking for. It is far from comprehensive, but the real prizes are sometimes hidden in the blank spaces in the mosaic."

"What do you consider the real prize?" Isabelle asked before he could turn away. If he had some other pressing matter, his attention would be divided. "Sorcery?" He'd spent his life searching for it. No one in all the world wanted it more than he. Was he aware of Ingle's experiments? If so, he did not seem to have undergone the procedure. He had no bloodshadow, no trepanning scar on his forehead.

Lael didn't quite turn all the way to face her. "Sorcery is a very primitive kind of power. Real power comes from the mind. When someone wants to keep you powerless, the first thing they do is try to control what it is permissible for you to think. They write your story for you without your consent and tell you this is how you must believe until even your own thoughts seem like alien things in your head. They hem you in so there is no escape or relief, until in desperation you step off the page, out of the story, into a place their narrative cannot find you. Then can you see the world as it really is.

"Sorcery is a prerequisite for power today only because it was something our ancestors had that the clayborn did not. If the first rulers of the world had been blind, we would elevate the sightless and people would pluck out their own eyes for a chance at power. Your idiot brother would certainly do so; he prefers the blindness of ambition to the light of reason. Builder keep."

"Savior come," Isabelle said, and watched him go. The gears in her mind turned with the quiet sort of clicking that often preceded the understanding of a proof. What did he just say?

Guillaume.

Merde.

Just because she knew her brother was an idiot didn't mean the whole world did. Guillaume had never left l'Île des Zephyrs before coming here, and even if he had, far-wandering Lael should never have heard of a second-rate comte's insignificant twit of a son. Not unless Lael had gone to l'Île des Zephyrs.

Mistwaithe had gone to l'Île des Zephyrs, so had Hailer Dok, and so had the Harvest King.

Two of those men were accounted for, Mistwaithe and Dok had faces and histories to go along with their names.

Isabelle grabbed her speculation by the throat and throttled it before it had a chance to become fact in her mind. If Lael was the Harvest King, how had he gotten to l'Île des Zephyrs?

She faced Hasdrubal. "How did Lael rescue you?" Lael had disappeared into Skaladin territory last year, but where had he gone from there?

Again in the warbling undertones of goat, Hasdrubal said, "He ambushed the caravan my master was leading, and took away the prize they were carrying. When he discovered me amongst his booty, he set me free."

"You were amongst the cargo?" Isabelle asked.

"I was pulling the wagon," Hasdrubal said. "Bound in the shape of an ox."

Isabelle was appalled, and yet this deed spoke well of Lael, at least if one discounted the purpose of the ambush, which was theft.

She said, "No one should be kept in such bondage. What was the prize he sought?"

"Some trinket of knowledge," Hasdrubal said. "My master was always digging things from the sand. I spent enough time as a beast of burden that I all but forgot how to think as a man."

Yet he spoke fluently in le Langue, a language he had presumably only recently encountered.

"So how did he come to bring you here? Rocher Royale is a long way from anywhere in Skaladin."

"We took ship from Ishkelon," he said. "I learned to become a gull. It was the first skin I ever took for myself. The cohort Ild'Sar never allowed their slaves to fly."

"Ishkelon. The name is familiar." It scratched at the back of Isabelle's mind like a rat.

Sagax Quill said, "It's one of several Skaladin words for the Treacher's Coast."

"Ah," Isabelle said. That was the site of the Great Betrayal where the Gyrine had turned on the Kindly Crusade. "I thought that stretch of land was supposed to be uninhabitable, the farthest place from anywhere anyone would want to be. It's one of the reasons the Gyrine made their ambush there."

"There are people who prefer their privacy," Quill said. "The desolation suits them well. Smugglers, for example. The Gyrine come there to trade their plunder, and slave ships carrying kidnapped sorcerers stop there to resupply before they reach the City of Gears."

A link clicked into place for Isabelle. Not the last piece of the puzzle, but the one that brought her speculation into focus.

"What ship could you find there that would bring you here?" Isabelle asked. "We don't allow Skaladin ships in our ports." This was technically true, though Skaladin goods made it into port all the time from various ports of ill repute.

"The Gyrine go where they will," Hasdrubal said.

At last all the bits finally lined up. Lael had gone to Ishkelon to meet the Gyrine. He donned the mantle of the Harvest King and sailed to Brathon, where he met Mistwaithe, and then on to the *Conquest* . . . and what in all the ten thousand Torments had he wanted there? Not the treasure, surely. Something to help him make sorcery?

A bell chimed, dragging Isabelle out of herself. Isabelle joined the rest of the guests in filing into the main hall for the official inauguration of festivities.

Lael appeared amongst the guests, and gathered the partygoers around him to begin the toasting. A servitor came by with a tray of drinks and Isabelle took one just to have something to hold. Thankfully the metal was something her spark-hand could hold. She still had the l'Étincelle notebook in the other hand. On any other day she would have found a quiet corner somewhere and buried her nose in it. Now it dangled like an afterthought.

"Madames and messieurs," Lael said. "Good evening to you all. Little did I know how many friends I have in Rocher Royale. *Vini Amicitia!*"

There was a rumble of approval from the crowd. Everyone drank. Isabelle looked around for Bitterlich. He ought not be hard to spot unless he'd changed shape again.

Lael went on. "My friends. This is an auspicious occasion. Today marks the end of my father's seventy-fifth year, a triumph of longevity to be sure. Once there was a time I looked up to him. He was the sun in my sky, illuminating the world and driving away all shadows. When he stretched out his mighty hand, the world trembled, and I imagined in my naivety that by his touch, he made things right in the world."

Lael paused to stare into his goblet as if into a divinatory well. "When I learned the truth, it shattered me. My father cast me out, not for being evil, or rebellious, or even incompetent. He cast me out for being unsightly, like a clay pot with a thumbprint. I came to realize that the beauty and order he brought to the world was nothing but a painted shroud on a corpse, hiding the rot underneath. I tried to reason with him. I tried to shock his conscience. I raged at him as any son would who only wanted his father to refrain from the atrocities he daily committed.

"For years I hated him," he said. Blotches covered his cheeks and tears stood in his eyes. "By all the saints I hated him, and I stormed around the world in my anger, searching for the truth: the clear, cold, sharp, and brilliant answer that would both cure him and bring him pain."

Lael wiped at his eyes with his sleeve, managing not to spill his drink as he did so. Either his emotions were genuine, or there was an acting coach who needed a medal.

"Yet no anger can burn forever, and when mine finally died to ash, I came to realize that his faults came not from wickedness, but from weakness. He was blind to the world, blind to the injustices he created. He painted the shroud because he could not comprehend the corpse beneath it. In time I came to pity him, and the meanness of his world. I could no longer in good conscience stay away."

All the hair on the back of Isabelle's neck stood up. Lael's speech was prettier than anything that her father or brother had ever said, but it dripped with the same tones of self-exculpation: *I'm sorry you made me do this. I didn't want to have to hurt you, but you didn't give me any choice.*

Like them, Lael's diatribe was directed as much at himself as at his audience—Grand Leon wasn't even here—convincing himself of his rightness. He had not made a threat, but every version of Isabelle from eight years old to eighteen wanted to bolt from the room, to put as much space between herself and that tone as possible.

Twenty-seven-year-old Isabelle held firm, though her skin chilled down to the muscle.

Lael said, "I came back to fix what was broken. If only I could cure his vision and pull the cobwebs from his eyes, then perhaps the world could be right again, corruption swept away and daylight let in."

He paused and looked out on the room with eyes gone hollow with despair. "Imagine my pain to think I may have come too late. As you all know by now, last night in a ballroom dance, my father fell. My people tell me he was seized by some kind of fit, as if the Breaker herself at last had her claws in him."

A fearful murmur rippled through the room. Isabelle's stomach tightened at the reminder. Did he have the shadow rot? If Grand Leon fell there would be chaos.

Lael raised his cup. "Let us drink to my father's health. May his recovery be quick, for there be no justice without healing. *Viva le roi!*"

Isabelle raised her toast but did not drink. She could not have stomached water just now.

Bitterlich emerged from the crowd behind Isabelle and spoke softly in her ear. "Is it just me, or was that the most self-serving tribute ever uttered?"

A series of knots unwound along Isabelle's spine at Bitterlich's arrival. She had no desire to be alone in this place right now.

"I'm sure it's a contender," she said, and twitched her nose toward the main doors.

She led the way outside to the patio. The wind whistled by, a relentless chilling tune, and she took shelter behind one of the great blocky uprights of the colonnade.

"You first," she said. "Did you learn anything interesting?" She wanted to hear what he'd found out before presenting her speculation.

Bitterlich's whiskers twitched. "There were a great number of disturbing rumors being circulated about Grand Leon's health in particular but also branching out into similar occurrences. It turns out Monsieur Possel's eldest brother passed out at a soirée the other evening, and Monsieur Feradame's sister-in-law has taken to her bed. And then I heard Madame DuVinter say that she thinks Monsieur Alibert has the black cankers. 'Why else would his bloodshadow have holes in it?' were her exact words."

Isabelle stomach shrank in dread; even the rumors of plague and pox could start riots and burn cities to the ground. During the reign of the gray pest, the fear of the disease had led to almost as many deaths as the pest itself.

Bitterlich went on. "I got close enough to Lael to get a whiff of him. He's very sick. He smells of liniment, and dried blood. His breath carries the taint of the Miasma and he has a fever you could fry an egg on. His sweat has the bitter fume of moon milk, and there's a smudge of Jasper's weed on the sleeve of his robe." A pain suppressant and a vitalizer.

"Do you think he's dying?" Isabelle asked.

"I don't know," Bitterlich said. "I've seen people survive gut wounds and I've seen people die from flesh wounds. You go when it's your time, but I'm surprised he's upright."

Isabelle chewed her lip. "All I have is coincidence," she said, "but I think Lael is the Harvest King." She told him how Lael had let slip Guillaume's name, and how Lael could have known that. She would not be surprised if Bitterlich called her mad. "The problem of course is that I have no proof and my word is worthless."

"Not to me," Bitterlich said. His ears twitched in agitation. "But we'll need more tangible evidence, witnesses. I should follow him and see if he leads me to your brother and sister-in-law, but I don't like leaving you unescorted at a time like this."

"I don't like being unescorted at a time like this." She was no porcelain teacup, but she also knew the difference between bravery and bravado.

Something brushed her leg. She started and looked down. She did not see but rather felt a tendril of air curl up her leg and tease the hem of her skirt. It flowed up her back, slithered along her neck, and tickled her ear. From this tongue of air came Hailer Dok's reedy voice. "Princess Halfagain. Ye and yours be in danger. You brother and sister be taken, I be betrayed, and a bloody foe plots against yer roi. Meet me at yer mother's crypt, and mayhap we'll see what can be done to change the winds."

"Dok," Isabelle said, swiveling her head as if she might see where the whispering wind had come from. "Can you hear me?" But the voice faded and the wayward zephyr disappeared into the prevailing wind.

Bitterlich's eyes had gone round. "What happened?"

"Hailer Dok," she said, staring in the direction of the Rivencrag. Speaking of witnesses. Aside from her brother, he was the one person who might be able and willing to identify Lael as the Harvest King. "His fortunes have taken a turn for the worse and he wants to talk."

CHAPTER

Eighteen

Washed and scraped with his hair clipped and a fresh new uniform conjured from the Imperial stores, Jean-Claude fancied he looked like one of those creaky old officers who pinned his medals on every day and harassed the younger generation with stories of famous cavalry charges in which he had not actually participated.

"You'll pass for respectable as long as you don't open your mouth," Impervia said.

"I need it open to breathe," he said. "I feel like an overstuffed sausage." This year's fashions reminded him that he was not as svelte as he had once been, or ever.

"We didn't have anything sized for a cart horse."

Several tart replies flitted through Jean-Claude's mind but did not pass his lips. He missed being able to spar with her, and other things. Her presence made his trousers even tighter. She hadn't let herself go like he had. Her skirt had a long hidden slit so that when she strode or turned, it flashed a strong shapely leg clad in sheer white stockings. Jean-Claude remembered those legs intimately and wished he did not. He kept having to remind himself that none of her display was aimed at him.

They sat opposite each other in her coach, a narrow one built to accommodate the Pilgrims' Road.

Impervia said, "We'll observe the play first, try to identify anyone associated with production who's not part of the acting troupe, interview as many as we can without being obvious, then my people will track them wherever they go after the production."

"If you have people, why expose yourself at all? Won't the presence of Grand Leon's spymaster put them on their guard?" Jean-Claude asked.

"In my experience, anything that makes people uncomfortable makes them more likely to betray their secrets, not less."

Jean-Claude could not disagree with that. "How did you find out about this soirée?"

"My daughter-in-law is hosting. It has become the fashionable thing to do."

"That would be Henri and his wife, Giselle," Jean-Claude said.

Impervia smiled somewhat more warmly. "I may even sneak off for a few moments with my grandson, wind him up for his mother if nothing else."

Jean-Claude kept her going for a while with questions about her offspring, a subject about which she was dry but effusive. He tried to imagine what it would have been like for her children at the sharp end of her tongue. Yet apparently they were much loved, for she more than once bemoaned how far away the younger three lived, and how would the grandbabies ever get to know their grandmamma?

"What about you?" she asked. "Will Isabelle's children call you grandpapa?"

Jean-Claude shook off his complacency. "I don't know that she plans to have children." Isabelle wanted children, but had much to fear from childbearing. Her mother and her grandmother both died in childbirth, and then there were the hazards that might come from passing along her highly distilled sorcery. Did she want to give birth to a child who would very likely be torn apart by competing sorceries even if it was not murdered for being an abomination? None of these concerns were his to divulge, however.

Le Comte de Marchand's chateau was a stately pile built out from the cliff face on one of Rocher Royale's highest terraces. It overlooked Chisel Lake, a deep narrow ribbon of water pooled in a dammed-up rent in the side of the Rivencrag.

Impervia's carriage wound its way through a garden of ornamental fountains, all of which sported frozen plumes, jets, and fringes of icicles lit up in spectacular hues of green and gold by beams from colored lanterns.

They debarked in a wooded courtyard and were led into a sumptuous hall with a parquetry floor in three shades of rare wood and a groined roof painted to look like a forest canopy. It was held up by what looked to be the cores of actual trees. In this city of limestone, it was the poor who walked on marble floors.

They were met just inside the doors by Impervia's son Henri and his wife, Giselle, who barely had time to greet their mother before a five-year-old pelted across the floor squealing with delight for his grandmamma. While Impervia twirled the youngling around, Jean-Claude did due diligence with his own introduction. He was greeted with the stiff politeness of people being saddled with a social inferior they could do nothing about. Jean-Claude dearly hoped that their decision to host tonight's play was the sum of their involvement in the Harvest King's plot.

Jean-Claude cast his gaze over the sea of guests. Clayborn servants dressed in black waited on saintborn nobles, mostly Sanguinaire decked out in white, their bloodshadows pooled at their feet like docile hounds. Like jewels upon this snow were cast a scattering of different colors: silver-eyed Glasswalkers in their short jackets and soft caps, a Fenice with bright yellow and orange plumage that made him look like a firebird, even a Goldentongue with his gloriole on full display.

Jean-Claude made conversation with the guests, who took note of his uniform and concluded that he must have special knowledge of Grand Leon's mysterious illness. In return, he heard tales of uncles with tattered shadows, sisters with strange fits, the friend of a friend who had committed suicide. How long would it be until these whispered rivulets joined into a flood of panic?

The clock had rung the eighth hour when the orchestra struck up a tune and the center of the great hall cleared out to make room for the dancers. Jean-Claude limped toward the edge of the room to continue his interrogation of his fellow bachelors when a hand caught his sleeve.

Impervia turned him around and her lips scowled up at him. "You aren't planning on stranding me, are you?"

Jean-Claude shrank at the thought of taking her on the dance floor. "My pardons, but I do not so much dance as wallow, and I don't wish to embarrass you. Plus, I'm supposed to be canvassing the room."

She snorted. "I am assured these will be stately old-people dances, and we need to coordinate our efforts."

Jean-Claude braced himself for awkwardness—this was part of his duty, nothing more—and extended his elbow in the approved fashion. "May I have this dance, madame?"

"Why yes, you may, monsieur."

As he guided her onto the floor, she asked, "Have you learned anything so far?"

"More of what we already know," he said. "Half a dozen people have mentioned Grand Leon's sickness, at least two have mentioned bloodshadows with holes in them. You?"

"My grandson is obsessed with birds. He can name about thirty species of them, some accurately. Aside from that there is at least one young gentleman here who is thrilled his uncle has taken ill. In his mind, this moves him a step closer to inheritance of some sort. And several people have asked me about Grand Leon, trying to position themselves if the worst comes to pass. I also asked Giselle why she decided to host the *Harvest King*. It was recommended to her by a friend, a socially ambitious woman with a wealth of opinions stacked on a paucity of facts. I deduce that she hopes to take a share of the credit for tonight's performance."

They reached their mark on the floor just as the music started up. It was a couples' dance, slow enough that he could manage it on his bad leg, but far too intimate for his comfort. The absurd difference in their size didn't help. Every time her thigh brushed his, it sent a thrill up his spine, and he found himself twisting to try to avoid the contact.

"Relax," she said. "It's like trying to dance while holding a python at arm's length."

"I told you I was bad at this," Jean-Claude said.

"Only because you're fighting it," she said. "You used to love this sort of thing. What happened to you?"

"I got old," he said, and when had that become his preferred excuse?

"There's a difference between old and stale," Impervia said. "What happened?"

"I hurt you." The words fell out of Jean-Claude's mouth, as raw and bloody as if he'd just spit out a rotten tooth.

Impervia gave him a look that suggested spluttering anger without the actual spit. "Oh. I see. You hurt me."

Jean-Claude tensed. Why was she angry? "Yes."

"And then what," she said. "Did you imagine you broke me? Did you imagine you shattered my poor little life? Do you think I've spent all these years weeping in a corner? Do you believe you had such power over me?"

She leaned into him, gliding her hip up his thigh in a way that set off every rutting urge in his body.

"I was there," she whispered fiercely. "It wasn't a mistake. I wasn't a mistake, and I'm not your damned victim."

Jean-Claude's mind whirled dizzy with more than just the dance, and now he felt truly the fool. Of course she'd been insulted. In his hubris he'd diminished her.

The tenor of the music changed mid-dance as the sound of shepherds' pipes wove their way into the melody. New dancers appeared and interspersed themselves amongst the guests.

Dressed in furs and leaves, their hair ornamented with flowers, the newcomers danced with a vigor that pulled the tempo along with it until Jean-Claude's heart hammered and his leg felt like it was going to twist off. More dancers appeared from the sides of the room, plucked the wallflowers from their comfortable plots, and dragged them onto the dance floor. Primal drums joined the woodwinds and the lights around the edges of the room were snuffed by fleeting players. The sudden isolation drove the dance floor into a different world, a primitive place without the trappings of civilization. The growls and cries of wild animals filled the air, along with the shrieking of birds.

Jean-Claude tried to watch every which way at once, but he wasn't even sure what he was looking for. This play had been performed dozens of times before and never once had some great conspiracy been revealed, nor any crime more serious than adultery committed. For all he knew, the villain they were chasing had been inspired by the play and not the other way around.

Impervia, better at adapting to the music than he was, shimmied up against him. He flinched. A spasm of pain jolted his thigh and he collapsed in a graceless heap, clutching his leg and hissing.

Impervia knelt, horror-struck. "What happened?"

"Damned leg," he growled between gritted teeth. The dance swirled on around them.

"Let me help you," Impervia said. She clasped his arm and hoisted him up. She was surprisingly strong for someone of her diminutive stature. He managed to balance, but his leg throbbed mercilessly. Two more players darted in. One of them whisked him off the dance floor and the other twirled Impervia back into the dance.

"Are you injured, monsieur?" asked the player who helped Jean-Claude onto a chair at the side of the hall.

"I broke my pride in three places," Jean-Claude said. The youth plied him with wine. Jean-Claude took the cup but found the libation too sweet for his mood. Besides, he did not need alcohol on top of pain muddying his thoughts.

Impervia adapted to her new, more graceful partner with ease. The dance made permissible physical suggestions that would have been otherwise quite salacious. The pair made some very suggestive passes, brushing each other lightly in a way that filled Jean-Claude with an entirely unreasonable envy. He'd wanted to be elsewhere when he was out there; it made no sense to want to be out there when he was elsewhere.

So how did one apologize to someone for discounting their vital honor?

The question failed to suggest its own answer. At last he tore his gaze off Impervia. He had business to attend. Scores of people had been murdered, including Orem, and this play must hold a clue as to why.

From his spot in the shadows he watched the story unfold. He was no connoisseur of the theater, but it was not hard to see how much effort had gone into this production. The story was a legend about a great king who rose to power and found himself at the top of the highest mountain. Still unsatisfied, he challenged the gods themselves, and was cast down for his pride. His fall left the world in ruins, but he had left his seed behind in the belly of the World Mother and was reborn to begin the cycle anew.

The themes were not subtle, and a whole range of sins were enacted. Still, the actors entertained, and the audience was involved at every stage, drinking blood wine and disappearing into sacred groves only to appear later much disheveled. The impregnation of the World Mother took place within a cyclone of whirling banners, but Jean-Claude had no doubt that it actually took place.

It was all too easy to see how the *Harvest King* was meant to be a taunt to Grand Leon. "You have reached for godhood and you will fall." Yet aside from the decidedly lascivious production, this was hardly different than any number of other morality plays, and none of the references were pointed enough to warrant charges of sedition.

When the last act was done and the Harvest King awakened, the house lights came up and the actors took a bow to thunderous applause. Jean-Claude pried himself out of the chair and strolled to the door from which most of the actors had emerged. A door ward made to block his way, but he pointed to the golden thundercrown emblazoned on his blue tabard. The door ward's eyes rounded and he stepped aside.

Jean-Claude stepped into a drawing room cum costume shop where a half-dozen players were in the process of changing clothes. Several of them looked up and one fellow said, "Monsieur, you're not supposed to be . . . oh."

Jean-Claude pointed to that one and asked, "Is there anyone in charge here?"

The man looked nervous. "Madame Veva is our producer. She's still on stage."

Madame Veva. The name rattled around in Jean-Claude's brain for a moment before thumping into a memory. Shocked, he asked, "Is she . . . I mean, did she have a relationship with an Aragothic Ambassador?"

"Cubilla?" said the man. "Yes, but he died. She's really upset about it."

Jean-Claude felt like he'd been kicked in the gut by a particularly ornery mule. For the past three days he's been hunting the Harvest King because he'd had the power to create sorcerers, but now he had a whole new thread to pull. Cubilla connected to Veva connected to the Harvest King. Cubilla had committed suicide because he'd lost his sorcery. Coquetta was losing her sorcery. Saints and Torments, somehow the play itself was the vessel for the pest. Was it the wine? The sex?

"Take me to her," Jean-Claude said.

"But—"

"Right now," Jean-Claude insisted, and followed the man out into the grand hall.

He found Veva, who had played the part of the World Mother, loosely robed and still barefooted, in conversation with a pair of avid young Sanguinaire would-be studs.

Jean-Claude cleared his throat and barged in. "Madame Veva, if I might have a word? Messieurs, excuse us."

One of the young men, who was already listing hard to port wine, turned a belligerent gaze on Jean-Claude and said, "Clayborn piss-drinker, I'll—"

Jean-Claude laid him out with a belt to the face before he could do anything even dumber, and chased his friend off with a growl.

"Thanks for that," Veva said, clutching her robe tight at her throat. "If his kind don't pay in advance, they don't pay at all."

"You're welcome," Jean-Claude said, drawing her into an alcove off the main hall, "but I need to talk to you about Ambassador Cubilla."

Veva grimaced. "Poor Mateo. Why would anyone do that to him?"

"You loved him?"

Veva barked a mournful laugh and tears stood in her eyes. "Yes, and damn the saints for it, him a saintborn and me soulless clay. But he didn't care. He didn't mind I've ridden more studs than a cavalry regiment. Where do you find a man like that? He was going to take me glasswalking. I was going to get to see Om and the great Temple."

"I'm sorry for your loss," Jean-Claude said.

Veva pulled her cape around herself a bit more tightly. "Thank you, but why does a King's Own Musketeer want to know?"

"I'm looking for the man who assassinated him," Jean-Claude said.

All the color drained from Veva's face. "I thought that maid killed him."

"No," Jean-Claude said. "She was set up."

Veva's hand flew to her mouth. "Oh saints."

"Did Ambassador Cubilla ever come to watch your play?"

Veva grimaced and shook her head. "No. He wasn't jealous but there were some things he didn't want to watch."

"How did you get involved in the play?" Jean-Claude asked. "Who is paying for all this?"

"I answered a casting call. The producer calls himself Monsieur Rexmessis."

The Harvest King, Jean-Claude translated from the Saintstongue. "Where can I find this Rexmessis?"

"I don't honestly know. I only met him a few times, when he hired us on, and at one or two rehearsals. We did the show for him once, and then he said, 'Go forth and cast down the grasping king.' After that we've just got our pay by messenger, along with notes about our performances."

"And you don't think that's a little odd?"

"I'll put up with a little odd for a lot of silver," she said. "Besides, nobles do that when they want to put on a play but don't want to be sullied by association with the theater. When we started, I never thought we'd be this successful."

"How many times have you put this play on?"

"Maybe forty times over the last few months. But what does the play have to do with anything?"

"I think your patron is responsible for Ambassador Cubilla's death, and I need your help to prove that."

Veva looked horrified. "But . . . how?"

"Was there anything special Monsieur Rexmessis gave you, some prop or another that he absolutely insisted you use?"

Veva looked stunned, like someone trying to remember what happened when they were drunk. "The ritual," she said slowly. "We put our blood in the wine. It's just a drop—you can't even taste it—but it's got to be real, and the sex, too. That's written into the contract. What's all this about?"

Jean-Claude's head swam with the understanding; the Harvest King must have infected the troupe, turned them into a weapon. Actors were almost all clayborn so none of them were affected, and they didn't know they were diseased. Veva had passed on the shadow rot to Cubilla through sex and to others through blood. Then the infected audience members spread the disease to their lovers, and so on. Given how randy the court tended to be, it was only a matter of time until the pest found its target, the great billy goat himself: Grand Leon.

"Jean-Claude," Impervia said, appearing from the crowd. "Have you found something?"

"Yes," Jean-Claude said. With a horrid sinking feeling he asked, "Have you had any of the wine?"

"A few sips," Impervia said, and she must have read the dismay on Jean-Claude's face, for she looked to Veva and demanded, "What did you do to the wine?"

Veva fell to quivering. "Nothing. A drop of blood."

"That's how it's being spread," Jean-Claude said, and now Impervia had sipped the poison, and there wasn't a damned thing anyone could do about it.

Impervia's bloodshadow lanced out and pinned Veva's shadow. Veva's back arched like a bow pulled to the breaking point. Her mouth gaped in a silent scream. The bloodshadow held her paralyzed down to the roots. "Who sent you?"

"Impervia, stop!" Jean-Claude snapped. "It's not her fault. She was duped!" Of course Impervia was furious, her sacred soul had been infected.

Impervia's rage all but blistered on her face, but she dragged her bloodshadow back and Veva collapsed to the floor mewling in pain.

Jean-Claude got between Impervia and Veva. "The Harvest King set them up, the whole troupe without them knowing it."

Impervia's teeth clenched. "Even if that's true, she's still passed that vile pest on to me. I've seen what it's done to Coquetta." She looked down at her bloodshadow as if expecting it to evaporate on the spot.

"Which means we have to stop it from spreading, and we have to warn Grand Leon. You go do that, and I'll round up all the players." If he didn't get them out of here, if news of what they had done, however unwitting, got out, they'd be torn to pieces and reduced to soul smudges.

"And my son and my grandchildren," Impervia said, fury burning in her gaze. "I gave little Elliot a sip of my wine."

"Impervia," Jean-Claude said. "Perv, listen to me."

The old nickname got her attention. "I am not a perv," she said.

"No, just slower than a sack of snails. This anger, this outrage is exactly what the Harvest King wants. He wants us to panic and lose our twice-cursed minds."

"Says the man who hasn't been poisoned," Impervia snapped.

"So what in all ten thousand Torments are you going to do about it? Do you want me to bring in all the players so you can burn them into soul smudges? Who will that help? We need to find the Harvest King, and for that we need live witnesses."

Impervia forced her posture into its usual proud position. "I wasn't going to kill her."

Jean-Claude glanced down at the woman who was curled up in a fetal position, her skin nearly white and becoming translucent.

"There are worse things than death," he said.

"Or turn her into a bloodhollow," Impervia said defensively.

Jean-Claude decided to let that be true. Sometimes the truth wormed its way backward in time and memory. "I need you to go warn Grand Leon. I'll get this lot out of here to someplace I can question them."

Impervia closed her eyes for a moment, breathing deeply. At last she said, "Call me Perv again and I'll nail your ankles to your ears."

"How about Imp?" Jean-Claude said.

She glowered at him, but it was a friendly glower, or at least not full of rage and despair. "Find him," she said. "Quickly. Find out if there's anything to be done."

Jean-Claude watched her out of the alcove. Saints but his soul ached for her, but she needed his sympathy less than she needed his action. He grabbed the nearest player by the arm and said, "Madame Veva needs your help."

In ones and twos, out various exits, Jean-Claude stole the players away and herded them to a storehouse filled with barrels of precious salt. They were all distressed by what had happened to Madame Veva, but none of them knew any more than she did about the Harvest King. At long last he summoned the city watch and put a guard on them lest they try to flee and inadvertently spread the pest to some other city.

He had just finished arranging for the captive troupe to be fed and watered, when an Imperial messenger approached, his pennon snapping in the breeze. "Monsieur musketeer."

Jean-Claude looked around, but alas saw no other musketeers to whom the man might be referring.

"A message for you, monsieur," said the rider, passing down a scroll tied with a red ribbon and marked with Coquetta's seal.

With dread in his heart, he broke open the seal and squinted at the paper, which was covered in squiggly blurs. He put on his spectacles and tried again. His heart lost its grip on his ribs and sank down to crush his lungs.

Come quickly. I need you.—Coquetta

What more needed to be said? Coquetta's bloodshadow was dying, and rare it was for the sorcerer to survive such a shriving. Jean-Claude asked, "From whom did you receive this?"

"From Mademoiselle Josette, her own hand."

Jean-Claude's hand clenched and unclenched. His first priority, his only one, was to find the Harvest King and find out if this pox had a cure, but just now he had no leads . . . but Coquetta might know which nobles would sponsor a play like this.

"Off your horse, monsieur," Jean-Claude said.

"Beg pardon," the messenger said.

"I'm needed at le Ville Céleste, so unless you have another horse in your saddlebags, I'm borrowing yours and your pennon. Meanwhile you take charge here, those actors are to be well cared for, but they are not allowed to leave until I say so."

He took the time to lengthen the stirrups so that he could sit without hunching over like a jockey, then guided the horse around so he was a little uphill of it, which made getting his foot in the stirrup possible without help.

Alas that galloping away in a cloud of dust was not an option. He had kilometers to go, and all uphill. He lifted the horse into a quick walk and gazed up, and up and up, where the quondam towers of le Ville Céleste thrust up above the ragged lip of the Rivencrag. Please let Coquetta be alive when he got there.

Nineteen

When Isabelle and Bitterlich rode into the graveyard, the sky was so clear that the stars seemed to hover just beyond the reach of Isabelle's upstretched fingers. The white moon Kore peeked out over the lip of the Rivencrag while the red moon Threin lingered on the horizon.

Bitterlich had already done a survey of the grounds as an owl, and reported no sign of any ambushers. There were mourners amongst the graves tonight, and the slow sad procession of a moonlight burial taking place. Given the size of the city and the limited slice of land, only the fortunate could afford a burial, and only the rich could hope for an undisturbed rest.

The mounted party had attracted the attention of the gravediggers. Foreman Jillette hurried toward Isabelle and Bitterlich, waving a lantern to make sure they saw him. They adjusted course and he approached to a respectful distance before doffing his hat and making a deep bow.

"Princess," he said. "Good to see you again. Wasn't expecting you so soon. We put the corpses on ice, just like Sergeant Pierre said."

"Corpses?" Isabelle asked.

"Aye, the sorcerers. Sergeant told me that a musketeer told him to keep the corpses on ice so you could have a look at 'em."

"Ah," Isabelle said.

Bitterlich looked to Isabelle and asked, "Corpses first or Dok?"

Isabelle said, "Corpses, I think." She wasn't at all sure how Mistwaithe's corpse might inform her interrogation of Dok, but she wanted all the physical evidence she could gather. Dead men might tell fewer tales than living ones, but they had at least forgotten how to lie.

Jillette led Isabelle and Bitterlich into a cave in the cliff side that had been converted into an icehouse. Bitterlich explored the cave first, declared it devoid of anything more dangerous than low temperatures, and led the way in. The adit went back only a dozen meters or so and the entire left-hand side was bricked up with ice blocks. Before this frigid façade was a long slab of ice on which were laid out several bodies, whole and partial.

Jillette hung his alchemical lantern on a hook. The light got into the ice and made the whole room seem to glow as if Kore were trapped inside.

"These five here are yours," he said, gesturing to the worst of the lot, including two that were better described as bits than bodies. "These others came from Screaming Hall."

The chill of the dead house got in under Isabelle's mantle and made her skin prickle. Jillette seemed impervious to the cold of the place, and Bitterlich's fur had become longer and more luxuriant. *Cheater.*

To Jillette she said, "Would you mind showing Capitaine Bitterlich to my mother's tomb? I have no idea where it is. She was Comtesse Vedetta des Zephyrs, though I suspect she may be buried with her father's family, du Piagets."

Jillette brightened at this very ordinary request. "Yes, mademoiselle, I know just where that is. Funny, but you know you're not the first person to want that crypt of late."

"Really? Who?"

"There was a Monsieur des Zephyrs. Your kin, perhaps? Begging your pardon."

"My brother," Isabelle said. "When was he here?"

"About a three days ago. Seemed powerfully upset when he came out. I imagine he must have loved your mother greatly."

"She gave him life," Isabelle said, the truth at its simplest level. To Bitterlich she said, "You can see if our quarry awaits us." She wanted to add, *be careful,* but did not want to offend him by suggesting timidity.

Bitterlich said, "If I do not return very swiftly, I beg you to leave without a second thought."

"I know my part," she said. *But I will definitely think twice.*

As soon as they had left, Isabelle collected another alchemical lantern and took a closer look at the ghastly cadavers.

The most intact corpse, presumably Mistwaithe, was just complete enough to be truly horrific. He'd been a thin man with high cheekbones. His eyes and guts had been torn out by scavengers, but there was no mistaking the slice in his throat for anything but a surgical cut. Isabelle put on her *gant de acier* and pulled aside the skin flap and cartilage. Mistwaithe's tongue had been removed at the root. His Goldentongue, the organ of his sorcery. He also had a hole in his head, right at the place Ingle's drawings showed the sorcerous nodule ought to be, and there was a void in his brain where the Builder's node had been excised.

Understanding bloomed in Isabelle's mind, bringing with it the fetid stink of horror.

It took her only a brief survey to discover that the other two sorcerers' skulls had trepanning wounds. The scorched skeleton's breastbone had been surgically sawn in half and ripped open.

Sickly sure she understood now what was going on, she moved to the corpses from Screaming Hall and uncovered Monsieur Elliot Odson, the Seelenjäger who had attacked Jean-Claude and Marie. Gretl had found the hole in his head, but that was all she'd been looking for. Isabelle pulled off the sheet covering him, and found a long incision across his abdomen. The scar was healed, but still raised and rough. She drew her blood cipher and took a sample of the dead man's blood.

She was still staring at the results when Bitterlich returned in the form of a bat and unfolded into his normal handsome self, tipping his hat to her. "Dok is at your mother's crypt," he said. "He appears to be alone. He had the look and the smell of a man on the run."

"Good," Isabelle said, not looking up from the cipher. She gestured to the corpses. "What do you see, or smell?"

Bitterlich said, "I smell death and decay, and charred bone, which is also what I see. This fellow had his throat cut, though not in the usual way of a back-alley murder. What do you see?"

Isabelle showed him the blood cipher.

He regarded it uncertainly. "I don't understand."

"This is a blood cipher," Isabella said. "It says this man is a clayborn, not un-hallowed, not saintborn by any degree. Maybe that's why he was chosen. As a test, to make sure it would work before Lael subjected himself to it."

"Subjected himself to what?" Bitterlich asked. "I think you've skipped a few steps."

Isabelle took a deep breath. Yes, she'd gotten ahead of herself, ahead of Bitterlich, but still far behind her foes.

She gestured to Odson. "We've been operating under the assumption that Ingle figured out how to awaken sorcery in the unhallowed. This man is clayborn but he has been given sorcery."

She entered Odson's name in the cipher's store, then cleared its face to make it ready for a new subject. She reopened Odson's head wound, positioned the cipher very precisely over the Builder's node, and took a sample.

The cipher displayed one word: Seelenjäger. There was no name attached to it, ergo the Builder's node came from a different person.

"That's why he calls himself the Harvest King," Isabelle said, her mouth dry. "He harvests the organs of sorcery from one person and puts them in another. He isn't awakening sorcery in the unhallowed, he's stealing it from the blessed."

Bitterlich's whiskers pulled back flat against his face. "How? You can't take an organ out of one person and stick it in another like transplanting a tree."

"You can if you have in your possession a salve that can heal any wound or sculpt flesh and bone: Primal Clay." She tapped on her own silvery stump with her flesh hand. "The man who did this to me used the stuff to seal off my arm, healing it instantly. It can also be used to meld disparate parts." The one person Isabelle had met who'd had his whole visage changed by the clay had been given the eyes of a Glasswalker—so clearly the transplant had taken root and thrived with no ill effects—but he had no power because he lacked the brain nodule Ingle had discovered was essential to making sorcery work.

Bitterlich's nose wrinkled as if he'd smelled something fouler than corpses. "Can you imagine the butcher's market that could bring? For the paltry price of murder, you too can be a sorcerer. I can think of a hundred clayborn men who would happily kill for such a chance."

"Or one in particular," Isabelle said. "You said Lael smelled sick—moon milk and liniment and fever—what if that was just the smells of his surgery? Even with the Primal Clay I ran a fever for days after my arm was severed."

"What I smelled was more than just a little surgery," Bitterlich said.

"How about a lot of surgery," Isabelle said. "My brother seemed to think he might be granted all the sorceries."

"He'd make himself an abomination." Bitterlich's voice was incredulous.

"I imagine he'd do worse than that," Isabelle said. "I need to talk to Hailer Dok and persuade him to testify that Lael is the Harvest King, find out what he knows about the *Conquest*."

The path to the crypts snaked along the foot of the cliff. Isabelle and Bitterlich climbed a stone stair to the arched entrance to another tunnel cut into the cliff face. It was guarded by statues of Saint Umbar, patron saint of the dead, and an iron-banded gate, currently askew.

The catacombs were darker than the night outside, filled with the sort of blackness that seemed to get into Isabelle's eyes and fill them with ink. Even her spark-arm barely illuminated the foyer. They fetched two alchemical lanterns off a rack by the door and sparked them to life. Their yellow light pushed the shadows back and made them squirm as if they were angry.

"This way," Bitterlich said. His feet turned into paws, and he padded forward. Isabelle trailed after, her boots clunking and her spurs clinking on the stone floor. The catacombs themselves were surprisingly uncomplicated, being a main adit with branch tunnels going off at right angles. Every wall was filled with burial niches, like bookshelves loaded with corpses, each one closed off by a panel of wood or stone, painted or graven as the relatives of the deceased could afford.

Several times they passed insets where some very wealthy family had carved out crypts with one or more graven stone sarcophagi lined up within, as if extravagant grief were somehow superior to the ordinary kind.

They reached a side tunnel no different than any other, and Bitterlich motioned her to stop. He set down his lantern and whispered, "Give me a moment to find a good watch point, then call him."

"How long?"

"Count slowly to fifty."

Bitterlich crisply folded himself into the shape of a bat and flittered away.

Isabelle counted. Her taut nerves made it hard to tell how fast she was counting, so she switched to base eight so at least she had to work at visualizing the numerals.

She picked up Bitterlich's lantern with her spark-hand and called out, "Hailer Dok. I know you are here."

"Aye, mademoiselle," Dok replied from the corridor. "Yea best come here. It's no as if I can drag the casket out."

Isabelle rounded the corner into the largest crypt she'd yet seen, a semi-circular room with a half-domed ceiling. A few young stalactites hung over a low-walled round font, their occasional drip plinking loud in the silence. In arched alcoves along the curved walls lay seven stone sarcophagi, with space left over for two more.

Hailer Dok sat on the sixth one, a covered lantern glowing dimly behind him so that he was nothing but a silhouette in the darkness.

"Your folk worships death, mademoiselle, building shrines such as this," he said in a tired voice.

Isabelle held up her lantern to illuminate his face, and found him haggard and worn, his eyes in deep pits . . . or perhaps that was just the effect of the insufficient light.

"As of the last census there are more than twenty-million Célestials," Isabelle said. "We don't all even have a language in common, much less funerary traditions, but you said you had information about a plot against le roi."

"Aren't yea going to summon your beastly capitaine? Yea wouldn't be down here without a guard, and you surely wouldn't be carrying two lanterns all by yer lonesome."

"You didn't invite him," Isabelle said, setting her flesh-hand lantern down on the edge of the font. "I'm not even entirely sure why you summoned me."

"Outcast or no, ye've le royal bugger's ear, or so I've heard."

Isabelle folded her arms. "I'm hardly unique in that respect."

"Maybe, but ye haven't any other friends, neither. Yer on no one's side but your own."

Isabelle declined to disabuse him of this notion. Her friends were her joy and salvation. "In other words, you judge me weak enough that I have to bargain with you rather than simply take you by force."

"The mademoiselle is wise," he said.

"Then what is it you want?"

"I want what was promised afore," Dok said.

"A ship, to bring back *Conquest*'s treasure," Isabelle said.

"Clever wench, too," Dok said.

"I will help you," Isabelle said. "I'll get you an audience with le roi, but only after you tell me what you know about the Harvest King. I know he hired you to help him reach the *Conquest*."

Dok shook his head as if bothered by flies. "That's a burst bag and a flaming basket, but yes. I meets a Goldentongue says he knows a man who looks to hire a ship to recover the *Conquest*'s treasure. He's got a special orrery shows the way. A splinter of the *Conquest*'s bone keel in the matrix, he says. Got sympathetic resonance, just like chartstone. He shows us the location of the ship, north into the Twilight Circle, onward past the Bittergale.

"First I say he's mad. No one challenges the Bittergale, but then I sees the orrery. There's sure something there, and it had to get there somehow. He says he goes with us right through the Bittergale to prove he's not lying. Risks his own neck, see. So I gets to thinking about the pay chest, and it won't lets me go. I gets to thinking I can change the world."

This was not what she was expecting from Dok. "How so?"

"Ye believe me not," he said, "but I means to give the treasure back, back to the Temple in exchange for lifting the curse upon the Gyrine. After three hundred and fifty years we'll take back our goodlands, find soil for our seed."

Isabelle was stunned. "I thought you were the masters of the sky, the lords of the air, the emperors of the wind, the ad of the infinitum."

"But I'm nay fool. Twenty million Célestials, yea say. There be maybe eighty clans of Gyrine left, and our numbers decline. If we sticks with our pride, we dies out like fire and passes on like smoke.

"Yet I sees more skyships aloft now than ever afore, and skyships needs fair winds. Methinks there's more treasure to be had singing a ship back and forth to Craton Riqueza than stealing the cargo. We is rich with the chance if we can get it."

"That . . . sounds like an admirable goal," Isabelle said, but he was right about one thing: she didn't believe it. Chances were that even if he meant every word he said now, he'd double-cross the Temple in the end. It's what the Gyrine did.

"What did the Harvest King want?" she asked, the one crucial question.

"He wants just one thing," he said. "All the gold is ours, and the plunder, and the Azurite to do with as we will, but for one thing of his choosing amongst the spoil, something he called the saint eater."

The word unfolded before Isabelle's mind's eye. "Saint eater. In the Saints-tongue it's sanctivore." She stopped short, like a condemned criminal hitting the end of her rope, for she'd heard that word before.

Nobody really knew what the sanctivore was. It was just one mention in one line of one of the most controversial books in the *Instruction*. One version of an oft told tale read: *And so the Eldest Circle named Skalexes heretic, and banished him from the land. The Builder cursed him and withdrew the protection of his mighty hand. Thence did the Breaker unleash the sanctivore, the beast consumed the gift Skalexes had abused and condemned his line forevermore to the clay.*

It was one of those lines that theologians, especially drunk theologians, liked to argue about endlessly, for the sanctivore was nowhere else mentioned or described. It was generally assumed to be one of the Breaker's many minions, a spirit loosed from Torment, a metaphor to modern sensibilities.

Yet what if it was a real thing, a weapon the Risen Saints had used against Saint Skalexes to rob him and his people of their power? It might have been one of the artifacts salvaged after the annihilation of Rüul, stored in the quondariums in Om, and loaded onto the *Conquest* to be used against Skaladin and their cullborn.

Centuries later, Lael had spent a great deal of time in the quondariums, looking for something he didn't find. Somehow he learned or guessed what the sanctivore was and how it had been lost.

"What did this saint eater look like?" Isabelle asked

"Strange," Dok said. "It looks like water in a glass tube, but without the tube. There be a belt about its waist of the old metal. Turn it this way up and the water sloshed down and it's green. Flip it the other way and the water turns the color of a plum."

Isabelle's brain hurt trying to imagine that, but at least she had most of the story now. "What happened between you and Guillaume after you tried to hoodwink Grand Leon?"

Dok looked offended. "Twasn't I lying to yer roi. An honest dealer I am, but yer brother be trying to skin out of a murder."

Isabelle waved this away, her spark-hand trailing motes. "The question is what happened next? And how did you end up down here?"

"We lay low at his townhome getting ready to wait out the month until he gets made comte and I gets me ship, when two of them Praetorians show up, say le roi's changed his mind and tries to arrest us. Guillaume says they be working for the Harvest King. They gets him but I jumps off the cliff and my shadow falls away where they can't gets me. I don't know who's after me so I hides down here."

"Why here?" Isabelle asked.

"Cause yer brother's already been here, see, and he comes back ta me and says it be gone, his mother's tomb's been robbed, the Harvest King must have took it, his mother's gift. So I don't know what that is, but if he's been here and the Harvest King has been here, then I figure they've got no reason to come back."

"Who is the Harvest King?" Isabelle asked.

"That's something only yer roi needs ta know," Dok said.

Isabelle advanced on him. "No. It's something I need to know, and I need to know it now. I said I would help you and I will. You're welcome to the *Conquest* and whatever treasures it holds. I don't care that you helped my brother cover up my father's murder. I don't even care if you stuffed Arnette like a game hen, but if you want my help, you will tell me what I need to know. The Harvest King was on your clan balloon for months from what I understand; he could not have kept his secret for that long."

Dok shrugged his skinny shoulder. "Fine. He's le royal bugger's bastard, Lael, as I suspect ye already knows."

Isabelle let loose a breath she seemed to have been holding for hours. "If you will testify to that before Grand Leon, I will see that you get your chance to lift the curse on your people."

Dok snorted. "I'm not that much a fool."

Out of curiosity she examined her mother's stone sarcophagus. The lid had been graven with the full-relief image of her mother in her funerary gown. Her arms were folded across her chest, but instead of the spindle and distaff that were standard fare on such memorials, she bore a mirror and a makeup pot, an eternal tribute to her overweening vanity.

Except it wasn't really a makeup pot. It was Kantelvar's gift to her, a jar of Primal Clay. Had she been buried with it?

The whole lid sat askew, as if whoever had last opened it saw no reason to close it again. There were claw marks on the side of the lid. Presumably Immacolata had opened it. Immacolata who had not been seen since the Golden Swain. She was even more elusive than the Harvest King.

"Did Lael have a Fenice with him aboard your clan balloon?" she asked.

"Nay," Dok said. "He came alone."

Isabelle lifted her lantern above the sarcophagus opening and her stomach lurched. Inside was indeed a corpse. The burial shroud had been pulled away, revealing a skeletal figure tightly bound in blackened shriveled skin. The dermis was split in some places, showing bone and ligament. The lips were pulled back from the teeth in an eternal snarl. Such was the fate of the most beautiful woman in the world.

Isabelle was usually more fascinated than repulsed by the grotesque, but she could not apply the concept of "mother" to this pathetic corpse.

The deceased's arms were folded across her breast. A mirror was locked in the bony grip of her right hand. It looked to have been wired in place, but her left hand cupped . . . nothing. Clearly it had once been wrapped around something round, but that something had been removed, and none too gently judging by the severed wires and broken fingers. The Primal Clay had to have been taken weeks ago to give the Harvest King time to try out his transplant technique on Odson before using it on himself.

The sound of bootsteps interrupted and Isabelle turned to face the entrance as two Sanguinaire walked in: Roland and Serge. Fear turned Isabelle's marrow to slush. "Saints be blessed," said short dark Serge. "If it isn't the foreign spy Hailer Dok, and look who his contact is, the ever-unfortunate Mademoiselle des Zephyrs."

"Luckless," Roland confirmed.

Dok snarled at Serge. "Treachery. You double-crossing dogspawn!"

Isabelle's heart galloped like a runaway horse, but she stepped out of the alcove. "What are you two doing here, unless you think I have a diary hidden in a sarcophagus? Who sent you?"

A slow smile oozed across Serge's face. "Lord Colonel Hachette sent us, of course. We are placing you under arrest for harboring an enemy of the crown."

"I assume you can produce a warrant for this absurd charge," Isabelle said, willing them to see her fury rather than her fear. "No? But then you aren't working for l'Empire anymore, are you? Your honor is dust, and your loyalty sold to the lowest bidder. But Grand Leon can be merciful. If you turn witness against Lael, I guarantee you will be neither hollowed or hanged."

"You are in no position to make promises," Serge said. "And Grand Leon's days number less than a beggar's handful. Soon we will have a roi who understands power, and who will not tolerate upstart clayborn, degenerate foreigners, shrill women, or the Breaker's get."

"Undesirables," Roland said, making a slow circuit of the font, peering into the shadows in search of Bitterlich.

Serge said, "No more Parlement. No more politics. Once again the strong will rule the weak, as it should be."

"Unfettered," Roland agreed.

"Then by your own admission, you are both traitors."

Serge smiled. "You know, I might have let you live, but for that. The traitor is le roi who's gone soft, not the man who throws him down. The traitor is the Breakerborn who thinks to put herself above righteous men, the Seelenjäger that thinks it's better than a Sanguinaire."

Roland said, "Here, kitten."

Serge said, "Let's flush him out, shall we?" His bloodshadow licked toward Isabelle. "Let's hear you scream."

Down from the ceiling, Bitterlich exploded into the shape of a bear, if such a beast ever had horns and a long snakelike tail with a bony sting. So swift was his change that the air seemed to shudder with his passing. One great paw tore into Roland's back and removed his spine with a meaty rip. The stinger flashed for Serge's eye . . . and stopped just short. The smaller Sanguinaire had thrown himself to the side and lashed out with his bloodshadow, catching Bitterlich just before his blow struck home.

Bitterlich reared up, yowling in pain. The bloodshadow slammed him against the wall, and pinned him like a bug in some collector's box.

A look of utter stupefaction on his face, Roland's corpse folded in half and slumped to the floor, blood spilling in a wide pool.

With a high-pitched wail, a great wind kicked up from nowhere and Hailer Dok shot from the room like a crossbow bolt, riding his own private gale.

Isabelle cursed Dok's cowardice even as she hauled back to throw her lantern at Serge.

"No!" Serge said. A lance of his bloodshadow pierced Isabelle's shadow and stripped away all control of her body. She collapsed. Pain flooded her mind, as if she was being scraped clean from the inside out.

Serge regained his feet and advanced on Bitterlich, yelling at the top of his lungs. "Animal. Beast. You dare attack a Sanguinaire!" He released his hold on Bitterlich just enough to let him scream, then drew him back and slammed him into the wall again.

Serge's bloodshadow infiltrated Bitterlich's ordinary umbra like fire chewing its way through thin parchment. Bitterlich's tawny fur faded in color and turned gray, leeching toward the translucency of a bloodhollow.

No! Isabelle howled in her mind. Once before she'd been pinned, forced to watch as her friend was made a bloodhollow. Not again!

There was no hope fighting a bloodshadow, but Isabelle reached into her body anyway, seeking self like a drowning woman would seek air. Her spark-arm tingled. A brief moment of wondrous clarity bloomed in her mind. Her spark-arm was made of luminous energy and therefore cast no shadow, the bloodshadow couldn't affect it . . . and she still clutched the lantern. She shifted her grip. She had no angle. Only one shot. She pushed her sorcery into her spark-arm to make up in sheer strength what she lacked in leverage. Her sparks flared and shot off glowing embers like a kicked campfire.

"Stop that!" Serge snarled. His bloodshadow tightened its grip, razors of fire sliced deep into Isabelle's every nerve. She recoiled from the agony. Her mind took the only path available to it, shooting out along her sorcerous limb.

Her awareness turned very strange as the root of her senses left her body. Her vision liquefied, all colors smearing like chalk paintings in the rain. Her hearing became muddy. She reached the end of her fingertips and kept going, dragging her sparking nebula with her, straight into the lantern.

Her bones sang like violin strings.

Like a spider dancing on a silken thread, she felt her failing body far behind her, but she also extended into glass and metal. She'd gone into the lantern, merged with it. Being inside brass was like riding a ripple on a warm smooth pond. Glass was stiff but pliable like taffy, shot through with tendrils of pressure pushing and pulling in every direction. She had possessed the lantern, become it.

Oh. So that's how l'Etincelle works.

If this was her body now . . . she turned her attention outward. She needed to see. She remembered eyes, remembered what it felt like to blink, to squint, she chewed on the taffy glass to soften it, pulled and stretched it into shape. Her shape. Her eyes.

And there was Serge, his eyes mad with fury, shadowburning Bitterlich. *No.*

Isabelle pushed her whole face into the glass, like making a mask in soft wax. She forced her tongue into the lantern's phlogiston core. It felt filled with fiery thorns. Parting her glass lips was like blowing bubbles in tar. She took a deep breath, drawing air into the lumin reservoir. Brass and glass glowed with pink and purple sparks. She spat with all her might.

A great rush of flame roared from her mouth and engulfed Serge. He caught fire like a torch, screaming and flailing in his panic. The fire clung to him like a beast, igniting his felt hat, his powdered wig, his perfumed clothes. He caromed off one of the crypt's decorative pilasters and then another.

Her energy spent, Isabelle recoiled into her body along the thread she'd gone out on. The bloodshadow had let go, but it left a hollow creaking pain in its wake. She forced herself to uncurl from the agony. Slow purposeful breathing gradually flushed away her agony like a hand pump draining a mine of water.

Serge's mad dance stopped, and his screaming died to a low animal moan. Isabelle forced herself up on her hand. Her left hand. Her spark-arm had vanished. Spent. Would it ever come back?

On the floor in front of her lay the husk of her lantern, remolded into the shape of her face, her lips still puckered from spitting fire. The ceaseless inventor in the back of her mind started bubbling with ideas for things she might create, now that she knew the way.

She balanced on her knees, weirdly off-kilter with her spark-arm gone. The spark-arm didn't weigh anything—she'd measured to be sure—but she was always aware of it, always accounting for it, until she couldn't feel it anymore.

She reached out for the lantern, but her merest touch made the glass crack and crumble to dust. Apparently l'Étincelle was not gentle with the objects it animated, or perhaps she just hadn't learned to be gentle.

Too shaken to stand, she crawled around the font to where Bitterlich lay mewling. He had returned to his erstepelz and was curled up in a fetal position. His fur was all but white. His eyes were slits, but he was still breathing. She peeled back one of his eyelids, His pupils were pin pricks, but thank the saints his irises were still the color of honey. He would recover. He would need warmth. She pulled off her heavy cloak and draped it over his body.

Isabelle braced against the wall and slowly, laboriously, half climbing the stones, forced herself upright.

She staggered to Serge. The fire had gone out, but he had not yet managed to expire. His face was burned down to the bone and his eyes were ruined, blistered pits. His bloodshadow was a tattered remnant, frayed like a flag left out in a gale. The stench of him brought up her bile and nearly undid her.

She leaned against the wall to settle her gorge and then pulled her maidenblade. She toed Serge onto his back, and put her knee down on his squelching chest to keep him from moving. "Can you hear me, Serge? Because if you can, I have a new deal for you. Tell me where you took Guillaume and Arnette, where I can find Lael, and I'll cut your throat clean and quick. Otherwise, I leave you here to die alone in the cold, the damp, and the dark."

Serge thrashed. His bloodshadow, wispy as it was, whipped around and raked Isabelle's shadow. Pain lashed across her back. She gasped and fell, failing to catch herself with the spark-arm that wasn't there. Though his bloodshadow could hurt her, he hadn't enough control to paralyze her.

He sat up and flailed toward her. His clawlike hands clutched the air, and he heaved up flecks of lung with his aspiration. Isabelle rolled away and rose to her knees.

There was a swish, a flash of pale green light from the darkness. Serge's charred head toppled from his shoulders and landed with a thump, the scorched pits of his eyes staring into Torment everlasting. Blood spurted from the stump of his neck until the last stillness overcame him and his blood-shadow faded to gray.

From the darkness of the tunnel emerged Brunela, carrying an old-fashioned longsword made of arcanite, a jade-tinted metal last drawn from the soul forges in the age of Rüul. The edge of the blade was so thin and sharp as to be transparent, flickering green and trailing a smear of emerald, like a wound left in the air. It was quite a weapon for a fugitive to have. There couldn't be more than a dozen of its kind left in the world. Of course the Fenice were experts at handing things down from generation to genera-tion. But wasn't such an heirloom the sort of thing she'd want to hide if there was a bone queen looking to identify survivors of her line?

Brunela flicked the blade. Serge's blood sloughed off and landed in little splats that hissed like grease on a frying pan.

Brunela sheathed the sword, strolled to Isabelle, and extended a hand. "Well met, sister, though I think you could use a more substantial blade."

"I wouldn't know what to do with one." Isabelle accepted the hand up and put away her maidenblade. "Thank you for coming, but what brings you here?" It was a damn strange place for her to show up.

"I was actually following these two knaves, who have offended my em-ployer. Why were they trying to kill you?" Brunela lightly kicked Serge's sev-ered head, rolling it facedown in the blood pool.

Isabelle looked down at the mangled corpses and frowned. "I don't think they were, not at first. I think they were hunting the same person I was."

"That Windcaller who left in such a hurry," Brunela said.

"Yes." Isabelle picked up the one remaining lantern and slowly circled the font on her way to tend Bitterlich. She passed her mother's sarcophagus with the claw marks on the open lid. "Could you put this back for me?" she asked.

"She's not quite as comely as I remember her," Brunela said, lightly shift-ing a ton of marble and lead back into place.

A chill raced up the nape of Isabelle's neck. Yes, Brunela qua Lorenzo had known Vedetta in every sense of the word, but there was nothing on the sarcophagus that actually identified its occupant. Brunela already knew who she was.

Isabelle's pulse quickened. Lael had spent a great deal of time in the quondariums in Om, looking for something, looking for the sanctivore. Somehow he had learned it was on the *Conquest,* and who in this day and age could have known that? Who had helped catalogue the quondariums? Who had marched in the vanguard of the Kindly Crusade when the sanctivore had been taken aboard the *Conquest?*

Who had only appeared after Immacolata had disappeared? Who had intimate knowledge of the bone queen?

And yet Brunela couldn't be a bone queen; she'd given blood to the cipher . . . unless there was some part of her that hadn't dried up. And her name was already set in the matrix. What if she hadn't set it there herself? That meant she had encountered the cipher before, when it had been in Kantelvar's possession.

She had to be wearing a glamour charm. As disguises went, the charms were nearly perfect, altering color, shape, smell, and even sounds in the minds of those who viewed them.

Yet Goldentongue glamour charms had weaknesses, cold-forged iron, the bearer's blood, the fickleness of the Goldentongue maintaining the enchantment, and water. Isabelle glanced at the Fenice's reflection in the pool.

Isabelle's heart came as near to stopping as it ever had. The Fenice in the pool was definitely the same woman, but covered in feathers the color and stiffness of bone. The hardened scales rasped ever so slightly as she moved, and many of the longer plumes were ragged and broken, scarred like the limbs of some ancient tree. Her teeth were yellowed and jagged. Only her bright green eyes remained unchanged, and her lips still had the color of life. Marie had said she'd kissed the cipher.

Isabelle tried to be quick, but Brunela . . . Immacolata caught her gaze in the pool and frowned, bone feathers creaking.

"Too clever by half, sister," Immacolata said. "Too clever by half."

Jean-Claude huffed onto the landing outside Coquetta's chambers and found himself in the company of a dozen or so worried onlookers, including handmaids, a man with a lawyer's green sash, an imperial messenger, several courtiers, and a pretty young man with a shadelings collar. Jean-Claude announced himself by clearing his throat. When that garnered no response, he said, "Excuse me, le roi's business."

The reluctant herd parted before him. He considered rapping on the doorframe, decided against it, and let himself in. Inside, Josette lurched up from her seat at a writing desk, her bloodshadow shooting halfway across the floor before she realized who he was.

She called her bloodshadow to heel and glided over to him. Her eyes were red-rimmed behind her next-to-nothing veil, and her voice was hoarse. "I know my mother summoned you, but she's not herself. I'm not saying you shouldn't come in, but . . ."

"Thank you for the warning," Jean-Claude said, but the worst was why he was here. Josette pushed aside the curtains to Coquetta's bedroom and Jean-Claude ducked inside.

To Jean-Claude's surprise, Coquetta was out of bed, dressed for the day, and moving rather briskly around the room, sorting and packing clothes and other paraphernalia into a series of large trunks. In strength and fortitude, she looked infinitely better than she had yesterday. The only difference was the absence of her bloodshadow. Gone was the crimson tint to her skin and the long liquid train of the umbra itself, and in its place a quite ordinary gray shadow.

Jean-Claude hesitated at the doorway, unsure what to make of her unexpected industry. He had been preparing himself to face her death, not her packing.

Josette's voice cracked, "Mother, Monsieur Jean-Claude to see you."

Coquetta looked up. Her eyes were dry, and her smile professional. "Yes, dear. Now please stop blubbering." She came round the largest chest and reached out to embrace Jean-Claude. "Bonjour, my friend. Thank you for coming."

Only when he gathered her to his chest did Jean-Claude feel the tension within her, shivering like taut rigging in the wind. "Of course," he said. "And how may le roi's strong right hand serve you today?"

"I need you to take a message to Grand Leon for me," she said, returning to her packing. "Tell him that I'm going on a pilgrimage to the shrine of Saint Guyot in Laindeaux. I would have asked Josette to deliver the message, but she would insist on embellishing and besides it . . . it will make more sense coming from you. This has the proper symmetry."

From their first adventure together, he'd had to get her and her warning of an assassination attempt to Grand Leon on his annual pilgrimage. "As long as I don't have to drag you through a pig yard in a downpour again."

That actually won a sharp brittle laugh from her. "Oh saints, the stench! I thought I would never be free of it. You always did choose the most scenic routes."

Josette watched the whole exchange with the bafflement of any adult child hearing for the first time of her mother's misspent youth.

Coquetta said, "I've given all my papers to Josette, and settled all my other accounts. She is my designated heir and, if my will be done, will take over my gossip-sifting duties amongst the Trefoil."

Josette's hands clenched and unclenched and her bloodshadow rippled. Of the two women, she looked more ready to burst into tears. Jean-Claude gestured her close. "If your mother and I might have a moment alone."

Josette allowed herself to be herded out of the room and Jean-Claude drew the curtain shut. When he faced Coquetta, she'd gone back to her packing, or rather now unpacking, flinging a selection of expensive gowns onto the bed. "Forgot I need colors. Can't wear white now. Sumptuary laws. Someone will suspect. I should travel light, but not too light. Perhaps I'll be a merchant's wife on a pilgrimage. Or a widow . . . but no, widows attract grifters like dung attracts flies."

"What do you plan to do?" Jean-Claude asked. "Really?"

She looked up as if surprised to see him there. "Oh, I thought I sent you to Grand Leon."

"You told me to tell him you were going to Laindeaux, to the shrine, but where are you really going?"

"Home," she said.

"Your lands in Ambrouse?"

She stopped flinging clothes and gripped the edge of her trunk. "They aren't my lands anymore. I gave them to Josette, a name day gift. It's bit early I know . . . but I never much cared for that place. It's too . . . too . . ."

"Sunny," Jean-Claude said. "Warm, even in the winter."

"I find that I miss winter," she said, her voice growing tighter, "as I get older. And mountain peaks. And goats. My mother needs me, you see. Father's been dead five years and Mother is half blind. I imagine the chamberlain is robbing her cold."

Jean-Claude put a gentle hand on her shoulder. "Coquetta—"

"Not Coquetta," she said. A dam broke inside her and tears welled up and overflowed her eyes. "Not comtesse. Not even first mistress of the bedchamber. Just Matilde. Matilde Matilde, born of the plow. Matilde Matilde, named after a sow. That's what they used to sing about me. Someone made it up and all the children sang it."

She turned away from Jean-Claude and covered her face and her eyes in an effort to hold back sobs and hide her anguish. "Don't see me like this," she pleaded. "Please just go away."

Jean-Claude instead strode to her, turned her to face him, and pulled her to his chest. "I may depart from time to time," he said. "But I never abandon my friends."

She clutched at his doublet and wept until her lungs grew tired and her tears ran dry. "I thought I was going to die. I was *supposed* to die."

"No. You are not supposed to die. You still have children to disappoint, grandchildren to spoil, and enemies to thwart."

She plucked at the bedcover where her ordinary shadow lay. "Unless they choke themselves laughing, my enemies have nothing more to fear from me."

"Far be it from me to point out the obvious, but your bloodshadow was never your greatest strength."

"But without it I am nothing," she said. "Without it I have no rank, no title. I'll be no better than—"

"Than a clayborn," Jean-Claude said.

Coquetta winced but said, "I am only speaking as my enemies will. Grand Leon will dismiss me. Parlement will give him no choice, not after that fiasco with Lael." She buried her face in her hands and took deep breaths to keep from bursting into tears again. "Perhaps this is the Breaker's punishment for abetting that crime."

Jean-Claude said to Coquetta, "Don't do anything drastic until you've talked to Grand Leon personally."

"He will not appreciate me putting up a fuss."

"Hearing his judgment from his own lips hardly counts as putting up a fuss. Besides, he needs your help, and so do I."

Coquetta stared at him as if he'd grown a second head. "Jean-Claude, I—"

Jean-Claude gave her no chance to protest. He'd trod all over Impervia's honor by underestimating her; he wasn't about to do the same for Coquetta. "This pest was released on purpose, as a weapon against the l'Empire. The play was the vehicle for it."

"The play?" Coquetta said, clearly playing catch-me-up. "You mean the ritual."

"The wine, the sex, yes," Jean-Claude said. "But the play had an anonymous sponsor, someone from the nobility."

"That could be anyone," Coquetta said.

"Which is why I need you, and the fact that you know everything about everyone, to help me find a rice grain in the snowdrift."

Coquetta held up her hands as if trying to grasp the air. "I can't. Not like this."

"You can, like this. There are others who need you. You are not the only one to be afflicted with this disease. So far I know of half a dozen others, and there must be more. The shadow rot is spreading."

Coquetta looked at him in shock, displaced for a moment from her own misery. "That's horrible."

"Yes. They are losing their gifts and they are terrified. Several have committed suicide. That death toll is likely to grow. What those people are going to need is not so much a reason to live, but an example of living through it."

Coquetta gave him a disbelieving look. "And you think I should be the standard by which they measure themselves?"

"Why not. If you can overcome this, that will give hope to the afflicted."

"You make it sound so simple, but the fact of the matter is that by law I will be stripped of all status."

Jean-Claude said, "Maybe not. I'm sure there is some duty that you can perform better unhallowed than hallowed. Perhaps Grand Leon will make you his ambassadress to the City of Gears."

Coquetta made an appalled noise. "Saints what a horrible thought, but it's just the sort of thing he'd do. I pray you don't give him that idea."

"Would I ever do such a thing?" he asked innocently.

"In a heartbeat."

There came a commotion from the room outside, Josette's voice rising in outrage. "What do you mean under arrest?"

An unfamiliar male voice said, "Precisely that, mademoiselle, both you and your mother. I recommend you do not resist."

Jean-Claude's pulse raced. Coquetta blanched. Jean-Claude held up a hand to forestall any action on her part and peeked through the curtain into the receiving room. Three Sanguinaire Praetorians had pushed their way into the room and backed Josette into a corner. She'd pulled her bloodshadow into a defensive ring, but was hard-pressed to hold its shape against the Praetorians' incursions.

"I assume you have a warrant," Josette said, her back straight and her chin up, despite the fear in her voice.

"We don't need one," said the first Praetorian.

Jean-Claude withdrew quickly into the bedroom. "Palace coup," he hissed. Grand Leon never would have sent his men without a proper warrant in hand.

"There's no other way out," Coquetta said. If she'd been ready to throw her life away a few minutes ago, this threat had quelled that urge.

"Don't panic," Jean-Claude said as much to himself as her. It wouldn't be a minute before the Praetorians sent someone in here to search. He had to be ready. He spied a bit of curtain cord and a plan bloomed in his mind. He tossed one end of the cord to Coquetta. "Wrap that around your wrists and try to look distraught."

Coquetta looked him in the eye. "Once more unto deceit, my friend."

Jean-Claude pulled his secret weapon from his pouch and towed Coquetta, weeping, into the receiving room.

"Parley, Messieurs," Jean-Claude said, holding up his free hand to demonstrate that he had nothing in it. "I have the prize you are seeking."

All three Praetorians looked up at him. Their leader, a lieutenant, flicked his shadow in Jean-Claude's direction but did not instantly burn him. "The musketeer."

"Not anymore," Jean-Claude said, stoking his genial expression to a blaze. "Not after what Grand Leon and the cursed Parlement did to my Isabelle. But now I have a hostage worth a promotion in the new regime, what say you?"

Josette's face nearly blistered with rage. "You traitor!" Her shadow lashed toward him, and tangled with one of the Praetorians. The floor churned with shadows.

Josette's honest vehemence sold Jean-Claude's act more convincingly than he ever could. He said, "Shall we discuss price, lieutenant?"

The Praetorian cast a glance at Josette, shrieking and thrashing and Coquetta weeping inconsolably. He gave Jean-Claude a would-be shrewd look and said, "Hand her over and we will talk."

Jean-Claude hesitated and the lieutenant extended his hand emphatically.

Jean-Claude let his breath out. "I hope you deal fairly." He placed the cord in the lieutenant's hand, and pressed the glamoured coin he'd palmed against the man's bare flesh. The lieutenant's face went slack as he was sucked into the glamorous world of Célestial infidelity between Arnette and Dok. Using the ensorcelled officer as cover, Jean-Claude drew his pistol, aimed at the second Praetorian's head, and fired. The bang deafened, and smoke choked the air as blood, skull, and brains painted the far wall. The third Praetorian whirled about, but in that instant Josette was no longer outnumbered and her bloodshadow tore into his. Jean-Claude whipped out his main gauche and cut the lieutenant's throat while he was still trying to surface from the illusion and tipped his body on the floor.

Coquetta shrugged off her fake bonds and stormed toward the last Praetorian who was still struggling with Josette. She twitched her hands, reflexively trying to summon a bloodshadow that was no longer part of her. A flash of agony and loss passed over her face, but she directed her ire at the Praetorian. "I know you, guardsman Lange. You were on discipline for theft, and now this."

Lange snarled, "Damn you and your discipline. I have debts."

Jean-Claude began reloading his pistol in full view of Lange. "We might be inclined to overlook your theft, if you tell us who sent you and who else is coming."

Lange's eye was drawn to the pistol. "Nay, musketeer, whether you kill me or not, Grand Leon's cause is lost." He shoved hard against Josette's blood-shadow but could not throw her off. "You have nothing to gain, but help me capture these two and I will see to it that you are rewarded."

Jean-Claude paused as if giving the matter some thought. "To whom will I be bending my knee?"

Sweat beaded on Lange's brow. "Monsieur Lael."

Coquetta winced. "Fool boy."

"Ah," Jean-Claude said. "And what's to stop me from killing you and delivering the women myself?"

Lange said, "You'll never get out of this building without me. They've seized the main entrance and the back route."

Jean-Claude tamped a ball into his pistol and pulled out the rod.

"Good to know," Jean-Claude said. "And what triggered this coup d'état? Why now?"

"Grand Leon fell again, his seizure on display for all to see, and now the whole city knows his bloodshadow is dying. He is no longer fit to be roi."

"Still more fit than the Harvest King," Jean-Claude said, pointing his pistol at Lange's face. "Send my regards when you meet him in Torment."

After the bang, Lange slumped to the ground, leaving a bloody smear on the wall. Jean-Claude's heart hammered and his ears rang from the gunshots.

Josette faced him, her visage drawn and pale. "I think I owe you an apology. I thought . . . I was so scared that you might actually be turning my mother over to them."

Coquetta scoffed, "Hardly. That was just a bit of a lark by our old standards."

"More a vulture than a lark," Jean-Claude said. "Josette, I want you to get your mother out of here, or at least hide until you can move."

"I know a way," Josette said. "They may be sitting on all the ordinary doors, but once you get out of the timberworks the inside of the spire is a maze."

"Don't get lost," Jean-Claude said, looking around as if the native architecture of the quondam structure might suddenly reveal itself. There was an entirely different world just beyond the thin wooden walls humans had built to make themselves comfortable. They had no more understanding of the nature of the structure in which their dwelling was built than did cliff swallows nesting under the eaves of a Temple.

"What are you going to do?" Coquetta asked.

"Extract Grand Leon," Jean-Claude said.

"Well, you can't just send me off with the baggage."

"Yes, I can. Right now you're the only one of the Trefoil who we know is still at large. As long as you stay that way Lael can't win, not completely. I, on the other hand, am of no particular political importance."

Coquetta looked frustrated, but Josette said, "He's right, Mother. We need to go now."

"If you see Isabelle before I do," Jean-Claude said, "tell her I would not have traded a moment."

Coquetta nodded. "You make sure that I don't have to."

They touched hands. "Builder keep you until the Savior comes."

Coquetta and Josette departed, leaving Jean-Claude alone to deal with a whole tower full of sorcerers and other guards. All of Grand Leon's enemies would be converging on him if they hadn't reached him already, and Jean-Claude was ill-prepared to fight them in bunches.

Each of the Praetorians wore a nonstandard belt favor in red, probably to help the traitors recognize each other. Jean-Claude found one with no bloodstains on it and took it for himself.

Jean-Claude unfastened his medical and munitions pouches and got to work improving his armaments. He had to borrow a sparker, a small alchemical lantern, and some sugar from Coquetta's tea service, but he doubted any of it would be greatly missed. If he was to go out in a blaze of glory, he might as well set things on fire.

CHAPTER

Twenty-One

Immacolata reached for Capitaine Bitterlich.

Isabelle tried to intervene but the bone queen nudged her aside. It was like being shouldered by an ox.

"Don't hurt him," Isabelle said.

Immacolata hefted the comatose capitaine over her shoulder as lightly as if she was slinging a feather pillow. "Killing him would be counterproductive. As long as he's alive, I shouldn't have any trouble from you. Now come unless you want to prove me wrong and render him disposable." She strode away down the tunnel, leaving Isabelle to hurry along behind.

Past the bend in the corridor, they came upon Hailer Dok, lying in a heap with a broken jaw. Immacolata picked him up and flopped him over her shoulder atop Bitterlich. "He was so busy looking back for danger that he forgot to look ahead."

"What are you going to do with him?" Isabelle asked, astounded that she could carry two grown men without apparent effort.

"For what they did to us, the Windcallers and all their ilk deserve annihilation. Practicality, however, demands he be spared until his lungs and nodule can be harvested."

"That's insane," Isabelle said. She must escape, must warn Grand Leon about the traitors in his own Praetorian guard.

"Need I remind you he is a condemned man. Even if I could forgive the crimes of his ancestors, which I am disinclined to do, your own laws would still hang him for piracy. Did you ever ask him how many people he's killed in his time, or how many ships he has plundered? To recover some use from his corpse repays but a token toward his true debts."

Isabelle followed along in silence until they reached the point where the horses were tied. Kore showed her whole face over the rim of the Rivencrag. Three-quarters waxing, she filled the graveyard with a stark cold light. Offshore, clouds gathered, another blizzard on the way.

"What happens now?" Isabelle asked, while Immacolata roped Bitterlich and Dok over the saddle of a horse.

"If you really wanted to know my plans, you could have had them all days ago," Immacolata said. "But you have rejected your heritage."

Immacolata finished tying off her unconscious captives and mounted her horse.

Isabelle watched helplessly. She could not believe she was compliant with her own kidnapping, but all the alternatives were futile just now. Perhaps she could escape en route to wherever Brunela meant to take her. Fleeing meant she'd have to abandon Bitterlich and let Immacolata carry through with her threats to kill him or worse.

Her heart rebelled at the idea, yet what other choice was there? If she let herself be dragged into the enemy's lair, she'd never come out again as herself and Bitterlich would be butchered for his organs. Both she and Bitterlich served l'Empire and would lay down their lives if need be in its defense. Yet that wasn't the same as laying down somebody else's life, abandoning a friend.

She needed help, and she could not count upon any second chances if she did not take the first one that came along. Yet even if she could escape, how would she get word to Grand Leon? She'd have to try for the harbor garrison and hope they could be persuaded to send a message.

"Get up," Immacolata said.

Isabelle climbed into the saddle, but no sooner had she settled herself than

Immacolata seized her forearm and twitched a braided leather cord around her wrist.

"Stop it!" Isabelle yanked against the hold, but it was like pulling on a mountain.

Immacolata was logarithmically stronger than a normal human. She tied Isabelle's wrist to her saddle horn and took her reins. "You were getting ideas."

Isabelle fumed but said nothing. Immacolata cued her horse into a walk. Isabelle relaxed her posture and tried to ride as if she was not tied to the horse. If she didn't feel so much like a captive maybe the slimy fear crawling up the back of her neck wouldn't stifle her mind.

"You really should consider accepting the vitera willingly," Immacolata said. "A willing and prepared recipient becomes the inheritor of a deeper history. She inherits her previous lives as an estate of the mind over which she is the master."

"And an unprepared mind?"

"An unprepared mind may be swept away and subsumed. A resistant mind can lead to a battle that both sides lose . . . ultimate foolishness."

"You think it's foolish for someone to defend themselves?"

"Consider the alternatives. A gravebound mind is destined for oblivion. Not so a Fenice's mind. If a gravebound is given the chance to host a Fenice's vitera, the worst that can happen to it is that its present memories will be carried on into the indefinite future as part of a greater more glorious whole. Fighting back gains the gravebound nothing, for they are most likely to be destroyed in the battle, their mind ruined."

"But if I die you die," Isabelle said. "Just not right away." Immacolata had no other kin. As a bone queen she could have no children of her own. Unless she passed on the seed of her consciousness to Isabelle, this body would be her last.

"That is why you cannot in good conscience refuse. Not only would you die, but so would I, and a hundred generations of your ancestors. Preserving them is your duty."

"A duty I never asked for."

"No one ever asks to be born," Immacolata said. "We are pushed into this world without permission and afflicted with all of its hurts and handed duties we may not want, but they are our duties nonetheless, and the first of these is to secure the line, no matter how we are hunted."

That was a thread that hadn't surfaced for a while, and Isabelle tugged on it. "You never did say who is hunting you." They exited the graveyard and joined the flow of traffic down the Serpentine way toward the bottom of the city.

Immacolata's expression became grim. "The rest of my kind."

"All the Fenice?" Isabelle asked. "Why?"

"You mean you haven't worked it out? I'm disappointed."

Isabelle was flummoxed for a moment, but the only thing she'd said about her past was that she'd been part of the Kindly Crusade.

Oh. Isabelle had been shocked enough today that one more shouldn't bother her, but this . . . "You . . . You mean to tell me you're Maximus Primus. But he died. He never made it . . ." She stopped herself in mid mind-tumble. "You didn't have to make it back, just your vitera did. You knew you were about to die, so you gave your vitera to someone. They escaped and took it back to the goodlands."

"To Om, where my son was waiting to receive it, except that he did not. You see, my people, the ones who my brother and I had led to victory and glory, the ones who we had finally united into a single empire, blamed us for the defeat. They blamed us for losing tens of thousands of lives and the treasure of a century on a quest they demanded we take. They blamed us rather than the Windcallers who betrayed us, and they took their revenge upon our families. My only living relative was a bastard son I had sired for just such an emergency. He became your fifteen times great-grandfather, but he was never free of the pursuit, nor were his children or his children's children, not until Lorenzo decided to stop running. He made a deal with Kantelvar to pass his vitera down to his daughter, and then allowed himself to be assassinated to throw off the trail at last."

Isabelle pulled the threads together. "But you didn't know you had two daughters. You didn't know the bone queen your enemies had sent to assassinate you was your child or that Kantelvar had made a deal with her to obtain her father's vitera. It must have been quite the surprise to both of you, when Lorenzo woke up in Immacolata's head." Now father and daughter, killer and slain were locked in the same skull in the same dying body, with no way to escape it or each other except through Isabelle.

"So that is what you want for me," Isabelle said. "You want me to endure your pain. I will experience everything you have gone through, murdering your own father, the flensing worms eating your flesh from the inside out."

"The memory of pain is not the same as pain. I want my sister to live. I want my daughter, my granddaughter to join with me in immortality. Is that not generous?"

"Generosity can never be imposed, only offered," Isabelle said.

Was this fear of death the truth of Immacolata's soul? If so, it seemed a small dim light for such a long life. "What will you do with all this life? You told me that Fenice are blessed with skipping the tedious business of re-learning all that is known. If that was true, the names of Fenice should be at the top of every list of famous inventors and empirical philosophers. Yet of all the advances in the past few hundred years, the best inventions, and the most interesting math has flown from the imaginations of clayborn minds unfettered by the inescapable opinions and false certainties of their fore-bears."

Immacolata pointed out the coast, where the navigation lights of skyships bobbed on turbulent skies. "Do you see those ships with their aetherkeels and their orreries and their cannons? Are they not the greatest product of this new empirical age that so enamors you? Are not they driven by the al-chemist's knowledge of fluids, the engineer's understanding of the preferences of metal and wood? Are they not all stitched together by the cat's cradle of mathematics? They are magnificent, and yet they are but different tools for the same tasks we have always faced. The more clever your philosophy, the better weapons men build, the more supplies they can shift, the bigger armies they can field, the more destruction they can wreak."

"Not everything is about war," Isabelle said.

"Yes, it is," Immacolata said. "A good general knows every wheat field is a weapon, food for one army or another. So is every road, every bolt of cloth, every book. Wars are won in the warehouse before they are ever fought on the battlefield."

"Then who is your enemy?" Isabelle asked.

Immacolata made a scimitar smile, helped along by the glamour covering her bonefeathers. "War itself. I intend to finish what Secundus and I started. We united the Risen Kingdoms, and we would have united all of the Craton Massif if not for the damned Windcallers."

"You didn't unite them; you conquered them."

"And how else will they ever be united? Do you imagine each petty king will set aside his own interests to work together for the greater good of hu-mankind? Throughout our history, every peace had failed, every armistice has been broken, if not in a year then in a century. Peace can never be bargained for; it can only be imposed. The only way to put an end to the fighting is to win, to throw down every king, to behead every tyrant and to unite all peoples under a single, or in our case double, immortal overlord. You and I, sister, will be known forever as the generals who defeated war."

Isabelle blanched at this description. It was just barely possible that her sister, life piled upon life, mind upon mind, was completely insane.

The current of traffic had shifted while they spoke. Almost all of it turned against them. The volume of the crowd chatter rose.

A military horn sounded up ahead. With it came the rippling snare of a drum, and the clomp of feet. The crowd on the street stirred and parted as a platoon of infantry came along double-time. They wore the blue and white parade coats of a regiment belonging to le Duc d'Orange, but they'd put their battle kit on over it. Their muskets were shouldered but had wicked bayonets attached. They shoved out of the way anyone not swift enough to clear the path on their own. The column thundered by like a herd of very disciplined oxen.

Their grim determination made Isabelle's skin chill. She'd seen this kind of maneuvering in Aragoth in the confusing days surrounding a failed coup attempt.

Isabelle looked up the face of the Rivencrag toward le Ville Céleste. As far up as she could see, all the traffic on the Pilgrims' Road, picked out in bobbing lanterns, was descending. The upper third of the road was dark save for the intermittent guide lanterns.

"They've closed the road at the top." To Isabelle's left, above an outcropping, a light flashed in timed pulses, the upper stockade's semaphore tower sending to the naval base, "Le roi is alive. Interdict coastal zone. No ships to leave. Le roi is alive."

"It has begun," Immacolata said. "The irredeemable pest had touched le roi. And now l'Empire crumbles."

Isabelle could hardly breathe through the anger and denial that filled her like a toxic fume. Grand Leon could not crumble. Every potential heir would look to their claim. Some would try to flee to their lands to gather their forces. Others would seize whatever hostages and positions they thought would grant them an advantage. With Rocher Royale already groaning under the burden of so many extra people, the city would become a slaughterhouse. It was the sort of peril that had many people of Isabelle's rank asking questions such as, "To whom should I offer myself as a hostage?"

And what of Jean-Claude? Where was he in all this mess?

Immacolata took Isabelle by the shoulder. Even through thick gloves and layers of fabric, her talons pricked Isabelle's skin. "Come. Events will be proceeding swiftly now."

"What does the Harvest King intend to do?" Isabelle asked. Immacolata had not mentioned her supposed employer at all. Perhaps there was a wedge to be driven there.

Immacolata said, "Before the Breaking of the World, Iav's great sin was to take from the Builder powers she had not been given. Lael has made the same transgression. He was unhallowed, unworthy, and should have had the humility to recognize his own weakness. Instead he has rebelled against his place. His entire quest, from first to last, has been to overthrow the Builder's order and to put himself in the Savior's place, to sit in judgment above all who have despised him."

Isabelle's wrist chafed in its bond. "How is he going to manage that?" And what good would it do Isabelle to know if she couldn't escape?

"He knows that saintborn who are losing their sorcery will do anything to keep it. Those who swear loyalty to him will be cured of their affliction. Those who refuse, or who are too dangerous to let live, will be replaced by his hand."

"And then you will depose him," Isabelle said.

"I doubt he'll let me get that close. You, on the other hand, he will be unable to resist. He's already interested in you. He intends to bring you under his sway, to display Grand Leon's favorite cousin as a jewel on his crown."

"That's revolting," Isabelle said.

"But very useful," Immacolata said. "It will make it very easy for you to seduce him, have him make you his queen. You can be the voice of reason in his reign of terror, gather allies to you. Then when Lael's madness claims him and his sorceries burn him from the inside out, you can cast him down and become the savior of l'Empire."

Isabelle let all the implications of this sink in. "You're not working for him; you're using him. If you were the usurper, you would be seen as the enemy. But if he is the usurper, you'll be seen as the savior."

Immacolata grinned. "Some people have ambition and just need a little nudge into corruption. Men like Lael already have corruption, but just need a little ambition to guide them. Once I told him about the sanctivore, he was eager to believe he came up with all the rest by himself."

Isabelle was beyond feeling anger, pity, fury, or outrage. How did one deal with this . . . this delusion? Why were all her relatives so senselessly cruel?

Immacolata continued. "Of course, Lael should get some credit in his own downfall. He asked me to make him a Sanguinaire, and so I did. So enamored of his newfound power was he that he asked me to make him a Volshebnik, and a Seelenjäger, and a Windcaller, and a Goldentongue. Five different surgeries, five new brain nodes, and four new organs. Of course, he already had the skin of a Sanguinaire, but his nodule was atrophied and underdeveloped.

"Everyone knows the Temple outlawed miscegenation between sorcerous bloodlines because such crosses are likely to give rise to abominations. What nobody realized until Prior Ingle pointed it out is that sorceries interact with each other as well as with the brain. Two nodes is three times as complex as one, and three is six times as complex."

"So five nodes is fifteen times as complex," Isabelle said, expanding the sequence automatically.

"All that complexity is hard to control, and sorcery is like a fire in the mind. Stoke it too hot, leave it untended, and it will escape. Abominations lose control because they have two nodes and no way to balance them. With five, Lael's decay should be rapid and spectacular."

Isabelle had not thought anything could make her feel even a little sorry for Lael, but the disintegration of a mind was always tragic.

By the time they clip-clopped down the switchback to the lower city, a great shiver had gone through Rocher Royale like a frigid wind through winter-dead grass. Criers ran through the city shouting, "Le roi has fallen, le roi has fallen!" and they carried with them stacks of posters, which they nailed up on every signboard. Everywhere they went, people milled like sheep before an oncoming storm.

"Grand Leon Has Fallen: The Breaker Reclaims His Own!" screamed the headline. Isabelle was not close enough to read the rest.

Isabelle closed her eyes to block out the chaos and clear her thoughts. Was there any way to reach Immacolata . . . or was Immacolata the wrong person to be talking to?

"Was there ever really a Brunela?" Isabelle asked.

"I am Brunela," said Immacolata. "That was the name this body grew up with."

"You're something much bigger and older than she," Isabelle said. "Brunela was just a woman, a Fenice who didn't know who her father was. What was she like before they put the flensing worms on her and made her into a bone queen?"

"She's part of me now."

"But she wasn't once," Isabelle said. "She was my sister."

"Studious," Immacolata said grudgingly. "No skill at all in war. She was a physician. A surgeon."

"Is that where you got your surgical skills?" Isabelle asked.

"Yes." The word was dead on Immacolata's lips.

"I would have liked to meet her."

In a low pained voice unlike anything Isabelle had yet heard from Immacolata, she said, "It was her own family who gave her to the flensing worms. They found out her heritage and turned on her. They didn't want to be accused of harboring one of the Maximi, so they invited her over for a family dinner, drugged her, and delivered her to the abattoir. They watched as the purifiers tore out her feathers and, into each bleeding wound carefully inserted a larval worm. Hours she spent begging them to stop, professing her love and her loyalty. They never even told her why she was being cleansed."

"After that, why did she work for them?"

"By the time worms finished their work, she was half mad, and they told her that killing Lorenzo was the only way to make the pain stop. As it turns out, that was a lie. She was in so much pain by the time she took me in, that she was all too happy to relinquish her body, and withdraw behind the wall of sleep into the everdream."

Isabelle tried to imagine the internal politics that must take place when more than one person occupied a mind. She didn't want to find out in person, but how to escape? There was nothing she could do about the cord around her wrist, or the reins in Immacolata's hand. The other weak point was the horse's bridle. If she could slip the strap off over the beast's ears, he'd be able to pull his head out of confinement. Yet she didn't have enough slack in her tie to reach.

The once crowded streets were now mostly empty as all but the bravest and most foolhardy shrank back into their houses like turtles into their shells. Only those with strength of arms or numbers were abroad. From down at the docks rose a sullen orange glow of massed lanterns as people rushed to the sky cliff, looking for passage out but finding no ships at any price.

The tramp of feet drew Isabelle's attention to a platoon of red-jacketed soldiers on the march crosswise through the next intersection before her. If she could reach them, would they help? It was an awful chance, but she would not get another. She prayed for swiftness, and strength, and forgiveness from those she must either fail or abandon.

"Hyah!" She whipped her right leg up and scraped her heel along the horse's head, caught the bridle with her heel, and shoved. The horse screamed and reared. The bridle slipped free. Isabelle nearly pitched from the saddle, but leaned in hard and clung to the horn.

Go! she willed the beast, trying to get her balance and spur the horse into a gallop at the same time. Immacolata's hand shot out like an arrow. Her talon severed the cord tying Isabelle to the saddle and seized the loose end. The horse bolted. Isabelle hit the end of her tether. Her arm nearly yanked from its socket, and she was jerked from the saddle.

Immacolata let go the cord and Isabelle hit the cobbled pavement like a sack of bricks. The world went black and then flickered back in again, though all the colors seemed to be missing. She'd stunned all the breath from her body but couldn't remember how to inhale.

Immacolata alighted beside her and seized her by the throat. "Brave try," she said. "Clumsy, slow, and stupid, but brave."

Isabelle would have spit at her, but her lungs seemed to be trying to prolapse through her mouth. Immacolata bound her hand and foot, stuffed a rag in her mouth, and tied her across her own saddle like the carcass of a slain hind.

"It's important for you to remember that you brought this on yourself."

Her body awkwardly bent, her ribs compressed, her mouth gagged, Isabelle spent the rest of the jouncing ride fighting to breathe and little else. She was dimly aware of being hoisted from the saddle, carried through a door, and lugged up several flights of stairs. By the time Immacolata flopped her down on a pallet in an otherwise empty stone room, she could hardly identify which way was up.

Immacolata squatted beside her and took the gag from her mouth. She shook her head sadly, illusory peacock-colored crest feathers bending with the motion. "I am truly sorry it had to come to this. I gave you every chance. I gave you every reason to cooperate, and still you have betrayed me, betrayed your sister, your father, and your family."

Isabelle coughed and spat. "You are not my father," she wheezed. "Some dead part of you provided the seed, but you neither tended the fields nor pulled the weeds. You will not reap the harvest."

"You will not escape your duty. You could have thrived. We could have worked together as a family. We could have shared the glory that is to come. Yet you leave me no choice but to erase you." She pulled a small glass phial from her belt pouch and examined its contents—it held a viscous liquid—and gave it a shake before pulling out the stopper. "This is called slave oil. It will dull your mind and make it impossible for you to resist my vitera. I would rather have made you my partner in this, but I have no time and cannot take chances. This ensures a peaceful transition of power, and I think we can both agree that's important."

Isabelle jerked and twisted away, but she was still bound and there was nowhere to go. Immacolata caught her, bent her head back, and forced her mouth open. Isabelle thrashed uselessly against her steel sinews. Immacolata raised the phial to Isabelle's mouth. A drop of the oily liquid splashed onto Isabelle's tongue, and another. It tasted of anise and ant bites.

Immacolata clamped Isabelle's mouth shut and held it. "There you go. Good girl. Take your medicine."

Wild with terror, Isabelle tried not to swallow but the vile stuff spread out through her flesh, a stinging tingling, that seemed to lift her mind out of her body like oil floating on a rising tide of black, bitter water. The harder she thrashed, the muddier her mind became, until her body went limp as a wine sack, and her awareness floundered around inside it like a goldfish out of its pond.

Immacolata reached around to the back of her own head and pulled on something. There was a creak like overstressed wood and then a crack as she removed the bonefeathers covering her vitera and drew forth the symbiote. It was a ball of segmented bonefeathers about the size of her palm. It uncurled into a shape much like a beetle, its foreparts bony needles and its abdomen a distended sack like the body of a bloated tick. Its legs ended in tiny hooks that flailed at the air.

Isabelle's mind recoiled in a soupy kind of horror. No. Please no.

Immacolata arranged Isabelle gently facedown on the pallet, and her words came in slow as molasses. "It's a shame, really, that we'll lose most of what makes you Isabelle, but it's impossible to integrate without full cooperation. I can assure you, however, that your sacrifice is not in vain. You will be remembered as a worthy opponent, a reluctant hero, and a dear sister."

Immacolata placed the vitera beetle on the back of Isabelle's neck. It was warm, damp, and slimy like a slug in the sun. Its hooked legs took a grip on her skin, then its body heaved up and crawled slowly along the back of her neck, dragging its sack up her spine. It reached the base of her skull, rooted around for just the right spot, and jabbed her with a needle of bone.

Instantly, another presence, another consciousness rushed into Isabelle's mind, brushing her aside as it grew to fill all the spaces where she used to live.

The Other pressed against Isabelle's consciousness like an acidic fog, infiltrating her memories, corroding and dissolving everything it touched. Its presence of mind seeped into hers. It was old, and dense, and heavy with memory. She remembered standing on the hills above great Byphon, watching the city burn. Remembered the hot stink of blood as she rammed her spear through the heart of the terrible beast of Goran, remembered setting the crown on the head of the first King of Vecci and later cutting that king's head from his shoulders. She had slain monsters, seduced queens, given birth, betrayed lovers, united empires, written treatises, burned libraries. The Other was vast. It was deep. It was Maximus.

Isabelle's consciousness thinned and dispersed like ink in a stream. She clung to memory, to Jean-Claude and Marie and all her friends, and all her thoughts. She conjured around herself a wall of mathematics, of equations she'd solved and proofs that she'd made, deeds that belonged to no one else before her. These must be *me*. But her strength faded, like holding her breath under water, and she had no way to replenish it. Maximus curled in around the edges of her defenses, absorbing even her most precious and personal memories, eroding her.

Down she spiraled, into blackness, until all she was aware of was a faint buzz in the distance. Pink and purple sparks in the dark.

Her sorcery. L'Étincelle!

She reached for the sparks, called her power. Her spark-arm ignited like banked coals in a new breeze, but l'Étincelle was no use against a thing of flesh and blood. Only metal and stone. She could only flee. She groped beneath herself with her spark-arm. Her sorcery passed through flesh and caught on metal. The Other bore down on her like an avalanche. She turned her face toward the far point of light and jumped.

CHAPTER

Twenty-Two

Jean-Claude hurried through the undulating twisting hallways of le Ville Céleste's timberwork interior toward Grand Leon's chambers, pausing by every corner to listen for other traffic. Twice he ducked aside as footsteps approached. Both times they were packs of servants looking for shelter. From the edges of hearing came the sounds of battle, and soon he stumbled across the aftermath, soul smudges creeping amidst the fallen bodies of a squad of Thunderguard. Several men still lived, though barely. There were a few of the usurper's men amongst the dead as well.

There was no hope to avoid being spotted going forward; someone would come to tend the wounded or relay messages to some other front in what had to be a very confused battle. Jean-Claude straightened his tunic and then strode out as if he owned the place. He'd bluff his way into Grand Leon's presence. He only prayed that the conspirators did not all know each other by sight.

Yet hardly had he rounded the first bend in the corridor than he felt the lash of a bloodshadow. It gripped his shadow from somewhere behind and paralyzed him so that he could not even whimper. Panic rose in his breast.

He couldn't move, couldn't fight. If he could only talk for just a moment then he might have a chance.

The shadow slid him across the floor like a token on a game board and into a narrow space that opened up between two wall panels. The panels slid shut again with a click.

"Jean-Claude," said Impervia. "You idiot, what do you think you're doing?"

She released him from her shadow's grip and he fell to his knees, quivering. "On my way to rescue Grand Leon."

"By yourself? No, never mind." She helped him to his feet and turned him around. They were in a low-ceilinged, curving corridor with not quite enough room for a man's shoulders. Her tattered clothes were covered in blood and her wig was missing. "Did you ever have a plan that didn't consist of rush in and see what happens?"

"It got me this far," he protested. "I notice that you are not currently accusing me of being a traitor."

"Was I supposed to?" she asked, arching an eyebrow at him. "I don't think so. Anyone trying to turn you would find himself holding the wrong end of a hydra. He would never know which head bit him."

Jean-Claude said, "Likewise you could have killed me already if that was your purpose. So what happened to you? I stopped Lael's traitors from taking Coquetta."

"He sent men after me, too," Impervia said. "The problem with most Sanguinaire is that they rely far too much on their bloodshadows. They never really learn how to fight without it. They assumed I would be the same way." She unsheathed two blades about the length of her forearms. "I snuffed the lights, and then I snuffed them."

Jean-Claude nodded. "Do you have a plan?"

"I have a shortcut to the throne room," she said. "Come on."

They hurried along the narrow corridor. Jean-Claude said, "So your plan is 'Rush in and see what happens'?"

"Sneak in," Impervia said. "It's totally different."

"For the record, my plan was talk my way in," Jean-Claude said, surprised at his own cheer; this was just like old times.

"This gets a bit tight," Impervia said, squeezing through a slot between a wood wall and a tilted plane of quondam metal that pinched off the corridor at about shoulder height.

Jean-Claude eyed the slot. "I'm not going to fit."

"You have to, there's no other way."

Jean-Claude sucked in everything that would suck and applied himself to the opening. He imagined this was what sausage must feel like being stuffed into a casing. One small scrape at a time he pushed himself along until Impervia made a hissing noise and said, "Shh. Someone's coming."

"I thought this was a secret passageway," Jean-Claude whispered.

"So did I. Damn. Stay still, I'll try to lead them away."

Impervia scuttled off, leaving Jean-Claude to contemplate a selection of futures, the worst of which involved him being permanently wedged here, alone in the dark. He would die of thirst long before he starved down enough to unstick himself, and then who would give him the rite of last watch. Not that he necessarily believed in ghosts, but why take chances?

What would Isabelle think if he just disappeared like that? And where was she now? He prayed she was not taken by surprise, and that she found allies and safety. Except she wouldn't seek safety. She'd seek the heart of the problem, stop it if she could, and there was not a damned thing he could do to protect her.

There came the sound of hurrying feet, and whispered voices in a conversation too filled with echoes to understand. Jean-Claude held still within himself, trying not to breathe.

A light appeared from the direction of the voices, and the speech grew more excited. "There's one," said a voice. "Colonel was right."

Somebody shined a light in Jean-Claude's eye. "It would seem we have found a rat in the wainscoting. I believe this one's name is Jean-Claude and he's Grand . . . the old roi's favorite weasel."

Jean-Claude cursed the man, but kept his tone genial. "I think of myself more as a badger. Stout, near-sighted, and generally grumpy. Would messieurs mind extracting me."

"Just stick him now," suggested the not-lieutenant.

"Then we'd have to drag his carcass out or leave it to stink," said the lieutenant. "Better he walks out under his own power. Besides, the new roi will want to question this one."

With the lamp in play, a bloodshadow reached out and dragged Jean-Claude from the hole, scraping a rash on the side of his face and shredding his musketeer's tabard. The shadow pinned him fast while they deprived him of sword, main gauche, and pistol, then kept him corralled as they marched him through a series of corridors that did everything but turn upside down before emerging at last into Grand Leon's throne room.

Not Grand Leon's anymore.

Lael, resplendent in white, with a thick bloodshadow draped down his left side, sat upon Grand Leon's throne. Broad of shoulder and narrow of hip, Lael all but glowed with masculine vigor. Jean-Claude had never questioned his own attraction to women before now, but . . . but damn this was no ordinary magnetism. It was a Goldentongue's gloriole. When Jean-Claude looked away, the man he saw from the corner of his eye was still handsome but not compelling. But what about the bloodshadow? Goldentongues couldn't use their glamours on themselves, which meant he couldn't be faking the bloodshadow. Somehow he had obtained two sorceries.

Jean-Claude forced himself to take in the rest of the room.

By Lael's side stood a hulking Seelenjäger with scimitar horns sprouting from under his homespun hood.

At the foot of the dais stood Grand Leon, surrounded by three more Sanguinaire: le Comte de Maersh, a nobleman Jean-Claude didn't recognize, and Lord Colonel Hachette, the lead of the Praetorian Guard. All three had hooked Grand Leon's bloodshadow with their own and stretched it like a canvas. Grand Leon's posture was erect and his manner poised, but there was an unfamiliar strain on his face, and beads of sweat formed a crown on his forehead.

Behind him, Sireen was likewise pinned by three Praetorian Sanguinaire. Down on one knee, her arms crossed before her, she held her shadow together against their attempts to shred it. Two nearby soul smudges suggested loyal guards already dead.

Despair gnawed at the root of Jean-Claude's spirit, but Grand Leon still lived and breathed, so hope yet remained. It would not be too late for Impervia to show up with a regiment of reinforcements.

Jean-Claude had apparently come in the middle of an exchange. Lael's face was avid, his eyes gleaming. ". . . Simply because of the order of their birth. This is not about revenge. It has never been about revenge. This is about justice. From now on, power will be taken from those unworthy to hold it and given to those who can use it to the best effect."

Grand Leon's manner was composed but his bloodshadow was full of holes and his face was haggard, his attention divided. Jean-Claude got the impression that he was fighting a battle on two fronts, one with Lael and the other deep inside. The shadow rot was the sort of foe he had never faced before, an enemy he could not outwit or bargain with or crush.

"And who shall you deem unworthy?" Grand Leon asked. "If you value loyalty, you could certainly do better than Colonel Hachette there. I must say this comes as a personal disappointment, Acel. I thought you a better man."

Hachette squirmed under his gaze, but spread his bloodshadow, displaying a jagged edge. "I would have given my life for you, full willing, but not my soul. I won't go to Torment."

The respect Jean-Claude had once held for Hachette bled away. *Coward.* Clayborn faced death and Torment with courage every day, without any hope of salvation until the Savior came.

Sireen yearned toward Grand Leon with her gaze and surged against her captors, staggering one of them before he heaved back with a force that made her snarl in pain.

Grand Leon gestured to the Praetorians. "And to the rest of you. Will you serve a man who has threatened your very souls, for his is a poison with no antidote. He will never grant you freedom or trust, only forbearance. He begins by asking you to overthrow your roi, and what will he ask you to do tomorrow? What will you do when he orders you to betray your own kin, to slaughter your own children? And when he is finally finished with you and he strips your power anyway, what good then will all your groveling have done?"

Several of the Praetorians shuffled nervously.

"Rubbish," Lael said. "The desperate wheezing of an old man who has forsaken wisdom for the path of lies. Never once in all his life has he ever served anything but his own vices: lust, greed, and vanity."

"You forgot my greatest extravagance," Grand Leon said. "Mercy."

Lael's anger burned on his face and sent a hot wind through the room. Was that a real wind? Jean-Claude glanced over his shoulder and saw it kick up dust and shake the curtains. A Windcaller's power. Three sorceries!

Lael roared at Grand Leon, "You dare speak to me of mercy. You who cast me out for no crime other than being unhallowed."

Grand Leon twitched his nose toward le Comte de Maersh. "As I recall, de Maersh put forth a motion to have you executed for sedition against the crown. I quashed that motion."

Jean-Claude's hope dared peek up from its bolt-hole. Lael might have a huge club to wield, but Grand Leon had a hundred smaller levers. This, not his sorcery, was how he had maintained his power for so long, turning his foes against each other. Could he throw the coup into confusion through words alone?

De Maersh twitched and looked at Lael. "Monsieur . . . m-my liege. I was forced into making that motion."

Lael said, "Quit whining. The old goat is only trying to confuse and frighten you. His words are meaningless. Under his rule, all ambitions save his own were stymied. Even the saintborn were herded like cattle."

With the heat of battle glowing in his breast, Jean-Claude reached up with his bound hands, and doffed his hat in an awkward bow. "Messieurs, at least under Grand Leon's rule the saintborn were not slaughtered like cattle. Lael has murdered the Volshebnik Ambassadress Ustina, the Goldentongue Earl Mistwaithe, and several others who had not offended him. They were literally butchered like sheep."

Jean-Claude expected the lash of his captor's bloodshadow, but it made him scream nonetheless. Pain like a thousand white-hot needles jabbed into every inch of his body pitched him forward onto his knees.

Lael turned his gaze on Jean-Claude. "And here is more proof of Grand Leon's corruption. To the saintborn was given the responsibility to rule. To the clayborn the duty to obey, and yet Grand Leon has given this one the power to judge his betters, but we will teach his kind to be humble, and cleanse the stain of their ambition from the world."

Just for an eyeblink Lael's gloriole flickered. Like an image glimpsed through a break in a forest, Jean-Claude got the impression of a figure wholly transformed, a bestial face and a hunched back, wisps of black smoke leaking from open wounds as if they were vents for some infernal forge.

The grotesquery vanished so quickly Jean-Claude could not be sure he'd seen it at all. Lael's magnificent image reasserted itself and his bloodshadow oozed across the floor toward Jean-Claude slow and thick as molten wax.

Lael said, "Let my father watch as his favorite creation—"

"Fire!" yelled one of the Praetorians. Black smoke roiled up from a grate in floor and rose in a choking plume. The spires of le Ville Céleste were impervious to fire. Not so the wooden hive within. A conflagration could kill everyone inside.

"Extinguish it!" Lael roared at one of the Practorians, who grabbed one of his fellows and ran for the spiral stair. "Take my father. Kill the others!"

Jean-Claude's heart hammered and time became very slow. His captors had bound his hands still in his thick gloves. He ripped off his right glove and his hand popped free.

A door behind the dais flew open and Impervia lunged through. She flicked her bloodshadow in an arc around the throne and seized Grand Leon by the shadow to yank him away from his captors. It might have worked if only Grand Leon's bloodshadow hadn't ripped nearly in half from the force of her tug. He cried out in pain and fell to the floor convulsing. Impervia's eyes rounded in horror.

The goat-headed Seelenjäger crouched. His body bulged and distorted like someone cramming a sack full of live pigs. His legs became haunches, his hands claws. His head sprouted a long beak with a serrated edge. Part bird, part bear with the horns of a ram, he leapt over the throne and drove Impervia back through the door.

Jean-Claude flicked his sparker out of his sleeve and lit the fast match he'd threaded through his bandolier. The Sanguinaire behind him raked him with his bloodshadow, and paralysis stole the will from his body. But the burning fast match reached Jean-Claude's first cartridge and it burst into flame. The heat seared him even through the leather strap and his layers of clothing, but the sugar- and lumin-infused gunpowder spat out clouds of smoke like a firework, diffusing the light and confusing the bloodshadows. Where did one shadow end and the other begin? The bloodshadow lost its grip on him.

The smoke stung Jean-Claude's eyes. Lael and Hachette seized Grand Leon and dragged him toward the main entrance. Sireen shrieked as her captors redoubled their efforts. One of them drew a long knife. Jean-Claude sparked the lantern on his belt and dropped it behind him as he raced for Sireen.

Lesser Sanguinaire might have been utterly baffled by Jean-Claude's smoke, but the Praetorian behind Jean-Claude had most likely seen battlefields before and fought through gun smoke. He whipped his shadow back as fast as a frog's tongue and drove it forward in a wedge, plowing the smoke aside.

Jean-Claude leapt on his good leg. He passed over the bloodshadows of Sireen's attackers, howling as they burned his trailing shadow, and by sheer force of momentum knocked Sireen from the circle.

With a deafening bang, the lantern exploded. The gunpowder and shot he'd filled it with sprayed lead and glass all over the room. Jean-Claude's Praetorian died in a shower of meat and blood. All of Sireen's attackers were stunned and one went down. A flake of glass creased the back of Jean-Claude's neck.

He heaved himself to his feet, knees shaking, and hauled Sireen up after him. Across the room, Grand Leon fought a losing battle with Hachette and Lael. They tore his once proud bloodshadow to ribbons as they hustled him out the door. Jean-Claude was out of weapons and there were too many for Sireen to make a difference.

He grabbed Sireen's arm. "Come on!" he said, loud enough that he could hear it over the ringing in his own ears.

Sireen took a step toward the usurpers. "Leon!" she screamed. She yanked at Jean-Claude's grip, but at least she didn't rake him with her bloodshadow.

His pulse thundering like a battery of cannons, Jean-Claude got low, wrapped his arms around Sireen's thighs, and threw her over his shoulder. Stumbling into a run he hurtled for the secret door on the far side of the room just as one of the flanking Praetorians regained his wits and slicked his blood-shadow at them.

Enraged and no longer outnumbered, Sireen met the Praetorian force for force with her own bloodshadow and smashed him into the far wall. Jean-Claude threw open the hidden door, spun through, grabbed it shut, and slammed down the bar.

They were in a narrow corridor, barely wide enough for one person.

"Put me down!" Sireen shouted.

It was all Jean-Claude could do not to drop her. His lungs wheezed like a bellows cramp, his eyes stung from gunsmoke, every nerve felt shadow-burned, and his damned leg wanted to collapse like a house of cards. "That won't hold them," he said, gesturing at the door.

"We can't leave Leon!" Sireen shouted.

"We're getting reinforcements," he coughed. "Lael won't kill him. Wants him alive."

Something large and heavy rammed into the door, throwing splinters into the narrow passage.

Sireen glared at the bulging door, then seized control of herself. "Right. Yes. This way." She gestured at Jean-Claude to follow, hiked her skirts, and hurried down the corridor, grabbing a stashed lantern as she went.

Through twisted passages they ran, too swiftly for Jean-Claude to think past his aching leg and his burning lungs. The sound of pursuit goaded him on. Fortunately, Sireen knew what she was about, taking swift turns and barring doors until they reached a place where the human-built structures ran out and the corridor emptied into a vast dark shaft crisscrossed with struts and spirals of quondam materials.

Jean-Claude wheezed to a stop beside Sireen at this bridgeless gap. "Wrong turn?" he asked.

"No, just a bare chance. This section of the spire is still alive, still trying to do whatever it was doing before the Breaking of the World. The original shrine where people used to come to worship is on the other side of this."

Jean-Claude stepped as close as he could to the edge, but the depth of it made him dizzy. His stomach churned and he wanted to swoon. He had no idea why heights affected him this way, but no amount of effort had ever served to overcome it. "How do we get across?"

"It goes through its cycle every seventeen minutes or so. There will be a platform of sorts. It's hard to explain, but we'll have to jump for it."

Jean-Claude's spirit sank. There was no way he was going to be able to leap into that void. At best he would fall. At worst he would still be standing here when the Praetorians caught up with him. Neither was an ending he fancied.

"What happens after you jump on?"

"You jump off at another doorway that leads to the shrine, and then to the outside. Grand Leon had it barred shut years ago, but it's not guarded."

"Probably not," Jean-Claude said.

"Even if Hachette had turned every guard in le Ville Céleste to his service, he'd either have to send someone by this route to guard the gate or send them halfway down the back side of the mountain to get in from the outside."

Jean-Claude wanted to know what she planned to do when she got out, but decided against asking her. He didn't want to know in case he got taken alive.

Somewhere in the corridors behind them there was a muffled crack as yet another door gave way. Jean-Claude reached for his sword, remembered he didn't have it, and said, "We don't know how long it will take this convey-ance to get here, but it will surely take less than a quarter hour for the trai-tors to catch up to us. I will lead them away from here." That, at least, would be a last act worthy of a musketeer.

Sireen whirled to face him, shock in her eyes. "You mean to leave me?"

"I mean to protect you," he said, and to preserve his honor, threadbare gar-ment though it was. Another crash sounded behind them, closer this time. "When you see Isabelle—"

A thrum in the darkness grabbed his attention. There came a great low hum in several chords. A diffuse glow in many colors converged from many directions. Jean-Claude reached for his spectacles but found them smashed. Only when the glow congregated at a single point, a body length away and down from the ledge where they stood, could he see that it was made up of many individual lights, odd-shaped bits of crystalline matter that clung to each other in a three-dimensional lattice, like aethercoral.

"Be ready." Sireen clipped her lantern to her belt. "When the color becomes solid we jump."

Jean-Claude stared into the shaft. The fall called to him, its allure stronger by the heartbeat. "I . . . can't," he said, hating himself for his cowardice. "I can't jump." Already his knees felt like jelly. His skin went cold and clammy. "I'll fall."

Bootsteps thundered in the corridor behind them. Someone shouted, "There they are!"

Sireen's baffled expression turned stern. "I will help you." Her bloodshadow reached out and grabbed his shadow. His soul stung, but the touch was light. He was a passenger in his puppet body as he crouched. Sireen turned. The multitudinous colors shimmered and solidified into a uniform mauve. Sireen and Jean-Claude both leapt from the doorway into darkness.

The construct was bigger and more stable than it looked. Jean-Claude landed hard on the uneven surface. The bloodshadow released him, and by sheer reflex he hooked his arm through one of the illuminated loops. Sireen had done the same. The whole strange chariot began to descend, spinning slowly along a diagonal axis that had Jean-Claude scrambling to stay on top.

A shout from above made Jean-Claude risk a glance up. Two Praetorians appeared in the small rectangle of light of the doorway from which they'd leapt. They cursed and fell into arguing with each other.

"See how well your new roi deals with failures!" Jean-Claude shouted at them while climbing around the construct. "He'll let your sorcery die!" Hopefully that fear would keep them from swiftly reporting Sireen's escape.

Sireen worked her way beside him. Their combined weight did not seem to deter the construct at all. She said, "We need to be on top. Getting off again is another jump. Are you ready?"

"With your help." Jean-Claude managed to stand on top of the spinning construct, balancing like a timberjack on a rolling log.

The leap onto the outgoing landing was no less terrifying than the leap onto the construct had been, but Sireen managed it for both of them with no broken bones. The construct spiraled into the center of the shaft and then broke apart into a swarm of separate pieces that dispersed and diffused into the dark.

Jean-Claude shook his head in wonder. "What in all the world is that thing?"

"Ask the Builder," Sireen said. "Pilgrims used to call it the dancer. Its shape is never the same twice, and it never appears or disappears in precisely the same spot."

"So we got lucky," Jean-Claude said.

"Very."

The platform on which they sat had the ruin of an altar where long ago pilgrims had left offerings, most of them long decayed. A semicircular room behind them was an iconarium with niches for statues of the Risen Saints. All of these had been removed except for the statue of Saint Emberine the unlucky, which always faced the back of the niche and was never removed once ensconced.

A rickety bridge led Jean-Claude and Sireen out of the spire below ground level, and a long narrow tunnel took them to the surface. It was the dead of night when they emerged into a stony grotto on the inland slope of the royal plateau. The light of two of the three moons showed a landscape every bit as rocky as the coastal cliff, just not as a steep. Here and there a few hardy shrubs eked out a living in the nooks and crannies where sandy soil collected. In the narrow valley far below, a thin smudge of deeper black hinted at trees. Behind them, upslope, was the Plateau de Céleste on which the festival grounds stood and from which the twisted quondam towers kinked their way skyward.

Sireen, exhausted, snuffed her lantern and sat on a boulder in the shelter of the grotto. "Rest a moment, musketeer, and advise me. We must find allies amongst the high houses."

Jean-Claude sat down across from her and stared out across the ragged peaks of the Hoarteeth mountains, which carried their glittering ice caps even in the heat of a threefold summer. He said, "The high houses will be the ones most terrified of being stripped of their sorcery. Any one of them may decide to hand us over to Lael in exchange for his protection."

"Then we must make our first ally someone who can protect us from our second ally. Gather enough behind us, and they will endure their fear for a time."

"May I suggest le Duc d'Orange. I saved his father once, before he was conceived. He owes me enough to at least listen to me."

Sireen said, "And his brother is a Praetorian who was not amongst Lael's treacherous crew. Yes. D'Orange, then Chardin, and then Janders. That will give us a solid base. What I need you to do is help me contact them. No doubt they will be watched. It's possible Lael may have already tried to assassinate or suborn them."

"You don't happen to know a secret way into Rocher Royale, do you?" Jean-Claude said.

"No, unfortunately, and I imagine the Pilgrims' Road is barred to us."

"Then we'll just have to get them to come to us." Jean-Claude's knees protested mightily as he stood up and offered Sireen a hand.

Sireen took his hand and made a tired smile. "Leon always said you make the average weasel look like a stunned sloth. I suppose it's time I got to see that in person."

Jean-Claude surveyed the upward slope in dismay at its rocky steepness. He rubbed his leg in anticipated agony. "We'd best be going."

"I might be able to help you with that," Sireen said.

"Eh, what?" Jean-Claude said.

"Your leg," Sireen said as she sparked her lantern to light, set it on a stone behind him, and knelt to peer at his shadow. "The nerve is damaged."

"You can see that in my shadow?" Jean-Claude said, incredulous.

"Not all Sanguinaire are created equal," she said, "or trained equally, or equally curious. Hold steady. This is going to hurt."

"Now wait just—" Jean-Claude's protest turned into a muffled wail as a wire-thin spike of Sireen's bloodshadow lanced into his shadow. It felt like someone had jabbed his leg with a white-hot, ice-cold knitting needle. Twice she stabbed him, and a third time. He would have collapsed save that her bloodshadow held him fast. At last, with the sensation of someone removing a long-embedded nail, the shadow spike withdrew and she let him go.

He clung to her arm as the pain faded. His shadow leaked for a few seconds, spilling darkness like ink until the wound, if you could call it a wound, healed over.

One tendril of Sireen's bloodshadow held a clot of darkness, an irregular lumpy scab of his shadow. Her bloodshadow teased the clot apart, picking it into smaller pieces until it dissolved completely.

Jean-Claude put weight on his leg and for the first time in a year it didn't ache. "What? How did you do that?"

"The Builder gave me this gift," Sireen said. "But he never explained what it was for. No one else ever seemed to question it. My family and my teachers and every other Sanguinaire I met were content with the power it gave them, a weapon and a symbol of status, but I always wondered if the Builder would truly have given us a gift that could only be used to hurt people. I sought out others who felt the same way, and found a few who had discovered, through great effort, how to read shadows. Once I've sampled someone's shadow, I can see things within it, things that shouldn't be there, wounds invisible from the outside, and sometimes, if the problem is simple enough and I can see how everything fits together, I can effect repairs."

Jean-Claude walked around in circles, to the left and to the right. Astoundingly it didn't hurt. "That's amazing. Are you teaching this to others?"

"Slowly," she said. "One major obstacle to getting Sanguinaire interested is that so far it doesn't seem to work on other Sanguinaire."

"And why should they be interested in helping clayborn?" Jean-Claude grunted.

"We are the order of the Succoring Shadow," Sireen said. "I had hoped to dedicate it as an Imperial Order. The status would make it more appealing to ambitious sorcerers."

She did not have to tell Jean-Claude how forlorn that hope had become. They would be lucky to survive the night . . . but at least now they might make it up the hill.

CHAPTER
Twenty-Three

The waning red moon Threin crept up over the Hoarteeth. The temperature dropped like an icicle, sharp and piercing. The various camps around the parade grounds had been broken down in haste, all the merchants and revelers herded into the city below. All that remained atop the plateau were several regimental camps that had chosen to dig in rather than redeploy.

From the wreckage of the civilian camp, under cover of darkness, Jean-Claude had gleaned blankets and water and a large brass platter that he deemed would serve his purpose well enough. He rejoined Sireen at their hiding place at the farthest spinward edge of the plateau, a downward stair-step in the stone that made the ridge above them look like the precipice of the cliff to anyone who wasn't standing right on the lip. The position put the stockade between them and the le Ville Céleste with the Pilgrims' Road well beyond that.

Sireen, huddled in the dark and shivering, hissed to get his attention and drew him into the cramped hideout. "Where in Torment have you been? Three patrols have been by since you left."

Jean-Claude threw the blanket over her. "There were these three patrols I had to avoid," he said. "Lael has search parties out looking for us, but he hasn't involved any of the other camps. They all have patrols out tracking his search parties and watching each other. It's just not a proper cock-up without at least a dozen factions."

Sireen sniffed. "He should have lined up his support long before this, been ready to move into place."

"You're wishing he was more organized?" Jean-Claude crawled forward as far as he could before the vertigo overcame him, and scanned the coastline for the naval base. There it was, all watchtowers lit.

"No," Sireen said bitterly. "I only wish I had seen this coming in time to kill it in the crib. I have people in all of the high households who should have warned me if a coup was afoot."

"So really, he took great care to avoid you." Jean-Claude motioned for her to join him, and plunked the unlit lantern down. "Bend over this, make a tent. We only want light getting out in one direction."

"Who are you signaling?"

"I have a friend in the navy," Jean-Claude said. As soon as he was satisfied that there would be no light leakage to give them away to the stockade or any passersby, he sparked the lantern, positioned the brass plate, and flashed to the naval semaphore tower below. The problem with this method was that if the navy yard flashed back to him, the stockade would see it and send a search party, so Jean-Claude began, "Blackout message. Do not respond. Repeat. Blackout message do not respond. Urgt Msg Cmmd Jerome . . ."

It took some time for Jean-Claude to get the whole message out in his rusty flash code. He sent the key bits of it several times, just to be sure. Every time the wind shifted and brought with it the sound of boot treads from the plateau above, his arse puckered a little tighter until the noise moved away again.

Finally, his back aching and his hand cramping, he finished the message and flicked the lantern off. The naval yard below remained dark. The *other* problem with this method was that he had no way of knowing if it had been received, or if it had been believed, or even delivered to the right person.

"And that's it," Sireen said. "Coquetta always made your adventures together sound so exciting."

"Stories like this are always better looking back than when you're living them."

"Because if you are looking back, you guessed right." She held up the edge of the blanket for him and he squeezed in tight for warmth. There was nothing to do now but wait.

He asked, "Are you sure you can secure the high houses' support?"

Sireen stared into the distance, surveying some political landscape Jean-Claude could not quite see. "I'll be able to get le Duc de Cheron, and anyone else in the line of succession who Lael is likely to kill out of hand. For the rest . . . I never would have thought Hachette would turn against us. Lael claims the Builder's power for himself, the ability to give and take souls. What can make a man stand up to that?"

"Are you saying it can't be done?" Jean-Claude said.

"No, only that the usual suasions won't work."

Jean-Claude grunted. "If a man gave me a disease I knew would cripple me without a cure only he could give, I would kill him and take the cure from his corpse."

"And if you didn't know what the cure looked like, or how to apply it?"

"I would still kill him," Jean-Claude said, "just to stop him from hurting anyone else."

"That is because your instinct is to protect," Sireen said. "These people are nobles, there is not one amongst them who would not rather forget his own name than lose the seat of his soul."

—

Immacolata sat up and stretched her arms . . . arm. The phantasmal arm connected to her right stump had only the faintest sensation to it, like being aware of a hole in the air. It was unfortunate that she had to inhabit yet another damaged body, but saints how good it was not to be in pain. She'd all but forgotten what it was like to be able to move without feeling like every muscle in her body was made of shattered glass.

"Who rises from the ashes?" asked Maxima Immacolata. Her bone queen sister progenitor sat on a stool next to the door. She'd taken off the glamour charm that covered up her all but mummified face and her ragged crown of bone feathers. She looked like an ancient, one of those Fenice lucky enough to see the end of their second century. It was shattering to think she'd reached this state before she was forty.

The new duplicate of Immacolata stood up and curtsied, giving the traditional response. "I am Maxima Celestina ne Immacolata." This was the name she had come up with before the act of transferring the vitera had sundered her life into two different branches. "For the sake of our plan, however, I must remain Isabelle to the rest of the world." She and her sister needed Isabelle's identity to seduce and depose Lael.

"*Qui sit omnium maximus?*" Immacolata asked. She had been worried that the vitera would fail, or that Isabelle would find some way to fight it.

"*Ipse est qui autem mundus est unus,*" Celestina said, with the proper tone and accent.

At last Immacolata relaxed and her ruined mouth bent into a smile. "How does it feel?"

Celestina went down on her knees before her sister and took her armored hand. "It doesn't hurt. I had forgotten what it was like not to be in pain. Saints I wish I could share this with you."

Immacolata squeezed her hand gently. "And what about Isabelle? Does she have anything to tell us?"

Celestina turned her attention inward. Usually when a vitera inhabited a host it was either absorbed into the consciousness of its recipient, all of the great lineage becoming part of the new, or the host's personality was destroyed, leaving behind a jumble of memories like the ruin of a city or town. But not this time.

"She's not here," Celestina said with a frown. "There's almost nothing of her left."

"Like it was with Brunela?" Immacolata asked.

"No," Celestina said. "Brunela was still there, just so damaged that all we could do was encyst her. Isabelle is just . . . gone. I felt her flee, she leapt into the void." Her complete absence was unnerving.

"She chose annihilation over assimilation?"

"Apparently." Celestina would have preferred Isabelle cooperate with her, but fighting back was her choice, and death was her consequence. What a waste. Yet Celestina wished she had some ground on which to place a grave marker to a brave foe.

"Do you have enough of her to play your part?" Immacolata asked.

Celestina picked herself up and smoothed out her dress. Having only one real hand was going to be damned awkward. "Not if we were trying to fool anyone who knew her well, but the only one we really have to convince is Lael. We'll be playing on his weaknesses, not her strengths." Lael wouldn't be able to resist the chance to seduce Grand Leon's favorite cousin, even if she was his own second cousin. "One day, the world will have peace, and we will have glory."

"Shall we put it to the test?" Immacolata asked. She reaffixed her glamour charm, recapturing poor Brunela's lost youth and beauty.

Celestina led the way out of the monk's cell. Knowing where she was going was another way of assuring her sister that she was in fact in charge of this body. The vitera symbiote still clung to her neck, pincers itching. It would remain there for several weeks, orchestrating the transformation of her mind and body until her first crest feathers came in. Only then would she be able to summon her armored coat and the first stirrings of her sorcerous strength. Until then, she was just as vulnerable as any clayborn.

They tromped down to the chapel, which doubled as Lael's audience chamber within the spiral ziggurat. Two Neverborn surgical grotesques stood guard by the archway. Their faces were saggy and puffy in places and their eyes seemed to be staring out through the holes in a fleshy mask, which wasn't far from the truth. Immacolata's supply of the precious Primal Clay was strictly limited. She had used just enough on each of her creations to ensure that their new organs, in this case the skins peeled off a couple of visiting Sanguinaire, were not rejected by their new owner. And if they spent the rest of their lives shambling around in ill-fitting skins, at least they had blood-shadows and the souls to go with them.

The grotesques looked at Celestina suspiciously but Immacolata waved them off before they could protest her presence. Like most Temple chapels, the Azure Flame's was a circular domed chamber with a font in the center and niches for the saintly icons all around. Only these had the Azure flame's obscurantist take on them. None of the icons were in the right order and instead of being clearly represented they were merely hinted at by visual puzzles.

Also in the chamber were Isabelle's brother and her sister-in-law. They saw Immacolata come in and bunched up like a pair of cornered sheep. So fixated were they on the obvious Fenice that it took Guillaume a moment to recognize Isabelle.

"Greetings, brother," Celestina said neutrally. Guillaume was neither terribly bright nor reliable. Lael had given them sanctuary on the pretext that they were enemies of Grand Leon, and had offered them a place in his new regime. What he had failed to tell them was that their place was to be as skin and nodule donors for some of his loyalists. Immacolata had made no objection to this plan if only because she wanted to find out if Celestina could fool them.

Guillaume made no attempt to hide his contempt. "What are you doing here? Shouldn't you be up at le Ville Céleste getting deposed with your roi?"

Celestina recoiled in pure visceral dislike of such petulance, but said, "He ceased to be my roi when he fed me to the wolves. What is your excuse?"

Guillaume eyes narrowed. "So much for your vaunted righteousness."

His vastly pregnant wife, Arnette, peered around him like a recently fed python lurking behind a sapling. "Grand Lael has made Guillaume le Comte des Zephyrs, and he will make you his slave."

Celestina arched an eyebrow, and wondered at the futility of trying to fool someone whose point of view did not connect with reality. It was like starting in a hole and trying to reach the surface by digging. "I wish you all the best," she said, with all the insincerity they would expect. She passed them by without looking back. She and Immacolata approached a niche that contained not an icon but a bloodhollow in a gray dress, her hands folded in her lap, her skull visible beneath her translucent flesh.

The bloodhollow had once been a Goldentongue. It was the first one Lael created once Immacolata had replaced his withered nodule with a functional one. Lael then compelled the Goldentongue's power, reduced though it was by her condition, to cover himself in the illusion of health and beauty.

Immacolata produced a glass rod and delivered a galvanic jolt to the bloodhollow's head to get Lael's attention. After a moment, the bloodhollow stirred and sat up, its face molding into a likeness of Lael's.

"There you are," Lael said. "Where have you been? We could have used you last night."

"You sent me to retrieve Hailer Dok, which I did. I also brought back Princess Isabelle, who would like to speak with you. I take it the assault did not go as smoothly as you had hoped."

The bloodhollow shrugged. "We have my father, that's all that matters. I have summoned all the great houses to pledge their allegiance to me at the stadium this afternoon."

"So soon?" Immacolata asked; this hadn't been in their plans.

"The momentum is all on our side. All must see my father humiliated, his spirit crushed and his soul destroyed. They must be made to understand that the old ways are dead, and that the mere fact of birthright no longer entitles them to power. From now on they must earn their place in the world, beginning by swearing their allegiance to me."

Celestina said nothing—it wasn't her turn—but Lael was frightened, scrambling to cover up a failure before it became obvious.

"Did you capture the Trefoil?" Immacolata asked; that was nearly as key as capturing Grad Leon himself.

"Hasdrubal knocked Impervia down the Swallowing Well. The others are trapped in the spire."

"So one might be dead and the other two are still at large," Immacolata said. "It sounds like you could use some reinforcements, to which end I give you Princess Isabelle des Zephyrs."

Lael shifted his attention to Isabelle. "My apologies for meeting you like this, but duty presses. It was high time my father and his corrupt regime be brought down."

"You will get no disagreement from me," Celestina said. "But will you be any better?" It was an Isabellish thing to say, a bit dangerous, but she was in a hurry.

Lael said, "My reign is already an improvement. No one will be punished without just cause, nor rewarded without due effort. No saintborn will be denied their due because they were born second, or unhallowed, or a woman."

Given how many blameless bodies Lael had literally butchered to achieve his triumph, the notion of him dispensing justice was laughable. Isabelle, however, wasn't supposed to know that, so Celestina asked, "And what guarantee do I have that I will not be swept up in the general purge? You father is my cousin, and that puts me closer to the throne than is comfortable in times like these."

"If you join me on the podium today, and remind the lords of the great houses of the matter we discussed, then I shall accept your loyalty as genuine."

Celestina said, "Of course," but what in all the most creative Torments had he discussed with Isabelle? She would have to improvise.

Guillaume pushed in beside Celestina. Celestina reflexively elbowed him in the face, but her phantom arm passed right through him.

Guillaume said, "Your Majesty, I beg you not to believe my sister. She is a liar of the first order, corrupted by her damned musketeer."

Immacolata whipped the emerald sword *Ultor* from its sheath and stabbed it through Guillaume's bloodshadow. Guillaume screamed and clutched at his belly as if she'd stabbed him through the gut. There weren't many things that could hurt a Sanguinaire through his bloodshadow, but *Ultor* had been birthed in the soul forges of antiquity. Alas that the soul forges had burned out and the ritual for igniting them had been lost even before Rüul fell.

Immacolata loomed over his squirming form. "You will respect your betters." She yanked the blade free and Guillaume lay there moaning.

Lael said, "He has a point, though. The musketeer Jean-Claude did trouble me yesterday."

Celestina invented quickly, "So that's where he went. He abandoned me in my moment of greatest need. I hope you killed him."

Lael gave her a measuring look, which she returned. "He is dead."

"Good," Celestina said. Assuming Lael wasn't just trying to shock her into a revealing display of emotion, that was one less person who knew Isabelle intimately enough to be a problem.

Lael looked over his shoulder at someone who wasn't there. "Have them wait. I'll see them in a moment." Then he returned his attention to Immacolata and said, "I have petitioners here. Come to the stadium, and we'll discuss our next move. Builder keep you."

"Until the Savior comes," Immacolata and Celestina said at the same time. The bloodhollow sat back down in its niche and became inert.

Arnette helped her groaning husband to his feet. "How dare you attack le Comte des Zephyrs? He is favored of the new roi."

"No," Celestina said, "he really is not. Lael has many faults, but he's not such a fool as to promote such imbeciles."

Guillaume peered into Celestina's eyes as if trying to see through them. "Who are you? You aren't my sister. She loved that damned musketeer like a father."

"That's worth knowing," Celestina said; she held out her left hand toward Immacolata, who placed *Ultor*'s pommel in her hand. "Unfortunately you've become as much a danger to me as you generally are to yourself and others."

Celestina didn't yet have her Fenice strength or speed, but with *Ultor* she hardly needed it. A quick stab pierced all three of them; man, woman, and unborn; with hardly any more resistance than slicing butter. She whipped the sword out cleanly and watched them gape with astonishment as their life blood spilled in a crimson sheet. Arnette opened her mouth to say something but only frothing blood came out. Guillaume's bloodshadow reached for Celestina, but she sliced across it with the blade and sent him reeling to the floor for the last time. It might have been faster to behead them, but dying was an important part of life, and it would have been cruel of her to deny them the experience.

She stepped back so as not to get her shoes bloody and returned the sword to Immacolata. It wasn't the sort of thing Isabelle would carry, not yet. Once she became reine, that would be different.

She quieted her mind and listened, waiting for the echo of horror that Isabelle certainly would have felt if any part of her had been lurking in this body. She was met with only silence.

"Not there?" Immacolata asked. Their minds were still so closely synchronized that it was nearly possible for each to tell what the other was thinking. That would pass with time and differing experience, but the time of twinning was always to be treasured.

"Nothing," she said. "I've heard of people claiming they would rather die than be united, but I've never heard of anyone succeeding to this degree."

"It's unfortunate; she had useful skills."

"And we liked her."

They left the remains of the des Zephyrs clan where they lay and strode out the sally port into a bitter predawn. The sky grew lighter, but a thicker darkness off the spinward coast heralded another storm on the wing. Snow-laden clouds rolled down from the winter vortex, spicules of ice ranging ahead to sting and harry.

Celestina shivered as the gathering damp got into her clothes. She reflexively twitched her skin to extend her close feathers for warmth, but of course they hadn't grown in yet.

On the landward side of the ziggurat waited a regiment of fifty Azurites, their blue robes looking black in the quivering light of their lanterns. Their heads were tucked in deep cowls away from the cold, and all of them had shouldered muskets.

Ahead of the regiment was a donkey cart to which the Seelenjäger Praetorian and Hailer Dok were shackled. Iron spikes had been driven through the Seelenjäger's wrists to keep him from shapeshifting, and his whole body was bent in agony. Dok's broken jaw had been bandaged shut. The wound would kill him eventually, but he only had to be kept alive long enough to have his lungs harvested.

Both were inferior species of sorcerers, devoid of any refinement of character.

The Windcallers would be exterminated down to the last infant for their treachery during the Great Betrayal. The Seelenjägers, though, she would keep for their utility as shock troops.

The Seelenjäger twitched and looked up at Celestina. His bleary eyes grew wide. "Isabelle. Oh saints, I had hoped you had escaped."

"I'm well," she said. "Take heart and follow my lead once we get to the plateau." Making these two sacrifices to Lael's new order would help cement her loyalty in the new roi's eyes. Once she got past Lael's suspicions, it was just a matter of keeping him in line until she was ready to eliminate him.

At the head of the column was a mounted contingent of Neverborn grotesques in their bicorn hoods, each of them showing the blazon of his stolen sorcery: four Sanguinaire and two Seelenjäger.

Celestina and Immacolata mounted a pair of waiting horses and called the column to advance. It was time to give Lael his moment of glory. If you were going to push someone off a peak it was important to make sure they had a good view of the fall.

—

When morning's pale light washed night's ink from the sky Jean-Clause lay belly down on the cold stone and watched the semaphore tower at the naval yard through eyes sore from lack of sleep and stung by the wind.

"Hurry up, will you," he muttered to the distant signal station.

Had they even seen his message last night? Bright as they were, handheld lanterns were no match for the barrel-sized lenses of the semaphore towers loaded with purified lumin and quicklime. Had anyone even been looking his direction? Such were the fears of an exhausted old man who was fresh out of tricks.

Activity atop the plateau had picked up with the dawn. Lael had sent out heralds from le Ville Céleste announcing to all and sundry his ascension to the throne, and calling on every Sanguinaire who wished to keep his or her power to pledge their service to the rightful roi. "All loyal subjects are expected to behold their monarch and receive his blessing!"

Sireen cursed quietly at the heralds. She was worried about Grand Leon, and not just because he was the lynchpin that held l'Empire together. She'd been with him for most of thirty years, given him seven children of whom four still lived. Her oldest was probably in one of those armed camps, making his own calculations about how to survive this debacle. Her youngest was five hundred kilometers from here in a private finishing school surrounded by loyal guards, though even that might prove insufficient protection if the coup succeeded. All of this had come out of her during the night, each piece of her history taken out and examined for flaws, as if she might identify some mistake that had brought the world to this dire pass.

Mostly, however, she had plotted a defense against the coup. "Lael has picked up a weapon he doesn't know how to use. He set loose the pest knowing it will drive people to seek a cure, but if he gives them a cure he loses power over them. If he refuses to give the cure then he will drive people to our side. He's put them all on desperate ground."

"He's courting all the second sons and unhallowed kin to turn on their fathers and brothers."

"That will work on a few of the most toxic ones," Sireen said. "But in the battle between loyalty and ambition, loyalty wins most of the time. Even the unhallowed love their parents and don't want to see their family humiliated."

Jean-Claude continued to watch the naval yard, but had almost given it up as a lost cause when the semaphore tower flashed, "Watch Change. sixth bell. All stations secure. Requested delivery en route."

"Thank the saints." Jean-Claude blew out a long breath in relief and rolled over on his back, gazing up at the long twisty fingers of le Ville Céleste kinking skyward until they faded into the upper airs.

Sireen gave him a hopeful look. "Commodore Jerome came through?"

"So it would seem. You should give him a promotion, or at least a bigger hat."

"If we live, I'll get him a hat so big it needs its own rigging."

Jean-Claude rolled to his side and sat up, because straight sit-ups were no longer in the cards. There was nothing now but to wait and worry about things he could not affect at all. Where were Isabelle and Marie? He could count on Djordji to keep Marie safe, but that Seelenjäger Praetorian had been very keen on taking Isabelle to Lael's soirée. Had he delivered her all unwitting into the usurper's hands?

"What do you know of that Seelenjäger Praetorian?" he asked. "Is he one of Hachette's creatures?"

"Capitaine Bitterlich? No."

"How can you be sure?"

"He's an outsider, a Seelenjäger orphan whose family's lands were given to a Sanguinaire invader. On the surface, no one has a better reason to hate l'Empire than he does, and would-be usurpers have been trying to turn him since he was a boy. He just follows them back to their leaders, and then leads them into traps."

Jean-Claude tried to be reassured. Had Coquetta managed to remain hidden? Had Impervia escaped?

Sireen, huddled next to him, wrapped the blanket around his shoulders, and they sat wrapped together, waiting and listening and keeping their heads below the lip of the overhang to their gully. The morning sunlight painted the highest tips of the spires and sent mauve and gold auroras streaming away from the quondam metal. Slowly the glow expanded down the metal skin, like candles burning low.

Then the sky began to close in, the colors of the world turning gray as the first flakes of a new storm whisked across the plateau. Every now and again a horn sounded as noblemen and their regiments came up the Pilgrims' Road. How many would answer Lael's summons? How many would offer him their knee and kiss his ring?

The sound of a boatswain's whistle wiggled its way through the wind. All hands on deck.

Jean-Claude's head came up. "That would be our cue." He levered himself up and offered Sireen a hand.

They peeked up over the top of the gully and saw the fairgrounds slowly coming back to a semblance of life. It was a resurrection without any sense of vitality or joy. Across the broad swath of the plateau, a dozen new retinues in the liveries of various noble families staked out territories. Closer to hand loomed the bulk of the army stockade, sloped walls of fitted stone that looked like someone had started a pyramid but quit about six meters up.

A column of marines marched up the rim road behind a pair of wagons loaded up with barrels and crates. Jean-Claude and Sireen hustled up to the shallow end of their cut where it ran parallel to the rim road, stepping onto the plateau just in time to intercept the column.

Strong hands hoisted Sireen and Jean-Claude aboard the carts, folding them under the tarp into a space between the crates no bigger than a fat man's coffin . . . as well it might yet be.

"Do you mind," Sireen said. "You're sitting on my foot."

"My pardons, madame," Jean-Claude said, squeezing himself out of the way.

"Not quite the most glamorous coach ride I've ever had," Sireen said.

The small space quickly grew close and stuffy. Jean-Claude closed his eyes and tried to listen through the jouncing and creaking to hear what was going on outside. Even so he had no warning when the cart suddenly creaked to a halt, and the marching stopped. Someone threw back the tarp, and the light stung Jean-Claude's eyes.

"Sorry catch you are. Ought to throw ye back," said a skeletal silhouette. Jean-Claude squinted up, but neither his eyes nor his ears deceived him. "Djordji! What are you doing here? Where's Marie?"

"Girl's inside, as you should be, and you, madame." Djordji extended a hand and helped Sireen up and off the wagon, and into the wagon yard of the Monk's Measure. "Privy council's waiting in the back room."

"Thank you, musketeer," Sireen said. Indeed Djordji had donned his King's Own Musketeer's tabard, even if it did flap about him like a flock of seagulls.

No one helped Jean-Claude, so he scooted to the rear of the cart and let himself down. Sireen faced a semicircle of marines, all of whom were saluting proudly as she praised their perseverance and discipline.

"You will all be remembered," she said. Damned ironic, in Jean-Claude's point of view, as she didn't know their names, and they could very well have been dragooned by the other side, who would have blessed them with similar words. Men like this were loyal first to their mates, second to their service. The actual nobles who sent them into battle rated a distant third. Yet this day, this hour, they were Duchess Sireen's men.

Jean-Claude caught up with Djordji. "How'd you end up on this trip?"

The Old Hand shrugged. "The news comes down that Grand Leon's fallen. The city clenches up. Naval yard is the closest military station to the challenge courts, so I heads there. Plus I has this young voice in my ear saying I must find Jean-Claude."

"And what of my apprentice?" Jean-Claude asked.

Djordji paused to light his pipe, cutting and tamping and sparking, puffing until he got the texture of the peppery weed just right.

"She'll do," he said, which was high praise coming from Djordji.

They entered the building through the storage area. There amidst the dusty sacks and barrels was Marie. She spotted Jean-Claude and strode toward him. She'd discarded her skirt in favor of pantaloons tucked into rugged calf-high boots, all of which bleached white in her presence. Around her waist was hung a pistol rig with a half-dozen guns.

Her expression was as neutral as ever, but she planted herself in front of Jean-Claude and said, "I am glad to see you safe."

Jean-Claude resisted the urge to hug her. She was supposed to be his apprentice and one did not hug apprentices, even if one had known them since they were little girls.

"Djordji says you have potential."

"I intend to prove that word inadequate. Do you know what happened to Isabelle? She never returned to the lodgings."

The words hit Jean-Claude like a hammer to the heart, but missing wasn't necessarily bad. It could just mean gone to ground.

"No," he said. "But she's smart."

"Smarter than both of us put together," Marie said, which ought to be more encouraging than it was.

"Jean-Claude," called Lord Commodore Jerome, emerging from the conference room. "Sireen wants your testimony."

"Right away," Jean-Claude said. "And thank you for your timely rescue."

Jerome shook his head. "We're not in safe harbor yet."

Marie said, "I'll stand watch."

Djordji said, "Aye. And there's a right way and wrong way to do that. I'll show you the right way before Jean-Claude gets round to showing you how he does it."

Jean-Claude snorted, but allowed Jerome to draw him away.

Sireen was holding court in a low-ceilinged private room behind the kitchens. Around her stood a colorful panoply of l'Empire's highest nobility, or rather their bloodhollow emissaries. Depending on how many bloodhollows they had, any one of these blessed nobles could be involved in several conferences just like this one, and the only way Jean-Claude would know about it is if one of them ratted out the others.

Sireen gave the crowd a grave look and said, "I call upon King's Own Musketeer Jean-Claude to testify to Lael's treachery."

The Duc d'Orange, son of the man who had put Jean-Claude into the musketeer academy all those years ago, peered out from the translucent face of his bloodhollow.

"Very well, musketeer, what happened?"

Jean-Claude took a moment to decide where to begin. "I was in conference with Comtesse Coquetta when a trio of suborned Praetorians burst into her receiving room . . ."

Jean-Claude gave them a full report of the events as he'd experienced them, including his decision to escape with Sireen.

"Was it not your job to defend my grandfather?" asked le Duc de Cheron accusingly. "You left him to die."

"No," Jean-Claude said. "I left him to fetch help, and here we all are, assuming you agree to fight for your family."

The Duc d'Orange said, "How is he spreading this pest, and how can it be cured?"

Jean-Claude shook his head. "He set the pest loose in the population and now it spreads where it will. We know it can be transmitted by sex with an infected person, but we don't know about sneezes. You'll have to ask Lael about a cure, preferably at gunpoint."

"And what if he snatches away our sorcery before we get the chance? You have no idea how powerful he is."

"The pest takes time to work, or it would have been noticed long before now. He can't just reach out and snatch your gift. As for his power, that's mostly in your heads. He's already demanded you come to him, in person. He is not going to ask for your fealty; he is going to demand it. He is going to make you beg for your lands, your titles, your sorcery, and your souls. And what will he give you in return? Will he give you honor? Will he give you glory? No. After you have debased yourself to him, he will let you slip away like whipped curs until the next time he calls you to heel."

The audience stared at him owlishly, unimpressed with his political acumen.

De Cheron put on a petulant look. "That's all well and good for you to say, clayborn; you have no soul to lose."

Jean-Claude's temper rose. "You cannot save your soul by selling it—"

"Thank you, Jean-Claude," Sireen put in. "Messieurs, now that we've heard from the musketeer, let us discuss an alliance . . ."

"That went well," Jerome said dryly when the door had closed between Jean-Claude and the emissaries. "If your next trick is eating your boots, I want to sell tickets."

Jean-Claude rearmed himself with sword, main gauche, and a brace of pistols. "Did you manage to bring all the supplies I asked for?"

The two of them began a circuit of their inner perimeter, checking on guard stations. The wind had picked up and snow flurries hurried by in herds. "Yes. Fortunately for you, I had gotten myself involved in the process of provisioning a ship for a trip to the Twilight Circle because some madman wanted to get into a snowball fight with the Breaker's own Torments."

"That could still happen," Jean-Claude said. "In fact, when you get back to the naval yard, I suggest redoubling your efforts in that direction, in case Sireen needs a longer retreat."

"And when do you imagine this retreat will take place?"

Jean-Claude jabbed a thumb in the general direction of the privy council. "Sireen says she trusts to loyalty in principle, but I wager at least one of those nobs is too scared of losing their sorcery to stand up to Lael. It has no doubt occurred to that individual that only the first person to sell us out stands to gain from it. That means we have to be ready to vanish in an instant. Did you bring those turvymen I asked you for?"

"Yes, and if you asked for them for the reason I think you did, we don't have enough rope to descend the Rivencrag."

"You don't have to make it all the way down to the bottom. The road zig-zags past this point about a hundred meters down. Another half kilometer on and there's a wooden bridge you can cut behind you."

"You sound like you're not coming with us."

"You know what heights do to me. Besides, somebody has to lead the distraction. I'll take the carts and try to draw the enemy away. Then I'll make a run for the backside of the mountain. Who knows, I might even make it, but I'll need some volunteers."

"I'll go," Marie said, emerging from the window well where she'd been keeping watch on the foreyard.

"No, you won't," Jean-Claude said. "This is where that oath you swore comes back to bite you. I swore to stand the sleepless watch and defend l'Empire. You swore to defend Isabelle, so you get Sireen to safety, and then you go find Isabelle."

"But . . ." Marie began, then paused. It was the first time he'd ever seen her hesitate over words. "I need you."

Jean-Claude gestured her toward a bench and then sat down beside her. He searched his heart for words that were not glib or clever, words that might actually help.

"I don't know exactly how old I am. In my village, we didn't keep track of the years that way. I was born in the year when the frost came early and the black bull broke his leg. But I must have been around ten when my father died. I needed him. Peasants are supposed to be dull and taciturn, but he loved to talk. He was always bringing in things he thought were interesting, different kinds of rocks, old knotty roots, animal bones. Once he found a rock with what looked like a fish pressed into it. 'Well, isn't that a puzzle,' he'd say, and my mother would call him a magpie. He never solved any of those puzzles, as far as I know, and then one winter he died of the drowning lung."

Jean-Claude wiped a tear of remembrance from his eye. "I didn't stop needing him then, and though it took a while to understand it, I found I could still hear his echoes in the hollow space inside, and I could still lean on his ghost in the wee hours."

"Do you still need him?" Marie asked.

"Less," Jean-Claude said. "But it's nice to know he's still there. What really changed for me was finding someone who needed me as much as I'd once needed him."

"Isabelle," Marie said.

"Yes. In taking care of her needs I found most of mine fulfilled. If you ever want a good day, find someone who really needs help and give it to them."

Jean-Claude realized his speech had wandered off into the woods and he made a valiant effort to bring it back around. "But I don't mean to die today."

"See that you don't," she said, and angled her body slightly toward him. He put his arm around her shoulders even though it wasn't how a master was supposed to treat his apprentice.

A few moments later, a bugle cry sounded from across the plateau. It was followed by the sound of drums, the royal march rolling in against the wind.

"Unless I miss my guess," Jean-Claude said, "I think Lael has figured out where we are." He climbed up on the bench and peeked over the wall. Down from le Ville Céleste came the usurper's host: a contingent of Thunderguard, the Praetorians, and the regiments of three or four comtes lining up in battle array.

"Go to Sireen," he said to Marie, holding out his hand palm down. "Builder keep you."

She completed the gesture palm up under his. "Until the Savior comes."

Jean-Claude watched her retreat into the Monk's Measure, then checked his sword in its sheath and marched to the barricade at the front gates of the inn yard to greet the coming storm.

Twenty-Four

"Bring out the traitor whore, Sireen!" Lael bellowed, his voice rolling like thunder across the rocky plateau. Someone had cast a glamour that made him seem three meters tall and wreathed in flame, striding before his army, pulling them along like leaves in his wake. The chill wind did not touch him.

He shouted, "Your names are known to me, de Cheron, d'Orange, de Chardin, and de Monde. Your treachery is written in the book of betrayal, your lives are forfeit, and your lands, and your families down to the last generation if you defy me. But I can be merciful. Hand over Sireen, renounce your wicked alliance, and you will be spared!"

Lael's battle line spread out in two wide wings. Blocks of infantry set up with lanes for artillery backed up by cavalry. He had maybe twenty cannons, which were twenty more than he needed against the inn's thin walls. He also had shadowpults, massive alchemical floodlights good for projecting blood-shadows hundreds of meters across the battlefield. Even as Lael delivered his threat, the artillerists sparked the floodlights to life. It would take them a few minutes to warm up to full brightness. Jerome had about that much time to evacuate Sireen before these defenses folded.

Jean-Claude clambered up on the barricade. "Greetings, usurper! Greetings to all you traitors who follow him! Greetings, oathbreakers! I see now the true colors of the Praetorian Guard, who swore an oath to protect their rightful roi, and who have broken that oath, burned it to the ground, and pissed in the ashes. Do you imagine you have saved your souls by shitting on them? Take yourselves away from here or face the wrath of righteous men." The longer he could keep Lael blustering, the more lives Jerome could save, down the ropes and away.

Jerome appeared at Jean-Claude's side, and he'd brought with him d'Orange's bloodhollow.

"The royal party is away," Jerome said.

Jean-Claude nodded. "Good. Start evacuating your men. I only want one rank left on the wall. Two volleys and then retreat." Then he turned his attention to the bloodhollow. "And what can I do for you, monsieur?"

"You will need someone with you who is not afraid to die."

Jean-Claude nodded. "It will be of use." The clan d'Orange had ever been true to Grand Leon and Jean-Claude.

Lael seemed to grow another foot and the flames around him grew brighter.

His voice rolled like thunder across the plain. "By your own words you have condemned yourself. The Builder has withdrawn his mighty hand and the Breaker has claimed her due. She has stripped Leon the Tyrant of his sorcery and burned his soul to ash. The oaths you cling to are blasphemy, and in the Builder's service, I will cleanse you from the face of the world. For l'Empire! For the Builder!"

As he spoke, his regimental commanders ordered their troops forward, bugles sounded, and the snares kept time. Artillerists jerked the flintlocks of their cannons. They spat fire and smoke. A deadly roar.

Jean-Claude dropped behind the barricade and yelled, "Down!" Marines threw themselves flat.

Cannonballs smashed into the inn yard wall, shattering stone and sending splinters flying. An unlucky marine screamed in pain.

Lael's Sanguinaires threw open the shutters on their shadowpults and stood in the beams. Columns of light cast bloodshadows on the inn yard's wall. The bloodshadows flowed over the top of the wall and dripped down like tentacles reaching for victims.

Jean-Claude scrambled back from the barricade and yelled, "Firewall!"

Marines ducked forward and thrust flaming brands into the long pile of tar-covered, oil-soaked wooden debris that had been stacked along the front of the wall. Greedy flames raced along the befouled wood, belching out a huge pall of black, gagging smoke to confound the bloodshadows.

Jean-Claude clasped arms with Jerome, and shouted to be heard over the clatter of gunfire. "Until we meet in Torment."

Jerome answered, "And crack the Breaker's hold."

Jerome drew his saber and set off down the line, slapping men back into line with the flat of his blade. "Stand and prepare to repel boarders!"

His heart thundering, Jean-Claude ran toward the wagons. D'Orange followed at the lumbering-through-knee-deep-water pace that was the best a bloodhollow could manage. A cannonade blasted overhead, smashing the roof, shattering the top of the inn yard wall. A flying stone nearly brained Jean-Claude. He had nearly forgotten just how much he hated open battle.

At the edge of the yard awaited four horsemen and a cart with a team of four, exactly the sort of unit one would expect to use if one was trying to make a break for freedom with a valuable noble on board, though the canvas-covered bulge in the bed of the cart was considerably more explosive than even the most volatile duchess. A teamster handed Jean-Claude the reins to the four-hitch, saluted, and ran for the down ropes. Jean-Claude scrambled into the driver's seat, turned, and hoisted d'Orange up after him.

"Messieurs," Jean-Claude said to the horsemen. "Ride fast and don't die. We're only pretending to be heroes."

They saluted him in return. He aimed his team at the open side gate, flicked the reins, and whistled them into a canter. A cannonball punched through the inn wall and shattered a water barrel. Jean-Claude's wagon launched through the gate onto the battlefield, the four horsemen lined up in escort position.

D'Orange said, "This reminds me of the way a lot of old stories end."

"In those stories, do we live or die?" Jean-Claude asked. He looked over his left shoulder. Lael, towering in his rage, spotted them and shouted an order. A cavalry regiment broke from the back of the usurper's army and kicked into a gallop on a course to intercept them.

"It's about evenly split," d'Orange said.

"Better than I would have thought," Jean-Claude said. A dozen other armed camps ringed the plateau, the personal regiments of nobles who were mostly hoping to wait until the smoke cleared and then line up with the winning side as if they'd been there all along. Jean-Claude aimed between the two nearest camps.

Lael's cavalry surged, looking to head Jean-Claude off before he shot the gap. Jean-Claude whipped his team into a breakneck gallop, pulling ahead.

"Take over!" he yelled, and thrust the reins into d'Orange's hands. "Around the edge!"

The bloodhollow was slower than a human, but not so slow that he couldn't control the horses, or so Jean-Claude hoped. Jean-Claude half vaulted, half crawled into the back of the wagon just as one of Lael's men drew alongside and raised his lance. Jean-Claude whipped out his rapier, cut the rope holding the wagon's tarp down, and flung it in the man's face. The cavalryman yelped and his horse bolted sideways as it was assaulted by the great flapping canvas rectangle.

Beneath the canvas was a crate of mortar shells with fuses in, and a barrel loaded with naval signal rockets. Saints bless Jerome! Jean-Claude snatched up a mortar shell. Another cavalryman pulled even and aimed his pistol. Jean-Claude dropped flat. The cavalryman's shot blew a hole in the side planking.

Jean-Claude rolled to his knees. The cavalryman slashed with his saber. The blade cut into Jean-Claude's hatband but scraped and sparked off the chainmail coif sewn inside. Jean-Claude drew his pistol, aimed, fired. The gun spat fire and smoke. The cavalryman fell from his saddle.

Three of Jean-Claude's escort riders were still up, peeling off in different directions. Half a dozen enemy riders bore down on Jean-Claude. Jean-Claude cocked his pistol and used the flintlock's sparks to light his mortar fuse. He lobbed the projectile overboard, ducked his head, and almost counted to two before the bomb went off, picking up the back end of the wagon and filling the air with chunks of iron.

He groped for another bomb and sat up again . . . and stared. Up in the sky, a second Solar seemed to have risen.

Burning through the icy air was a massive lion with eagle wings the size of a galleon's sails, all made entirely of fire. Its glow cast the whole battlefield in shades of orange like the last embers of a dying world. It swooped around the circle of encampments, trailing an endless streamer of black smoke.

"Behold!" it roared in a voice that shook the sky and rattled the stones on the ground. "Behold the Builder's chosen voice. Behold power. Behold your emperor!" As it passed over the Monk's Measure it spat a bolt of fire that shattered the tiled roof and cracked the main beam.

All around the plateau, soldiers pointed and shouted at the glorious terror wheeling above them. Some threw down their weapons and ran. Others prostrated themselves in prayer. Officers ran amongst them, slapping them with sabers and trying to whip them back into line.

Jean-Claude was stunned. That was Lael. How in the . . . what sorcery had he obtained? Or sorceries. Seelenjäger and . . . hadn't Ambassadress Ustina mastered the element of fire?

Lael made another pass at the inn and spat more fire, a gout that was hot enough to make the stones glow like the inside of a forge. Twice he'd hit the front of the building, but if that monster circled out beyond the edge he'd see Sireen's party escaping down the cliff face. They'd be helpless as sitting birds.

"Horses are almost done!" d'Orange shouted.

Lael's cavalry opened fire and Jean-Claude felt a bullet whiz by his ear. Jean-Claude's terror yielded to the urge to action. He sparked the match to the signal rockets nestled in metal tubes in the barrel. Another bullet punched through the side of the cart. A grim-faced rider got close enough to slash at Jean-Claude with his saber. Jean-Claude parried and thrust. Missed.

The rocket barrel belched fire. With a great rush of smoke the first rocket shot straight up, and then the second one, smoke trails glowing red and black like streamers tossed in some infernal celebration.

The cavalryman screamed and slashed Jean-Claude across the left forearm. Pain shot all the way up to Jean-Claude's teeth, but he trapped the blade against the wagon with his main gauche and stabbed the man in the shoulder.

The third rocket shot from the barrel just as the first exploded, a brilliant ball of white light that throbbed in the air. Then the second rocket exploded all in red. Across the plateau, Lael turned, saw the flares, and came rushing down the wind to investigate.

The wagon lurched and bucked. They'd run into rubble. Jean-Claude whipped around only to see d'Orange's bloodhollow slide off the driver's seat with a hole in its head.

"*Merde!*" He lunged for the reins just as the wheel came off the wagon.

⁓

The sound of cannon fire jerked Celestina's attention up the side of the Rivencrag. A few hundred meters ahead and hanging over the edge of the cliff like a dark gargoyle was the inn that had once been a monastery. A halo of orange light around it suggested a fire. Beams of light cutting bright cones through the blowing snow spoke of Sanguinaire shadowpults.

Irregular cackles of gunfire filled the space between the louder report of cannons. But who was fighting whom? Celestina had no spyglass and could only squint at the spectacle as people suddenly started jumping over the side of the cliff. But instead of plummeting to their deaths, they descended slowly and steadily on ropes to land on the Pilgrims' Road just a few hundred meters up from Celestina's caravan.

Immacolata had seen it, too. "Enemies. Lael's forces wouldn't be holding the inn."

"We'll take them before they get organized on the trail," Celestina said, the thrill of battle surging up in her breast. Too long had it been since she'd experienced open battle, the clash of sinews and the elation of victory. In all her lifetimes and all her experiences, those were the moments worth having. Cursed had she been for so long without a worthy foe.

"I will," Immacolata said. "You're still soft from the shell. Wait here."

Celestina bristled at being denied this chance, but of course Immacolata was right. Damn that she could not put on her *mantello di piume* or even extend her talons. Indeed, the only thing she had to defend herself with was the ridiculous little maidenblade. She couldn't even use Isabelle's l'Étincelle, as she had no memory of how it worked. She was not yet hardy enough to play the fool. There would be time enough for that when the new age of conquest began. The world had grown much larger than the last time she had nearly dominated it, but the larger arena would only make her victory more glorious.

Immacolata marshaled her Neverborn grotesques and cultists and the whole column stormed off at a quick march, leaving Celestina with two gloomy Azurites, the brick-jawed cart driver, and the prisoners. She consoled herself that it wouldn't be much of a fight. With more than half a dozen surgical sorcerers in Immacolata's contingent, a swift strike ought to be able to overwhelm the enemy coming piecemeal down the cliff.

The fire atop the plateau got brighter, and Lael wheeled overhead, a monstrous fiery feline. By the Eldest, what a monster! She had done well. He was her work of art, a great sculpture of sorcery and madness. Even his limp left arm, paralyzed by one sorcerous inset too many, hardly detracted from his incendiary magnificence.

How long would it take him to realize that the more sorceries he extended, the harder it would be to reel them all back in or separate each from the other? Every sorcery ran the risk of consuming the sorcerer, and the strain would be much worse when all were competing for the same resources of body, mind, and spirit. It would not be long until Lael found himself trapped in his own powers, bestial, enflamed, shadow-ridden, and deluded. It was Celestina's job to hold him together until she and Immacolata could secure all l'Empire's levers of power. Then it would be her joy to slay him.

Lael wheeled away without looking down.

"What have you done with Isabelle?" It was the Seelenjäger who spoke. His back was bent in pain and his fur was still pale from being shadowburned, but his beastly eyes were clear.

"Shh, Bitterlich," she said. "I have everything under control."

"No," he said. "Isabelle would never contemplate such treachery as I have heard from your lips."

Celestina had forgotten how good the Seelenjäger senses could be. Even with the whistling wind, the stomp of boots, and the clopping of hooves he'd overheard her planning with Immacolata. Even in his agony, he'd somehow paid attention. She could use such a tool. Alas that his dedication was so misplaced, and she had no time to entertain the chance of turning him.

It had been part of the plan to use the beast-born as a tool against Leon. In the eyes of the Sanguinaire, the elevation of a Seelenjäger was one more piece of evidence for the fallen roi's corruption. Unfortunately, she could not allow this animal to make Lael suspicious that "Isabelle" was more than Grand Leon's favorite cousin.

Celestina dismounted and approached the beast-born from the flank. As brave as his words were, the spikes through his wrists and the lingering effect of his shadowburn had left him trembling and weak. He barely twitched away when she grabbed the thicker shock of hair atop his head, and yanked it back to expose his neck.

"I am Celestina, and I have taken from Isabelle that which is my right and my due. Be thankful I make this quick." Celestina slid the maidenblade from its sheath.

Her phantom-hand stung as if she'd grabbed a nettle. Distracted, she looked down just in time for a rush of light and heat to boil out of the knife and flood up her arm, coursing along her spine and slamming into her brain like floodwaters from a burst dam.

The presence thundered into Celestina's consciousness and drove her from the center of her body's flow, ripping away control of her limbs. *Isabelle!* Where had she been hiding? The knife? Celestina tried to hurl the maidenblade away, but she had no control over her phantom arm.

Celestina pushed back against the invader. This surge of strength couldn't last. She enfolded Isabelle's pink-and-purple presence, snuffed the sparks, absorbed the force of her charge.

—

Isabelle's thoughts bloomed as she unfolded into her own skull. Thank the Builder she had learned to push herself out of her body. Thank the saints she was so familiar with that knife that she'd been able to squeeze herself in and hide there until the Other, Celestina, drew the blade.

Wrestling Celestina was like trying to strangle a bear, but at least this time she had a toehold. This time there was no slave oil. Celestina flowed through her, around her, dissolving and dispersing her, breaking her up into incomplete and impotent pieces. She pulled back, clinging to her core self, fighting one bit of Celestina at a time.

Yet already Isabelle's onslaught weakened. All her energy had been stored in the knife, but she had no way to replenish it. Celestina had a constant source. The vitera.

Isabelle surged for the light and sound of consciousness. She opened her eyes, saw a cart. There was Bitterlich. Alive. Thank every saint that ever lived.

She reached back with her flesh hand, seized the vitera, and yanked the monstrosity from the base of her skull. It felt as if someone had ripped through her brain with a white-hot saw blade. Isabelle screamed like a Torment unchained. Celestina dragged Isabelle back into the depths of her mind, back where she could be disassembled, rendered into nothing more than memory. The whole world shrank to a pinprick of light.

Like a drowning woman in deep water, Isabelle reached for the light, for the surface, for air and breath and the strength to fight. Up there in the light was her mind, the landscape of her imagination and all the structures of her personality. They might both reach that surface and continue their battle and lay it all to waste. Even if she won, what would be left of her?

Celestina sank in her claws, crawled over Isabelle, and pushed for the surface. *Not for the grave am I.*

Isabelle seized Celestina and held her back. She turned from the light and dove into the depths, dragging the struggling fiend down into the dark and the cold, where there was no goal but to outlast. Isabelle burned with fatigue, with yearning for the light. Celestina's struggles became a desperate frenzy. The cold seeped in and numbed Isabelle's thoughts.

Isabelle conjured memories, certainties, the rock and roots of her being. Jean-Claude spoke to her as a friend, saved her life, taught her to laugh at the darkness. Young Marie tagged along on every adventure, eager to be talked into mischief. Gretl had given Isabelle her trust in the face of a monster. Julio had given her his precious word. Bitterlich had given her fire under snow.

Isabelle clung to her friends, their warmth in the cold, their life in the crushing depths, their calm in the face of panic. Celestina cracked and frayed, each part of its composite being seeking its own escape. Its presence frayed in Isabelle's grasp, coming apart like sodden paper in the frigid deeps until holding on to it gave it more form than letting it go.

Isabelle let Celestina go, to dissolve and vanish. She allowed herself to drift, directionless, in a space with no up or down. She held only to herself and her dear ones, until, almost imperceptibly, light filtered into the darkness like the glow before dawn, and she found herself in familiar surrounds.

She took a deep breath. There were her lungs. There was her heartbeat. There were her limbs and her aching head.

She opened her eyes. She was flat on her back on the road, staring up at Bitterlich who was curled over the back of the cart, trying to protect his head and cruelly shackled arms while the Azurites beat him with the butts of their muskets.

"Stop!" she croaked, and struggled to rise. "I said stop."

The Azurites hesitated. Isabelle grabbed the back of the cart and hauled herself up between them and their victim, forcing them to back off.

"Why are you beating this man?" she gasped, still trying to reacquaint herself with the idea of balance.

"He attacked you," said the first Azurite, a man with jowls like a bloodhound.

"I slipped," Isabelle said. "He never touched me." But she was supposed to be a cruel master, wasn't she. Immacolata's mental twin, so she added, "Still, your reflexes are commendable, and I shall remember your swift action on my behalf. Well done."

Bloodhound puffed up a little with pride.

His partner knelt down and reached for something on the ground. "What's this?"

The vitera. Isabelle bent and snatched up the ticklike horror before the Azurite could lay hands on it.

"This is mine," Isabelle said, stuffing the vile thing in her messenger bag.

Isabelle took stock of her situation. What else was she missing? A stinging wind flung flecks of ice at her face. Breathing hurt. Bitterlich still lived, though his fur was torn and bleeding. His wrists were a ruin of blood and matted fur that made her cringe right down to her soul. She must get him out of those bonds . . . but then what? He was in no shape to fight, and she had no way of getting him out of here.

Gunfire in the distance echoed off the cliff face. The wooden shelf road shook beneath her feet. Steel clashed and men shouted. Immacolata did battle with the cliff people. Soldiers and horses screamed and several went over the edge. A shout of triumph erupted through the storm. Immacolata and the Azurites raised their voices and their weapons in cheers. Immacolata reached down and hoisted a woman in white by the throat.

It was Duchess Sireen. She clung to Immacolata's arm, trying not to choke to death as Immacolata carried her back through the press of Azurites, showing her off like a prize catch.

It was all Isabelle could do to keep her expression from revealing her despair as Immacolata strode toward them with her trophy. Captured was better than dead. Captured could be rescued, but how? Isabelle could not face Immacolata alone, much less surrounded by all her minions. And Sireen wasn't the only person they'd taken captive. The Azurites disarmed and bound up several soldiers and—it was all Isabelle could do to choke down her horror—they had Marie. She bled from several wounds, walked with a limp, and cradled her right arm.

Despair clawed at Isabelle's mind, but at least Marie was alive. Had Jean-Claude been with them? No, he would never have made it down that cliff.

Grinning, Immacolata lifted Sireen high in a salute to Isabelle. "Victory!"

Isabelle had no choice but to play along.

She thrust her fist skyward and shouted, "Victory!" That was what Immacolata wanted. That was what the Maximi had always craved, another foe to fight, another land to conquer. Celestina had left memories behind in

Isabelle's head, not all of them, but certainly all her recent ones. Every act in her life, every skill was bent in service of the next battle.

Immacolata tossed Sireen on the baggage cart and said to the driver, "Stuff her in a barrel. I don't want her shadow getting loose."

Stunned and wheezing, Sireen put up only the weakest of struggles as the Azurites poured most of the water out of a water barrel on their supply wagon, folded Sireen up, and crammed her in. Before they wedged it shut Sireen caught Isabelle's gaze and spat, "Traitor."

Isabelle felt like she'd been gutted, but she had a part to play. "Traitor is what history calls the loser."

Marie never wore an expression on her face, but she never stopped staring at Isabelle while the Azurites chained her and the other captives to the cart behind Bitterlich.

Isabelle could not stand to watch, so she turned to Immacolata. "A fine catch, sister."

Immacolata said, "Lael will be pleased, but I wonder if we should keep the duchess in reserve. As long as she is alive and on the loose, Lael will not sit easily on the Célestial throne."

Isabelle combed Celestina's memory. The original plan had been to infect Sireen with the pest, and then have Lael rip her bloodshadow to pieces so as to prove his power to the other nobles. Even as Isabelle imagined it, a vision of the sanctivore appeared in her mind, a cylinder of green and purple fluid. Around its belt at its girth flowed characters in the Builder's speech, which even the greatest scholars could not read. Lael permitted no one to touch it, but kept it chained to his person.

Isabelle blinked through the memory and said, "We want Lael secure on the throne so there is no doubt of the succession when he hands the reins of power to me. Let Sireen be my special gift for Lael and it will cement his trust in me."

If Isabelle was to have any hope of rescuing her friends, of salvaging l'Empire, it had to be today. It would be harder to dislodge Lael once his grip was firmly established. The nobles of the high houses might knuckle under to him for any number of reasons from terror to ambition, but once they bent their necks to a new master they would find them difficult to straighten.

Also, once Lael forced the high houses to swear fealty to him, it would forever drive a wedge between those who joined with him and those who resisted. Even if the tyrant was thrown down, those fractures would remain to weaken l'Empire for ages to come.

"Well reasoned," Immacolata said. Then she turned to the color guard. "Move us out."

The bugler blew a call to form up, and the Azurites who were picking through the dead and dispatching the wounded hurried to their places. Isabelle remounted her horse and trotted to the front of the line. The drummer snapped out a marching beat. Up the road they tramped and stamped, through puddles of blood and past dozens of dead bodies from both sides. Wasted lives. A little way up the road, an old man under a pile of Azurites groaned. He wore the tabard of a King's Own Musketeer. He was no one she'd ever seen, but her heart went out to him nonetheless. Not that she could show it.

An Azurite stepped smartly out of formation to skewer him with a bayonet.

"Stop!" Isabelle said. No trained spy would have risked her cover like this, but Isabelle could not let a helpless man be stabbed to death.

. . . *ignorance begets* . . . came a thought in a voice quite different from the one she usually found in her head. Isabelle's heart nearly stopped in terror that Celestina had somehow re-formed and taken up hiding in the crannies of her mind.

The bayonet-wielding Azurite looked at her in confusion. "But—"

"Chain him up with the others," Isabelle said.

Immacolata gave Isabelle a skeptical look. "Why save the musketeer?"

Isabelle's heart hammered so loudly she imagined Gretl could have heard it. "Grand Leon loves his musketeers. It will pain him more to see one killed than to see one already dead."

Immacolata snorted. "As you say."

"Strategy is the seed of warfare. If I cannot have battle, I can at least plan for it," Isabelle said, paraphrasing a quote from Maximus Primus's own *Stratagems*.

That seemed to dispel Immacolata's incipient doubts. Ironically it did nothing for Isabelle's. She had no idea what she was going to do when she faced Lael in his might. And where in all the world was Jean-Claude?

CHAPTER

Twenty-Five

Jean-Claude hurt all over. Sharp fresh pain. He opened his eyes. One of them was not swollen shut. The world had gone sideways. No. He was just lying on the ground. Amongst rocks. Sharp rocks. And snow. He remembered the wagon tipping over, the front end clipping a stone. The whole thing flipping up in the air.

He ought to be dead.

He contemplated lifting his head, but he was not entirely sure it was still attached to his body. Inconvenient if it had rolled away. He had a brief weird vision of his headless body groping around in the rubble, trying on different rocks for size.

But no. Many of the parts of him that hurt were well south of his neck, which indicated that there was at least some nominal communication with the outlying provinces. Perhaps a treaty was being worked out.

He rolled onto his back, dislodging at least a knuckle-length of snow. How long had he been unconscious? The wind whistled around him and he could hardly see his hand in front of his face. The front of the blizzard must have come on quickly, hiding him under its cloak.

With a sound like a tremendous flag rippling and snapping in the breeze, Lael the fire lion rushed by overhead, but so thick was the snow that all Jean-Claude could see was the glow of his passing. He circled the plateau in great swoops, roaring at the regiments and demanding the nobles attend him or be destroyed.

Judging by the path of disturbed rocks behind Jean-Claude, and the fact that the ones beneath him slipped every time he shifted his weight, he deduced that he'd been thrown from the wagon and tobogganed down the opposite side of a spoil heap until he slid to a stop at the bottom of a quarry.

Jean-Claude forced himself to his feet. His clothes and skin had been shredded. His head ached and he could not balance on the slippery stone. He crawled, several times throwing himself flat as the ground shifted beneath him, once sliding halfway back down the slope. The wind chilled his bones and the snow accumulated to the thickness of his arm. Still he crawled on. To stop was to die. Cold could sneak up on a man, turn the blink of an eye into a drowse, turn just-for-a-minute into the grave.

He could not have said how long it took him to realize he had crawled out of the pit, but it finally occurred to him that he must have done, for the rock had stopped shifting under him, and pinpricks of light penetrated the snowstorm. Lines of alchemical lanterns trudged antlike through the gloom, all converging in the distance at a single larger glow: Grand Leon's stadium.

Jean-Claude braced on an up-thrust rock and climbed to his feet. His legs didn't want to hold him, but he shambled on anyway, toward what fate he could no longer guess. He had no weapons, no allies, and little strength. He ought to be finding someplace to shelter, to recoup strength, not staggering defenseless into the heart of his enemy's power. Yet if this was l'Empire's final day and Grand Leon's last hour, he could not turn away. He must find a way to make a difference. If he could not fight, he must at least bear witness. He only prayed that Isabelle was safe somewhere—still fighting, because she would—but at least surrounded by allies. *Builder let her live.*

On through the dark he stumbled, until he literally tripped over a corpse. It was one of the cavalrymen who had chased him down earlier, already half buried in snow. Jean-Claude took the chance of kneeling down and divesting him of his long coat. The man's weapons were missing, but at least now Jean-Claude had a disguise.

It was harder than he'd expected to stand up again, and the coat fit him like a small skin on a fat sausage, but he belted it on and continued his trudge. The stadium could not have been more than a kilometer away from the quarry, but it seemed to recede from him almost as fast as he approached it. He angled his march toward one of the flickering lines of lanterns.

A small, loosely assorted band of stragglers clung to the back of the nearest column. None of the marchers were carrying their weapons. Lael must have demanded they be left behind. Jean-Claude joined in their nearly blind determined slog.

At last the great stadium loomed out of the blow. Lanterns dotted the lip of the wide wooden bowl, outlining its squat round shape. It seemed madness for Lael to hold his triumph here in this weather, but ten meters from the entrance Jean-Claude passed through a great staggering swipe of wind, and stepped into calm air. No snow stung his face. He was not alone in looking up and around with wonder. The whole stadium seemed to be covered by a dome of stillness, one that repelled the snow. It was a Windcaller's powers.

A picket of Praetorians guarded the entrance to the stadium, glaring into the crowd, seeking out known troublemakers. Jean-Claude sidled up to a struggling soldier and got a shoulder under the man's arm to help him along. This allowed him to duck his head and hide his face behind the brim of his hat and he limped by the security cordon.

He kept on helping his new friend until he slipped on a patch of ice in the corridor leading out onto the floor of the stadium. Almost instantly two other men hauled him up, steadied him, and assisted him out into the arena.

Jean-Claude took a moment to be profoundly grateful for ordinary people. Many of the men lined up in colorful blocks all across the stadium floor were conscripts, dragged from their shops and farms, stuffed into uniforms and made to fight and die for a glory in which they would not share and for prizes they would not be given.

Yet reaching down to help a fallen comrade was as reflexive for them as breathing. Yes, they were lowly, crude, drunken, and dim. They'd fight each other over money or women or insults or just because they liked a good brawl. They'd drink themselves into the grave and piss away whatever fortune fell into their hands. But when you fell down, they'd pick you up again.

And they were the ones who would suffer the most under a tyrant like Lael. The saintborn might have to suck his cock to keep their powers and their lands, but it was the clayborn who he would hurl into war, their farms he would pillage, their bodies he would use to shore up the walls of his empire.

Jean-Claude made his way to the back of the crowd and up into the lower part of the stands to get a better view. Below him, across a field extensive enough for a cavalry charge, was a patchwork quilt of high house regiments, rank-and-file in uniforms of blue, gold, red, and green. At the head of each block was a small band of men and a few women in white. The Sanguinaire with their red shadows. How many of them were already suffering under the shadow rot, in fear for their status and their souls?

Across from them were the black-clad Praetorians and two regiments of the Thunderguard, though both units were thinned out either by execution or desertion. They would have been horribly outnumbered if they weren't the only ones who were armed.

When the last of the high houses had crowded in, but before they had settled down, a troop of trumpeters sounded a royal entrance and a herald cried, "Behold, His Magnificence le Roi de Fue, Defender of the Enlightened, Rightful Ruler of the Risen Kingdoms, Emperor Lael!"

A sudden heat prickled along Jean-Claude's back as if he'd just walked by the open door of a furnace. With a tremendous rush of hot wind Lael rushed by overhead, trailing flame and smoke like a skyship on fire. The tarry reek of it settled over Jean-Claude like a shroud and tried to crawl into his lungs.

Lael cut across the center of the arena, just in case there was anyone there who he hadn't gagged, and alit in the royal box, a platform two stories high.

Even as he touched down Lael's form grew blurry around the edges as a Seelenjäger's did when he was changing form, but instead of a smooth flowing transformation, his reversion into his human form jerked and twisted through several contortions as if there was a badger inside him trying to get out. His flames, likewise, took time to gutter and die. As many powers as he possessed, he was untrained and unpracticed in all of them. It was a weakness, albeit one Jean-Claude did not see how to exploit from here.

Yet the figure who emerged from these contortions was nothing less than a demigod, standing head and shoulders above ordinary men, with flowing black ringlets, and a visage that encouraged bitter envy and unnatural lust at the same time. His bloodshadow draped over his shoulder and fell in a ruby pool at his feet.

He held up a hand for silence, and a hush fell over the stadium, settling thicker than the snow outside.

His voice was clear and deep and strong enough to be heard even in the highest seats. "Welcome, my subjects. I see amongst you stalwart defenders of l'Empire's long traditions, and also those with the vision to comprehend a glorious future.

"Yet I see that some of your number are missing. Where are the houses of Cheron, and d'Orange, of Lefebvre and Gauthier and Trintignant? Are any of them amongst you?" He paused and was answered by only nervous shuffling.

Lael continued, "Let it be known that unto my hands and mine alone has been given the power of judgment everlasting. The Builder has turned his back on l'Empire. He has let loose the Breaker to send her scourge to strip the unrighteous of the sorcery they have betrayed.

"Yet the Builder is merciful, and he has given unto me, the one who was castigated, scorned, and outcast, the ability to forgive, to restore the Builder's protection and drive off the Breaker's pest. It is a mercy I will grant to all those who submit to my rightful rule, for only I am without sin."

Jean-Claude's bile rose, for he had stood in judgment of men and executed men without trial. It was never a duty without sin. Jean-Claude soul was tarnished, stained through and through, and he knew better than to ask for forgiveness from saints, Builder, or roi. Forgiveness missed the point. Once you'd forgiven yourself the first time, once you'd given yourself permission, what was to stop you from doing it again? If there was any truth at all in the business of bloodletting, it was that the bloodstains must remain. They might not show on the outside, but they were always right there, under the skin, a reminder of the cost of power.

For all his faults, Grand Leon understood the matter of bloodstains. He never denied the evil he did in the service of l'Empire and accepted the cost to his soul.

"Behold the Tyrant Leon," Lael declared, and with a wave of his hand, a troop of Praetorians marched out from a tunnel just under the royal box, bearing on long poles a wooden platform on which huddled Grand Leon. His head and arms locked in a pillory. He had been stripped of his robes and regalia, even his wig, leaving nothing but a bald, wrinkled old man in his smallclothes. The post supporting the pillory's crossbar was too tall to allow le roi to kneel without choking himself, and too short to allow him to stand, so he had curled into a feral crouch, bracing his knees on the post in an attempt to relieve the strain, though even that probably pained him less than the loss of his bloodshadow. Lael and his cohort had torn it to shreds. Under the influence of the pest, it had not regenerated.

A fire sprang up around Lael and he seemed to swell. "See you all now the dread tyrant Leon, the man who has ruled l'Empire Céleste with an iron fist for the last sixty years. This is the spinner of webs and the master of intrigues, warlord and conqueror, the most powerful sorcerer the world has witnessed in a thousand years. This is the man you all feared right down to the bone. See him as he truly is: base, disgraced, weak, and worthless. This is the worm you have obeyed."

Visceral revulsion shook Jean-Claude's innards at the glee leaking out through Lael's ringing tones. Jean-Claude would bet his other leg that Lael was staining his codpiece with joy.

The rest of the crowd muttered and mumbled. Soldiers shifted their weight uneasily. Grand Leon was the only roi any of them had ever known, and the common soldiery respected him.

For all his many faults, Grand Leon had always been a shrewd cultivator of the clayborn. He'd kept the saintborn nobles in his own tight orbit and off their people's backs. He had sent these men into battle, yes, but he had also fought beside them, bled in the mud with them.

Jean-Claude was willing to bet that there was not one common soldier here who did not have some story, perhaps handed down like an heirloom from some drill sergeant about that time he saw Grand Leon down in the muck of the breastworks, or dragging a whole platoon to safety with his bloodshadow. These were not men who hated Grand Leon. These were men who looked up to him. He was their roi, but he was also one of their mates, and when your brother-in-arms falls down . . . you pick him up again.

Jean-Claude's heart beat a little quicker as he surveyed rank upon rank of men watching their great leader being degraded. Oh yes. Jean-Claude needed a weapon and he was going to recruit one.

He stepped smartly up to the end of a row of men in the regiment before him. From their uniforms they were le Comte de Jardin's men, called the Stonemasons for the circumvallation they had constructed at the Battle of Dembres.

"They can't do this to le roi," Jean-Claude growled, by no means under his breath. "I was at Dembres. I remember His Majesty holding the breach by himself when the old comte took that bullet to the knee. The damned lowlanders came at us in waves but he held them back. Grand Leon's shadow plucked a cannonball out of the air this far in front of my nose." He placed his hand like a blade in front of his nose.

The man next to him stopped fidgeting nervously and started fidgeting angrily. "My pa told me he was there at Havoc Ridge, when Grand Leon turned the line."

"They can't do this to him," Jean-Claude said, and another listener, farther into the rank, told how Grand Leon had saved his brother at the Battle of Toloup.

Jean-Claude slipped away to set other hearts aflame. But even if he started a conflagration, could he wield it? Could he aim it? He searched every regiment for familiar faces, men he had met long ago but kept in touch with over the years. Alas, faces changed and rarely was a soldier's career a long one.

Jean-Claude eased forward several ranks and started again. "They can't do this to le roi." To le Comte de Maersh's Flying Huns, Jean-Claude recalled Grand Leon's exploits at the Battle of Bone Bridge. To de Hauet's Gravediggers he recalled the threefold winter of 1654 when Grand Leon had lived and starved along with his troops in the fabled Fort Nowhere in the Forest of Sorrows. These were storied regiments of renown and Grand Leon had given many of them their names.

"Be ready to fight," Jean-Claude said.

There should have been officers stationed at the corner of every platoon, but they would have been the ones trusted enough to be left behind with the weapons cache, and so while Jean-Claude had to dodge the occasional lieutenant, their presence was thin on the ground.

He was just making his way along the lines of Comte Morel's Iron Fist brigade, when a massive hand seized him around the neck, and a great square shape blotted out the stadium light.

"Troublemaker," growled a ruined voice. The owner of the voice looked like someone had stuffed a mountain ogre in a sergeant's uniform. It was Sascha!

Jean-Claude's spirits soared, but before he could overcome his surprise, the sergeant squeezed. "No. Talking. In. Line."

Jean-Claude's eyes bulged and the world went dim. His breath was a frantic whistle. He let his body sag and yanked away the giant's thumb. "Sascha, it's me, Jean-Claude."

Sascha recoiled as if shot. Jean-Claude pushed back the brim of his hat. Sascha's eyes went round. "Jean. Claude."

"What in Torment is going on back here," said a more refined voice, annoyed and nasal. It was a damned officer. "Sergeant, why are you out of line?"

Sascha slugged Jean-Claude in the stomach and he doubled over, retching. Sascha casually shoved Jean-Claude to his knees and turned to face the officer. "This. Man. Sick."

From his hunched position, Jean-Claude should only see the officer's boots, which had the sort of polish one could only get from other people's spit.

"Drunk, more than likely," said the officer. "Have him flogged when we get back to camp."

Sascha hefted Jean-Claude and carried him to the back of the formation before setting him down. "Why. You. Here?"

Jean-Claude regained his balance and clasped a hand on Sascha's shoulder. "To stop this coup. I need your help, but it's going to be dangerous."

Sascha slapped his hand on Jean-Claude's shoulder in return. "Say. No more. What. To do?"

"Just follow my lead," Jean-Claude said. *You'll know when I do.*

"Will. Do. Iron. Fists. Are. Yours."

"May the saints bless all your children," Jean-Claude said.

A blast of trumpets announced new arrivals. A herald cried, "General Brunela! Princess Isabelle des Zephyrs!"

Isabelle? She was alive. She was here? Of course Isabelle was here. Where else would she be. She must have insinuated herself amongst the traitors, but to what end?

Isabelle rode into the arena alongside her sister at the head of what looked like a triumphal procession. Behind them rolled a cart to which were shackled a half-dozen prisoners. There was the Seelenjäger Bitterlich pinned like bug, and Marie holding up Djordji, who looked pale as death. But where was Sireen? Where was Jerome? Had they escaped or were they dead?

Sascha said, "Follow. Your. Lead."

"Thank you, my friend," Jean-Claude said. "Builder Keep."

"Savior. Come," Sascha said, and lumbered away.

A regiment of Azurite monks marched in behind the prisoners, muddy and bloody as if from battle. Two more of the hooded kind rode at their head. One of them had a bloodshadow, the other a physique that screamed Seelenjäger to Jean-Claude's mind. The regiment turned smartly and formed up with the Thunderguard, who looked none too pleased at their inclusion.

General Brunela and Isabelle lined up their prisoners as offerings to Lael, in full view of Grand Leon.

Saints but Jean-Claude hoped Isabelle had a plan.

—

Isabelle maintained her disguise mostly by maintaining her silence through the long ride up the Rivencrag. Her heart ached for Bitterlich, Marie, and all the others chained to the prison cart, whipped when they did not move swiftly enough for the driver, and poor Sireen crammed in that barrel.

Every moan or cry tore at her mind, but she dared not look back. Not only would it be out of character, but the sight of their suffering would likely undo her. What if they died on this trek before she even tried to help them?

. . . *loss of the wretched* . . . muttered the voice from nowhere.

Every time the voice spoke, Isabelle sought its source within her, but the vile and vicious sentiments always appeared in the midst of her thoughts like acid dewdrops from the air with no particular point of origin. If they were not the result of madness, they would surely be the cause of it. The vitera had begun to change the secret architecture of her thoughts before she ripped it away. The damage was done, but how far would it spread, and how much of her would it destroy? She imagined a cup of wine spilled on white fabric, the stain continuing to spread long after the cup was pulled away.

Yet her own fate hardly mattered if her friends and family all suffered, if l'Empire fell. She set her teeth and carried on through the storm. She must bring down Lael, but even he was not the ultimate problem, not even with all his new powers. Nor was Immacolata.

The problem was the pest, the Breaker's curse. The saintborn were paralyzed, rendered helpless by fear of a foe that got inside them that they could not fight. She must liberate them from that fear.

But the only chance she saw seemed very slim.

At last the procession reached the stadium. Isabelle was as shocked as anyone to pass out of the blizzard and into the dome of still air. The swirling snow overhead reflected the light of the great stadium lanterns, reducing the whole world to this one small hemisphere.

The royal herald took their names and then with fanfare announced them. No cheers greeted their arrival, only a tense silence. On Isabelle's left were arrayed dozens of provincial regiments and their Sanguinaire lords. Where was Jean-Claude? If he still lived, he would find a way to be here, and he would find a way to make himself felt, but she saw no sign of him amongst the colorful crowds.

Perhaps he was on her right, hidden amongst Lael's forces, the Thunderguard and the Praetorians. Lael stood above everyone in the royal box. Below him, humbled and quivering, hunched Grand Leon in the pillory. His eyes looked dead in their sockets.

Isabelle felt his despair as if it was her own. This was the man who had given her her first great challenge, who had made her Ambassadress to the Grand Peace. Always had he used her for his own ends, but they were worthy ends and she had made them her own.

When they drew even with the royal box, Immacolata saluted with one fist upraised. "Hail the Emperor. Glory to Lael!"

Isabelle gave a more modern salute. She was supposed to be Celestina pretending to be Isabelle. "All glory to l'Empire!"

The man who stood in the royal box ought to be a horror to look upon, a monster stitched together from bits of many people. Instead he was regal, strong, with nigh godly pulchritude. The glamour he compelled from his Goldentongue bloodshadow hid his flaws and his gloriole made him stunning to behold. Nor was it her imagination that the wind swirled around him without touching him, for he had within him a Windcaller's lungs. How many times had Isabelle noticed the wind skirling around him, the breath of air that seemed to accompany him like a fawning hound? It was the one blazon his stolen glamour couldn't hide, but she had never thought it anything more than one of Rocher Royale's persistent drafts.

It's the little mistakes one regrets.

Isabelle's party dismounted and made obeisance before Lael as if he were their rightful roi. Lael smiled down upon them. "Be welcome, General Brunela, my most faithful subject. Well met, Princess Isabelle, who has come before us to be the first amongst the great to prove her vision and loyalty to the new order. Isabelle, are you prepared to renounce your oaths of fealty to the tyrant Leon?"

A low mutter spread throughout the assembly. It was nobler to die than to spit on an oath, even if honoring that code was the exception rather than the rule. To break her oath publicly would forever stain her, no matter what her better purpose might be.

Isabelle gazed up at Lael in all his finery, his magnificent whites, looking for the sanctivore. Celestina's memories suggested he always carried it with him, disguised by his glamour. She must find a way through the illusion. She must get close to him.

"I am," she declared, "and I do! I, Isabelle des Zephyrs, do hereby renounce my loyalty to the tyrant Leon, and to all his work. Too long was I blinded by ambition. Too long was I bound by fear. No more."

Breaking the oath felt like breaking one of her own legs. Even when the Parlement had condemned her as a lawbreaker, they had never accused her of being an oathbreaker.

"And are you prepared to swear your life and your service to me?" Lael asked.

"I am," Isabelle said.

"Kneel," he said, and when she did, he said, "Isabelle des Zephyrs, do you recognize me, Emperor Lael, the Voice of the Builder, and the Shepherd of the Enlightened as your rightful master?"

"I do," Isabelle said.

Liar, said the voice from nowhere, leaving behind the stink of self-loathing.

Lael said, "And do you swear to me your utmost obedience, even unto death?"

"I do," Isabelle said. *I don't!* Had that been her own defiance or the Other's?

"Then rise, my servant, and prove your oath in blood. Behind you stand ten prisoners. Ten tools of the tyrant's corruptions. Their lives are forfeit, their souls annihilated, but their hearts beat on. Ere I raise mine hand in protection over you. Ere I grant you the honor of service, you shall slay one of these."

Dread and loathing near choked Isabelle, but she had expected this. She turned away from Lael and strode to the line of prisoners, Bitterlich, Dok, Marie, and seven she didn't know. She approached Bitterlich and pulled out her maidenblade. He lifted his gaze to hers.

"Isabelle, are you you?"

Isabelle wanted to weep. Instead she put her blade to his throat. "I am exactly what I seem."

. . . Cut deeply the slithering! . . . said the voice from nowhere, incoherently.

Isabelle's hand quivered with the urge to stab, but that was not the plan. Instead she made her way along the line, prodding every would-be victim in turn. The show was the thing, the spectacle was what would convince Lael.

She stopped before Marie, who peered up at her with her ever expression-less white-on-white eyes. "I serve you still. If you must kill someone," she said, "kill me."

Isabelle nearly cracked then, in the face of such loyalty, but she kept her composure and did not falter.

Down to the end of the line she prowled, inspecting her possible victims like cuts of meat in a butcher's shop.

"Any of these would be worthy of the knife," she said, pitching her voice to carry. "But I have something even better." She climbed on the back of the prisoner cart where the barrel holding Duchess Sireen had been put. "General, if you will lend me a hand or two."

Isabelle prayed that Sireen had neither frozen nor suffocated. She pulled off the lid and Immacolata qua Brunela tipped the barrel over onto the platform where Grand Leon was bound. Sireen slid out with a wet thump. She coughed, quivered, still alive, but showed no other sign of coherence.

Isabelle summoned all her worst thoughts, every dram of hatred that had ever washed into her mind and gave it voice. "I give you Duchess Sireen, first and most dangerous of the Tyrant Leon's supporters. I will cut her throat if you wish, but it seems too kind to allow her to die with her soul intact." And just what would she do if Lael called her bluff? How low would she stoop for the chance to stand by his side?

Along with Sireen, the last dregs of water spilled out of the barrel, making a great puddle on the wooden platform. Isabelle's pulse raced and she stepped to the side, peering at the puddle at just the right angle—

In the reflection in the water was Lael without his glamour. His posture was crooked, his whole body hunched, and his left arm dangled uselessly at his side. His face resembled that of a lion, but his left eye was milky white and sightless. His skin was pocked with smoldering sores.

Yet there on his belt, just in the reach of his good right hand, the sanctivore hung from a chain at his waist, the green and purple pseudo-liquid bubbling.

"Well done, Isabelle," Lael boomed. "You have brought me a worthy prize indeed. Come and stand by my side."

Immacolata gave her the barest smile, and spoke that no one else might hear. "Well done, sister."

"We are only getting started," Isabelle said.

As she passed by Grand Leon, he looked up at her with a sullen hatred. "Traitor. There is no retreat from this."

"Retreat," Isabelle said, because every ear was listening, "is for the vanquished."

Isabelle ascended to the box where Lael stood. The Praetorians there divested her of her maidenblade before directing her to stand on Lael's left side, away from the damned sanctivore. How was she supposed to get it away from him without being instantly killed? She could reach through him with her spark hand, but then what?

Lael gave her a beatific smile that would have made her want to melt if she wasn't on the verge of puking with loathing and terror.

"Behold Princess Isabelle, who shall be my left hand as General Brunela is my right."

Isabelle would never get a better introduction than that.

"Your Majesty," she said. "Before we go any further, I must bring to your attention a betrayal from within your own ranks. Your right hand, General Brunela, means to have you killed."

A great murmur went through the crowd, for no matter what side they were on, no one could have anticipated this, least of all Immacolata.

Lael stepped away from Isabelle as if she was a viper. "What do you mean?"

"I mean exactly what I say. Your General Brunela is a Fenice, and Fenice pass on their memories and personalities through their vitera. Last night she tried to pass on her memories to me, to erase Isabelle and make me her puppet twin."

Immacolata gawped at her, but only for a second. "Your Majesty, this is a lie."

Isabelle drew the vitera, somewhat worse for wear, from her bag and held it up for all to see. But it was Immacolata with whom Isabelle's eyes locked. "A lie, is it? You tried to steal my mind. You tried to erase me. You wanted to use me as a puppet to seduce Emperor Lael, to make him my husband, and then to stab him in his sleep."

Immacolata's gaze locked on the vitera, her visage melting into an expression of horror as she realized that Isabelle had escaped her grasp, that the final fate of five hundred years of lifetimes rested in Isabelle's vengeful hand.

Immacolata's gaze flickered back and forth between Isabelle and Lael. "Majesty, stop her. She's—"

"I end you," Isabelle said. Squeezing down hard on the vitera. She could not crack the impervious bonefeathers, but the soft underbelly splattered like an overripe plum. She tossed the carcass over the rail.

Immacolata screamed and lunged for it, but it hit the ground with a wet plop. She knelt and picked it up, her lungs heaving and her eyes welling. She glared up at Isabelle, teeth bared. "I will kill you." She reached to her side and her gleaming emerald blade sang from its sheath, whining as it sliced the air.

"Seize her!" Lael shouted. "Seize the general!"

Immacolata darted for the base of the royal box. Two Praetorians shot their bloodshadows out to block her, but quick as lightning she knelt and scribed a circle in the ground with her blade, bisecting the shadows before they could grip her. The Praetorians fell back, howling in pain.

"Stop her!" Lael roared even as he shifted shape. His body bubbled like boiling tar overrunning its kettle as he grew into his lion shape. Flames leapt from his skin, and the heat seared Isabelle's face.

Isabelle grabbed Lael's chain belt with her spark-hand. Being this close to him was like stepping inside a furnace. Her spark-arm didn't care but the rest of her started to cook. She couldn't see the belt because of the glamour, but she swept her sorcerous limb through his molten mass until she hit something metal. Then she opened her mind and poured herself into the chain.

As fast as she'd retreated into her maidenblade yesterday she swam through the links of the chain. The iron was gritty but not like sand. There was a pattern to it. A grain. It had been hammered together in layers. Iron had a smell, old cold stone and hot charcoal. Its scale of rust itched her mind. The heat of Lael's fire bled into the chain, filling Isabelle's awareness with heat. It obviously wasn't hot enough to melt the metal . . . or was it? The heat was spread out through the whole chain. If she could concentrate it in just one link—

Seized with her inspiration, Isabelle gathered as much of the heat as she could and pulled back. Retreating toward her body, bringing the inferno with her. She concentrated all her mind in just one link, just one point. The metal glowed white-hot and ran like butter left out in the sun.

She yanked with all her might. Her mind snapped back into her body. The glowing chain came away in her spark-hand. The sanctivore wobbled along at the end of the tether.

Lael looked down at her in astonishment. "Thief! Traitor."

Then Immacolata cut the legs out from under the royal box and the whole platform pitched forward, toppling into the stadium. Isabelle clung to the chain even as the ground came up to meet her.

Jean-Claude watched Isabelle's charade in heartsick horror. She meticulously avoided killing any of the captives, but her treatment of Sireen was almost worse. How much must it hurt her to behave so cruelly? More than it hurt him to watch it, and it tied his stomach in knots. And then she made her accusation against Brunela, turning the usurpers against each other.

This was his chance. Jean-Claude broke into a run up the aisle between the regiments until he reached the open ground between Lael's men and the assembled nobility.

"Men of l'Empire," he shouted. "Soldiers of Céleste. All men brave and true. To le roi! For l'Empire. Charge!"

From the front row of his regiment, Sascha bellowed, "Iron. Fists. Charge!"

As one, the Iron Fists roared and surged forward, scattering their own officers and noblemen as they raced to defend their roi. Then, as if a dam had burst, came the Gravediggers, the Flying Huns, and the entire regimental mob all at once.

Jean-Claude raced toward Grand Leon as fast as his legs would carry him, while all around him unarmed men hurled themselves into the teeth of waiting guns. One unit of Thunderguard took aim and fired and a dozen men fell, but two dozen leapt over their bodies and crashed into the royal regiment before they could reload. Another unit of Thunderguard simply broke and ran.

The Praetorians closed ranks and flung out their bloodshadows, a crimson wave that swallowed the Flying Huns faster than they could pile on. The assault began to falter.

Suddenly half a dozen Praetorians fell, their chests erupting with blood as a wave of deeper bangs rolled across the stadium. There, up on the very rim of the stadium, a dozen old women with twist-barrel long guns as tall as they were: the Gray Spiders. They must have scaled the stadium from the outside.

Into the blood breach poured the remaining Huns, falling on the Praetorians like the Breaker's own Torments.

"For l'Empire," bellowed le Comte Morel, who had apparently decided he'd had enough of being bullied. "Sanguinaire, to me!"

Jean-Claude could not follow the whole battle. The regiments overtook him in their headlong rush to grapple the foe, and he was lucky they did not bowl him over. He fetched up against the prison cart just in time to see the royal box collapse. Lael leapt free of the crashing structure in his guise as a fire lion, but Isabelle went down with the platform structure and disappeared under the debris with Brunela.

"Jean-Claude!" Marie called, loud but calm. "Get us out."

Bitterlich had wrapped one bloodied hand around the chain holding him to the cart, and braced his boot against the boards. With a ferocious strength he pulled. The metal ring that held the chain shrieked in its distress. He caught Jean-Claude's eye. "Free Grand Leon!"

Jean-Claude snatched up a mallet out of the back of the cart and clambered up on le roi's platform. He smashed the locks on the pillory and caught Grand Leon as he slid out of the torturous device.

"Ah Jean-Claude," he said. "On you, at least, I may always depend."

"Thank me later," Jean-Claude said.

Bitterlich had shattered the ring holding the chains, freeing his fellow prisoners, but now curled in on himself in agony. Jean-Claude helped le roi into the arms of the other liberated prisoners. Then he went back for Sireen and pushed her into Marie's arms.

"Get them out of the way," he said.

"Yes," Marie said. "But Isabelle—"

"She's next," Jean-Claude said, but even as he spoke, Lael wheeled around and swooped over the melee, spewing a long gout of flame that burned le Comte Morel to ash and made the stones glow red hot.

"Traitors," be bellowed. "Gnats. You will bow down before me, or you will burn!"

One more pass like that, Jean-Claude judged, and the melee would become a rout.

Suddenly Lael's fire dimmed as a great red shadow enveloped him. He yowled in pain. On the far side of the stadium, wearing a Sanguinaire battle cloak to make her shadow bigger and using the blazing stadium lights as a shadowpult, stood Impervia.

"Die, monster!"

Lael howled and clawed at the air. The Gray Spiders' guns roared, and slugs the size of eyeballs slammed into him. Blood and sparks sprayed.

"Yes!" Jean-Claude cried, but too soon. Lael screamed and burned brighter, incandescent as the Solar. Impervia's bloodshadow evaporated like morning mist. He lumbered around in a ircle, spraying the rim of the stadium with fire. The Gray Spiders leapt from their perches, and Impervia's stadium light exploded in a fireball that shook the air clear across the battlefield.

Isabelle gasped like a landed fish. Her vision darkened. If only she could manipulate the beams crushing her chest, but the whole platform had been made of wood. Her spark-arm passed through them like mist. Her flesh arm screamed in pain when she tried to move it. Broken surely, and the right side of her face was burned and blistered, her right eye swollen shut.

Behind her somewhere that she couldn't see, a battle raged. No telling who against whom. Muskets rattled, men shouted, Lael roared, and fire cackled. It was everything Isabelle had hoped to avoid.

The wood creaked, and the log jam around her shifted. She sucked in breath that felt like someone had skewered her with a spear. Her ribs had shattered. Had they gone into her lung? She tried to scoot away from the tangle but her legs were still trapped and every twitch sent jagged black clouds across her vision.

The pile before her erupted, beams cracking and dust billowing as Immacolata emerged from beneath the collapse. Gone was her glamour and her true form lay revealed, bloody lips and exposed teeth beneath a mask of bone. Her crest feathers were nearly all shattered. One wayward piece hung on by a thread. She hauled herself upright, still clenching her wicked green blade. How close was she to her final desiccation into a husk?

"Wretched worm," she spat, wading through the interlaced timbers like a child kicking a pile of sticks. "I offered you sisterhood. I offered you immortality."

Isabelle wheezed. "Whatever you think you offered me, you offered my family nothing, my friends nothing, my people nothing."

"The grave-bound are nothing!"

Isabelle was tempted to reply in kind, but anger would not avail her here. For a few hours she had been Immacolata's twin. She knew how much Immacolata hurt, how she suffered, how she longed for glory.

Isabelle said, "Look at you. Once you were Maximus Primus, who conquered all the Risen Kingdoms, who no foe could withstand, who wanted nothing more than glorious battle, but what are you now? A rat hiding in the walls, scuttling from secret plot to cowardly intrigue, dreaming of battle but never risking it, yearning for glory but never taking it. And in spite of all your scheming, you're dying, just like me, or maybe worse."

Immacolata said, "You dare call me a coward? You know nothing of the trials I have endured."

"Yes, I do. I still have Celestina's memories, some of them, anyway. I remember the time we hid in the dung wagon to escape Don Pescelli's hounds." It was the strangest feeling of déjà vu for Isabelle, recalling long-ago events in which she knew she had never participated, in bodies she had never worn, with people she had never met. Those memories were hers now as long as she lasted.

Immacolata paused, her attention riveted to the shared experience.

Isabelle said, "I remember the time we seduced Don Basco's daughter despite the way she smelled. But more than that, I remember being afraid. Afraid that it would all come to an end before we had another chance at victory. Saints but we missed the battle. We missed standing before our enemies and defying them, laughing at them. Oh how we wanted to turn and face them just once."

Immacolata's breathing was heavy, but her voice lost some of its edge. "If you know that, then you also know why we couldn't."

Isabelle coughed and her chest burned. "Because there was only one of us, after Secundus died. No matter how we tried, never more than one of us survived into each new generation. We didn't dare fight, because we didn't dare lose, because there was never an extra one of us to spare, because that would be the end."

Immacolata voice trembled with more than physical pain. "We were betrayed. No one else had our vision. No one else could unite the world."

"And what would we have done if we had succeeded in conquering the world, when there was no one left to fight, no battle left to join? We never wanted to rule. We just wanted to win. Now you are drying out, dying. You are in pain the likes of which I shudder to remember. You've got just one fight left in you, one grand melee, one great duel, one more chance at victory and glory. My question to you is how will you spend your last coin. Will you skewer me as I lie here helpless, and then skulk off somewhere to die? That was never our plan. We created Lael so that I could become queen and you could slay him. I will never be queen, but you can still have the battle you wanted, fight the monster you created, a beast of fire and terror and death, of sinew and sorcery."

"A false choice," Immacolata said. "I can kill you first and still take that battle."

"Can you?" Isabelle asked. "Who else knows who you are? Who else can tell your story and spread your glory down through the ages?"

"A false promise," Immacolata said. "You are as grave-bound as any, there are no ages left for either of us."

"Are there not?" Isabelle said. "We have these things called books, now. And I have a printing press. I will give you your glory. I will tell your story, make you the hero you always wanted to be."

Immacolata stared at her mutely for a long moment. As weak as she was, Isabelle had little hope her seduction would work—if she wasn't stabbed to death, she'd likely drown in the muck of her own lungs—but it had been a damned good try.

At last Immacolata spoke. "How can I trust you?"

"Because I'm your sister," Isabelle said.

Immacolata sheathed her sword and bent down. With a grunt, she lifted a ton of debris off Isabelle, and then took her in her arms, light as a kitten.

"I have one other request," Immacolata said.

"What?" Isabelle asked

A grim smile twisted one corner of her mummified mouth. "Remember me as Brunela."

———

"Isabelle!" Jean-Claude stumbled through the billowing smoke, avoiding corpses, toward the royal box. All around him, the melee had devolved into pandemonium. Lael circled the stadium, setting the whole thing on fire, blocking all the exits, and then dived down to burn any living thing he saw.

"Traitors," he roared. "Betrayers. I am your emperor." Lael's rage had consumed his mind and he recognized neither friend nor foe.

"Isabelle!" Jean-Claude cried again, though his lungs were raw. It seemed like half the stands had come down with the platform.

A flash of green light clove a wall of splintered wood in two, and out through the breach stepped a bone queen supporting Isabelle with one arm. Isabelle's flesh arm dangled at her side, and the right side of her face was blistered, that eye swollen shut. In her spark-hand she held the strangest object Jean-Claude had ever seen: a green and purple liquid solid.

Jean-Claude raised a saber he'd scrounged, as if it would make the slighted difference against a bone queen. "Halt! Release Princess Isabelle."

Isabelle spotted him through the smoke. "Jean-Claude!" She tugged on her supporter. "This way. It's Jean-Claude."

To Jean-Claude's astonishment, the bone queen gently whisked Isabelle over the rubble and into Jean-Claude's arms. Isabelle's floppy weight nearly toppled him.

The bone queen stared into Jean-Claude's eyes and said, "See to it that she lives. She has promises to keep."

"There you are," boomed Lael, swooping by overhead. "The worst of the worst. The heart of all corruption. You thought you could bring me down. You thought you could betray me?"

"Run," said the bone queen, stepping smartly away from Jean-Claude and Isabelle. She brandished her emerald sword and bellowed, "Monster, I am Maxima Brunela, Terror of the Grinding Alps, Conqueror of the Seven Cities. I created you, and I will destroy you."

Lael soared straight up until he lost momentum, rolled over in midair, and dived at Brunela. "Burn!"

Jean-Claude and Isabelle ran, limping and stumbling. She winced and hissed at every step. The space behind them exploded. A fireball picked them up and tossed them across the arena to land in a sprawl. Isabelle howled in pain and could not rise. Jean-Claude glanced over his shoulder. The ground glowed from the heat of Lael's blast. Brunela's feathers were black and flames licked along their edges, but somehow she still stood. With one hand, she ripped the wheel off a flaming wagon, spun around like a discus thrower, and hurled it at Lael as he came around for another pass. It smashed his face and shattered to flinders, knocking him off course. He plowed into the stands and tumbled, furrowing through the superstructure and scattering flaming bits of timber everywhere.

Brunela leapt into the stands, fifteen meters through the air, and charged the downed beast, screaming like all the Breaker's Torments let loose.

Jean-Claude yanked his attention away and pulled Isabelle to himself. She was panting now, her face waxen and her breathing shallow. He shouldn't move her, but the middle of this arena was nowhere she ought to be. He stripped off his long coat, spread it on the ground, and rolled her onto it. She was so damned tall, he could barely fit enough of her. He finally got a good grip and pulled, dragging her across the arena floor, away from the battle.

Up in the stands, Lael regained his footing. Brunela had chopped off one of his wings and a ghastly black smoke poured from the wound. He limped around on three legs, belching fire. The very boards on which they stood blazed up and turned to ash. Brunela's foot punched through the board on which she stood, costing her her balance. Lael pounced.

Shadows loomed up around Jean-Claude and he found himself surrounded by soldiers.

"Everybody take a corner. You and you on the middle." That was Marie's voice. She'd gotten rid of her shackles and taken command of men who needed direction. Soldiers shouldered in around Jean-Claude, seized the long coat, and lifted Isabelle from the ground. Two other people hoisted Jean-Claude up by his armpits.

"Go," Marie commanded, and the troop carried Isabelle and Jean-Claude away, but not before Lael landed on Brunela, and the stadium collapsed beneath them.

Jean-Claude managed to regain his own footing and had almost reached a makeshift barricade composed of looted stadium seating when a thunderous blow shook the ground and a flash of green light burst from under the collapsed seating. A dreadful howl cut short, the dome of still air collapsed, and the blizzard came rushing in.

CHAPTER

Twenty-Six

The blizzard ended the battle if not the confusion and the dying. Marie and Jean-Claude—mostly Marie, Jean-Claude admitted—turned rope and boards into sledges and recruited stray soldiers to drag the injured to the army's stockade, it being the closest source of real shelter. Even from this distance, through howling torrents of snow, the stadium's blaze raged bright enough to guide their way.

The acting commander, a man named Martin, had already arrested his former commander, which saved Jean-Claude from having to do it. Grand Leon, Sireen, Isabelle, and the rest of the injured were safely ensconced in the officers' barracks, under Sascha's personal protection.

Marie tended the burns on Isabelle's face. Jean-Claude winced at the sight of the blisters. He could not be more proud of her, but why did she have to pay the price of bravery?

"I'll summon Gretl as soon as the snow stops," Marie said, ever practical.

"You comported yourself well today," Jean-Claude said.

"That is an understatement," said a soft mellow voice. Sireen and Grand

Leon were both sitting up in the former commander's bed, sharing a few blankets. Both looked exhausted, but neither looked to be on death's door.

Sireen said, "That Fenice sent six Sanguinaire to attack us. I could not fend off so many, even untrained as they were, but Marie stepped directly into the shadow flood and started firing." She mimed a pistol shot. "She killed three of them before they realized they couldn't hurt her and sent in a Seelenjäger to drive her off."

"I should have got four," Marie said. "I missed one shot."

Sireen said, "If you hadn't been there, they would have overrun us. They might have taken me alive, but we wouldn't have been allowed to surrender."

"On days like this, you take what victories you can get," Jean-Claude said.

Grand Leon coughed, and his voice was a rasp. "There were no victories today. Only tragedies."

Jean-Claude doffed his hat and bowed to his roi. "And survivors, Majesty. Planting comes after winter. Crops grow back stronger when the rhizoweed is burned. The trick is to keep everything in rotation."

Grand Leon snorted weakly. "I get the impression you are trying to tell me something without telling me I'm a fool, but I am a fool, Jean-Claude. Like all men, and I am very tired. So speak plainly and give me hope."

Jean-Claude put his hat back on, and bowed to Sireen. "The solution to all your problems is right beside you, Your Majesties."

Sireen's eyes rounded, and Leon gazed upon her. If Jean-Claude was not entirely mistaken, there came a thoughtful glint to his eye.

⁓

Isabelle leaned on a brass-handled cane as she waited for the reconstituted Parlement to render a verdict in her case. The faceless crowd of jurists, all hidden behinds white masks under black hoods, milled about in the parlementary gallery, muttering to each other, discussing, she suspected, everything but the actual evidence. At least they weren't all nobles now. The makeup of the Parlement had been changed to allow space for the clayborn. Lael had gotten at least part of his wish.

Yet the nature of politics hadn't changed. This group would declare her guilt or innocence based on what they felt would be to their own best advantage, whatever that might be in this new regime.

. . . the stinking hates all drowning rats . . . said Nowhere, as she had come

to call the noxious rambling voice, a memento from her sister. Hers to keep. Nowhere's voice was bad enough on its own, but the emotions, and urges it brought along were nothing less than terrifying. What if she forgot that the ideas it put into her head weren't her own? What if she acted on one without thinking? She could kill someone, destroy a negotiation, ruin yet another friendship.

Three weeks she had been bedridden, sometimes delirious, while her body fought off the drowning lung, three broken ribs, a broken arm, and a burned face. Her arm remained in a splint, and the skin on her face was finally starting to regrow. She would have to add disfiguring scars to her list of notable attributes. She supposed she could count herself lucky that she'd survived and kept her eye.

She'd saved the day.

Mostly.

Grand Leon and all the others who had lost their sorcery wouldn't be getting it back.

The sanctivore was actually very simple to operate. In one of her moments of lucidity, she'd dredged the process up from Celestina's memory and told Sireen, and volunteered herself as a test case. Just take a spoonful of the purple end to inflict the pest, or the green end to cure it. In either case, the recipient's bodily fluid became so thick with the serum that even a drop of their blood in, say, a common pot of wine, could infect a whole family. Likewise a particularly lecherous monarch could disseminate the pest through a goodly number of sexual partners before he ever realized he was ill.

Yet even after the sanctivore stopped the progression of the pest, it couldn't repair the damage already done.

Once the new monarch's privy council was convinced Isabelle spoke the truth, Reine Sireen ordered every person in Rocher Royale, saintborn or clayborn, inoculated whether they wanted it or not. A week on and no new cases had been reported. Those known to have the disease reported no further decay in their gift. The capital began to breathe more easily, to forget their solidarity in terror, and resume their habitual internecine struggles.

Hence Isabelle's current predicament, called to answer to Parlement for her oathbreaking on Burning Day. At least it had been a proper trial this time, with lawyers for the accused, and evidence and witnesses. Isabelle was not allowed to testify on her own behalf owing to her previous conviction, which no one seemed interested in voiding.

. . . merciless beggars groveling and grinding . . . said a voice from over her left shoulder. She glanced that way, but it was Nowhere again. Isabelle had to resist the urge to hit herself in the head; that wouldn't make it stop.

At last, the dictator of Parlement rapped his staff on the floorboards and called the jury to order. Isabelle risked a glance up into the observer's booth where waited those who had stood with her throughout the trial, Jean-Claude, Impervia, Coquetta, and Marie. Jean-Claude had his arm around Impervia's shoulder, and she leaned into him. Something had mended, there.

Bitterlich had not been to see Isabelle, even after they released him from the infirmary, and that hurt more than it should. She'd only known him a few days, but she'd delighted in every moment of his company. But she had left him shackled to the back of that cart with those awful spikes through his wrists. She got phantom pains just thinking about it. One of the worst things in her head was the memory of the way she'd treated him, even if it had only been an act. It would have been different if he'd known what she was up to, or even if she'd had a chance to explain it after the fact . . . but he'd never come around, never answered any of her messages.

The dictator intoned, "Has the lawful Parlement here assembled reached a verdict?"

"We have," replied the speaker of the jury.

"The first question before the jury remains: did the defendant, Isabelle des Zephyrs, forsake her oath to l'Empire Céleste, then willingly pledge her allegiance to the usurper, Lael the Abjured, and thereby commit treason against l'Empire Céleste? To this question, is she guilty or innocent?"

. . . betrayal of kind brings grief to the forsworn . . . Sometimes Nowhere seemed to be trying to tell her something, but the more she tried to interpret it, the less sense it made.

Isabelle did her best not to tremble, for treason brought with it the penalty of death by exposure.

. . . the disintegration ends in graves . . . Nowhere's voice was a chorus whose members came and went.

"If I die, you die," she muttered, and maybe that was what the damned thing wanted. It couldn't finish dying until she did. If it wanted anything. If it wasn't just random bits of emotion broken loose and sliding around her brain like an unsecured cannon in a pitching ship.

"Not guilty," said the speaker.

Isabelle let out a long shuddering breath that led to a coughing fit that had her down on her knees spitting into a brass pot. Thank the Builder. Thank the saints, but this wasn't over yet. After the coughing fit subsided, she pushed herself back up again, and went back to leaning on her cane like someone twice her age.

The dictator said, "The second question before the jury remains: did the defendant, Isabelle des Zephyrs, knowingly and willingly murder her brother, Guillaume des Zephyrs, and his wife, Arnette?"

Considerably less time had been devoted to this question in the arguments than had been to the matter of her oathbreaking. It had been treated almost as an afterthought. Traditionally this sort of thing would have been seen as family matter, but given that the disposition of a countship was involved, it had to be taken up by the Parlement. Isabelle argued self-defense. Of course Celestina had been in charge then, but Isabelle owned the memory, and it felt like a stain on her soul, a bit of corrosion logic could not buff away.

The speaker said, "For the crime of murder, not guilty. For the commission of fratricide, guilty."

Isabelle's stomach clenched, for this peculiar language deemed that while she could not be condemned for her act, neither should she be allowed to profit from it.

The judges said, "For the commission of fratricide, the defendant, Isabelle des Zephyrs, is stripped of her family name. She may make no claim to the family's lands, titles, or incomes from any source."

The dictator turned to face Isabelle directly. "Do you understand the penalties levied against you, for your despicable act?"

"I do," Isabelle said. Indeed, aside from the stripping of her name, all of those penalties were redundant with the ones already imposed upon her.

"Do you wish to appeal?"

Isabelle turned to face the royal box, where sat the newly crowned Imperatrice Sireen, la Reine de Tonner, and her husband consort, Leon. There had been a great deal of political wrangling in the weeks following Burning Day, and several important laws had been amended. No one would ever again lose their nobility simply for not having sorcery.

And if the unhallowed could be nobles today, might not the clayborn tomorrow? Isabelle had managed to sneak in language that suggested it was possible.

The law was passed on the unwritten agreement that those, like Grand Leon, who had stoutly defended the principle of requisite sorcery, step aside. That had in turn been agreed to only after Grand Leon had been allowed to select his own heir.

The outrage that flared up after he chose Sireen proved remarkably short-lived, likely because none of the other candidates were nearly so well-respected. The subsequent royal marriage had led to the accusation that Grand Leon was still clinging to power despite his protestations of giving it up. To some, this came as a blow to their own plans to marry the new reine and claim authority over her as her husband. To others Sireen's marriage to Leon came as a secret relief. Better Grand Leon steer the ship of state at one remove than put a woman at the helm.

Isabelle could appeal her fratricide verdict to la reine, but that would put Sireen at odds with the re-formed Parlement, a complication the new monarch didn't need.

Sireen tilted her head and gave Isabelle a questioning look.

. . . *drowning crowns sink claws in deep hate* . . . Nowhere said. Sireen had forgiven Isabelle publicly, but who knew what la reine felt in her secret heart.

Isabelle returned her attention to the dictator and said, "I do not appeal."

The dictator looked stunned. "You are aware that this decision is final?"

But Isabelle had already turned away. She climbed down from the stand, and limped for the door as if nothing of consequence had happened. As if she had not just been slapped in the face by the people she'd saved from a true tyrant. As if she had not just been robbed of her very name.

She was halfway to the spire's exit with no idea where she would go after that when Marie caught up with her. Isabelle slowed to let her friend fall in step beside her. She'd taken to the delightfully outlandish habit of wearing pantaloons, six guns, and "boots you can kick somebody with." Her wounds were well on their way to being healed, and she'd resumed combat training with Djordji.

"Isabelle," she said in her perpetual deadpan. "That was unfair. They had no right."

"They had every right," Isabelle said. "In fact it's why they exist, to make judgments, even despicable ones. Better to have them making mischief by procedure in controlled conditions than out in the wild with no one to watch them."

Marie digested Isabelle's opinion for a long moment. "So what will you do now?"

. . . feigning friendship to envision secret betrayal . . . A prickling like many centipedes scuttling across her scalp made her shudder in revulsion.

"That's the big question," Isabelle said. "Math, I suppose, and writing. I'll do the accounting for the candleworks. I get some income already from Martin DuJournal's writing, and I have to write Brunela's tale as well. I imagine people will want to buy that one." One of her few trips outside in the bitter cold of the threefold winter had been to see the molten crater where the battle between Brunela and Lael had reached its conclusion. Both of them had been charred down to the bone. Brunela's gutted husk still knelt with her head bowed and her sword rammed through Lael's skull. The sword, *Ultor*, somehow unharmed by a blaze that had managed to melt stone, had been removed after three days when it was finally cool enough to handle.

"What about you?" Isabelle asked. "A disgraced recluse like me isn't likely to need a bodyguard, and from what Jean-Claude says, you'll be good at it. Djordji says you're a fast learner, and apparently that's not something he ever says."

Marie said, "I like the training. Fighting isn't something you can memorize. You have to teach your body how to do it, and let your mind get out of the way. I've never been this sore or this strong in my whole life. But I chose this path because I wanted to be with you and Jean-Claude, and I wanted to be useful."

Isabelle understood how hollow Marie must feel right now. Everything they had ever done or dreamt of was over. The future was like sailing into a fog.

Words failed them both and they walked in companionable silence until they reached the spire's tilted exit, donned heavy capes, and stepped out onto the porch overlooking the courtyard.

The craton still turned and the Towering Coast had drifted much farther north, so that even at midday the sky was dark, and the glowing curtains of the auroras danced overhead.

What could cause them to glow without heat? Isabelle felt a knot in her soul unwind. It was the first spontaneous empirical question she'd had in weeks. She'd have to write it down, but she'd have to use the *gant de acier* because her left arm was still mending.

The air stung Isabelle's face, made her lungs ache, and turned her breath to mist, but she had no desire to step back inside just yet. The auroras were too beautiful, the stars too bright.

Not a damned thing anyone had done in the past few weeks had served to shift the heavens from their course. The moons still performed their synchronized dance, one week, two weeks, and four. The planets still wandered their elliptical paths. The world beneath her, Caelum, sped around the Solar at speeds unimaginable. The craton made its ponderous pirouette.

It was comforting to know the vastness of Creation was bigger than any human event, and that it played by its own rules, indifferent to the designs of rois and reines. If only she could keep some of that vastness inside her, then perhaps this world wouldn't hurt so much.

"Isabelle," Jean-Claude said. "It's cold out here."

She turned and smiled at him and he embraced her very gently owing to her still mending wounds. His arms felt good around her. Safe harbor.

"How was your business?" she asked.

He led her back inside to a room where someone had set up benches around an alchemical stove. They all three took seats.

"Business was . . . difficult," he said. "I made sure that Jerome got a posthumous promotion and his widow gets his full admiral's pension. Sireen said he deserved a bronze statue. I said only if you melt it down and make coins for the widow. Sireen doubled his pension and reserved two places for his children in the academies if they can qualify. She said she'd build the statue from her own purse. I said make sure he has a really big hat."

Isabelle leaned her right shoulder against him. Strange to think that her amputated limb was the one that wasn't injured. "I'm sorry about your friend."

Jean-Claude shook his head. "I talked him into this. I should get the blame, except if I hadn't recruited him, there would have been no one to rescue me and Sireen from that ledge, and no one to help her escape down the Rivencrag, and if Sireen hadn't been captured who knows how any of the rest of it would have worked out. As my mother used to say, good planning is seeing where you ended up and saying that's where you meant to be."

Isabelle snorted. "Your mother had a saying for everything. I suspect much of her wisdom is posthumous."

"I'll tell her you said that next time I visit her grave. We'll see what she has to say about it then."

This brought Isabelle to another difficult question. "So what will you do now? I certainly no longer qualify for the protection of a King's Own Musketeer."

"What a coincidence; I no longer qualify as a King's Own Musketeer. I'm too old, too slow, too damaged."

Isabelle was appalled. "She dismissed you?"

. . . *comes crawling in the night, laced for* . . . Nowhere seemed to be breathing on her neck.

Jean-Claude said, "She offered me a *grade de capitaine* in the Queen's Own Musketeers, permanent deferral."

"What does that mean?" Isabelle asked.

Marie spoke up. "It means she made him an Old Hand, like Djordji."

"Ye saints, not like Djordji," Jean-Claude said with a shudder.

"It's brilliant," Marie said with all the outward enthusiasm of a statue. "It's essentially a license to stir up trouble."

"And what is the caveat?" Jean-Claude asked, in the tone of a teacher prodding his student.

"Don't get caught," Marie said.

Isabelle breathed more easily. "It sounds like a perfect fit."

. . . *Quick! Quick!* . . . Nowhere's directionless urgency made Isabelle twitch.

"So where do you plan to go?" Isabelle asked, and chided herself for giving credence to Nowhere's taunting.

Jean-Claude made a noncommittal gesture. "So far I have seen no evidence that you are capable of keeping yourself out of trouble."

A tremendous tension eased from Isabelle's heart and she placed her head on his shoulder, to weep in joy. "Thank the saints."

"I'm no saint," he said, hugging her gently.

"No, that would be boring," Isabelle said.

Someone rapped on the curtainway.

"Enter," Isabelle said.

Through the curtain stepped Capitaine . . . no, Major Bitterlich. Isabelle's heart lifted with delight to see him.

. . . *to be skinned alive and bereft of familiarity* . . . Nowhere whispered, as if delivering a salacious secret or spiteful gossip.

He was physically much improved. His spotted golden pelt was back to normal, his eyes were clear. He seemed to be able to use his hands, shooting his cuffs before doffing his hat.

"Mademoiselle Isabelle," he said in snooty official tones. "Madame requests and requires your presence for an exclusive audience."

. . . *twist the knife gently* . . . Nowhere said.

Isabelle smiled politely through her discomfort and rose from the bench. "Yes, Major. Congratulations on your promotion."

"Thank you," he said in that same ponderous voice. He gestured her outside and then fell in beside her, the same escort position he'd assumed the first day they'd met, but without any of the perky curiosity. His nose had a definite upward tilt.

"Do you know what la reine wants with me?" Isabelle asked. What more could Sireen want to squeeze out of her? She had nothing left to give.

"She did not confide as much in me," he said, which didn't technically answer the question she'd asked, but didn't invite her to repeat it either. He really didn't want to talk to her. But why had he been sent to fetch her in the first place? Surely a major had more important duties. She wished he would give her some sort of clue about how he felt about her.

It only took a few dozen steps and a few turns of the corridor for the silence to become unbearable.

"I'm sorry," Isabelle said. "I know that's not enough. There isn't any excuse for what I did, but—"

Bitterlich put a finger to his lips. "Shhh . . . you're spoiling the moment."

Isabelle frowned at him in confusion. "Moment. What moment?"

"I'm being very serious," he said. "Profound even, as befits my shiny new rank."

Isabelle shook her head in befuddlement. "You mean you're just having me on."

"You couldn't tell? Please say it isn't so. I'd hate you to think I could really be that stiff."

"I just thought—I mean, you aren't mad at me." Relief battled indignation.

"Whatever for?"

"For leaving you chained to that prison cart. For all those horrible things I said."

"What choice did you have? Once I figured out what was going on, once you showed off that brain bug, I thought you were brilliant. You are brilliant."

Isabelle kept putting two and two together and getting boiled oats. "But if you're not—If you don't—You never came to see me. You never answered my messages."

"Ah. Yes. I was on a secret mission. In fact, I was forbidden to talk to you."

"What kind of secret mission?"

"If I told you that—"

"It wouldn't be a secret." Isabelle had to allow him that one. "But why couldn't you talk to me about other things?"

"Sireen wanted to keep me as far away from you as possible—and believe me that was the last thing I wanted—not because of you, but because of all the people circling like vultures around your soon to be political corpse. Now that the worst has happened, and I am deeply offended on your behalf, by the way, they won't be paying as much attention. Nobody wants to hang around a funeral."

"So . . . you're really not—"

Bitterlich turned and put his finger on her lips. "Isabelle." He leaned in very close, so close she could feel the warmth of him, see all the caramel patterns in his golden eyes. "You're already a hero. You don't need to be a martyr."

"I don't want to be a martyr," she said. "I just . . ." Just what? *Like you a lot*, seemed too juvenile for this fascination.

He said, "Did you know your eyes glitter like your arm? They've gone rose and violet and there are stars in them."

Isabelle's pulse raced and her blood seemed to fizz. She wanted him to come closer. He couldn't come any closer without actually touching her.

"I don't have any arms," she said, her voice but a breath.

"Beg pardon," he said.

"My left arm is broken and tied to my side. My right arm is intangible. That means that if you want to kiss me as badly as I want you to, you're going to have to take some initiative."

He smiled a slow smile, cradled her head, and drew her in. His lips were warm and just rough enough, and every bit of her was awake to him.

They took their time, a long silky caress. Isabelle wished she could get her hand up and run it through his hair. He was very careful with her injuries, and she positively purred when he massaged the back of her neck. *Please do that forever.*

All too soon he eased away. "Mademoiselle. That was—"

"Yes. It was," she breathed. "Very much so. But not perfect, I'm afraid."

"Not perfect?" he asked, looking comically stricken.

"No. We'll need lots of practice." And because she was giddy, she leaned in, nibbled his earlobe, and whispered, "Lots and lots and lots."

Bitterlich looked stunned, and she was pleased to see she had his tongue.

And then her mind caught up with her mouth. Half of her wanted to beg off and plead momentary madness. The other half wanted to put the first half in a trunk and lock it.

He brushed his lips to hers. "I am yours to command."

A brief touch was all they took, just then. They had been summoned by la reine after all. They repaired themselves and continued on their way.

"So, ah, how are your injuries?" Isabelle asked by way of moving the conversation into less intimate territory.

He pulled up his sleeve to display the scar on his wrist. It was long and pale through the gold and brown pelt. "When I am injured, the damage is conserved from shape to shape, but with practice, one can learn to distribute the injuries more widely so they heal more quickly. It's especially useful to be able to turn into something like a snake, which doesn't have wrists to begin with, and so can't have injured wrists at all."

"I wish I could do that," Isabelle said, shrugging her broken arm.

"You were right about me," she said. Yet that wasn't the only sort of pain she'd caused him. She'd driven him away from her true center. If she wanted to get closer to him, she had to let him in. "I am Martin DuJournal: empirical philosopher, mathematician. I'm sorry I yelled at you. I'm just used to keeping it a secret. It's funny how big secrets get when you feed them fear."

"I knew it," he said gleefully. "You talk like he writes." After a more somber moment, he added, "I'm sorry I snapped at you about Littlepaws."

Isabelle let the silence hang. She hadn't asked him to reveal anything, though she was dying to know.

After another fraught minute he said, "I was eight years old when Wolfgang's assassins stormed our manor house. The heralds dubbed it the Night of the Black Claws. All I knew at the time was that I woke up to a yowling. A kitten had gotten into my room and curled up beside me for warmth, but now he was standing there with all his hair on end, screeching at the monster in the window. One of Wolfgang's killers came at me. He was huge and hairy, with a mouth as wide as an open grave and rows and rows of teeth. I leapt away, but there was nowhere to run. He pinned me in a corner. I screamed and I screamed.

"Then from nowhere came Olbrecht, my father's guardsman, a Seelenjäger himself. He rammed the assassin aside, and yelled, 'Run!'

"I don't know why I grabbed the kitten. I don't know how I stopped from crushing him in my terror. That night I ran through fire, slipped in blood, and hid in a wet ditch under a mound of corpses holding that kitten inside my nightshirt."

The rough edges of his soft recital made his old pain sound fresh.

"Eventually, Grand Leon's men found me and took me away. I found out later that my whole family was slaughtered along with most of their retainers and staff. Grand Leon took me in and brought me to live here. I brought the kitten with me. We were orphans together. I named him Littlepaws.

"I was an outsider at court, honored in name, despised in practice. Littlepaws was my solace. He slept on my pallet, walked with me in the garden, kept all my secrets and looked on every day as an adventure . . . or so I imagined."

He paused a moment, like a porter getting ready to hoist a heavy load, and his breathing became heavier. "I was fourteen when Serge and Roland nailed him to a post and set him afire." His hands twitched and his lip trembled. "I smothered the flames with my jacket, screaming for someone to help, but they just circled around laughing at their great jape. They were not allowed to hurt me, you see, but this was just a cat. I got the fire out, but there was nothing I could do for Paws. He was mad with pain and terror, but I took him in my hands and he recognized me. He heard my voice and looked at me. He reached out a paw. He asked me to make it stop."

Tears welled up unbidden and rolled down Bitterlich's nose. He did not wipe them away or even acknowledge them.

"A Seelenjäger's first soul hunt is supposed to be a feat of valor. His first kill gives him his erstepelz, so young sorcerers go to great lengths to make their first hunt a deed of legend. They stalk the deepest woods, the highest mountains, and the farthest jungles to find the strongest, the fiercest, the most honorable prey. Great names have been won on these hunts: Großerbär, Schwarzwildschwein, Stolzenlowen.

"My first kill was Littlepaws." Bitterlich stared at his hands as if they were foreign to him. "I reached out and I ripped his soul from his dying body. I drank it all in, all his pain, all his fear, all his love. I took his form. I took his skin."

Bitterlich clenched his hands and sucked in a deep breath, expanding his lungs to make room for grief and then compressing it down somewhere deep in his body.

"That's why they call me Littlepaws." He adjusted his sleeve cuffs. "Kittenslayer, and the ever-so-clever double-entendre catamite. It's also why

I can never go back to my family's lands. The Seelenjäger sneer at a man whose first kill was a domestic cat."

Isabelle heart burned with rage piled on outrage, all of it years too late. She fixed his gaze with hers and it was all she could do to steady her shaking voice. "That. Was. Valor. And honor. None of those men or women has ever earned a better name than Littlepaws."

He peered into her eyes. Looking for any sign that she was having him on. She wanted to throw her arm around him; damn her injuries.

He took off his hat, placed it over his heart, and bowed to her, breaking eye contact without shame. "I underestimated your kindness, Isabelle. Thank you."

"You underestimate your own compassion. It raises you greatly in my esteem."

One corner of his mouth turned up in a crooked smile. "A worthy prize, your esteem."

They arrived at the landing outside Grand Leon's . . . Reine Sireen's audience chamber. Isabelle wondered if Sireen would leave the extravagant sculpted door, with its images of Grand Leon, in place or replace it with one of her own.

The two of them were apparently in good time despite their delay, for they were still kept waiting by the door wardens for several minutes.

Eventually the doors opened on silent hinges, and women's voices emerged, preceding the women themselves.

"She's lost her mind," Josette said. She was pale with shock and walking as fast as a lifetime of decorum would allow.

Alongside came her mother Comtesse Coquetta, test case for the new more generous devolutionary law. "Of course she hasn't," Coquetta said. "Now stop panicking."

"I am not panicking."

"You're forgetting to breathe, dear," Coquetta said. "Ah Major, Isabelle, how good to see you both. We have the best news."

"Mother!" Josette said, and Isabelle could not help but wonder what had the stolid Josette so flustered. Josette hadn't been kissing Bitterlich, after all.

"May I inquire as to the good news?" Bitterlich asked.

Coquetta beamed. "Josette is going to be named the new crown princess. She's the new heir. Sireen is intent on not making the same mistake Leon made."

"Yes," Josette said. "She's making an entirely different mistake."

"Congratulations," Isabelle said. "That's amazing. When will the official announcement be made?"

"Next week," Coquetta said. "Sireen is going to take her under her wing so that she'll be ready to take over seamlessly when Sireen abdicates."

"Abdicates?" Isabelle asked, alarmed. "She just ascended."

"Not anytime soon," Coquetta said. "But she says she doesn't intend to die harnessed like a donkey to a mine-cart, either."

Josette regained her composure and recited, "She said only by the Builder's grace and the work of his messengers did the crown pass without the death of a monarch. It's a tradition she intends to encourage and continue, along with picking an heir who is not of her body."

Coquetta picked up, "It was a good speech. What she means to do is make sure that no future generation ever knows life without the rule of law."

"And what do you think?" Isabelle asked.

"I think great works require great people," Josette said.

"Perhaps," Isabelle said. "But great people require great teams. If you want my advice—"

The door warden said, "Mademoiselle Isabelle, la reine requests your presence."

Isabelle walked toward the stairway leading up to la reine's audience chamber, but said over her shoulder, "Find people who love you enough to oppose you."

Bitterlich joined Isabelle on her trip up the stairs. Given that he hadn't been stopped, he must have been invited.

She rose up through the floor of the audience chamber, still wondering what more Sireen wanted from her.

. . . *means to destroy your crest* . . . Nowhere said.

Sireen sat the throne as if born to it. She filled the space without sprawling and wore her bloodshadow over one shoulder like a senator at some ancient forum. Beneath the thundercrown on her brow, she'd parted her veil like a curtain, showing one dark eye, her nose, and her generous mouth, leaving the rest a mystery.

Isabelle curtsied rather awkwardly and Bitterlich made a leg.

"Rise and be welcome," Sireen said, and her operatic voice filled the room.

Isabelle stood. "And how may I serve Your Majesty?" It was the question of the hour.

"Someone of your abilities? The mind boggles. But before we move on to that, I would like to thank you for your performance in Parlement today. The dictator wagered rather a lot of his political capital on getting me into a dog fight over that ridiculous verdict. It's a wager he lost and I intend to collect on."

"I'm glad to have been of some use," Isabelle said. "It's too bad I'm not allowed to have honors. I think I've qualified for a golden scapegoat with fig leaves."

. . . spat from the churning council. . . Nowhere said.

Sireen ignored her wit, such as it was, and said, "In point of fact, the matter of the events surrounding my rise to the throne still has one loose end on which I require your advice."

At her signal a footman strode forward with a long ornate wooden box and opened it to display the sanctivore, the pseudo-liquid cylinder and its ever-shifting shadow-writing resting on a velvet cushion.

Isabelle twitched at the sight of it. How many lives had been destroyed by that thing?

Sireen asked, "If it were up to you, what would you do with it?"

Isabelle stared at the quondam device. It was a rare and precious artifact, of historical, empirical, political, and military importance. Some said it was product of the Builder's own hand. How else could it still be working after several thousand years of abuse and neglect? The writing swirling around like ghosts under its skin could keep a legion of scholars busy for a dozen lifetimes. If its mechanism could ever be deciphered, it might reveal the inner workings of the Builder's gifts in a way butchery like Ingle's never could.

Isabelle gathered her best arguments. "The problem with it isn't that it's powerful or dangerous. The problem with it is that it is unique and irreproducible. Only it can unleash the Breaker's pest, and only it can stop the pest from spreading. Whoever holds it has a kind of ultimate power.

"But the problem with ultimate power is, when would you ever use it? When would you risk letting it get away from you? And how will you keep it? As long as you have it, someone will try to steal it. I would be surprised if there were not already plots being hatched to that effect. If I may turn the question around, imagine el rei in Aragoth had it. How much effort would you put into obtaining it? It's a weapon no ruler can allow any other to possess.

"Worse, the fact that you have it, and the idea that you might be tempted to use it, will hang as a cloud over every act of diplomacy in which l'Empire engages. It's a loaded gun you can never stop pointing at people. If it were me . . . I would cast it into the Gloom."

"Despite all it might teach us?"

. . . *dread sucking the brightness below.* . . Nowhere tugged at Isabelle's attention like a cat clutching her skirts.

"Even so," Isabelle said. "If the mysteries locked within the sanctivore are things that can be discovered, empiricists will find them out in due course, but only when we have followed the path and earned the knowledge of everything that underpins those mysteries. Only when we understand it can we predict it, and only when we can predict it can we hope to control it. We are not ready for that." She gestured to the box.

"Your point is well taken. As it so happens, I agree. As soon as we make sure the pest is truly gone and not just slumbering, it will be disposed of in a very public and very well-attended ceremony," Sireen said, and waved the footman away.

"Thank you," Isabelle said.

Sireen folded her hands in her lap. "I've had several people tell me to keep it, several suggest targets to use it on, one suggest I give it back to the Temple, and a few wise souls advise me to get rid of it. What is truly amazing is the number of people who seem to think I should regard it as a gift because it put me on the throne. Only one so far has seen the other truth."

Other truth? The thing had inadvertently cleared Sireen's way to the throne, but that had never been her goal. She'd always served alongside . . .

"It hurt the ones you love," Isabelle realized. "Grand Leon."

"My husband and several of my children. It hurt them to the bone and nearly broke their spirits. I would not have my grandchildren or their grandchildren go through that again."

"Who was the person who saw that truth?"

"Marie," Sireen said. "That girl is an absolute treasure. You must take care not to get her killed."

"I am in no position to protect her. Not that I have any plans to endanger her."

"Which leads me to our last piece of business. I do believe, in his bewilderment, the dictator of Parlement failed to notice the rather sizable loophole he left in the restrictions he put on you. Honors, lands, titles, and offices all have very distinct and specific legal definitions. If Parlement thinks you should not have those, I shall have to find some other power to give you. Do you have any suggestions?"

Isabelle was feeling three steps behind just now. "I'm afraid I don't."

"How about you, major?" Sireen asked.

"It occurs to me," Bitterlich said with the stuffiest dignity Isabelle had ever seen. "That the dictator forgot to mention military rank. I doubt it ever crossed his mind that you would commission a woman as a naval capitaine."

Isabelle goggled at him. "But I'm no soldier." She dipped to Sireen. "I'm sorry, Majesty, but I serve peace."

"All good soldiers do," Sireen said. "I have no intention of sending you off to war, but you will be capable of defending yourself on your mission. Behold."

At some invisible signal, the floor behind Isabelle began to quiver. With a brassy clinking of hidden gears, a large section of the floor sank and split apart, allowing a large orrery to rise from beneath. The aetherglass globe, used to track aeronautical fleets and skylands in the deep sky, was twice Isabelle's height and bound in brass. With a final clank and a long gassy hiss, the mechanism settled into place, the floor closed up around the pedestal, and the sphere filled with greenish lumin gas.

While not nearly as large as the famous Naval Orrery in San Augustus, which took up a whole building, Sireen's orrery was clearly just as sophisticated. Given the number of feathery sympathy-vanes that spread like flower petals around the bottom of this sphere, Isabelle calculated la reine could track thousands of ships at once from this room.

The pressure rose higher and higher according to the gauge, increasing the scale of the simulation by orders of magnitude. The galvanic arc inducer touched the glass. Disorganized lumin gas gathered and resolved into cloudy simulacra. The first thing to resolve was a maplike image of the Craton Massif, the rotating disk on which the Risen Kingdoms stood, spinning in the northern hemisphere, nearing the northernmost point in its biannual migration.

As the orrery's pressure continued to rise, Craton Massif shrank, and another land mass appeared in the southern hemisphere. Its crescent shape was rendered in much less detail, owing to yet incomplete mapping. This was the Craton Riqueza, claimed half a century ago by Aragoth and fiercely defended by them, with all others cut off from trade by their mercantile policies.

"This is the state of the world today," Sireen said. "One craton old and overcrowded, the other wild and untamed. We could fight the Aragoths for it, but war is bad for progress. Diplomacy will work better, but even diplomacy requires leverage."

At this point, Hailer Dok entered the room. He was dressed in his clan motley, but had a brace in his mouth that held his jaw in place while it healed. He bowed gingerly to la reine, and produced a long thin needle of bone. That must be the sliver of the *Conquest's* bonekeel he'd told Isabelle about. Dok knelt by the dynamic nesting chamber attached to the pedestal and opened the hatch. He slotted the needle into a miniature model, and twisted the whole thing into one of the hyperbaric berths. The aether repressurized and a third great land mass appeared, an oblong disk spinning in place at the north pole.

"Behold the final resting place of the *Conquest*," Sireen said. "And more importantly the Craton Auroborea."

Isabelle shook her head, trying to make room for this claim: a whole new craton, ready for exploring. *Please let me be first!*

"Amazing," Isabelle said. "But won't it be frozen solid?" What would it be like? Even an icy wasteland would be amazing. Would anything live there, and if so what form would it take? Did the great Auroras touch down there?

Sireen said, "We are informed by Hailer Dok that the craton is lush and green, with plentiful plant and animal life. Confirming the accuracy of this testimony is a key component of our bargain. Should the craton prove otherwise, Hailer Dok shall not have his prize."

Trickery, muttered Nowhere.

So this was the scope of the Imperial vision, first Grand Leon's and now Sireen's. They looked not to the treasure of a lost century, but to the wealth of centuries yet to come.

Sireen said, "The *Conquest* is still up there, past the Bittergale on Craton Auroborea. The lands are still waiting to be explored. I would also point out that land you claim yourself, even in the name of the crown, is not covered under your verdict. If Craton Auroborea proves to be a fruitful land, and not a great barren wedge of rock and ice, you have Our permission to put down a flag. And after Auroborea, there are other regions of the great sky as yet uncharted."

Isabelle swallowed. To be in command of her own ship. To feel the pitch of the deck, and to run before the wind. To seek the ends of the sky.

"When?" she asked.

Bitterlich said, "The refits on the *Thunderclap* should be complete within the month. She'll be ready for her shakedown as soon as the air warms up enough that her keel won't ice."

Isabelle cocked an eyebrow at him. "That was your secret mission."

"Indeed."

"How very aeronautical of you."

"I've spent three weeks immersed in a language I call 'what does that bit do?' By the end of the month I'll be wearing an eye patch and sporting a parrot."

"You could just become a parrot," Isabelle said. "With an eye patch."

"Major Bitterlich," Sireen said, intervening before this byplay could get out of hand, "will be in charge of your marines."

. . . *because mutiny festers* . . . Nowhere said. Saints, was there no way to make it shut up?

"Do you accept this commission?" Sireen asked. "Capitaine Isabelle."

Isabelle took a breath for balance. She was not today where she had hoped to be last year, or expected to be this morning. But she was here. Now. And adventure beckoned.

"I do," she said.